CHRISTMAS
with my
COWBOY

BOOK YOUR PLACE ON OUR WEBSITE AND MAKE THE READING CONNECTION!

We've created a customized website just for our very special readers, where you can get the inside scoop on everything that's going on with Zebra, Pinnacle and Kensington books.

When you come online, you'll have the exciting opportunity to:

- View covers of upcoming books
- Read sample chapters
- Learn about our future publishing schedule (listed by publication month and author)
- Find out when your favorite authors will be visiting a city near you
- Search for and order backlist books from our online catalog
- Check out author bios and background information
- Send e-mail to your favorite authors
- Meet the Kensington staff online
- Join us in weekly chats with authors, readers and other guests
- Get writing guidelines
- AND MUCH MORE!

**Visit our website at
http://www.kensingtonbooks.com**

CHRISTMAS KISSES
with my
COWBOY

DIANA PALMER
MARINA ADAIR
KATE PEARCE

ZEBRA BOOKS
KENSINGTON PUBLISHING CORP.
www.kensingtonbooks.com

ZEBRA BOOKS are published by

Kensington Publishing Corp.
119 West 40th Street
New York, NY 10018

All Kensington titles, imprints, and distributed lines are available at special quantity discounts for bulk purchases for sales promotion, premiums, fund-raising, educational, or institutional use.

Special book excerpts or customized printings can also be created to fit specific needs. For details, write or phone the office of the Kensington Sales Manager: Attn.: Sales Department. Kensington Publishing Corp., 119 West 40th Street, New York, NY 10018. Phone: 1-800-221-2647.

Zebra and the Z logo Reg. U.S. Pat. & TM Off.

First Printing: October 2020
ISBN-13: 978-1-4201-4801-5
ISBN-10: 1-4201-4801-X

ISBN-13: 978-1-4201-4803-9 (eBook)
ISBN-10: 1-4201-4803-6 (eBook)

10 9 8 7 6 5 4 3 2 1

Printed in the United States of America

Contents

Mistletoe Cowboy

DIANA PALMER

To my editor and friend of many, many years,
Tara Gavin, with love

Chapter One

He had a first name, but they all called him by his last name: Parker. He was part Crow. In fact, he had an aunt and uncle who still lived on the reservation. His parents had divorced when he was young. His mother was long dead, even before he went overseas in the military. He didn't know, or care, where his father was.

He worked on a huge ranch owned by J.L. Denton, near Benton, Colorado. He was the world's best horse wrangler, to hear J.L. tell it. Of course, J.L. had been known to exaggerate.

It was autumn and the last lot of yearlings had gone to market. The bulls were in winter pasture. The cows were in pastures close to the ranch so that they could be taken care of when snow started falling. That would be pretty soon, in the Colorado mountains, because it was late October, almost Halloween.

All the hands had to do checks on the cattle at least two or three times a day; more on the pregnant cows, especially on the pregnant heifers, the first-time mothers. Calves dropped in April. The pregnant cows and heifers had been bred the last of July for an April birthing date, and there were a lot of pregnant female cattle on the ranch.

Calves were the soul of the operation. J.L. ran purebred Black Angus, and he made good money when he sold off the calf crop every year. Not that he needed money so much. He was a multimillionaire, mostly from gas and oil and mining. The ranch was just cream on top of his other investments. He loved cattle. So did his new wife, who wrote for a famous sword and sorcery television series called *Warriors and Warlocks* that even Parker watched on pay-per-view. It was fun trying to wheedle details out of the new Mrs. Denton. However, even though she was a kind, sweet woman, she never gave away a single bit of information about the series. Never.

Parker lived in a line cabin away from the ranch house, where he broke horses for J.L. for the remuda, the string of horses each cowboy had to keep for ranch work. Horses tired, so they had to be switched often on a working ranch, especially during high-stress periods. He was good with all sorts of livestock, but he loved horses. He was blessed in the sense that horses also loved him, even outlaw horses. He'd had the touch since he was in grammar school on the Crow reservation up at Crow Agency, near the Little Bighorn Battleground at Hardin, Montana. His mother had encouraged him, emphasizing that sensitivity wasn't a bad thing in a man. His father said just the opposite.

Parker remembered his father with anger. He'd married Parker's mother, Gray Dove, in a moment of weakness, or so he'd said. But he had no plans to live on a reservation with her. So she went with him to his job in California until their son, Parker, was born. She and the child seemed to be an ongoing embarrassment to Chadwick Parker. He never stopped chiding his wife about her stupid ceremonies and superstitions. Finally, when Parker was six, she gave up and went back to Montana. It would have been nice if Parker's father had missed her and wanted her back. He didn't. He filed for divorce. Parker had never heard from him again. He doubted if the man even knew who he was. But it didn't matter. One of Gray Dove's brothers had taken him in when she died prematurely of pneumonia. He was part of a family, then, but still an outsider, even so. He fell in with a local gang in his teens and barely escaped prison by going into the military. Once there, he enjoyed the routine and found himself blessed with the same intelligence his absent father had. He was a mathematical genius. He aced any math courses he took, even trig and calculus and Boolean algebra.

Those skills after he graduated, with a degree in physics, served him well with government work. He didn't advertise the degree around Benton. It suited him to have people think he was simply a horse wrangler.

Parker had found work on J.L. Denton's ranch fresh out of the army, through an army buddy who'd been with him overseas in the Middle East. He had a knack for breaking horses without using anything except soft words and gentle hands. Word got around about how good he was at it, that he could do the job in a minimum of time and without injuring the animal in any way. He got job offers all the time, but he admired J.L. and had no plans to leave him.

He had a first cousin, Robert, in the home he'd been given after his mother's death. He kept a careful eye on the boy and made sure he had enough money for school and athletics on the rez. Robert graduated from high school and also went into the military. He was now a petty officer aboard a navy ship somewhere in the Atlantic. He wrote home, but not often. Parker often got the feeling that his cousin was ashamed of his poverty-stricken beginnings and didn't advertise them to people. It broke his parents' hearts that the boy didn't come to visit when he was on shore leave. But they adapted. People did, when they had to.

Money was never a worry for Parker. He had more than enough these days, now that his cousin had become self-supporting. He did send money to his cousin's parents. His aunt and uncle had been kind to him, and they'd had his cousin late in life. They weren't old, but they were middle-aged and Robert's father was disabled. Parker helped out.

Parker didn't drink, smoke, or gamble and he didn't have much to do with women these days. So money wasn't a problem. Not anymore.

He did like the occasional cigar. It wouldn't appear obvious to an outsider, but Parker had a mind like a super-computer. He could break any code, hack his way into any high-level computer that he liked, and get out without detection. It was a very valuable skill. His degree in astrophysics didn't hurt, either, but it was his math skills that set him apart in intelligence work. So from time to time, men in suits riding in black sedans pulled up at the cabin and tried to coax him out of Colorado.

Finally, he'd accepted an assignment, for a whole summer. The amount they paid him had raised his eyebrows almost to his hairline. Even after paying taxes, the cash left over was more than enough to invest in stocks and bonds and make him a tidy nest egg for the future.

That one summer led to other summers, and top secret clearance, so that now he could have afforded to retire to some nice island and laze in the sun and drink piña coladas for the rest of his life. But he didn't like liquor and he wasn't partial to beaches. So he gentled horses and waited for the next black sedan to show up. There was never a lack of them.

He was thirty-two and he longed for a home and a family.

But he didn't have many friends left on the rez. Most of the girls he'd gone to school with were long married, with lots of children. His best friend had died of a drug overdose, leaving behind two children and a wife who lived in the same condition that had caused his friend's death. He'd tried to get help for her, but she'd gone out of the rehab center the day after he got her in and she never looked back.

Life on the rez was hard. Really hard. They gave all this aid to foreign countries, spent all this money, making horrible weapons that could never be used in a civilized world, while little kids grew up in hopeless poverty and died too young. The big problem with the rez was the lack of job opportunities. What a pity that those entrepreneurs didn't set up low-impact manufacturing plants on the rez, to make jobs for people who faced driving hours to even find one. They could have offered jobs making exclusive clothing or unique dolls; they could have made jobs creating prefab houses and easily-set-up outbuildings; they could have opened a business that would make sails for boats, or wind chimes, or furniture. There must be a thousand things that people could manufacture on the reservation if someone would just create the means. Craftsmanship was so rare that it was worth diamonds in the modern world. It was almost impossible to find anything made by hand, except for quilts and handcrafted items. Well, there were those beautiful things that the Amish made, he amended. He had Amish-built furniture in his cabin, provided by a small community of them nearby, from whom he also bought fresh butter and cheese and milk. Now there, he thought, was a true pioneering spirit. If the lights ever went out for good, the Amish wouldn't have to struggle to survive.

* * *

Parker had been running one of J.L.'s new fillies through her paces while he pondered the problems of the world, and was just putting her up, when he heard fast hoofbeats and a young, winded voice yelling.

He moved away from the corral at the back of the big line cabin where he lived most of the year and looked out front. A palomino was galloping hell for leather down the trail. A youngster in boots and jeans and a long-sleeved flannel shirt and a floppy ranch hat, obviously chasing the horse, was stopped in the dirt road, bending over as if trying to catch his breath.

He kept his usual foul language to himself, not wanting to unsettle the young boy, who looked frantic enough already.

"Hey," Parker called. "What's going on?"

"My . . . horse!" came a high-pitched wail from the bent-over youngster. She stood up and a wealth of blond hair fell out of her hat. It wasn't a boy after all. She sat down on the ground. She was crying. "She'll make me give him back," she sobbed. "She'll never let me keep him. He knocked over part of the fence. She was calling the vet when he ran away and I was afraid . . . he'd hurt . . . himself!"

"Wait a bit." He went down on one knee in front of her. "Just breathe," he said gently. "Come on. Take it easy. Your horse won't go far. We'll follow him with a bucket of oats in a minute and he'll come back."

She looked up with china blue eyes in a thin face. "Really?" she asked hopefully.

He smiled. "Really."

She studied him with real interest. She must have been nine or ten, just a kid. Her eyes were on his thick black hair, in a rawhide-tied ponytail at his back, framing a face with black eyes and thick eyebrows and a straight, aristocratic nose. "Are you Indian . . . I mean, Native American?" she asked, fascinated.

He chuckled. "Half of me is Crow. The rest is Scots."

"Oh."

"I'm Parker. Who are you?"

"I'm Teddie. Teddie Blake. My mom lives over that way. We moved here about four months ago." She made a face. "I don't know anybody. It's a new school and I don't get along well with most people."

"Me, neither," he confessed.

Her eyes lit up. "Really?"

He chuckled. "Really. It's not so bad, the town of Benton. I've lived here for a while. You'll love it, once you get used to it. The palomino's yours?" he added, nodding toward where the horse had run.

"Yes. He was a rescue. We live on a small ranch. It was my grandmother's. She left it to my dad when she died. That was six months ago, just before he . . ." She made a face. "Mom's a teacher. She just started at Benton Elementary School. I'm in fifth grade there. The ranch has a barn and a fenced lot, and they were going to kill him. The palomino. He hurt his owner real bad. The vet was out at our place to doctor Mom's horse and he told us. I begged Mom to let me have him. He won't like it," she added with a sour face.

"He?"

"Mom's would-be boyfriend from back East," she said miserably. "He works for a law firm in Washington, D.C. He wears suits and goes to the gym and hates meat."

"Oh." He didn't say anything more.

She glanced at his stony face and didn't see any reaction at all. He'd long since learned to hide his feelings.

"Anyway, he says he's going to come out and visit next

month. Unless maybe he gets lost in a blizzard or captured by Martians or something."

He chuckled. "Don't sound so hopeful. He might be nice."

"He's nice when Mom's around," she muttered.

His face hardened. "Is he, now?"

She saw the expression. He wasn't hiding it. "Oh, no, he doesn't . . . well, he's just mean, that's all. He doesn't like me. He says it's a shame that Mom has me, because he doesn't want to raise someone else's child."

"Are your parents divorced?"

She shook her head. "My daddy's dead. He was in the army. A bomb exploded overseas and he was killed. He was a doctor," she added, fighting tears.

"How long ago?" he asked, and his voice softened.

"Six months. It's why Mom wanted to move here, to get away from the memories. My grandmother left us the ranch. She was from here. That lawyer helped Mom get Daddy's affairs straight and he's really sweet on her. I don't think she likes him that much. He wanted to take her out and she wouldn't go. He's just per . . . per . . ."

"Persistent?"

She nodded. "That."

"Well, we all have our problems," he returned.

There was a sound of hoofbeats. They turned and there was the palomino, galloping back toward them.

"Wait here a sec. Don't go toward him," he added. "It's a him?"

"It's a him."

"Be right back."

He went to the stable and got a sack of oats. The palomino was standing in the road, and the girl, Teddie, was right where he'd left her. Good girl, he thought, she wasn't headstrong and she could follow orders.

"Look here, old fellow," Parker said, standing beside the dirt road. He rattled the feed bag.

The palomino shook his head, raised his ears, and hesitated. But after a minute, he trotted right to Parker.

"Pretty old creature," Parker said gently. He didn't look the horse in the eyes, which might have seemed threatening to the animal. He held a hand, very slowly, to the horse's nostrils. The horse sniffed and moved closer, rubbing his head against Parker's. "Have some oats."

"Gosh, I couldn't get near him!" Teddie said, impressed.

He chuckled. "I break horses for J.L. Denton. He owns the ranch," he added, indicating the sweep of land to the mountains with his head.

Parker smoothed the horse's muzzle. "Let's see." He eased back the horse's lip and nodded. "About fifteen, unless I miss my guess."

"Fifteen?" she asked.

"Years old," he said.

"I thought he was only a year or so!"

He shook his head. He hung the feed bag over the horse's head and smoothed his hand alongside him, all the way to the back.

"You know about horses?" he asked Teddie.

She shook her head. "I'm trying to learn. Mom knows a lot, but she doesn't have time. There are these YouTube videos. . . ."

"You never walk behind a horse unless you let him know you're going to be there," he explained as he smoothed his way down the horse's flank to his tail. "Horses have eyes set on the sides of their heads. They're prey animals, not predators. Their first instinct is always going to be flight.

As such, they're touchy and sensitive to sound and movement. They can see almost all the way around them, except to their hindquarters. So you have to be careful. You can get kicked if you don't pay attention."

"Nobody said that on the video I watched," she confessed.

"You need some books," he said. "And some DVDs."

She sighed. "Mom said I didn't know what I was doing. He was such a pretty horse and I didn't want them to put him down. They arrested his owner."

Parker just nodded. He was seeing some damage on the horse's back, some deep scars. There was a cut that hadn't healed near his tail, and two or three that had on his legs. "Somebody's abused this horse," he said coldly. "Badly. He's got scars."

"They said the man took a whip to him." She grimaced. "They told me not to touch him on his front leg, but I was trying to look at his hoof and I forgot."

"His hoof?"

"He was favoring that one." She pointed to it.

He patted the horse's shoulder, bent, and pulled up the horse's hoof. He grimaced. "Good God!"

She looked, too, but she didn't see anything. "What is it?"

"His hooves are in really bad shape. Has a vet seen him?"

"I don't know. The animal control man brought him to the ranch for us. Mom was calling to get the vet, even before he knocked part of the fence down and ran away. She's going to be really mad."

Parker noted that the horse had no saddle on. "You didn't try to ride him bareback, did you?" he asked.

She grimaced. "Mister, I don't even know how to put a saddle on him. I sure can't ride him. I've never ridden a horse."

His black eyes widened. "You don't know how to ride?"

"Well, Mom does," she said hesitantly. "She grew up on a ranch in Montana. That's where she met my daddy. She can ride most anything, but she's been on the phone all day trying to get the movers to find a missing box. They think it went back East somewhere, but they haven't done much about finding it. It had a lot of Daddy's things. Mom's furious."

He shook his head. "That's tough."

"She said we'll . . . uh-oh," she added as a small SUV came down the road, pulled in very slowly next to the man and the child and the horse, and stopped.

"Who's that?" Parker asked.

"Mom," Teddie said, grimacing.

A blond woman wearing jeans and a black T-shirt got out of the SUV. "So there you are," she said in an exasperated tone.

"Sorry, Mom," Teddie said, wincing. "Bartholomew ran away and I ran after him. . . ."

"Bartholomew?" Parker asked.

"Well, he needed a fancy name. He's so pretty. Handsome." Teddie cleared her throat. "He did."

"He broke through a fence. I was on the phone trying to find a vet who'll come out and look at him, and when I went out to tell you what I found out, the horse was gone and so were you!"

"I was afraid he'd run in the road and get hurt," Teddie said defensively.

China blue eyes looked up at Parker. "Oats, huh?" she asked as she saw the feed bag over the horse's muzzle.

He nodded. "Quickest way to catch a runaway horse, if he has a sense of smell," he added with a faint smile.

"She's Katy," Teddie introduced. "I don't remember

who you are," she added with a shy smile at the tall man with the long black ponytail.

"Parker," he said. He didn't offer any more information, and he reached out to shake hands.

"You work for Mr. Denton, don't you?" Katy asked, and her expression told him that she'd heard other things about him as well.

"I do. I'm his horse wrangler."

She drew in a long breath. "Teddie, you never leave the house without telling me where you're going."

"Sorry, Mom."

"And obviously the horse doesn't need a vet immediately, or he wouldn't have gotten this far!"

"You know about horses, do you?" Parker asked her. She nodded.

"Come here." He smoothed down the horse's leg and pulled up the hoof. "Have a look."

"Dear God," she whispered reverently.

"If they lock his owner up forever, it won't be long enough," he added, putting the hoof back down. "There are deep cuts on his hindquarters, and on one of his legs as well. One needs stitches. I imagine an antibiotic would prevent complications from the hooves as well, if you got Doc Carr on the phone."

She made a face. "He's on another large-animal call. I left my cell phone number for him."

"Your daughter knows very little about horses," he began. "An animal that's been abused is dangerous even for an experienced equestrian."

"I know. But she was so upset," came the soft reply. "She's lost so much. . . ."

"She can learn how to take care of him," Parker interrupted, because he understood without being told.

"Yes, and I can teach her. But it's going to take time. I'm in a new teaching job. I'm not used to grammar school children. I taught at college level. . . ."

"We have a community college," he pointed out.

She gave him a long-suffering look. "Yes, I'm on the waiting list for an opening, but I couldn't wait. There are bills."

"I know about bills."

"So I got the only job available."

"You aren't from here," he said.

She nodded. "My husband's mother was from here. She was a Cowling, from the Dean River area."

"I know some Cowlings. Good people."

"She and my husband's father had a ranch in Montana where they were living when my husband was born. After her husband died, she came back here to live, on the family's ranch. She ran it herself until her death early this year. She left my husband the ranch. He was going to sell it, but he was . . . he . . . anyway. It took us some time to get moved here."

"It's a good place to raise a child," he said, and he smiled gently at Teddie.

"She's going on thirty," Katy said, tongue-in-cheek, as she glanced at her daughter.

He chuckled. "Some mature faster than others."

"We need to get Bartholomew home," Katy said, and she was staring at the horse as if she wondered how exactly they were going to do that.

"Give me a second to get Wings and I'll be right back." He didn't explain. He just went around the side of the house.

"Honestly, Teddie," Katy began, exasperated.

"I'm sorry. Really. But he ran away!"

"I know. But still . . ."

"Next time, I'll come get you first. I will." Her eyes pleaded with her mother's.

Katy gave in with a sigh. "All right. But don't let it happen again."

"I won't. Poor old horse," she added, looking at the palomino. "Mr. Parker said that he's been abused."

"He seems to know a lot about horses," Katy agreed, just as Parker came around the house leading a white mare.

"What a beauty," Katy exclaimed involuntarily.

"Wings," he said. "She's mine. Two years old and my best girl," he added with a smile.

The horse had a halter and bridle, but no saddle.

Before they could ask what he meant to do, Parker took the oats gently away from the palomino and put them beside the road. He caught the horse's bridle, led it to the mare, and vaulted onto the filly's back as if he had wings himself.

"Okay," he said. "Lead on."

They laughed. He made something complicated so simple. Teddie and Katy piled into their vehicle and led the way home, with Parker bringing up the rear riding one horse and leading the other. Both went with him as easily as lambs following a shepherd.

The house was in bad shape, he noticed as he stopped at the front porch and tied Wings's bridle to it. He patted her gently.

"Just stay right there, sweetheart. Won't be a minute," he said in a soft, deep tone, running his fingers along her neck. She looked at him and whinnied.

He went to get the palomino's bridle and led him, along with the woman and the girl, to the ramshackle barn.

He made a face when he saw it, along with the broken fence where the animal had broken through.

"I know. We're living in absolutely primitive conditions." Katy laughed. "But at least Teddie and I have each other, if we have nothing else." She said it with affection, but she didn't touch her daughter.

"Yes, we do," Teddie told her mother. "Thanks for not yelling."

"You never teach a child anything by yelling," Katy said softly. "Or by hitting."

Parker glanced at her and saw things she didn't realize. He put the palomino in a stall in the stable and closed the gate.

"We have to lock it," Katy said. She drew a chain around the metal gate and hitched it to the post with a metal lock. "He's an escape artist," she added. "Which is how he happened to be hightailing it past your place. I guess he learned to run away when his owner started brutalizing him with that whip."

"I'd love to have five minutes with that gentleman, and the whip," Parker murmured as he looked around the barn. "This place is in bad shape," he remarked.

"One step at a time," she said with quiet dignity.

He turned and looked down at her and smiled. He almost never smiled, but she made him feel like he had as a boy when he got his first horse, when he dived into deep water for the first time, when he tracked his first deer. It was a feeling of extreme exhilaration that lifted him out of his routine. And shocked him.

She laughed. "It's what my mother always said," she explained. "Especially when Dad got sick and had to go to the hospital. He had a bad heart. She knew it when they married. He had two open-heart surgeries to put in an artificial valve, and he had a host of other health problems," she added, not mentioning the worst of those, alcoholism. "They'd been married for twenty-five years when he died in a car crash. She said she got through life by living just for the day she was in, never looking ahead. It's not a bad philosophy."

"Not bad at all," Teddie agreed.

"Is this his saddle?" Parker asked suddenly, noting the worn but serviceable saddle resting on a nearby gate. The stable was empty except for the palomino, tack on the walls, and some hay in square bales in a corner.

"Yes," Katy said. "It was my grandfather's. I've had it for years. I brought it with us when we moved. It's been a lot of places with me, since my teens." She joined him and ran her hand over the worn, smooth pommel. "Granddaddy competed in bulldogging for many years with a partner, his first cousin, up in Montana. He was very good. But he lost a thumb to a too-tight rope and ended up keeping books for my husband's father. They lived near Dan's folks in Montana, but they had a relative who owned the ranch here. When Dan's father died, his mother sold the Montana ranch and moved back here, to her family ranch. Dan inherited it." Her expression was wistful. "His grandfather, who founded the ranch, raised some of the finest Red Brangus around," she added. "He was active in the local cattleman's association as well. So was Dan's mother."

"My boss is, too. He and the Mrs. are pregnant with their first child. She writes for *Warriors and Warlocks*, that hit drama on cable TV."

"Oh, my gosh!" Katy exclaimed. "It's my favorite show! And she actually writes for it?! And lives here?"

"Her husband's got a private jet," he explained with twinkling eyes. "He has the pilot fly her to and from Manhattan for meetings with the other writers and the show's director and producer."

"That must be nice," Katy said.

"Mom won't let me watch that show," Teddie said with a faint pout.

"When you're older," Katy told her.

"You always say that, about everything," the little girl complained.

"Wait until you're grown and you have kids," Katy teased. "You'll understand it a whole lot better."

"This place needs a lot of work," Parker said when they were back outside again. "Especially that fence, and those steps." He indicated a board missing in the front ones.

"It really does," Katy agreed. "We're trying to take it one thing at a time."

"Fence first, steps second. Got any tools? How about extra boards for the fence, or at least wire?"

Katy was shocked, but only for a minute. She went inside and came back out with a toolbox. "It was my husband's, but I have no idea what's in it," she apologized.

"No problem. Boards? Wire?"

"I think there's a bale of wire out in the big shed behind the house," she returned.

"Yes, that big one there," Teddie said, indicating a metal building that had seen better days.

"My mother-in-law used it mostly for storage," Katy explained. "She kept some of the Red Brangus, just the breeding stock, and hired a man to manage it for her. He still works for us. . . ."

"Yes, that would be Jerry Miller," he said, smiling. "I know him. Honest as the day is long, and a hard worker."

"He has two full-time cowboys and four part-time ones." She shook her head. "It takes so many people to work cattle. We'll have our first sale in the spring. I'm hoping we'll do well at it. I've forgotten most of what I know about ranching. But that's what we have Jerry for," she added with a smile. And it was just plain good luck that the last cattle sale had left her with a windfall that took care of all the salaries. Wintering the cows and heifers, and their few bulls, would be expensive, due to loss of forage from all the flooding in the West and Midwest, but she knew they'd manage somehow. They always did.

"At least we got the plumbing repaired and a new roof put on," she said, waving her hand to indicate some rough idea of where the work had been done.

"Expensive stuff," he commented, looking through the toolbox.

"Tell me about it," she said, tongue-in-cheek.

He took out a hammer. "Nails?" he asked as he got to his feet gracefully.

"Nails. Right." She looked around the building until her eyes came to a workbench. "I think he kept them in a coffee can over here."

She produced it. There was a supply of assorted nails. He picked out some to do the job. He got wire cutters from the tool kit and proceeded to heft the heavy bale of wire over his shoulder.

"Can I help?" Teddie asked.

He chuckled. "Sure. You can carry the hammer and nails."

She took them from him and followed along behind him to the pasture that fronted the stable.

"I could find someone to do it. . . ." Katy began.

"Not before the horse went through it again." He

frowned and glanced at them as he put down the wire and pulled out a measuring tape. "Why did he run?" he asked belatedly.

Teddie sighed. "Well, there was this plastic bag that had been on the porch. The wind came up and sent it flying toward the corral. Bartholomew panicked."

Chapter Two

Parker burst out laughing. "A plastic bag." He shook his head. "Horses are nervous creatures, to be sure."

"You said they were prey animals," Teddie reminded him shyly.

"They are."

"How do you tell that?" the little girl wanted to know.

"Prey animals have eyes on the sides of their heads, not on the front like humans do," he replied. He went on to explain about the evolution that produced such a trait.

Katy was watching him curiously.

He gave her a dry look. "Oh, I get it. A horse wrangler shouldn't know scientific things like that, huh? I minored in biology in college."

She flushed. "Sorry."

He shrugged. "We're all guilty of snap judgments. Don't sweat it." He glanced toward the house. "Those steps need fixing as much as this fence does."

"Know any reliable handymen hereabouts?" Katy asked him.

He chuckled. "Sure. Me. I work cheap. A couple of sandwiches and some good, strong black coffee. It will have to be on a Saturday, though. Boss keeps me pretty busy the rest of the week."

She flushed. "Oh, I didn't mean—"

"He doesn't mind if I help out neighbors," he interrupted. "He's a kind man. So is his wife."

"You said she wrote for *Warriors and Warlocks*," she added, glancing at Teddie amusedly. "Teddie loves it. I have to keep her locked in her room when it's on, though. It's very grown-up."

He was grinning from ear to ear. "It is. If you saw the boss's wife, you wouldn't believe she was somebody so famous."

"I still can't believe we have somebody that famous here in Benton." She laughed.

"Yeah. Gave us all a start when we found out. Cassie Reed, now Cassie Denton, was working as a waitress in town. Her dad, Lanier Roger Reed, was working at the farm equipment place. None of us knew they were running from a big scandal in New York. Her father was falsely accused of "—he stopped and glanced at Teddie— "a grown-up thing. Anyway, the woman who accused him is now occupying a comfortable cell in state prison. J.L. married the writer and she came back out here to live. Her dad produces a hit show about a musical group from the seventies."

"Oh, my goodness, those are about the only two shows I watch on TV." Katy laughed. "What a coincidence!"

"She's a good writer. And she's a sweet person, too. She's very pregnant, so we all sort of watch out for her. It's their first child. Due pretty soon, too. J.L. says the baby's going to be a Christmas present."

"Is it a boy or a girl?"

"Bound to be."

She glared at him.

He grinned. "They don't know. They wanted it to be a surprise. So all the shower gifts they got were yellow."

"I didn't want to know, either," Katy said, smiling at Teddie. "But my husband did. So they told him and he didn't tell me."

"A man who could keep a secret. That's rare."

"He was a rare man," she said quietly. The loss was still fresh enough that she had to fight tears. "Okay, about the porch, I'll need to get lumber. Can you tell me what to get and where to get it?"

"I'll come back Saturday morning and do some measuring," he said.

"Thanks."

"And we could teach young Annie Oakley here how to saddle a horse," he teased, smiling at Teddie.

"That would be great!" Teddie enthused.

"So I'll see you both then."

"Thanks. I'd like to pay you, for fixing the fence. . . ." She stopped at the look on his face. She flushed. "Well, I'm not exactly a charity case and you work for J.L. Denton for wages, right?"

He pursed his lips and stared at her with twinkling eyes. "Sort of."

"Sort of?" she asked.

He smiled. "I work for him except in the summer. I go away to work for other people." He didn't elaborate. "I make a good bit then."

"Oh."

"So I can do a favor for a new friend"—he smiled at Teddie—"and her mom without having to worry about getting paid for it. Okay?"

She smiled. "Okay. Thanks, Parker."

"No sweat." He mounted the horse, turned it gently, and rode away, as much a part of the animal as its tail, using just his legs and the light bridle to control it.

"That's such a beautiful horse," Teddie said with a sigh as she watched the man ride away.

"It is. Wings suits her for a name," Katy agreed. She gave her daughter an irritated look. "But just for the record, if you ever do anything like that again . . ."

"I won't," Teddie promised. She grinned irrepressibly. "But I got us a new friend who knows all about horses," she added. "Right?"

It was impossible for her to stay mad at her daughter. "Right. Anyway, let me go and try to get the vet again. Your new friend Parker was right. The horse needs a lot of work done on him before you can ride him."

"It will cost money," Teddie said. "I'm really sorry. . . ."

"A vet bill won't break the bank," her mother said gently. "We have the money that comes from the service, after Dad . . . well, anyway, we have that and we have my salary. We'll get by."

"It will be nice to have him healed," Teddie said. "I didn't realize he'd need so many things done. I'm really sorry."

"He's a beautiful animal and he's been badly treated," came the curt reply. "I really hope his owner goes to jail. Nobody should treat a horse like that!"

"That's true," Teddie agreed.

"Come on inside. It's very cool out here."

The vet came out and looked at the poor horse, treated his cuts, recommended a farrier for the hooves, and gave Bartholomew an antibiotic injection. He promised to come back the following week and check on him, just to make sure he was healing.

"Going to be a scandal, when that man comes to trial," the vet, Henry Carr, told Katy. "In all my years as a vet, never saw a horse in such shape. He had two others, but the county animal control people took those away from him. Well, those horses, and about twenty dogs he had in cages for breeding purposes. They took those, too."

"Why isn't he in jail?" she asked angrily.

"Because his people are rich and they protect him," he said flatly, and with some anger. "If I get called to testify, they're going to get an earful from me!"

"Good for you," she said.

"You need to get the farrier out here before those hooves get any worse," he said.

"I'll call him today."

He smiled. "I'm glad you and Teddie decided to come and live here. Benton's a nice place to raise a child. I raised three, with my late wife. I miss her every day."

Katy took a breath. "I miss my husband. He was a good man."

"Life goes on," he said. "It has to. Have a good day."

"You, too. And thanks for coming out."

"No problem."

She watched him drive off and called the farrier. He agreed to come right out and check the poor horse's hooves after Katy had described the state they were in.

He cleaned them and replaced the shoes with new nails. "Hell of a condition for a horse to get in," he said.

"Yes, it is. They're prosecuting the former owner."

"I know him. Bad man. Really bad. I hope they'll get farther than they did with the last case they tried against him."

"Me, too." She watched him put in the last nail. "Do you know a man named Parker who works for J.L. Denton?"

"Parker." He rolled his eyes. "He's fine as long as he's not within earshot," he added on a chuckle. "J.L. has to keep women away from him."

"Why?" she asked, with some shock.

"His mouth," he replied. "Nobody cusses like Parker."

"But he caught Bartholomew–that's the name of the horse you're working on–and promised to help my daughter learn how to take care of him."

"Nobody knows more about horses than Parker," he agreed. "He likes kids. But he's hell on women. Tried to date a couple of local girls and when they got a whiff of his language, they ran for the hills."

"But he never used a bad word," Katy continued, trying to explain.

The farrier looked at her with total shock. "We talking about the same Parker? Big guy, long black hair, breaks horses for Denton?"

"Well, yes."

He caught his breath. "That's one for the books, then."

Teddie laughed softly. "Well, apparently my daughter has a good effect on him."

"I would say so." He finished his work, accepted a check for it, and said his good-byes after giving Katy instructions about keeping the horse in the stable for a few days until the worst of the damage healed. She didn't mention that the vet had told her the same thing.

"How is he?" Teddie asked when her mother came into the house.

"He'll be fine," she assured the girl. "He just needs to rest for a few days while he's healing. By Saturday," she added with a smile, "he should be ready for Horses 101."

Teddie laughed. "That's a good one, Mom. Horses 101."

"Well, let's get supper going. Then we need an early night. School tomorrow, for both of us."

"I know. It's not so bad here, I guess. I made a friend yesterday: Edie. She loves horses, too. She's got a palomino."

"I'm glad. You're like me, sweetheart. You don't warm up to people easily. Your father was the very opposite," she added with a wistful smile. "He never met a stranger."

"I miss Daddy."

She looked at her daughter with sad eyes. "I miss him, too. It takes time, to get over a loss like that. But we'll make it."

"Sure we will." She looked up at her mother hopefully. "I love you."

"I love you, too," Katy said, but she turned away quickly. "Now, let's get something to eat. Do you have homework?"

Teddie was resigned to never getting a hug from her remaining parent. She and her dad had been close. He hugged her all the time when he was home. But her mother almost never touched her. It was the only thing that made living with her hard. Teddie couldn't change it, so she just accepted it. "Yes. Math." She groaned. "And history."

"I used to love history."

"I would, if we didn't have to memorize so many dates. I mean, what does it matter if we don't know the difference?"

"It would if you ever started writing books and you had George Washington helping the men fight in Vietnam," Katy replied, tongue-in-cheek.

Teddie glowered at her and went to wash up for supper.

Saturday morning, Parker was at the door just after breakfast, while Katy was mending a tear in Teddie's jeans.

She went to the door and laughed. "You're early. I'm sorry, I meant to . . . Teddie's watching cartoons. Should I get her?"

"Not yet. I just need to do some measuring," he added with a smile. "For the steps."

"Oh, yes. Of course."

She went out onto the porch with him while he marked wood with a pencil and wrote figures on a piece of paper. He handed it to her. "That's what I'll need, to do the repairs."

It wasn't even a lot of money, she thought with some relief. The vet and the farrier had made inroads into her budget. "I'll phone the hardware store and tell them to let you get what you need. Are you going right now?"

"I am," he said. "Shouldn't take too long. Then I can show Teddie how to saddle Bartholomew."

"The vet said he should be all right to let out by today," she began.

"And you're worried," he guessed. He smiled. "Don't be. We'll keep him in the stall or the corral while we work with him. What did the vet say?"

"Not a lot. He gave him an antibiotic injection and stitched up his cuts. He gave me the name of a farrier, too, and I had him come out and clean Bart's hooves and replace his horseshoes."

"You're having to go to a lot of expense," he said.

"It's not so much," she replied. "And it's nice to see Teddie interested in something besides TV. She's been sad for so long. She and her dad were really close. It was hard for her, just having him in the service overseas. And after what happened . . . well, she wasn't looking forward to moving here. She's been very depressed."

"Not surprising," he said. "I still miss my mother, and

she's been gone for years. I lost her when I was twelve. Another family on the rez took me in and adopted me. We have good people there."

She cocked her head and looked at him. "Which one of your parents was white?"

"My father." He closed up. "I'll run to the hardware and pick this stuff up, then I'll come back and fix the steps. Don't bother Teddie right now," he added, and forced a smile. "Won't be long."

He went to the truck and drove away, leaving Katy guilt-ridden. His father must have been bad to him, she decided, because that look on his face had been disturbing. She was sorry she'd brought up something that had hurt him. It had been a casual remark, the sort you'd make to just an acquaintance. But it had really dug into Parker. Considering how little emotion escaped that face, it was telling that he reacted so quickly to the remark. She'd have to be careful not to bring up the past.

She recalled what the farrier had said about his language and she just shook her head. He hadn't said a single bad word around her or Teddie. Maybe he only cursed around people he didn't like. He was very good-looking, and very athletic. She smiled to herself. It was much too early to be thinking about men in her life. She'd tried to explain that to the attorney back home, but he hadn't listened. He'd invited himself out to see them next month, but he was in for a surprise if he thought he was staying in the house with Katy and her daughter. She didn't know him well enough, or like him well enough, for that sort of familiarity.

It was disturbing to think of herself with another man right now. Maybe, in time . . . but it still wouldn't be that smarmy lawyer, no matter how desperate she got. And that was a fact.

* * *

Parker was back in an hour with a load of lumber. He lifted it out of the truck with incredible ease. Katy marveled at how strong he was. Involuntarily, she mentioned it.

He chuckled. "I live at the gym when I'm not working. Muscles turn to pure flab if you don't keep up the exercise. I got used to it in the military and never really lost the habit. I have to keep in shape to do the work I do."

"You have an amazing way with horses," she commented.

He smiled. "I get that from my mother's father. He could outrun any horse on the place, but even the wildest ones responded to him. He never used a whip or abused his horses in any way. But he could do anything with them."

"I think that must be a very special skill," she remarked. "There's this guy on YouTube who works with horses like you do. It's a treat to watch him work an unbroken one."

"I know the one you mean. His father was vicious to him. He didn't understand that some people have talents that aren't mainstream."

"Like yours," she said softly. "Did you take a lot of heat for it, at home?"

He shook his head. "I was very small when my mother and I came back here to the rez." He smiled. "My people don't have the same attitude toward special abilities as some people off the rez do," he added. "We think of the supernatural as, well, natural. We have people who can dowse for water, people who can talk out fire. We have people who know more about herbs than laboratories do. We're a spiritual people in an age when it's frowned upon to believe in a higher power." He shook his head. "Nobody who'd been in combat would doubt there's a higher power, by the way. No atheists in foxholes, and that's a fact."

"You were in the army?" she asked.

He nodded. "It was a bad time. I saw things I wish I could forget. My old sergeant works near here. He's just taken in a three-legged wolf that was stalking calves over at the Denton place. Poor old creature was almost blind and couldn't hunt. They gave him to Sarge. He's a rehabilitator," he explained. "Except that you can't rehabilitate a half-blind, old, three-legged wolf. So the wolf lives with him now. Even watches TV, we hear," he added with a chuckle.

"My goodness! We had packs of wolves up in Montana who were predators. We lost cattle to them all the time."

He nodded. "It's hard to co-exist with wild animals. But the earth belongs to everything, not just to humans. Starving creatures will eat whatever they can catch. That's nature."

"I suppose so."

"Now, let's get those steps fixed before one of you breaks a leg on them," he said, and started ferrying lumber to the house.

Teddie spotted him and came flying out the door. "Parker!" she exclaimed. "Are we doing Horses 101 today?"

He chuckled. "Nice. Yes, we are. But first I have to fix your steps."

He put down the load of lumber and went back for another one. "Still got that fancy toolbox?" he added.

"I'll go get it," Teddie volunteered.

"Good girl," he said.

She brought the toolbox while Katy went in search of the coffee can where the nails were kept. Then Parker got to work with a skill saw and a pencil over one ear.

* * *

He was methodical, but quick. In less than an hour, he had the steps replaced.

"We can't stain them yet," he said. "That's treated lumber. It will last a long time, but you have to let it season before you can stain or paint it."

"That's fine," Katy said.

A truck came down the road and pulled up beside Parker's. A tall, well-built man in jeans and a denim jacket and a battered old hat came up to them.

"This is Jerry Miller," Katy said, smiling at the newcomer, who smiled back and offered a hand.

"Hello, Parker," he greeted.

Parker shook hands with him and smiled, too. "Nice to see you. I'm doing a few repairs."

"Looks good. I'd have offered, but I can't even measure, much less do woodwork," the other man said ruefully. "All I'm good for is nursemaiding cattle."

"Don't sell yourself short," Katy instructed. "You made us a nice nest egg with that crop of yearlings you took to auction for us. Which pays your salary, by the way." She laughed.

He grinned, tipping his hat back over sandy hair. "And my wife's hairdresser bills," he added.

"Your wife looks pretty all the time," Katy said. "And she's sweet, which is much more important than pretty."

"Yes, she does," Jerry had to agree. Then he asked, "Is there anything I can do to help?" He chuckled. "Well, except for offering to cut wood, which I can't do."

"Not a thing. All done," Parker said. "But we have some

leftover lumber. If you'll help me get it in the shed, it may come in handy for another job later on."

"Good idea."

The men moved the lumber into the building. Katy and Teddie put up the toolbox and the nails.

"So," Parker told Teddie, "Horses 101. Let's go."

"Yes!" Teddie enthused and followed Parker into the barn.

Parker put a bridle on Bartholomew and led him out into the corral that adjoined the stables.

"Where do your cowboys keep their horses?" he asked.

"Oh, Jerry keeps them at his place," Teddie said. "He and Lacy, that's his wife, have a big stable that his father built years ago. Mom says it's much nicer than ours, and he's got lots of room. There are two line cabins on the place, too, and the full-time men live in them with their families. They have a stable apiece. It was a really big ranch when my grandmother was still alive." She sighed. "They said she could outride any cowboy on the place, shoot a gun, rope a calf, even help with branding when she was in her sixties. But she broke her hip and she could never do it again. Mom says she lost heart and that's why she died."

"It's hard for active people to sit still," Parker replied. "I remember your grandmother," he added with a smile. "She used to sell milk and butter. My mother, and later my uncle and aunt, bought them from her."

"Your aunt and uncle, they still live on the reservation?"

He nodded his head. "Yes. They're the only family I have, except for their son, my first cousin, who's in the navy. He never comes home. I think he's ashamed of us," he added quietly.

"Why?" Teddie asked. "I mean, I think it would be awesome to be a member of a tribe and know all that ancient stuff that people used to know. It's such a heritage!"

He chuckled, surprised, as he looked down at her. "Where did you get that from?"

"My mom," she said. "She loves history. She had a friend who was Northern Cheyenne when she lived in Montana. They lost touch, but Mom knows a lot about native customs and stuff. She said that's how people were meant to live, in touch with nature and not with big stone buildings and pavement."

He pursed his lips. "That's exactly how I feel about it."

"Me, too. I hate the city. This"—she waved her arms around—"is the best place on Earth. Well, now that I've got Bartholomew, it is," she amended. She grimaced. "I didn't want to come here. I had a good friend where we lived, and I had to leave her. She sends me e-mails, though, and we Skype. So I sort of still have her. And I made a friend here named Edie. She has a palomino, too."

"You have two friends here. I'm one of them," he chided.

"Of course, you are." She laughed.

"So. First lesson. Horses 101."

"I'm all ears."

He went over the various parts of the horse, from fetlocks to withers, tail to ears, and he taught her the signs to look for when she was working with Bartholomew.

"Watch his ears," he told her. "See how he's got one ear toward us and another swiveled behind him? He's listening to us, but also listening for sounds that mean danger."

"Wow."

The horse looked back at Teddie and both ears swiveled forward.

"That means all his attention is on you," Parker said, indicating the horse's ears. "That's important, when you're training him."

"I guess he'll need a lot of training. Poor old thing," she added.

The horse moved forward and lowered his head toward Teddie.

"Poor horse," she said softly. She didn't make eye contact, but she let the horse sniff her nostrils. He lowered his head even more, so that she could stroke him beside his nostrils.

"He likes you," Parker said. "And he's intelligent. Very intelligent," he added, when the horse turned its head and looked directly at him.

He chuckled softly and put out a big hand to smooth over the horse's mane. "Sweet old boy," he said. Bartholomew nuzzled his shoulder.

"I was afraid he was going to be mean," Teddie confessed. "You know, because he was hurt and didn't trust humans not to hurt him anymore."

"Some horses can't be turned back after they're abused," Parker agreed. "But lucky for you, this isn't one of them. He's a grand old man. He'll make you a dependable mount."

"I wish I could already ride," she confessed. "Mom used to go for horseback rides with Dad when we lived back East, before he . . ." She swallowed. "But I didn't go with them because I was afraid of horses. But the first time I saw Bartholomew, it was like, well, I don't know what it was like."

"Like falling in love," Parker said, smiling at her.

"I guess. Something like that." She cocked her head and looked up at him. "You ever been in love?"

He averted his eyes. "Once. A long time ago. I lost her." He didn't say how.

"Maybe you'll find somebody else one day."

He smiled sadly. "Not on my agenda. I like my life as it

is. I have absolute control of the television remote and nobody to fuss when I don't take out the trash on time."

"Have you got pets?"

"Just Harry."

Her eyebrows went up. "Harry?"

He pursed his lips. "You scared of snakes?"

She shivered a little. "Oh, yes."

"Me, too."

"Is Harry a snake?"

He smiled. "Harry's an iguana," he said. "He's four years old and about five feet long."

"Wow! What sort of cage do you keep him in?"

He pursed his lips. "Well, that's sort of the reason I'm still single. See, he's a little too big to keep in a cage. I just let him go where he wants to. His favorite spot is the back of my sofa. He watches TV with me at night."

"An iguana who watches TV." Teddie sighed.

"Well, Sarge has a wolf who watches it. Maybe animals understand more than we think they do, huh?"

She laughed. "I guess so. Could I see your iguana sometime?"

"Sure. I'll invite you both over when we get a little further along with the repairs and your Horses 101 training." He looked down at her. "Is your mom afraid of reptiles?"

"Oh, no. She's not afraid of anything."

"An interesting woman," he mused as he turned back to the horse.

"That man's coming out here next month," Teddie said miserably. "For Thanksgiving, he said."

"That man?" he asked, trying not to sound too interested.

"That lawyer who helped her settle Daddy's business," she explained. "He doesn't like me. I really hope Mom doesn't like him. He's . . ." She searched for a word. "He's smarmy." She laughed. "I guess that's not a good word."

"It suits," Parker replied. "It says a lot about a person. But are you sure it fits him? Sometimes people aren't what you think they are at first. I hated Sarge's guts until we were under fire and he saved my life."

"Gosh!"

"Then I saved his, and we sort of became friends. So first impressions can be altogether wrong."

She drew in a long breath. "That would be nice. But it's not really a wrong impression. I heard him talking to another man, when Mom wasn't listening." She pulled a face. "He said that my daddy had lots of stocks that were going to be worth big money and that my mom wasn't all that bad looking. He said if he could get close to her, and get control of those stocks, he'd be rich."

Parker's black eyes sparked. "What does he have in mind, you think?"

"I think he wants to marry her. She doesn't like him. She told me so. But he thinks he can wear her down." She drew in a breath and looked up at Parker with sad eyes. "If she marries him, can I come and live with you and Harry?"

He laughed softly. "Come on, now. You won't have to do that. Your mom's a sharp lady. She's intelligent and kind and she has a sweet nature."

Teddie's eyes were widening. "You can tell all that, and you've only known us for a few days?"

He nodded. "I have feelings about people," he tried to explain. "You know how horses respond to me? It's like that, only I sense things that are hidden. My mother had the same ability. Nobody could cheat her. She saw right through confidence men."

"Maybe you could talk to Mom, if that man comes out here?"

He chuckled. "I don't mind other people's business, sweet girl," he said softly. "Life is hard enough without inviting trouble. But I'll be around in case I'm needed. Okay?"

"Okay," she said.

"Now. Let's go over the diamond hitch again."

She groaned.

"Might as well learn these things. You'll need to know them in order to be able to ride."

"There's bridles, and all sorts of bits, and ways to cinch a horse, and what to do if he blows his belly out when you tighten it . . . I can't remember all that!"

"You'll learn it because we'll go over and over it until the repetition keeps it in your mind," he said. "Like muscle memory."

"Dad talked about that," Teddie recalled. "He said it saved his life once when he was overseas and he got jumped by three insurgents. He said he didn't even think about what he needed to do, he just did it. He learned it when he was in boot camp."

"That's where all of us learned it," Parker said complacently. He indicated the horse. "And that's how you'll learn what you need to know about how to take care of Bart and ride him: muscle memory."

She laughed. "Okay. I'll do my best."

"That's all anybody can do," he replied warmly.

Chapter Three

Teddie was a quick study. She mastered the preparations for riding and was now learning how to get on a horse properly.

"There are all these programs that tell you to get on a stump or a stepladder so you don't overburden the horse's back. But you're small enough that it won't matter. Ready?"

She grimaced. She looked up to the pommel of the Western saddle she'd put on Bartholomew with Parker's instructions. "It's a long way up there," she said doubtfully.

He laughed. "I guess it is, squirt. Okay. Lead him over here."

Teddie led him to a stump near the porch, positioned Bart on one side of it, put her foot into the stirrup, and sprung up onto his back.

The horse moved restlessly, but Parker had the bridle. "It's okay, old man," he said softly, offering a treat on the palm of his hand.

Bart hesitated, but only for a moment before he took it. Parker smoothed over the blaze that ran down his forehead. "Good boy." He glanced at Teddie, who looked nervous. "You have to be calm," he instructed. "Horses, like dogs and cats, can sense when we're unsettled. They respond to emotions, sometimes badly. Give him a minute to settle down. And whatever you do, don't jerk the reins. Riding is mostly in your legs. Use your legs to tell him when to go, when to stop, which way to turn. The bridle gives you more control, but your legs are where your focus needs to be," he said as he adjusted her stirrup length.

"I have little scrawny legs, though," she said worriedly.

He smiled. "You'll do fine."

He had a calming nature, Teddie thought, because the words relaxed her. She noticed that Bart reacted to it. He tossed his head, but his ears stayed turned to the front, not the back. It was only dangerous when a horse had both ears flattened, because that meant trouble.

Teddie stroked his mane. "Sweet horse," she said softly. "I'm so happy I got you, Bart."

He seemed to relax even more.

"Okay. Contract your legs at the knee and see if he'll respond by going forward."

He did.

"Wow!" she exclaimed softly.

Parker chuckled. "Good job. Now, when you want him to turn left, put more pressure on your left leg and move the bridle very gently to the left. You don't want to hurt his mouth."

"Okay." She followed the instruction and so did Bart. "This is awesome," she said.

"Horses are awesome," Parker agreed. "Try turning him the other way. Same procedure."

She did. Bart followed through beautifully.

"How do I tell him to stop?" she asked.

"You pull back very gently on the reins."

She did that, and Bart stopped in his tracks.

"Nice job," Parker said.

"Can we go riding now?" she asked.

He smiled at her excitement. "Not just yet. First things first. You have to know what to do in case of an emergency. That's the next lesson. But we have to stop for now. Boss man is bringing over a few new horses for the remuda and I have to work with them."

"It's so nice of you to help me with Bart," Teddie said as she dismounted cautiously. "I could never have done this by myself."

"I love horses," Parker said. "It's no trouble. I enjoy working with this sweet old man, too," he added, patting the horse's withers. "So let's get him unsaddled and back into his stall."

"I'm with you," she said, and followed him back into the stable.

"How are you doing with Bartholomew?" Katy asked at supper one night.

"Really good," she told her mother. "Parker's so smart!"

"He knows horses, all right," Katy replied.

"No," Teddie corrected. "That's not what I mean. He's really smart. He had a phone call Saturday when he was over here. I only heard what he was saying, but it was way over my head. Something about Einstein-Rosen bridges and somebody named Schrodinger."

Katy's mouth opened. "Are you sure that's what he said?"

"Well, I think so."

"Did he mention a cat when he talked about Schrodinger?" Katy pressed.

Teddie frowned. "Yes. But the cat was alive and dead in a box until you opened the box he was in. Strange!"

Katy caught her breath. That was theoretical physics. And it was something she wouldn't have expected a horse wrangler to know anything about. Parker had said he graduated from college, but he hadn't mentioned in what field. This wasn't only over Teddie's head, it was over Katy's.

"Well," she said finally, as she finished her mashed potatoes and skinless chicken breast.

"I told you, he's real smart," Teddie repeated. She sighed. "Some man was trying to get him to go to the Capitol and do some work, but he said it wasn't summer and he couldn't spare the time, they'd have to get somebody else."

"Amazing," Katy said.

"What is an Einstein-Rosen bridge?" Teddie wanted to know.

"Over my head," Katy laughed. "It has to do with time dilation, and wormholes. I used to have a best friend when I was in college who had a degree in physics. She talked like that, too."

"And that cat?"

"It's a thought experiment," Katy replied. "There's a cat in a box. The cat is either alive or dead. But until you open the box and look in, the cat exists in both states."

"Weird."

"Very weird. That's the sort of thing physicists do. Einstein came up with the theory of relativity, and he was a physicist. Probably the most famous of all of them, although Stephen Hawking came close to that."

"If Parker's that smart, why's he breaking horses out in the country?" Teddie wondered.

"Maybe he doesn't like the city," Katy said. She made a face. "Truly, I didn't either, but your dad loved where we lived."

"He was a rancher, too," Teddie said.

"He was, but the military became his whole life after he went overseas. He was a doctor. He said having a practice here was fine, but good men were dying in other countries and he needed to be a combat physician to help fight for his country. He was the most patriotic man I ever knew."

"He was a good daddy."

"He was a good husband," Katy replied, fighting tears, as her daughter was. "We'll get through this, Teddie," she said after a minute. "It's going to take time, that's all. I thought maybe coming out here to live would make it easier for us. It's a wonderful ranch."

"Yes, it is. I made two friends." Teddie laughed. "Edie and Parker."

"You did. Parker's a kind person." She shook her head. "Theoretical physics and horses. Oh, my."

Teddie grinned. "Maybe he's dreaming up ray guns and stuff."

"Maybe he's trying for a unified field theory of relativity." She yawned. "I have to get some sleep. It's test day tomorrow. My students are dreading it. Me, too, I guess."

"You like teaching, don't you, Mom?"

She smiled. "I do like it. I didn't expect to. It's really different from teaching college students," she added. "But I have a good class to teach things to. Education is education, no matter the age of the student."

"Yes, I guess it is."

"How about you?" Katy wondered. "Is school getting any easier?"

Teddie nodded. "A lot easier, now that Edie and I can hang out together. We talk about horses. Everybody talks about horses," she chuckled. "Most of the kids in school around Benton are ranch kids, so most everybody rides. Except me. But I'm learning."

"Parker says you're doing well," Katy told her.

"There's a lot to learn," Teddie replied. "He said we have to do it with muscle memory, like in the army. You go over and over things until they're a reflex, especially if you get in a dangerous situation, like if your horse runs away with you."

"It's a good way to teach," Katy said. "I like Parker."

Teddie grinned. "I like him, too."

"You didn't eat your beans, Teddie." Her mother indicated the plate in front of her daughter.

Teddie made a face. "I hate beans."

"Eat just one and I'll say no more," her mother coaxed.

Teddie sighed. "Okay. Just one. Just for you. But only one."

"Only one."

Teddie glared at the bean before she lifted it to her mouth and chewed, as if she were eating a live worm. The face got worse.

"Swallow," Katy dared.

Teddie gave her a pained look, but she did as she was told.

"That's called compromise," Katy told her with an affectionate smile. "You did great. You're excused."

"Thanks, Mom! I'm going out to tell Bart good night."

"Watch for snakes. They crawl at night and I don't know how to kill one. We don't own a gun anymore." That was true. After her husband's death, Katy, who was mortally afraid of firearms, sold them to several friends of Teddie's dad.

"I'll watch where I put my feet," Teddie assured her.

"Okay. Don't be long."

"I won't!" she called back over her shoulder as she ran to the front door.

A few minutes later, there was a scream and a wail.

Katy, horrified, went running out the door onto the front porch, flicking on the porch light on the way. "Teddie! What happened?!"

Teddie was frozen in her tracks. She couldn't speak. She just pointed.

There, standing a few feet away, was a wolf. Even in the dim light, Katy could see that it was huge, much larger than the biggest dog she'd ever seen. It had an odd ruff around its head with black stripes running through it. As she looked closer, she noticed that the wolf had three legs.

"Teddie, come here. It's all right. Walk slowly. Don't run, okay?"

Teddie did as she was told. She was afraid, but she followed her mother's instructions. "He's so big," she said in a ghostly tone.

"Yes." Katy let a held breath out as Teddie made it to the porch. The wolf still hadn't moved.

Teddie would have run into her mother's arms, but they were folded over her chest. She never had understood why her mother didn't hug her. Her friends' mothers did it all the time.

As Katy stood there with her daughter, wondering what in the world to do, she heard a pickup truck coming down the road. It paused at the end of her driveway and suddenly turned in, going slow.

"It's Parker!" Teddie said. "That's his truck."

Katy wondered why he'd be here after dark, but she was so worried for her daughter that she didn't really question it.

He pulled up at the steps and got out. "Oh, thank goodness. You horror!" he said, approaching the wolf. "Your papa's worried sick!"

The wolf howled softly as Parker approached it.

"It's okay, old man, you're safe. Come on, now." As the women watched, Parker picked up the wolf as if he weighed nothing at all and put him in the passenger seat of the truck. He closed the door and only then noticed how upset Katy and Teddie were.

"It's all right," he said in a soft tone, the one he used with frightened horses. "He's old and crippled and almost blind. Sarge said he left the screen door open accidentally and Two Toes wandered off. Poor old thing probably couldn't find his way home again. He's got a lousy sense of smell."

"Oh, thank goodness," Katy said. "I thought he was going to eat Teddie. She screamed. . . ."

Parker chuckled. "That's what most people do when they come face-to-face with wolves. Some are aggressive predators. Old Two Toes, there, he's a sweetheart." He indicated the wolf, which was sitting up in the passenger seat without making a fuss.

"He's somebody's pet?" Teddie asked.

"My sarge. He's a wildlife rehabilitator. Two Toes lives with him, though, because the old wolf can't be released into the wild. He'd die."

"I remember now," Katy said. "You told me about him."

"I did," he agreed.

"That's so sad," Teddie said. "I'm sorry I screamed. I was really scared. He came out of nowhere."

"Everybody gets scared sometimes. It's not a big deal," he said softly, and smiled at her.

"Okay. I'm going inside. It's cold!" Teddie said.

"It is. You don't even have a jacket on," he chided.

Teddie just laughed.

He looked up at Katy. "You're not wearing one, either."

"She screamed and I came running," she said. "I didn't think about how cold it was." She looked frightened and sad and almost defeated.

He came up onto the porch, towering over her. "What's wrong?" he asked.

She drew in an unsteady breath. "Life," she said simply, fighting tears.

He pulled her gently into his arms, wrapped her up like treasure, and just rocked her. "Let it out. It's hard being the strongest person in your whole family. We all need a moment's weakness to remind us that life is like a prism, with many facets."

"Or like Schrodinger's cat?" she mumbled into his denim jacket.

He chuckled. "Who's been talking?"

"Teddie. She heard you talking to somebody about a cat in a box and an Einstein-Rosen bridge."

"Heavy stuff."

"Very heavy. Way over my head."

"Mine, too, at first. But I loved the concept of invisible numbers and tangents and cosine and stuff like that. Ate it like candy."

She drew back and looked up at him. He seemed different and she couldn't decide why until she realized that his hair, his thick, soft, black hair was loose. It flowed over his shoulders and down his back like silk.

"Your hair's down," she murmured.

He shrugged. "I was getting ready for bed when Sarge called. He's missing an arm and sometimes it bothers him at night. He asked if I'd go hunt for Two Toes, so I left supper hanging and came running. Driving. Whatever."

"Supper at this hour?"

"I don't live a conventional life," he said. "Supper's whenever I feel like fixing it. But tonight it was oatmeal." He made a face. "I think I'll pass on reheating it."

"If you'll come in, I can make you a nice ham and cheese sandwich. I even have lettuce and mayo."

His eyebrows arched. "All that on one sandwich?" he asked with a smile.

"All that."

"Okay. Thanks. But I have to take sweetums home to Sarge first."

"I'll be making the sandwich while you're driving. Want coffee?"

He nodded. "Strong and black, if it's not too much trouble."

"I'm grading papers," she replied. "Strong and black is how I take it, too."

He smiled. "Okay. I'll be back in a few."

"Sounds good."

"Is Parker coming back?" Teddie asked excitedly when her mother came inside.

"Yes, he is. He doesn't really want to reheat the oatmeal he left to go find his sergeant's wolf." She laughed.

"He's so nice."

Katy nodded. "And smart," she added with a wink.

Teddie smiled back.

Later, Parker knocked at the door and Teddie let him in.

"Your hair's down," Teddie said. "I didn't notice before. Gosh, it's long!"

"Warrior hair," he teased. "It's my 'medicine.' I've never cut it, except once."

Teddie's eyes asked the question.

"When my mother died," he said softly. "It's an old way of expressing grief."

"Gosh," she said, fascinated. "Well, I'm glad it grew back. It's beautiful!"

He chuckled and ruffled her hair. "You're good for my ego."

She made a face at him.

"Sandwiches and coffee," Katy said, bringing out a platter of them and going back for the coffeepot. The small table was already set. "Teddie, want a sandwich?"

"No, thanks. I have to finish my homework," she moaned.

"Feel okay now?" Katy asked gently.

She nodded. "I was just a little scared. He's a very big wolf."

"He's a big baby," Parker said as he took off his jacket and sat down at the table. "Sarge loves him to death."

"I guess he's just scary to people who don't know him," Teddie amended.

He smiled. "I'll take you over to Sarge's one day and you can get acquainted. He likes people. Loves girls."

She laughed. "That's a deal. I'll go do that horrible math."

"Math is not horrible," Parker pointed out. "It's the basis of all engineering."

"I don't want to be an engineer. I want to fly jet planes. Fighter planes!"

He rolled his eyes. "And here I'm teaching you to ride horses!"

"One step at a time," Teddie said with a grin. She turned and went down the hall to her room.

"Fighter planes." Parker shook his head as he bit into a sandwich.

"She's adventurous," Katy said, nibbling at a sandwich of her own.

"When I was her age, I wanted to be a cowboy and live on a ranch," he said.

Both eyebrows went up.

"Of course, when I was a little older than her, I was a cowboy and lived on a ranch." He chuckled, swallowing down a bite of sandwich with coffee. "Coffee's good," he said as he put the cup down. "Most people don't get it strong enough."

She laughed. "I like a spoon to stick up in mine."

"Me, too."

"You wanted to be a cowboy, but you already were one," she prompted.

"My point is, I'm happy with my life. So many people aren't," he added. "They're always chasing something they can't find, wanting things that are impossible to have. It's important to be satisfied not only with who you are, but where and what you are. After all, life isn't forever. We're just temporary visitors here. Tourists, really."

She burst out laughing and almost toppled her coffee. "Tourists! I'll have to remember that one."

He grinned. "I stole it from a pal, when we were overseas. He was a great guy. He was going to medical school when we got out of the service. He didn't make it back. A lot of guys didn't."

"I know." She did, too, because her husband had been one of those. "My husband was already a doctor, though. He loved his work. He loved being in the service. He said that patriotism was being sacrificed by people who didn't understand that freedom isn't free. He wanted to do his part." She bit her lower lip. "Sorry. It's still fresh."

He just nodded. "Life goes on, though," he said, studying her. "You have to pick up the pieces and keep going."

"You've lost someone," she said suddenly.

He hesitated. Then he nodded again. "The love of my life," he said with a quiet sadness. "She was eighteen, I was nineteen. While I was overseas, she was diagnosed with pancreatic cancer. She died before I even got home. We were going to be married that Christmas."

"I'm truly sorry," she said softly, and put her hand over his big one. She didn't understand why exactly, because she almost never touched people–not even her daughter, whom she loved. "I do understand how that feels."

His hand turned and clasped hers. There was a flash, almost electric, between them when he did that. She caught her breath, laughed self-consciously, and took her hand away. He seemed as disconcerted as she felt. He finished the sandwich and washed it down with coffee.

"I'd better go and let you get to those papers," he said, rising. "Think of the poor students who'll be disappointed to have to wait an extra day to learn that they failed the test." He grinned wickedly.

She laughed, the tension gone. "I guess so."

"Thanks. It was good coffee and a nice sandwich. Better than cold oatmeal," he added wryly.

"Anytime. Thanks for coming after our furry visitor. If he ever comes back, I'll know who to call."

"Where's your cell phone?" he asked.

She took it out of her pocket and placed it in his out-stretched hand. He put in his contact information and handed it back.

"That's my cell number," he told her. "If you have a problem, night or day, you call me. Okay?"

She smiled warmly. "Okay." She cocked her head. "Where's your cell phone?"

His eyebrows arched, but he handed it to her. She put her own contact information into it and handed it back.

"If you need us, you only have to call," she said quietly. "We'd do anything we could to help you."

He was unsettled. He hesitated. "All right. Thanks."

"I mean, if you come up with some unified field theory in the middle of the night and need to discuss it with someone who knows absolutely nothing about theoretical physics, I'll be right here. Think of it as ego building."

He chuckled. She was a card. "I'll do that."

"But if you get sick or something, you can call, too," she added. "I nursed my mother for several years before I married. I'm pretty good in a sick room."

That surprised and touched him. "I'm never ill."

"I knew that," she replied spritely. "But just in case . . . ?"

"Just in case," he agreed.

He started for the door. "Good night, Teddie. See you Saturday," he called down the hall.

"I'll be here, still doing horrible math!" she called back.

"Math is not horrible!"

"It is so! It has numbers that are invisible! I heard you tell that other man that."

He rolled his eyes.

"How do you see invisible numbers?" she asked from the hallway.

"I'm leaving," he told her. "It's much too late for philosophical discussions."

"I thought you said it was math," Teddie replied innocently.

"Just for that, you can learn two new ways to tie a

cinch on Saturday," he said formally, and then ruined it by laughing.

She grinned. "Okay. Good night."

"Good night," Katy echoed. "Thanks again."

"Thanks for the nice eats," he replied. His dark eyes were warm on her face. "Sleep well."

"I don't, but thanks for the thought."

He sighed. "I don't sleep well, either," he confessed. "I play solitaire and mah-jongg on my cell phone until I get sleepy. Usually, that's about four in the morning."

She laughed. "Me, too. Especially mah-jongg."

"I have four apps with it. I'm a fanatic."

"We should get a board game and teach it to Teddie. She doesn't like playing games on the phone."

"Not a bad idea. I'll pick up a Monopoly game, too. We might play one Saturday night if you don't have anything better to do."

"We just sit and watch old movies on DVD," she said, shrugging. "I watch that series that your boss's wife writes for, and the one her father produces, but nothing else. Well, maybe the Weather Channel and the History Channel. But that's about it."

He grinned. "Two of my favorites."

"I'll bet you sit and watch the NASA channel," she accused.

"I do. It's not the most stimulating channel on television, but I like seeing how far we've come in the space race."

"We're really having one, now." She laughed. "SpaceX fired the gun, and all the other space companies are piling into the game. I'm so excited about Starhopper lifting off!"

"Me, too. I like to watch those rockets land after they've lifted the vehicles into space. He landed two at once on floating platforms in the ocean. Do you have any idea how complicated and delicate a procedure that really is?"

"I do. It's amazing, what Elon Musk has accomplished."

"A man with a vision," he replied.

"A truly great man," she agreed. "He's revolutionized space travel."

"And in a very short space of time, as time goes." He cocked his head and smiled. "Well, good night."

"Good night, Parker." She frowned. "Do you have a first name?"

He made a face. "Yes, I do, and no, I'm not telling you what it is."

"Well!"

"Nobody knows what it is." He hesitated. "Well, the boss knows, because payroll sends me a check. But he's sworn to secrecy."

Her eyes twinkled. "Okay. We all have a few secrets."

He chuckled. "So we do. Good night."

"Drive carefully," she said, and then flushed. It sounded forward.

Both thick, dark eyebrows arched. "My, my, do you worry about me already?"

She turned absolutely scarlet and was bereft of words.

He grinned. "Don't sweat it. It's sort of nice, having somebody worry about me."

"Oh. Well, okay then."

He went down the steps to his truck. She watched him all the way to it before she closed the door and locked it. Her life was suddenly very complicated.

Chapter Four

It seemed a very long week before Saturday rolled around and Teddie was dancing with anticipation because Parker was going to take her riding down the fence lines today. He said Bart was as ready as he was going to be.

"I'm so excited," she told her mother. "It will be the first time I've ever really ridden him around the ranch!"

"You do exactly what Parker tells you, okay?" Katy said. "He won't let anything happen to you."

"I know that." She cocked her head. "You look really nice," she commented. "That's the first time I've seen your hair down in a long time, Mom," she added curiously.

"I rushed to get breakfast and forgot to put it up," she lied, hating the faint blush that was probably going to give her away to her daughter.

She was wearing jeans with a yellow long-sleeved sweater. She looked neat and trim but also very sexy. Her long blond hair was around her shoulders, soft and waving. She did look nice. It hadn't been intentional. At least, she didn't think it was. She was attracted to Parker and she didn't want to be. She'd only lost her husband a few months ago. It was too soon. Or was it?

Teddie watched those expressions pass over her mother's

face. "Parker's nice," she said. "Much nicer than that lawyer who's coming out here to see you next month."

"He's a nice man," Katy said, frowning. She'd forgotten that he'd invited himself out to Colorado. Now, she was regretting that she hadn't said no.

"Are we going to get to go trick-or-treating next week?" Teddie asked plaintively. "There's almost nobody near enough for us to ask for candy around here. Well, maybe Parker and Mr. Denton, but nobody else."

Katy grinned. "The school is going to be handing out candy next week. In fact, the businesses in town are staying open after dark so they can hand it out, too. Just between us, even the policemen have bags of it in their cars, and they'll be handing it out. So you'll get lots of candy. I promise."

"Oh, Mom, that's awesome!" She hugged her mother, who stiffened. She drew away at once, embarrassed. But she recovered quickly. "Mmmm." She sighed. "You smell nice. Like flowers."

"It's cologne. I haven't worn any in a long time." Katy felt uneasy. She'd never told Teddie why she didn't hug her like her father had. Someday . . .

"I like it when you dress up," Teddie said. She didn't add that she suspected it was for Parker's benefit, but that was what she was thinking. She grinned. "I'll just go check on Bartholomew."

"Okay."

Teddie went into the barn and Katy sat down in the porch swing and closed her eyes, listening to the sounds of nature all around her. It was the nicest place to live, she thought. She wondered how she'd ever endured city noise. She was certain that she couldn't go back to it after this.

"Asleep, are we?"

Her eyes flew open and her heart skipped. She hadn't even heard Parker come up on the porch. He was wearing boots, too.

"Goodness, you startled me." She laughed, putting a hand to her chest. "No, I was drinking in the sounds. It's so nice here. So different from the city."

"Amen," he agreed. He dropped down in the swing beside her, noting her long, soft hair with a warm smile. "You look pretty today."

She flushed and cleared her throat.

"Too much too soon?" he asked softly. "No sweat. You look cool, kid. How's that?"

She laughed. "Sorry. I was feeling a little self-conscious."

"Oh, I like the new look, don't get me wrong," he said. He cocked his head. "You and Teddie going trick-or-treating next week?"

"We were just talking about that," she replied. "They're having a big deal downtown in Benton. All the stores will be open and giving out candy. We're having a harvest festival at our school, too."

"Sounds like fun."

"Did you go trick-or-treating in town when you were a kid?" she asked.

He shook his head. "Too dangerous."

She frowned and her eyes asked the question.

He looked older than his years as he looked down at her. "I look like my people," he said delicately. "Back in 1876, some of my ancestors rode with the Cheyenne and the Sioux and the Arapaho and a few other tribes against Colonel George Custer. Old hatreds lingered, especially around the battlefield. We didn't come off the rez much when we were kids. Not until we were teenagers, at least.

I got in a lot of trouble, and I got given a choice—go in the army or go to jail."

She whistled. "Good choice," she said.

He shrugged. "It was the making of me," he said. "After the first couple of weeks, I settled down and really enjoyed the routine. I stopped being a juvenile delinquent and turned into a soldier."

She studied him curiously. "I thought we were getting away from prejudice," she said softly. "I have students from all races, all walks of life. They get along well."

"They do, if they're taught to, while they're young. You have to remember that the rez is for one race only: ours. We don't mix well."

"I'm sorry about that," she said with genuine feeling. "Someday, I hope we can look at qualifications and personality instead of gender or race or religion."

"Pipe dreams," he said gently. "People are what they are. Most don't change."

She made a face. "I guess I've lived a sheltered life."

"Nothing wrong with that."

She looked up into large, dark eyes. "The story of your life is in your eyes," she said quietly, and she grimaced. "Sorry. I blurt out things sometimes."

He smiled. "I don't mind. I'm pretty blunt myself from time to time. It sort of goes with the job description."

"And which one would that be?" she teased. "Breaking horses or working on a new unified field theory?"

He laughed. "Both, I suppose." He rocked the swing into motion and looked straight ahead. "The feds noticed that I had a gift for algorithms, so they send a black sedan to pick me up in the summer and take me off to D.C."

"Wow," she said softly. "What do you do there?"

He sighed. "It's all classified. Very top secret. I do code work. I'm not allowed to talk about it."

She winced. "I put my foot in my mouth again."

"Not at all. You didn't know." His dark eyes slid over her face intently. "Your major was what, English or education?"

"I did a double major," she said. "Both."

"What about your minor?"

She hesitated.

His thick black eyebrows lifted and he smiled. "Hmmm?"

She cleared her throat. "Anthropology. Specifically, archaeology. I went on digs for four years." She gave him an apologetic glance. "I know, your people think of archaeology as grave digging. . . ."

"I don't," he said. "I minored in anthropology, too, as well as biology," he said surprisingly. "I loved being able to date projectile points and pottery sherds. It was fascinating. You forget, I'm not all Crow. My mother was born on the reservation, near Hardin, Montana. But my father was white." His face closed up at the memory.

She never touched people. But her small hand went to his shoulder and rested there, lightly, feeling the taut muscles. "We all have bad memories."

His head turned. "I'll bet you don't."

"Well, my parents loved each other, they said, but they still had knock-down, drag-out fights every so often," she said. "I learned to hide in the stable until they calmed down."

He chuckled. "I never had to do that. But my father wasn't much of a father."

"Was he a teacher?"

He shook his head. "An astrophysicist," he said with distaste. "He still works in the aerospace industry. NASA, I think. I haven't had any contact with him since."

"I'll bet he'd be proud of the man you became," she said, and then flushed, because it was a little forward.

He looked down at her and frowned. "You think so?" he asked, surprising her.

"You're kind to strangers, you love children, you break horses without harming their spirit, you know about Schrodinger's cat. . . ."

He chuckled. "You're good for my ego. You know that?" he teased. "I guess a lot of us are prey to low self-image, especially people of color."

"You're a nice color," she said warmly. "Light olive skin. I'm just pink. I can't even tan."

He studied her fair hair, long around her shoulders, and her pretty, pink face. He smiled slowly, a smile that made her toes curl inside her shoes. "You're a nice color, too," he said huskily. His fingers went to her hair and touched it softly. "Your hair is naturally this color, isn't it?" he asked.

"Yes." Was that high, squeaky tone her actual voice? She was surprised at the way it sounded. "Well, I do use a highlighting shampoo, but I don't color it."

"It's beautiful."

Her breath was coming like a distance runner's. Her eyes fell on his mouth. It was chiseled, with a thin upper lip and a full square lower one. It was a mouth that made her hungry for things she barely remembered. Her late husband had been gone so much that intimacy had gone by the wayside, for the most part. At the end, they were more friends than lovers. And she couldn't remember ever feeling such hunger, even for him. Perhaps it was her age, or that she'd been alone too long. She felt guilty, too, just for entertaining the thought that Parker would be heaven to kiss.

He was staring at her mouth, too. His fingers tightened on her hair. "This would be," he whispered, "a very bad idea."

"Oh, yes," she whispered back, shakily. "A very, very bad idea."

But even as they spoke, they were bending toward each other. Her head tilted naturally to the side, inviting his mouth closer.

"I might become addicted," he whispered a little unsteadily.

"Me, too . . ."

He leaned closer, his big hand clutching her hair, positioning her face. His head bent. She could almost taste the coffee on his mouth. She was hungry. So hungry!

"Katy," he breathed, and his lips started to touch hers.

"Mom? Parker? Where are you guys?"

They broke apart, both flushed and uneasy. Parker got to his feet and moved away from Katy without looking at her.

"We're out here, sprout!" he called. "Ready to go?"

Teddie came barreling out the front door, dressed to ride. "Yes! I'm so excited!"

"We'll take it slow and easy the first time," he told her, grinning, although he was churning inside about what had almost happened. He managed to get himself together in the small space of time he had while Teddie rushed toward the stable.

He turned and looked at Katy, who was standing up, looking all at sea and guilty.

He went back to her, towering over her. "It's okay," he said softly.

She swallowed. "I'm . . . I mean . . . I think . . ." She looked up at him with her face taut with indecision, hunger, fear, guilt.

He touched her cheek gently. "We'll take it slow and easy, Katy," he said huskily. "No pressure. Okay?"

She took a deep breath. "Okay," she agreed, and her eyes grew soft.

He smiled in a way he never had. "Suppose I pick you and Teddie up on Halloween night and drive you around to the venues for candy?"

She hesitated just a second too long.

His face tautened. "Or is that a bad idea? You'd rather not be seen with me in public . . . ?"

She went right up to him and reached up to touch his hard cheek. "You know me better than that already. I know you do!"

He let out the breath he'd been holding. "Sorry," he bit off. "Life is hard sometimes when you're a minority."

"I've never been like that," she said. "I'd be proud to be seen with you anywhere. I was just worried about, well, gossip. Small towns run on it. You might not like being talked about. . . ."

He actually laughed. "I've been talked about for years. I don't mind gossip. If you don't." He hesitated. "That lawyer's coming out here next month, isn't he?"

"He's a pest," she said shortly. "He invited himself and I can't convince him that I'm not interested."

"No worries, kid," he teased. "I'll convince him for you."

She smiled slowly. "Okay," she said.

He chuckled. "I'd better go help Teddie saddle Bartholomew before she ends up in a pile of something nasty."

She smiled from ear to ear. "She'll love riding. Until she gets off the horse," she added, because she knew how sore riding made people who weren't used to it.

"You could come, too," he invited.

Her eyes were full of affection and something else. "Next time," she said.

He nodded. "Next time."

He turned and went toward the stable.

"Mom got all dressed up and let her hair down," Teddie said as she and Parker rode down the fence line, she on Bartholomew and he on Wings.

"I noticed. Your mom's pretty."

She laughed. "She thinks you're awesome, but don't tell her I told you."

"She does?" he asked, astonished.

"It was the cat," she volunteered. "She's keen on brainy people."

"It's a conundrum, the cat," he replied. "Einstein did thought experiments like that. Most theoretical physicists do. In fact. I follow two of them–Michio Kaku and Miguel Alcubierre. Alcubierre came up with the idea for a speculative faster-than-light speed warp drive. In fact, they call it the Alcubierre drive. One day, it may take mankind to the stars."

"Gosh, I didn't know that. You follow them? You mean, when you go back East to D.C.?" she wondered.

He chuckled. "I follow them on Twitter."

"Oh! Theoretical physics." She rode silently for a few minutes. "I still want to fly jet fighter planes."

"I knew a guy who did that, years ago. He said that when those things take off, your stomach glues itself to your backbone and you have to fight the urge to throw up. It's like going up in a rocket. The gravitational pull is awesome."

"I didn't realize that. Goodness!"

"It's something you get used to. Like the "raptor cough," if you fly F-22 Raptors."

She frowned. "Raptor cough?"

"That's what they call it. Nobody knows what causes it. But the guys who fly those things all develop it."

"Maybe I can get used to it," she said. "I love Raptors," she added with a sigh. "I think they're the most beautiful planes on earth."

He grinned. "They're not bad. But I like horses."

"Me, too!"

They rode along for a few minutes in silence. Bartholomew took his time, and he wasn't particularly nervous. Hopefully, being around Teddie relaxed him, because he didn't try to bolt with her. All the same, Parker was watchful.

"Will it offend you if I ask you something?" Teddie asked as they were on their way back to the stables.

"Of course not," he replied with a smile. "What do you want to know?"

"We learned at school that all Native Americans have legends about animals and constellations and stuff. Do the Crow have them?"

He grinned. "We do. My favorite is the Nirumbee."

"Nirumbee?"

He nodded. "They're a race of little people, under two feet tall. Some of the tales we have about them are violent and gory, but they've also been known to help people. I had a Cherokee friend in the service, and he said they also had a legend about little people that they called the Nunnehi."

"Do you think they really exist?"

"Some credible people have claimed to see them," he said. "My friend swore that he heard them singing in the mountains of North Carolina, where he grew up. And here's what's interesting. Archaeologists actually found evidence of a race of little people, no taller than three feet high. It made the major news outlets. They were called the "Hobbit" species, after Tolkien's race from the films," he said, chuckling.

"Wow."

"I think all legends have some basis in fact," he continued. "Like the Thunderbird. It's a staple of Native American legends, a huge bird that casts giant shadows on the ground. There was a lot of controversy about a photograph, a very old one, of several men holding what looked like a pterodactyl stretched out. I don't know if it was Photoshopped or legitimate, but it looked authentic to me. I saw it on the Internet years ago."

"I'll have to go looking for that!"

"I like legends," he said softly. "Living in a world that has no make-believe, no fantasy, is cold."

"I think so, too." She paused. "Do you speak Crow?"

He nodded. "A lot of us do."

"Is it hard to learn?"

"Compared to Dutch and Finnish, it's simple. Compared to Spanish or French, it's hard." He glanced at her whimsically. "We have glottal stops and high tones and low tones, double vowels, even a sound like the *ach* in German. It's difficult. Not so much if you learn it from the ground up as a child."

"I'd like to study languages in college," Teddie said.

"In between flying F-22s?" he teased.

She laughed. "In between that. I could go in the Air Force and go to college, couldn't I?"

"You could."

"Then I'll study real hard, so that I can get in."

"That's not a bad idea."

She fingered the reins gingerly. "Do you like my mom?"
He hesitated.

She glanced at him and saw his discomfort. "Sorry. I just meant she likes you. I hoped maybe you liked her, too."

"I do like her," he said. He sighed. "But you guys are getting over a big loss, a really big loss."

"She misses Daddy," she agreed. "But he wasn't the sort of person who'd want her to grieve forever or spend the rest of her life alone. He was always doing things for other people. Always."

"I wish I could have known him, Teddie," he said solemnly.

"Me, too."

"You're doing very well at riding, you know," he said after a minute.

"I am?"

He smiled at her enthusiasm. "Very well, indeed." He grimaced. "But you may not think so when we get back."

She didn't understand why, until they were at the stable and he reached up to lift her down. She stood on her feet and made a terrible face.

"You need to soak in a hot tub," he told her. "It will help the soreness."

"Mom never said it was going to hurt so much," she groaned.

"It only hurts when you haven't done it for a while," he explained. "Riding takes practice. You're using muscles you don't normally use, so they get stretched and they protest."

"I see."

"It will get better," he promised.

She drew in a breath. "Okay. If you're sure."

"I'm sure. Go on in. I'll unsaddle Bartholomew for you and rub him down, okay?"

"Thanks!"

"No problem."

She walked like an old woman all the way to the house. Katy was waiting on the porch and she made a face.

"I'm sorry, honey," she said. "I should have told you."

"It wouldn't have mattered. Honest. I'd have gone anyway. Parker said I'm doing great! I didn't fall off or spook Bart even one time!"

She laughed. "Good for you."

"He said I should soak in a hot tub, so I'm going to."

"Good idea," she replied. "Want me to run the bath for you?"

"I can do that. Thanks, Mom."

"You're welcome."

She hesitated and grinned wickedly. "He likes you," she said, and walked away before her mother had time to react.

Parker stopped at the steps where Katy was standing. "I'll be over Thursday about six to take you guys trick-or-treating," he said. "That okay?"

She smiled. "That's fine. Teddie will be looking forward to it. She loves Halloween."

"Me, too," he said with a grin. "I like anything to do with fantasy creatures, although I'm partial to dragons. But giant spiders and bats are okay."

She rolled her eyes. "You and Teddie," she mused. "I always decorate for all the holidays, but my favorite is Christmas."

"I like that one also," he said. "My mother was traditional.

She didn't celebrate regular holidays, but my cousin's parents were Catholic, so they always had a Christmas tree and presents. It was great fun."

She cocked her head. "Crow people have a proud tradition," she said softly. "I grew up reading about them in Montana."

"I forgot that you were raised there as well. Where?"

"Near Hardin, where the battleground is."

He whistled. "The rez is close to there," he reminded her. "That's where I was raised."

She laughed. "I'm surprised that we didn't know each other then."

"I'm not. I didn't venture off the rez until I was in my late teens. When I did, I got into all sorts of trouble. I'll bet you never put a foot wrong."

She shrugged. "My parents were strict."

"My mother died in my formative years. My cousin's parents were lenient; they pretty much let us do what we pleased," he confessed. "Probably not the best way to raise a child. But we're not big on heavy-handed discipline."

"I had a friend whose grandfather was Crow," she recalled. "I learned a lot from her."

His dark eyes searched hers. "Teddie wants to learn to speak it." He laughed. "I told her it was a lot harder than it looked."

She nodded. "I know it is. Most native languages have glottal stops and high and low tones and nasalization."

"Do you speak any of them?"

She shook her head. "I just have Spanish," she said. "I loved it from the time I was a child. I read a book that had Spanish words in it when I was in fifth grade. I took it all through high school and college."

"Are you literate in it?"

"Yes." She smiled. "I love to read books in the original language, books like *Don Quixote*."

"I envy you that. I can only read books in English. Well, and in Crow," he added, "and there are a few, mostly about legends."

"How about sign language?"

He chuckled. "I cut my teeth on that. My grandfather taught it to me."

"I learned just a few signs. I can't even remember them now."

"You need to brush up," he teased. "We can talk over Teddie's head without her knowing what we say."

"I'll get out my books," she returned, eyes sparkling.

He hesitated. "Well, I'd better go. I brushed Bartholomew down, by the way, and put him in his stall. He's doing fine. Tell Teddie."

"I will."

"Have a good night," he said.

Her eyes searched over his handsome face. "You, too."

He smiled and turned away with visible reluctance. She watched him all the way to his truck. When he drove off, with a wave of his hand, she was still watching.

Parker came to get them on Halloween night. Teddie went as Rey from the new *Star Wars* movies, complete with light saber. Katy was too self-conscious to wear a costume, although she did wear a pretty black silky blouse with pumpkins and lace, and nice-fitting jeans. She left her hair down, because she knew that their new friend liked it that way.

"The fire department is also handing out candy," he said

when they were on the way into Benton. "So we can make a lot of stops."

"Oh, boy!" Teddie said. "Endless candy!"

"Endless dentist visits," Katy groaned.

"Stop that," two voices said at once. Teddie and Parker looked at each other and just howled with laughter as they realized they'd said it at the same time.

"You two!" Katy said in mock anger. "I can't take you anyplace!"

"We'll behave," Teddie promised.

"Speak for yourself." Parker chuckled. "I never behave."

Their first stop was the side of the town square that contained a restaurant and a sports bar, along with a dress shop. The proprietors were wearing costumes and carrying pumpkin baskets full of candy.

Teddie held out her own bag and received handfuls of candy while Parker and Katy watched from the sidewalk.

"They really pull out the stops to do this, don't they?" Katy asked. "It's so nice of them!"

"It's dangerous for kids to go alone these days," he remarked. "And houses are spaced so far apart that it would take forever to go door to door."

"That's true."

"Hey, Mrs. Blake," a young voice called.

Katy turned. She smiled. The girl, a redhead with brown eyes, was in the class she taught. "Hello, Jean," she greeted. "You look very trendy!" she added.

Jean, who was wearing a Wonder Woman costume, laughed. "Thanks! My mom bought it for me!"

A woman joined them. She was tall and she looked irritated. "Honestly, all this fuss just for some candy we could have bought at the store," she muttered. "I'm missing my favorite program on TV!"

Jean flushed and looked as if she could have gone through the concrete with embarrassment.

"We all make sacrifices for the children we love," Katy said gently, making the tactful remark with just a faint bite in her tone.

The woman actually blushed as she looked from Katy to Parker. She cleared her throat. "Well, of course we do," she added belatedly. She forced a smile, and Jean relaxed. "Come on, Jean, there's another bag of treats waiting for you." She nudged her daughter forward.

"Good to see you, Mrs. Blake," Jean said.

"Good to see you, too, Jean," Katy said softly.

Parker made a face as the two of them went out of earshot. "My mother would never have complained like that."

"Neither would mine," Katy said on a sigh.

"Parker?" came an almost incredulous voice from behind them.

Chapter Five

Parker turned around and there was his former sergeant, Butch Matthews, grinning like a Cheshire cat as he saw his friend keeping company with a woman. A pretty woman, at that.

"How's it going, Sarge?" he asked, extending a hand to shake. "What are you doing here? And where did you leave Two Toes?"

"Safely locked in the den," the man replied. "Double locked. Is that Mrs. Blake?" he added.

"It is. Katy Blake, this is Butch Matthews. He was my sergeant when we served overseas. He owns Two Toes."

"Pleased to meet you," Katy said, smiling.

Matthews repeated the greeting and tipped his wide-brimmed hat. "Sorry he got onto your place and scared your daughter, ma'am. He's an escape artist. I was scared to death I'd find him in the road dead."

"He's a very nice wolf," Katy said. "My daughter was fascinated with him when Parker put him in the truck and drove him home. She said she'd love to meet him some-time."

The sergeant beamed. "I'd be delighted. Any time at all. I'm a rehabilitator for the fish and wildlife folks. I specialize in mammals, like wolves and coyotes, pumas, raccoons, and so forth."

"I imagine you stay busy," Katy said.

"Very busy." He sighed. "Too many people shoot animals without caring if they're just wounded. We get a lot of city hunters up here who aren't too careful about what they put a bullet in."

"True story," Parker agreed. "A hunter from Las Vegas came up here with a brand-new gun and shot what he thought was a white deer. It was Old Man Harlowe's prize goat. Talk about a lawsuit!"

"It wasn't just the money, either. He loved that old goat. Said the property was posted and everything and that idiot jumped a fence onto his property and just killed his goat. They caught him with it on the Benton highway. Said he was properly shocked when they told him what he shot."

"I hope they lock him up," Katy muttered. "I have no quarrel with responsible hunters, but I draw the line at idiots."

"So do I," Parker agreed.

The sarge looked from one to the other of them with twinkling eyes. "Well, I guess I'll go ask Lucy Mallory for a few toffees to satisfy my sweet tooth. She's got the cloth shop over there." He nodded toward the other side of the square. "I never miss Halloween in town," he added on a chuckle. "See you."

They waved.

"He's nice," Katy said. "What happened to his arm?"

"Blown off when we were in Iraq," he returned bluntly and then winced. "Sorry. He took a direct hit from a mortar. We didn't think he'd make it, but we had one hell of a battlefield surgeon. Saved his life. He's one of the best men I've ever known." He didn't add that he'd saved Matthews by running through a hail of bullets to recover him and been wounded in the process. Or that Matthews had saved his life by taking out an insurgent who had Parker in his sights. That was while Matthews was still recovering in the field hospital, too, before they shipped him home. A group of insurgents had actually attacked the field hospital.

"I would love to see the wolf again, now that I know he's not dangerous," Katy said.

"I'll take you and Teddie over there one day. Saturday maybe if it isn't snowing."

"Snowing?!"

"It's in the forecast, I'm afraid," he said on a sigh. "The nighthawks will be cursing."

"I don't doubt it."

"It's not something we mind, keeping watch over the cattle," Parker added. "I even pitch in when I'm not working with the horses. It's just the difficulty of getting equipment where it's needed if we have an emergency. . . ."

"Well, well," came an amused voice from nearby. It was the owner of the Gray Dove restaurant in town, a coincidence if there ever was one, because nobody knew it was Parker's late mother's name. "Fancy seeing you two in town."

Katy flushed, but Parker just laughed. "How are you, Mary?" he asked. "Katy Blake, this is Mary Dodd. She owns the restaurant in town."

"I'm very happy to meet you," Katy said. "You have wonderful food. Teddie and I ate there one afternoon just last week!"

"Thanks," Mary replied with a warm smile. "Parker, I don't think I've ever seen you trick-or-treating."

"I brought Katy and Teddie."

"Teddie?"

Parker nodded toward the little girl dressed up as Rey in *Star Wars* regalia.

"Why, isn't she adorable?" Mary enthused.

"Thanks," Katy said proudly. "She begged for the costume for two weeks, so I gave in. I have to admit, it does look pretty good on her, even if she is my daughter."

"That *Star Wars* stuff sells like mad at the costume shops," Mary agreed. "I used to go as Princess Leia. But that was years ago. Parker, did you ever dress up for Halloween?"

He shook his head. "We didn't celebrate it in my family," he said, and he was withdrawn suddenly.

Mary grimaced. "Sorry. Hit a nerve, didn't I? I didn't mean to."

"It's nothing," Parker said softly. "Really."

"We all have our bad memories of that golden childhood everybody talks about. I never had one."

"Me, neither." Parker chuckled.

"Sorry," Katy replied.

Mary pursed her lips and her eyes twinkled. "You're getting stares," she warned. "There will be talk."

Parker shrugged. "Won't be the first time I attracted gossip."

"Same here," Katy said, and she grinned.

Mary just laughed. "At least you have a good attitude about it. I'll go help my girls with the handouts. Don't forget to bring your daughter by the restaurant. We made Rice Krispies treats!"

"I wouldn't miss those for the world," Katy promised.

"You can have some, too," Mary promised, and patted her on the arm. "See you. Parker, you watch your mouth."

He put a finger to his lips and his eyes twinkled.

After Mary left, Katy looked up at him curiously. "Everybody says you cuss like a sailor, but I've never heard you say a really bad word."

"I'm on my best behavior, especially in front of Teddie." He glanced at her with real fondness. "She's a sweet child. You and your husband did a great job with her."

"Thanks. I'm very proud of her," she said, her eyes on her daughter, who was now talking with some other children who'd been brought to town by their relatives. She looked up at him curiously. "You're wonderful with Teddie. It's obvious that you love children. But . . . ?"

"But I never had any of my own, you were going to say, huh?" he asked, and his dark eyes were sad. "I didn't know until I got back home, out of the military, but my fiancée was pregnant with my child when she died."

"Oh, Parker, how horrible," she said under her breath. "I'm so sorry!"

He ground his teeth together. So many memories, all painful. He shoved his hands deep into the pockets of his jeans. "I got cold feet after that. All I could think about was how much it hurt to lose her, to lose my child." He laughed, but it had a hollow sound. "I withdrew from the world. I discovered," he added, glancing down at her, "that most women will avoid a man who can't say a complete sentence without a few really blue words. So I started cussing a lot, especially when the boss or the other cowboys had women relatives visiting." He pursed his lips and his eyes twinkled. "It worked very well."

She laughed. "Should I be flattered, that you don't use bad words around us?"

His big shoulders shrugged. "I guess so," he said after a minute. "I don't want to drive Teddie away. She's brought the sunshine back into my life." He looked down at her. "You're part of that."

She caught her breath as they stared into each other's eyes for just a little longer than politeness required.

"We're both carrying painful scars," he said after a minute. "You lost your husband. I lost my fiancée and my child. I've had longer to recover than you have, but it's still fresh, very fresh."

She drew in a breath and wrapped her arms around her chest. She felt a chill, even with her nice warm coat on. "My husband died doing something he felt a moral obligation to do. It was the most important thing in his life, even more important than us. He said that so few people could do his job, that many men would have died if he hadn't been there to do it. So I guess it evens out, in a way. But yes, it's still fresh. A few months' distance helps. It doesn't heal."

"It takes years for that." He lifted his head and looked where Teddie was opening her bag to another handful of treats from a merchant. "You know, when you have an old dog that you love, and it dies, they all say the best thing for the grief is to go right out and get a puppy."

Her heart skipped. "They do, don't they?"

He turned to her. "We're not speaking of dogs."

She just nodded. She was spellbound, looking up into those dark, dark eyes.

He moved a step closer, not intimately close, but enough that she could feel his breath on her forehead. "We don't have to get totally involved, just to have a hamburger together or take Teddie to a movie. Right?"

Her heart was going wild. It surprised and almost

shamed her, because she hadn't had such a violent physical reaction even to her late husband. "N-no," she stammered. "I mean, yes. I mean . . ." She just stopped, staring up into his eyes.

His jaw tautened and he averted his gaze. "Don't do that," he bit off. "It's been a long time. A long time," he emphasized. "I'm more vulnerable than I look."

She swallowed, hard. "Sorry," she said in a gruff whisper.

He shifted on his feet, feeling the hunger all the way to his toes. "I would love to drag you behind the nearest building and kiss you until you couldn't stand up by yourself."

Her lips parted on a shocked breath. She turned toward Teddie, not looking at him. "I would love it . . . if you did," she blurted out.

"Oh, God," he groaned.

"'Four score and seven years ago'," she began reciting Lincoln's Gettysburg Address.

She turned around again and he looked down at her in shock.

"It's what I did at school when I got all embarrassed and couldn't think of what to say to somebody," she explained, and flushed, and then laughed self-consciously.

He burst out laughing. "I started calculating the absolute value of Pi," he replied, and now his dark eyes were twinkling.

"Lincoln's address is much shorter," she pointed out.

He grinned. "So it is." He caught her hand in his and linked their fingers together. "People will talk," he added softly.

Her fingers tangled in his. "Let them," she said huskily.

He pulled her along with him and they went to find Teddie.

* * *

Teddie, of course, noticed the new attitude between both the adults in her life, and she smiled mischievously when they got back to the ranch house.

"Thanks for driving us, Parker," Teddie said on the front porch, and impulsively hugged him and then ran to unlock the front door. "Happy Halloween!" she called back as she went inside. "I'm going to eat candy and watch TV!"

"Not too much!" Katy called after her.

"Okay!"

Parker chuckled. "She doesn't miss a trick, does she? I guess we might as well be wearing signs."

"She's intuitive," she agreed.

He reached out lazily and pulled her to him. "How about a movie Saturday night?" he asked. "We can take Teddie to see that new cartoon one that came out."

"I'd love to go to a movie with you."

He bent his head toward her. "We can't make out in a theater," he whispered. "Probably a good thing."

"Probably a very . . . good . . . thing," she agreed as his mouth brushed slowly over hers.

"Come up here." He lifted her off the ground against him and his mouth grew gently invasive. "You taste like honey," he whispered, and smiled against her lips as he drew her closer.

She smiled, too. She loved the way he kissed her. He wasn't impatient or demanding. He was gentle and slow and seductive.

"I like this," he whispered.

"Me, too," she whispered back.

He drew in a quick breath and slowly lowered her back to her feet. "One step at a time," he said huskily, holding her just a little away from him. "We could get in over our heads too quickly."

She nodded. She was staring at his mouth. It hadn't been enough. Not nearly enough.

He read that hunger in her. "Too much too soon is dangerous," he said firmly.

She nodded again. She was still staring at his mouth.

"Oh, what the hell . . . !"

He swept her close, bent, and made a meal of her soft lips, pressing them back away from her teeth so that his tongue could flick inside her mouth and make the kiss even more intimate, more seductive.

She moaned helplessly, and he ground his mouth into hers, his arms swallowing her up whole, in a silence that exploded with sensation too long unfelt, hungers too long unfed, passion that flared between them like a wildfire.

Finally, when her lips were almost bruised, he eased her away from him. His heartbeat was shaking the jacket he wore with his T-shirt. He sounded as if he'd run a ten-mile race, his breathing was so labored.

She just smiled, all at sea, deliciously stimulated, feeling as if she'd finally taken the edge off a little of the hunger he kindled in her.

"Well, that was dumb," he muttered. "Now we'll have hot dreams of each other every night and I'll wake up screaming."

She laughed. "I'd love to see that," she teased.

He laughed, too. "If I do, I'll phone you."

"You could text me," she said. "Even when I'm at work. I wouldn't mind."

He smiled softly. "You can text me, too, even at two in the morning. I don't sleep much."

"I could?"

He nodded. He touched her cheek gently. "We have differences," he said. "My culture is not the same as yours.

Even though my father is white, I was raised a Crow, in a Crow community."

"I'll study."

He smiled. "That's the idea."

"But whatever the differences, I won't mind," she said. Her face was radiant. "I'll adjust."

He nodded. "I know you will. Meanwhile, we'll try to keep it low-key. Okay?"

She flushed. She'd started this. "I should probably feel guilty, but I don't," she added pertly.

"Neither do I. Some things are inevitable."

"Yes."

He drew in a long breath. "Well, I'll go home and try to sleep. If I can't sleep, I'll text you, and you can call and sing me a lullaby," he said outrageously.

"I actually know one," she said. "I used to sing it to Teddie when she was little. It always worked."

He brushed her mouth with his. "It will take a lot more than a lullaby to get me to sleep, I'm afraid," he said.

"Bad memories?"

"Very bad," he said. "And not all from combat."

She wondered if his father had anything to do with those, but it was far too soon in their very new relationship to start asking intimate questions about his life. Still, there was one question that kept coming up.

"Do you have a first name?" she asked.

He chuckled. "Yes."

She cocked her head. "Well?"

His dark eyes twinkled. "We need to keep a few secrets just to make ourselves more interesting."

"Spoilsport."

"If you're curious, you won't mind letting me stay around here."

"I wouldn't mind even if I wasn't curious."

"We'll still wait," he returned. "Tell Teddie I'll be here bright and early Saturday for her riding lessons, and that we'll go to a movie Saturday night."

She made a face. "No places to make out," she complained.

His eyes twinkled. "That's not a bad thing. We'll make haste slowly."

She let out a deep sigh. "Okay," she said.

He laughed. "We walk before we run."

"Some of us are still at the crawling stage, though," she said with a sting of sarcasm and a big grin.

He just shook his head. "Good night."

"Good night. Thanks for driving us."

"No problem."

He got in the truck and drove off with a wave. Katy watched him all the way out the driveway before she walked back into the house and locked the door.

Teddie was waiting in the hall as she started toward her own bedroom.

"Aha," Teddie teased.

Katy's thin eyebrows arched. "Aha?" she repeated.

"Your lipstick is smeared and your hair looks like rats nested in it," Teddie said with twinkling eyes.

Katy cleared her throat. "Well, you see—"

"It won't work," her daughter interrupted. She grinned. "I like Parker," she added, wiggling her eyebrows. She went back into her room and closed the door.

Katy laughed all the way into her own room.

It was two o'clock in the morning. Katy couldn't sleep. She kept feeling the slow, soft hunger of Parker's sensuous mouth against her lips, the warm comfort of his strong arms around her. She was restless.

She heard a buzz. She had her cell phone on vibrate so it wouldn't wake Teddie. She picked it up and disconnected it from the charger. There was a message on it. Are you awake?

Yes, she texted back. Couldn't sleep. You?

Same, he texted. Suppose you text me the Gettysburg Address? It might put me to sleep.

LOL, she texted back.

I had fun tonight, he texted. I don't go out much.

Me, neither, she replied. I had fun, too. Teddie mentioned that my lipstick was smeared, she added before she could chicken out and not text it.

There was a big LOL on the screen. I had lipstick all over my face. Lucky that I live alone, he added.

She laughed to herself. Sorry about that, she texted.

I didn't mind. But you might look for some type of lipstick that doesn't come off. You know, just in case we can't help ourselves one night . . . ?

I'll go right to the store tomorrow after school and search for one, she replied.

And the clerk will go right out and tell the whole town what sort you bought, he teased.

She laughed. Oh, the joy of small towns.

They're the backbone of the world, aren't they? he texted back.

They are. I'm sorry you can't sleep. Bad memories?

Oh, no. Delicious ones. I ache every time I remember those few minutes on your front porch.

Her heart jumped. She felt exactly the same. Delicious, she typed.

And addictive.

Definitely.

I have no plans to stop, he texted after a minute.

She felt warm all over. I don't, either.

There was a long pause, during which she felt as if he was right in the room with her and she was hungry and thirsty, but not for food.

Going to try to sleep now. You do that, too, he said. Sleep well, angel.

She smiled. You sleep well, too. Good night.

Good night.

She turned the phone off, but she felt safe and warm and content. She closed her eyes and went to sleep with the phone under her pillow.

"Mom! Mom, we're going to be late!" Teddie called from the doorway.

"Late?" Katy sat up in bed, looking all at sea.

"Late for school and late for work. Late, late, late!"

"Oh. Oh!"

She threw off the covers and got out of bed, groaning when she looked at the clock. She wouldn't even have time to make coffee . . . !

"I made you a cup of coffee and put it in your Starbucks coffee carrier," Teddie added.

"You sweetheart!" Katy called. "Thank you!"

"I figured it was the least I could do, considering all the candy I got last night. I had fun!"

"I did, too," Katy mused.

Teddie laughed. "I noticed."

Katy threw a pillow at the door.

Teddie ran, laughing all the way down the hall.

* * *

Teddie was waiting at the stable Saturday morning when Parker drove up. Katy, standing at the front porch door, hesitated to go out. She was wearing jeans and a frilly blouse, her long blond hair neatly combed and loose around her shoulders. And she'd found a variety of lipstick that would stick only to her lips and not to everything else. But she was suddenly shy of Parker. She noticed that he looked curiously toward the house before he went into the barn with Teddie to saddle Bartholomew and run Teddie through the basics once more.

They came back out of the stable, with Parker holding the bridle and Teddie sitting high in the saddle, back straight, arms in, eyes looking straight ahead instead of down.

Katy was proud of her daughter's seat when she rode. The child was a natural. She didn't tense up or watch the ground or even jerk on the bridle. She sat the horse like a real cowgirl, when she'd never done any riding in her little life.

Parker walked alongside, holding the reins. He had Snow with him this morning, and she was saddled. He spoke to Teddie and handed her the reins, instructing her how to hold them so that she didn't put too much pressure on the bit in Bartholomew's mouth.

When he was satisfied that she was sitting straight, arms in, he nodded and swung up into the saddle and turned Snow so that she and Bartholomew were parallel to each other.

Katy waved. Parker smiled. Even at that distance, it made her heart race. "I'll have lunch ready when you get back," she promised.

"What are we having?" he asked.

"Tuna fish sandwiches."

He made an awful face.

"You don't like fish," she began.

"I like tuna fish," he returned. "I just don't like most tuna salads."

She pursed her lips. "You need to taste mine," she said. "I put in a secret ingredient." She wiggled her eyebrows.

He chuckled. "Okay. I'll try it."

"That's the sign of a man with guts," she teased.

He laughed. "And other organs," he mused. "See you."

He turned to Teddie and gave another instruction. Then he went alongside her down the path that led to the road. Apparently, Katy thought, it was going to be a longer ride today. She went back inside to fix lunch. She could put the tuna salad in the fridge when she made it. It would keep nicely until they came back.

She put pickled peach juice in the tuna, along with mayonnaise and sweet pickles. It was an odd way to prepare it, but she'd learned it from her grandfather, who made the best tuna salad she'd ever put in her mouth. The taste was unique.

She finished her task and went to watch the latest news on TV.

Parker was riding beside Teddie as they wound around the ranch property. Both were wearing jackets, because there were actual snowflakes.

"Snow!" Teddie sighed. She laughed as she lifted her face to let the flakes melt on her soft skin. "I love it!"

"You wouldn't if you were a poor cowboy who had to nursemaid pregnant heifers," he teased. "It's a twenty-four-hour a day job. Even in the snow."

"Gosh, ranching is complicated."

"That's why I love it," he confessed.

She glanced at him and away. "My mom really likes you."

His heart jumped. "I really like your mom."

She grinned. "I noticed."

"We're going slowly," he said. "Nothing intense. We're taking you to a movie tonight, if you want to go."

"Oh, boy!" she exclaimed. "What are we going to see?"

"That new cartoon movie." He named it.

"I want to see that one so much!" she enthused.

He chuckled. "You make the sun come out, kid. You're always upbeat, always brimming over with optimism. I'd fallen into a deep place before I met you and your mother. I was so depressed that I didn't care about much."

She beamed. "I'm a good influence, I am," she teased.

"You truly are, Teddie," he replied. "I never thought I'd enjoy teaching anybody anything. But this is fun."

She grinned. "It is. I'm so glad you don't mind teaching me about horses. But gosh, it's complicated. There's so much you have to learn, about what not to do. It's a long list."

"You pretty much learn as you go along," he pointed out. "It takes time to get used to an animal you've never been around. But you're really getting the hang of it. You sit like a cowboy."

"Thanks. I love what you're teaching me," she told him. She ran her hand gently over Bartholomew's mane. "I love Bart, too. He's the nicest horse in the world."

Bartholomew actually seemed to understand what she was saying. He turned his head around toward her and made an odd snuffling sound.

"Smart horse," Parker remarked. He smiled. "I think he understands a lot more than we believe he does."

"He's so easy to ride."

"He's been through a lot," Parker said. He didn't add what he'd learned about the man who'd been so cruel to Bartholomew. It seemed that he'd escaped the abuse charge by daring them to prove it. It had maddened Parker, who knew the man was lying. But it was going to be hard to get any evidence that would stand up in court.

However, Parker thought, he knew people in the community who would keep an eye on the horse's former owner and tell Parker anything they learned. It might still be possible to put the man behind bars, where he belonged.

"You're awful quiet today," Teddie remarked.

He smiled. "I'm just thinking."

"You are?" She gave him a wicked smile. "Mom bought some lipstick that won't come off. The saleslady teased her about you."

He felt a ruddy color climb up his cheeks, but he laughed in spite of it. He knew there would be gossip about him and Katy. He didn't even mind.

"You're really nice, Parker," Teddie added with a fond look. "You and Mom look good together."

"Dark and light," he mused.

"You aren't that dark. But you look like a Crow. You really are handsome, like Mom says."

He whistled. "She thinks I'm handsome?" he asked, and laughed.

"I do, too. Now what about trotting?" she replied.

He jerked himself out of his ongoing daydreams about Katy and they went on to the next step in her riding education.

Chapter Six

While Katy was waiting at home for Parker and Teddie to come back, she had a telephone call from the vet who'd treated Bartholomew's wounds.

"I thought you needed to know that the man who abused Bartholomew had the charges against him dropped," he said with some rancor. "He's friends with the prosecutor, it seems, and since there were no witnesses, they dismissed the case. He's out again."

"He should be tied up in a stable somewhere and doused with recycled grass," she muttered.

"I agree. He says he wants his horse back. If I were you, I'd think seriously about getting an attorney. You're going to need help."

She drew in a long breath. "That's good advice. Teddie's so attached to the horse. It will kill her if they give him back to that . . . that animal. I won't let him take Bart. I'll fight him to the last ditch."

"I feel as if I should salute you," he teased.

"The army missed its chance when I didn't enlist," she said with a chuckle.

"Well, I just wanted to tell you what happened."

"Thanks, Dr. Carr. I really appreciate it."

"No problem. How are Bart's hooves?"

"Looking good. We keep them cleaned and the farrier came over again this week to have a look. He says Bart's healed nicely."

"Good news," he said. "I'll say good-bye. If you need me, night or day, you call."

"I will. Thanks again."

She hung up and thought about what the vet had said. She only knew one attorney, but he was very good. Despite her dislike for his relentless pursuit, Ron Woodley was a good attorney who won most of the cases he'd tried; and he was fairly famous, for a young attorney. He was sweet on Katy. It would be underhanded and unkind to play on that attraction, she told herself. Then she thought about Teddie and what it would mean to the little girl to have an abusive former owner try to reclaim his horse. She didn't know any local attorneys, and she was afraid that if the abuser had plenty of money, local attorneys in a small town might not be anxious to go up against him publicly. She needed somebody high-powered and aggressive in the courtroom. Teddie didn't like the lawyer, but she loved her horse. Katy thought about that.

After which, she picked up the phone and made a long-distance call to Maryland.

When Parker and Teddie came up on the porch, both laughing, she felt a sudden pang of guilt. She should have first discussed with her daughter what she planned to do. She had an impulsive nature that sometimes got her into complicated situations. This one would certainly qualify.

"I've got lunch ready," she said, leading the way into the kitchen. "How's Bart doing?"

"Very well, indeed," Parker said as he pulled out a chair for Teddie and then one for himself at the kitchen table. "His hooves look good. So does the rest of him."

"What do you want to drink?" she asked Parker.

"Oh, a fifth of aged scotch, a magnum of champagne . . ." He grinned at her expression. "How about coffee?"

She laughed. "That suits me, too."

She put the tuna salad on the table, along with a loaf of bread, a jar of mayonnaise, and knives at each plate. "Dig in," she invited them.

"We haven't said grace yet," Teddie reminded her with a pointed look.

Katy rolled her eyes. "Sorry, sweetheart. Let me start the coffee and I'll be right there."

She sat down and before she and Katy bowed their heads, Parker was already bowing his. "When in Rome . . . ?" he teased softly.

Katy smiled and said grace.

She got back up then and went to pour coffee into two cups.

"Cream? Sugar?"

"I'm a purist," he returned. "I take my coffee straight up mostly."

She grinned. "I do too."

"I don't," Teddie piped up. "Cream and sugar helps kill the taste! Can I have some?"

"When you're thirteen," Katy said, without missing a beat.

"Thirteen?!"

"That's when my grandparents said I could have it. My parents said it, too. Coffee's supposed to stunt your growth or something if you drink it earlier than that." She frowned as she put the cups down on the table. "That sounds very odd."

"It does," Teddie agreed enthusiastically. "So where's my cup?"

"When you're thirteen, regardless of why," Katy said easily and sat down.

They made sandwiches. Parker bit into his and his expression spoke volumes.

"Hey!" he said. "This is great!"

Katy smiled broadly. "Thanks. I learned how to make it from my granddad. He had a secret ingredient that set it apart from most tuna salad."

He lifted an eyebrow. "And . . . ?"

"Oh, no," she retorted. "I'm not giving it away. It's a secret," she said in a loud whisper.

He gave her a wicked look. "For now," he said, and the way he was looking at her made her flush.

Teddie noticed. She smiled to herself.

They ate in a pleasant silence, except that Katy looked guilty and Parker wondered why.

After lunch, Teddie asked to be excused to watch a special program on the nature channel. Katy agreed at once.

She put up the lunch things and put the dishes in the sink, worried and unable to hide it.

"What is it?" Parker asked when she sat back down at the table.

She managed a jerky smile. "The vet called. They let Bart's owner out of jail and dropped the charges."

He sighed. "I know. I just found out this morning. I was going to tell you earlier, but I didn't have the heart."

"He suggested I get an attorney."

"That's a good idea," Parker said. "He has one out of Denver," he added. "A relative who's a big-city attorney with a great track record." He sighed. "Problem is, getting you an attorney who can stand up to him in court."

"I thought about that."

"We have some good local ones," Parker continued. "But not one of them has ever gone up against a sophisticated city lawyer. Not to my knowledge. You need somebody comparable to the horse abuser's counsel."

"As it happens, I do know one back East." She gave him an apologetic look. "The attorney who handled my husband's affairs," she began.

He rolled his eyes. "Not the suit with the attitude problem who doesn't like Teddie?"

She winced. "Well, he's the only big-city attorney I know, and if Teddie loses that horse, I don't know what will become of her."

He made a face. He sipped coffee. "I guess it's not a bad idea." His dark eyes met hers. "So long as he keeps his hands off you."

Her heart jumped. Her lips parted. "Oh."

Both dark eyebrows lifted and he smiled wickedly at her expression.

She threw a napkin at him and laughed.

"As it happens," he said dryly, "I'm not kidding. If he makes a move on you, he goes on the endangered species list. I have squatter's rights."

Her whole face became radiant. "Really?"

He cocked his head and studied her. "I hadn't planned on getting involved with anybody, ever again, you know."

"Actually, neither had I."

His big hand reached across to hers and linked fingers with it. "Life goes on. Maybe we both need to look ahead instead of behind."

She beamed.

"I have a few things to do at home before we leave for the theater. But I'll be back around six. That okay?"

"That's fine."

He stood and drew her gently up out of her chair. His dark eyes looked down into hers, warm and soft. "They say it's a great movie."

"Teddie will love it."

He bent and kissed her very softly. "So will we. See you later, pretty girl."

She smiled with her whole heart. "Okay."

He winked and left her standing there, vibrating.

Teddie came bouncing into the living room when her program was over. Her mother was sitting on the sofa reading, but she was alone. "Oh, Parker's gone," she exclaimed. "Aren't we going to the movies, then?"

"Yes, we are. He had a few things to do before we leave. Sit down, honey."

Teddie didn't like the expression on her mother's face. She dropped down into the armchair across from the sofa. "Something's wrong, isn't it?"

Katy nodded. "Dr. Carr called while you and Parker were out riding." She sighed. "I hate having to tell you this," she added sadly.

"They let Bart's owner go, didn't they?" Teddie asked.

Katy nodded. "And he wants his horse back."

"No!" Teddie exclaimed. "Oh, we can't let him take Bart back! He'll kill him!"

"I know that. He's not getting him back. But he has a big-city attorney from Denver who'll be representing him. We don't have any such person in Benton who can go up against him."

Teddie looked unhappy. "What are we going to do?" she wailed.

Katy made a face. "I called Maryland," she said.

"No," she said miserably. "Not him!"

"Honey, if we want to keep the horse, we have to fight fire with fire. We need somebody who's formidable in court, and Ron Woodley is. He's practiced criminal law for ten years and he's only lost one case. He started out as an assistant district attorney. He knows what he's doing."

Teddie took a breath. "Okay, then. Is he willing to do it?"

"Unfortunately, yes," Katy said. "He said it would be better if he came out now than at Thanksgiving, anyway, because a rich client invited him to stay for a couple of weeks at his estate in the Virgin Islands over the Thanksgiving holidays."

"Lucky him."

"I don't like islands," Katy confessed. "They attract hurricanes."

"Not in November," Teddie teased.

"Anything can happen. I like dry land."

Teddie smiled. "Me, too. Well, I guess I can hide in the closet while he's here," she said. "He doesn't like me at all."

"He doesn't like children," she replied. "I guess he's never been around any."

"No, he doesn't like me, because I'm in the way. He said so. He likes you a lot." She studied her mother. "I like Parker, and I'm not in his way."

She smiled slowly. "I like Parker very much."

"I know he feels that way about you," Teddie said. "He's always talking about you."

Katy's heart lifted. "So, you're not mad at me, because I invited the lawyer out?"

Teddie shook her head. "I don't want Bart to die. Anything's better than that. Even the eastern lawyer."

Katy smiled. "That's what I thought."

* * *

The movie was hilarious. It was about a crime-fighting family of superheroes, and focused on the baby, whom nobody thought had any powers. There was a scene with the baby beating up a raccoon that had all three of them almost rolling on the floor laughing.

When they were back out on the street, they were still laughing.

"That poor raccoon," Teddie gasped.

"That poor baby." Katy chuckled.

"The poor parents," Parker commented. "Imagine having a child who could burst into flames or walk through walls?"

"You do have a point," Katy had to admit.

"It was so funny! Thanks for taking us, Parker," Teddie added.

"Oh, I like being around you guys," he said, smiling. "You're good company."

"So are you," Katy said softly.

He winked at her and she flushed.

"Are you going to have Thanksgiving with us?" Teddie asked.

Katy gave him a hopeful look.

His lips parted. He grimaced. "Well, you see . . ."

"Don't tell me. You don't celebrate it," Katy guessed. "You probably don't celebrate Columbus Day, either."

He laughed. "Caught me."

"But Thanksgiving is about sharing," Teddie protested. "Pilgrims and Native Americans sat down together at the harvest."

"At first," Katy agreed. "Afterward, when the vicious cold killed their crops and they exhausted the local game, they died in droves."

Parker pursed his lips. "Some of them were rather helped into the hereafter, I understand, after they attacked people who did have food and tried to take it from them."

"Gosh, I didn't know that," Teddie said.

"History isn't quite as pleasant as most people think," Katy said. "It's brutal and ugly in places, and some people in historical times don't stand up to modern scrutiny. Of course, historians are also taught that you can't judge the morality of the past by that of the present when you read history. And they're quite right. Can you imagine opium dens in today's world, or children working in mines?"

"We've come a long way," Parker agreed.

"Not quite far enough, it seems sometimes," Katy replied. She smiled at him. "It was a great movie. Thanks."

"We'll do it again in a week or so." He paused. "When does your eastern Perry Mason show up?" he added.

She burst out laughing. "I'm not sure. He said in about two weeks. He can't come at Thanksgiving because a rich client invited him to the islands."

"Nice," Parker said. "He'll get a suntan. Then he might look almost as good as I do," he added, tongue-in-cheek.

"Oh, Parker, you're funny," Teddie said. She hugged him. "I think you're just the right shade of tan."

He hugged her back. "Thanks, sprout."

Teddie sighed. It would be so nice if her mother ever hugged her.

"I'm going to play games on the Xbox. Okay?" she asked her mother.

"Tomorrow's Sunday. Just remember, we're going to church. Don't stay up too late."

"I won't," Teddie promised. She looked at Parker. "Do you go to church?"

"Of course," he said. "But not quite in the way you do."

"Can you tell us about it?" she asked excitedly.

He chuckled. "Plenty of time for that. What game are you playing?"

"Minecraft," she said. "It's awesome!"

He rolled his eyes. "It's maddening. I like sword and sorcery stuff, like Skyrim."

"That's ancient," she said.

"That's why I like it," he returned.

"No, it's ancient. Old. Out of date!"

"Not my fault," he said. "Tell Bethesda Softworks to get busy on Elder Scrolls VI and I'll give up Skyrim."

"As if," she said with downturned lips. "I'll be grown and married before we ever see it."

"Don't I know it," he agreed.

Teddie waved and went down the hall.

"Bethesda? Elder Scrolls? Skyrim?" Katy wondered aloud.

"I'm a finicky gamer," he said. He moved toward her, pulled her into his arms, and bent to kiss her very softly. "I'll have more chores for a week or two, so we may have to put Teddie's riding on hold, just for a bit," he said gently. "But I should be free by the time your attorney gets here, so I can defend my rights."

She laughed softly. "He's just going to help us keep Bart. I don't have any plans to move back to Maryland, whatever the temptation."

His mouth brushed hers. "You sure about that?"

"I'm becoming addicted to Benton," she said, and she sounded breathless.

"To Benton?" he asked at her lips. "Or to me?"

"Same . . . thing," she managed, just before his mouth covered hers and became drugging, deep and slow and arousing. He lifted her up against him and held her hungrily for a long time before he finally drew back and let her go.

"Wow," she managed unsteadily.

His eyebrows arched and he laughed involuntarily. "You're bad for my ego," he teased. "I won't be able to get my head through doors."

"You're bad for my self-restraint," she returned.

He pursed his sensuous lips. "That's a sweet admission."

"Don't take advantage of a weakness I can't help," she said firmly.

He smiled. "Not my style," he said gently. "I don't want anything that isn't freely given."

"I think I knew that already. But it's nice to hear." She lowered her eyes. "I don't seem to have much willpower when you're around."

"That works both ways, honey. Keep your doors locked, okay? We've got a pack of wolves roaming nearby. The feds don't think they'll pose a threat, but if we have severe weather and they get hungry enough . . ."

He let the words trail off. She knew what he meant. A wild animal was likely to look for food anywhere he could get it when he was starving. There were some horror stories about wolves and settlers, back in the early days of western settlement.

"We always lock the doors," she assured him.

"Make sure you keep the stable doors closed as well," he added.

She made a face. "That would be horrible, after all Bart's been through, to have him fall prey to a wolf."

"I agree. But if you take reasonable precautions, it shouldn't be an issue. Just don't let tidbit go out alone at night to see Bart, okay?" he said, meaning Teddie. "Not now, at least."

"I won't. Or I'll go with her."

"I know you don't like guns; you've said so often enough. But do you have a weapon at all around here?"

She sighed worriedly. "Not really."

"Then both of you stay inside and keep the doors locked. You've got my phone number. You can call me if you get afraid, for any reason, and I'll be right over. Okay?"

She felt warm and cosseted. She smiled. "Okay."

He moved closer. "I love the way you look when you smile," he whispered. He bent and kissed her hungrily one last time. He drew back almost at once. "I'm leaving. You're getting through my defenses. I fear for my honor."

She burst out laughing. "I feel dangerous!"

He made a face. Then he winked. "Sleep well."

"You, too."

She watched him out the window until he drove away. She felt as if she could have walked on air.

Ron Woodley arrived several days before he was expected. He checked into the local motel, after being told firmly by Katy that he wasn't living with her and Teddie while they fought for possession of Bartholomew. He showed up at her front door one Saturday morning in a fancy rented sedan while Parker was in the barn with Teddie, saddling the horse.

"Hello, you gorgeous woman," he enthused, and hugged her before she could back away. "It's so good to see you again!"

She drew back. "Good to see you, Ron. Thanks for coming. We may have to pay your fee on the installment plan—"

"Don't insult me," he interrupted. "I do some pro bono

work. This will add to my curriculum vitae," he added on a chuckle. "Got some tea?"

She was briefly disconcerted. "Hot or cold?"

"Hot."

"Okay. Come on in," she added with a glance at the stable. Parker and Teddie were looking in her direction, but they didn't come out.

"Where's your daughter?" Ron asked with barely concealed distaste.

"She's out in the stable with Parker."

His chin lifted. "Parker?"

She nodded as she boiled water and searched for a few scarce tea bags. "He's a horse wrangler for J.L. Denton, who owns the big ranch property next door. His wife writes for television, that *Warriors and Warlocks* series."

"Never watched it," he said, leaning back in his chair. "Do you think it's safe to leave a man you barely know alone with your little girl?"

She stopped what she was doing and turned to him, her pale eyes flashing.

He held up both hands. "Sorry. Obviously you know him better than I do. If you trust him, that's the main thing."

"The main thing is that Teddie trusts him," she said in a soft, biting tone.

He shrugged. His keen eyes looked around the room. "Primitive, but I suppose it's serviceable," he mentioned. "Some nice collectibles on that shelf," he added. "World War II?" he asked.

"Yes. My grandfather brought them back from Japan."

"They're worth some money," he said. "Do you still have those old Western pistols your husband had?"

"I sold them," she said. "I don't like guns."

"Neither do I," he agreed.

She finally managed to get a tea bag and hot water in the same cup. She handed it to him.

"Sugar's on the table," she told him.

He waved it away. "I learned to drink tea in Japan. They never offer sugar with it. You have to ask for it."

He sipped the tea and frowned. "What is this?"

"I'm not really sure," she said apologetically. "We don't drink tea. That was in a housewarming gift the Dentons sent over when we moved in."

"I prefer Earl Grey," he said, sipping it. "Or Darjeeling. But this is okay."

"I'm so glad." She bit her tongue to keep from making it sound sarcastic.

"So. Tell me about this horse."

"He's a beautiful old horse, a palomino. Teddie named him Bartholomew and she loves him dearly." She drew in a breath. "The previous owner had neglected him so badly that his hooves were clogged and infected, and he had deep cuts where he'd been abused with a whip."

Ron's eyes narrowed. "Can anyone prove that he inflicted those cuts?"

She sighed. "There were no eyewitnesses."

"Surveillance cameras?"

"Please. The man lives in a shack up a mountain."

"Sorry. I guess this is pretty far in the boondocks."

She didn't reply.

"All right," he said after a minute. "You said he was arrested and charged with animal cruelty."

"Yes. The animal control officer said that a neighbor reported him. It wasn't the first time he'd had such a charge leveled against him. But he has friends and relatives in high places, so the charges were just dropped."

He pursed his lips as he sipped tea and frowned, deep

in thought. "First order of business is to speak to the person who reported him, and have the neighbors questioned. If he has close relatives who live with or near him, they can be deposed as well. The local veterinarian examined him?"

"Yes. Dr. Carr."

"Would he be willing to testify?"

She smiled. "He said of course he would."

"You'd be amazed at how few people really will, even if they agree at first. Especially if the perp has connections."

"The world is a sad place."

He looked at her. "You have no idea how sad." He smiled at her. "Do they have any passable restaurants around here? If so, you and I could eat out tonight."

"I can't leave Teddie alone," she said, surprised.

"She's what, ten? She's old enough to stay by herself. You can just lock the doors," he said easily.

"Ron, it's very evident that you've never had a child," she said sadly. "It doesn't work like that. A child of ten doesn't have the judgment she'd need to handle an emergency."

"Bull. We had a five-year-old boy call nine-one-one after a shooting. He was a material witness in a murder case."

"This isn't the city. There are all sorts of dangers out here, including wolves."

"Wolves are sweet creatures." He sighed, smiling. "There's a wildlife center close to where I live. They have two wolves. I love to go and pet them."

She gave him a long look. "Have you ever seen a wolf in the wild?" she asked.

He smiled vacantly. "What does that have to do with it?"

She was about to explain, in rather biting terms, when she heard voices. Parker and Teddie came in the front door and stopped at the dining room entrance.

Ron stood up. "Ron Woodley," he introduced himself.

"Parker," came the droll reply, followed by a firm handshake.

"Parker what?" Ron asked.

Parker just smiled.

"Nobody knows that," Teddie said, smiling up at her tall companion. "He says it's a secret."

"You're Indian, aren't you?" Ron asked lazily.

Parker cocked his head. "Crow, actually. Or Absaroka, if you want the proper term."

"I thought Crows came from Montana."

"Mostly we do. I grew up there, on the rez, near Hardin."

"Reservations." Ron shook his head as he sat back down next to Katy. "It's sad that we have such a high civilization in the world, but we still have people living in abject poverty on reservations under government programs."

"Yes. Amazing that such a high civilization put us there in the first place, isn't it?" Parker asked. His voice was pleasant, but his dark eyes were saying something quite different.

Ron noted that the man was quite muscular and that he didn't back down from criticism. In fact, he looked rather dangerous. He cleared his throat. "Yes, isn't it?" he said, avoiding a confrontation.

Parker raised an eyebrow. "You practice law in Maryland, I believe?"

"Yes. Mostly in the Capitol," Ron replied. "You break horses, I hear."

"Most of the time," he agreed.

"He's teaching me how to ride," Teddie said.

"You couldn't do that?" he asked Katy.

"I don't have the time, and I'm too impatient," Katy

replied. "Besides, Parker knows more about horses than I do. I've forgotten a lot over the years."

"Pity it's a skill that doesn't travel well," Ron remarked when he noticed the way Katy was looking at the other man. He seemed to feel that a man who worked with horses was too stupid to do anything else. Not that he said it. He insinuated it.

Teddie was perceptive enough to be outraged on Parker's behalf. "You should tell him about the cat," Teddie told Parker firmly.

He grinned at her. "Patience is a virtue," he said gently. "We make haste slowly. Right?"

She made a face. "Right," she added with a covert glare at their other visitor.

"Well, I'll say good night," Parker told them. "I've got an old army buddy coming to visit for a while. We were in Iraq together."

Ron looked uncomfortable. He'd managed to keep out of the military. He didn't really like being around men who'd served. They made him look bad.

"Then we'll see you next Saturday, right?" Teddie asked.

He smiled. "Of course." He glanced at Katy, who looked uneasy. "See you."

"See you," she said, and forced a smile. Because even though Parker was polite and courteous, she sensed that he was drawing away from her because of Ron. She didn't understand why. At least, not then.

Chapter Seven

Katy had thought that Ron would start right away to interview people who knew the horse's owner, his neighbors and relations. But mostly what Ron did was drive around to see the sights and take Katy out to eat. He allowed Teddie to go with them, but the invitation was reluctant at best. He didn't like the child around, and it was painfully obvious.

A week after Ron's arrival, Katy came in with the mail and her expression was one of abject misery.

"What's wrong, Mom?" Teddie asked. "You haven't been yourself all the way home from school."

Katy put up her purse and car keys. She pulled out an opened envelope. "It's a legal document insisting that Bartholomew be returned to his rightful owner."

"But he can't! He just can't make us give Bart back!" she exclaimed.

"I'll discuss it with Ron as soon as possible."

"He won't do anything," Teddie said shortly. "He hasn't even asked anybody about how that man treated Bart."

"How do you know that?"

"My friend Edie told me," she said belligerently. "She says her mother and father are furious. They know at least two of the man's neighbors who would be willing to go to court to testify against him, but neither of them has even been asked."

Katy made a face. She was feeling worse by the day about her idea to have Ron come and do them this favor. He was pleasant company, but he spent their time together talking up Washington society and her gift for putting people at ease. She'd make a proper hostess for a politician, he insisted, and instead she was burying herself out here in the boondocks with filthy cattle and wild people.

She was glad Parker hadn't heard him say that. Sadly, Parker had kept his distance since Ron had shown up at Teddie's home. He excused himself because of the pressure of work, he said, but this time of year, ranch work was more attuned to watching over the cattle and repair work than breaking new horses.

"Ron," Katy began when they were briefly alone at the house, while Teddie was out in the stable grooming Bart, "we need to talk."

"Oh, yes, we do," he said.

He got up, pulled her up into his arms, and began kissing her hungrily.

She was too shocked to react, which was unfortunate, because just at that moment, an excited Teddie opened the door and came in with Parker.

Katy pulled back abruptly, feeling sick when she saw Parker's expression. It wasn't angry. It was disappointed. Sad. Resigned.

"Oh. Mom." Teddie flushed when she saw the glare Ron sent in her direction. "Sorry. I needed to ask a question."

Ron, furious, stuck his hands in his pockets and turned away to look out a window.

"What is it, Teddie?" Katy asked, almost shaking with indignation.

"Parker said Dr. Carr has a neighbor who actually saw Bart's owner hitting him with the whip, and he's willing to testify in court!"

Katy was still catching her breath. "He did?"

Parker's dark eyes went from Ron's back to Katy's flushed face. "He said that the man would have his attorney contact your attorney. When you get one," he added pleasantly.

Ron whirled around. "She's got one," he said tautly. "And just who are you?"

Parker lifted an eyebrow and smiled. "Forgotten me already? I'm just a horse wrangler. I'm helping Teddie learn to ride."

Ron made a dismissive sound and turned to Katy. "If you want my advice, you'll take the course of least resistance and let the man have his horse back."

"Did you not understand what was done to the horse?" Parker asked.

Ron shrugged. "Animals are just animals. Some people are abusive, even to other people. Teddie can always get another horse."

"You mean man!" Teddie burst out. "You don't even care about what happens to Bart if that man gets him back. You haven't done anything to help me save my horse! You only came here to try to get my mother to marry you. And if she does," she added, glaring at Katy, "I'll run away from home! I'd rather live at a shelter than have to live with you!" she cried, tears running down her face.

"Teddie, that's enough," Katy said quietly.

Teddie was sobbing. Parker pulled her close and held her. He stared at Katy with something akin to contempt.

She flushed.

"It's going to be a hard case to prove in court," Ron said breezily. "You have to call witnesses, it will tie you up in court, make you enemies in the community. The man is rich and he has powerful friends," he added. "You won't find a local attorney who'll even consider the case."

Katy turned to look at him, undecided.

"And it will cost an arm and a leg in legal fees," Ron added. "You'll face censure, your daughter will face it, and for what? An old, beat-up horse with hardly any time left to live anyway. It might be a mercy to just let the vet put him down. That's the course the owner favors, anyway. I spoke to him. He said he'll let the whole thing go, if you'll agree to let the vet do what's necessary."

"Nobody is putting Bartholomew down," Teddie said fiercely.

"You're just a kid," Ron said with faint contempt. "You don't have a say about this."

"She doesn't. I do," Parker replied.

"And you're a nobody around here, horse wrangler. You work for wages," Ron said with obvious distaste. "You're Indian, too, aren't you?" He smiled sarcastically. "That won't go over big with the locals, will it?"

"Oh, I've never been one to curry favor," Parker replied.

"Are you going to let them kill my horse?" Teddie asked her mother, with a dignity that sat oddly on such a young face.

Katy was torn. Ron sounded very logical. The horse was old. But that look on her daughter's face wounded her.

"It's painless," Ron said. "The horse won't even feel it."

"Why don't we get the vet to put you down first, and you can tell us if you feel it?" Parker drawled.

Ron looked outraged. "You have no right to even be here," he began.

"Parker is my friend," Teddie said. "The nicest thing you ever said to me was that it was a shame that my mother had a child."

Ron didn't deny it. He just shrugged. "I guess the local attitudes are corrupting your daughter, Katy," he said. "Another good reason to come back to Maryland where you belong."

Katy was feeling sicker by the minute, torn between logic and her daughter's pain.

"I have a simple solution," Parker told the child. "Give the horse to me." He looked up at Ron with a cold smile. "And I'll take on his former owner in court, with pleasure."

"I don't think a public defender will take the case," Ron commented smartly.

"Mr. Denton employs a firm of attorneys out of L.A.," he replied. "I've already spoken to him about the case."

"A rancher with attorneys in L.A." Ron laughed.

"His wife is the lead writer for *Warriors and Warlocks,*" Parker replied quietly. "Mr. Denton owns Drayco Properties."

Even Ron had heard of those. It was one of the biggest conglomerates of oil and gas property in the country.

"He also likes horses," Parker added. He looked down at Teddie. "You get your mother to sign Bart over to me, and I'll do the rest." He glanced at Ron. "I don't mind a good fight."

He was insinuating that Ron would run from one. And Ron knew it. His face flushed. "I could win the case if I wanted to," he said.

"We all need to calm down," Katy said, glancing from

one heated expression to the next. "Let's sleep on it and talk again tomorrow."

Parker bent and dropped a kiss on Teddie's hair. "Don't worry. We'll save Bart. One way or another," he added, with a cool glance at Ron and an even cooler one at Katy. He went out, with Teddie right behind him.

"You need to keep that man away from your daughter," Ron told Katy firmly. "He's using her to get to you."

But it didn't look that way to Katy. Parker had barely glanced at her on his way out, the sort of impassive expression you might expect from a total stranger. It had hurt. She'd felt guilty about her closeness to Parker and he'd backed off. Asking Ron out here had been the last straw, and she could see it. Parker thought she was serious about Ron, especially after he'd witnessed that impassioned kiss.

Ron approached her, but she backed away.

"I'm not interested in you that way, Ron," she said firmly. "I'm sorry if I gave you the impression that I was. I honestly thought you meant it when you said if I ever needed help, you'd come."

"Of course, I meant it," he protested.

"So you talked to the horse's owner, without telling me, and offered to have Bartholomew put down, knowing that I got you out here because my daughter loves the horse and wants to save him."

Ron cleared his throat. "I prefer negotiation to a stand-up fight."

"Oh, I can see that negotiation is certainly more preferable. It would have been a great solution when my great-great-grandfather was fighting off cattle rustlers up in Montana, negotiating with people pointing loaded guns at him." Her eyes were sparking now.

"Nobody rustles cattle anymore," he argued.

"Yes, they do. They use transfer trucks instead of horses, but they still use guns."

"Barbarians," he muttered.

Her eyes went over his expensive suit, his styled, neat hair, and his expensive jewelry. And she found that she infinitely preferred Parker's simple denims and long hair.

"Barbarians," she mused. She smiled. "That's what you think Parker is."

He wrinkled his nose.

"You should never judge people by the way they look," she said.

He made a rough sound in his throat. "I'm going back to my motel. I'll see you tomorrow. By then, hopefully you and that rude child will have come to your senses. Good evening."

She held the door open for him and watched him drive away in his expensive rented car.

She walked out to the stable to find Teddie still grooming Bart, tears running down her cheeks. Parker had already gone.

"Teddie," she began.

Her daughter looked at her with eyes that were red with tears and disappointment and anger. She put Bart back into his stall and put up the grooming tool.

"Daddy would be ashamed of you," Teddie said simply. She walked out of the stable and left her mother to turn off the lights.

Teddie didn't come out for supper. Her door stayed locked.

Katy was miserable. She shouldn't have listened to Ron. He was part of another world, another mindset. And yes, her late husband would have fought Bart's former owner to the Supreme Court, if he'd needed to. But he would have saved Teddie's horse. Even Parker fought for her, which was more than Katy had done.

She took a shower and dried her hair, put on a night gown, and sat down on the side of her bed. She picked up her phone and sent a short text to Parker.

It wasn't answered. She tried again and her number had been blocked.

She put the phone down, tears stinging her eyes. If she needed to know how he felt, that was her answer. Obviously, he felt that she'd taken the lawyer's part over her own daughter's, and he was disgusted with her. He'd witnessed that kiss, as well. It must have been painful to him, because he'd thought that he and Katy had something going for them. That kiss had shown him that they didn't.

She lay down and turned out her light. But she didn't sleep.

Parker couldn't sleep either. He was sorry that he'd blocked Katy's number, but he'd thought they were headed for a good placc together, and that wasn't happening. He'd found her in the arms of this eastern attorney whom she'd vowed that she disliked. It hadn't looked like dislike to Parker.

He got up and made coffee. It wouldn't help him sleep, but it was something to do. He heard a vehicle coming down the road. It stopped and pulled into his driveway.

For an instant, he thought it might be Katy. But it was only his boss. Odd thing, to find the boss out driving at this hour of the night, he thought as he opened the door.

"Hey, boss. How's things?" Parker greeted.

J.L. Denton came up on the porch, out of sorts and weary. "Got any coffee?" he asked.

"You bet. Come on in."

The two men sat at Parker's kitchen table sipping black coffee in a companionable silence.

"Okay, what's this about some lawyer from back East sucking up to the man who beat that horse that the Blakes rescued?"

"Him." Parker made a face. "Sleazy so-and-so. He's ambitious. Bart's former owner is rich and he has friends."

"I have a few of my own. I called Beck and Thomas in L.A. They're flying out here Monday. If the child's mother will give custody of Bart to you, I'll handle the rest."

"That's the thing," Parker said quietly. "She was all hugged up with the lawyer when I went over there earlier. Teddie begged her not to let the man take the horse. The lawyer said the former owner would drop the whole thing if they'd have the horse put down instead."

"What did Mrs. Blake say to that?"

"She told Teddie that it might be the best solution."

"Damn!"

"I said that and a few other things. Right now, I'm pretty sure I'd like to go home to Montana and live on the rez and be a real Indian."

"Baloney. You'd die of boredom in a week."

Parker laughed, but it had a hollow sound. "I could always move to D.C. and work for that letter agency."

"You'd die of stress in a week." J.L. chuckled. "Stay here and break horses. It's what you were born to do."

Parker sighed. "I guess it might . . . what the hell is that?"

They got up from the table and went out on the front porch.

"I don't believe it," Parker said heavily.

It was a little girl with a flashlight, leading a horse. It was Teddie, crying and muttering to herself.

"Oh, honey," Parker said, feeling her misery.

She handed the reins to J.L. and ran into Parker's arms. He lifted her and hugged her, rocking her.

"She's going to have him put down, I just know it. I can't let her kill Bart," Teddie wailed.

Over her head, Parker's tormented eyes met J.L.'s.

"Nobody's putting the horse down," J.L. said firmly. He pulled his cell phone out of its holder and started making calls.

A horse trailer arrived, along with a redheaded woman in a luxury car, about the same time Katy Blake came driving up in front of Parker's house.

She started toward Teddie, but Teddie, standing next to Parker, turned away.

J.L. Denton glared at Katy. "Nobody's putting this horse down," he said shortly. "I'm taking him home with me. Burt Dealy can get himself a damned good lawyer, because I'm going to put him behind bars and let him rot there if he doesn't! As for that child"—he pointed at Teddie—"if you were my wife, I'd divorce you for the misery you've caused her tonight!"

"Now, J.L., that's not helping," the redheaded woman said gently. She smiled at Teddie and went to Katy. "I'm Cassie Denton, J.L.'s wife," she said in her soft voice. "Apparently, there's a little trouble here."

Katy choked back tears. "I've been behind it all, I'm afraid," she managed.

Cassie pulled the other woman into her arms and rocked her while she cried. Katy was stiff and unyielding, and Cassie let her go almost at once. "There, there," she said gently. "We all have hard times. We usually live through them."

Katy moved away, dashing tears from her eyes. "Thanks," she said huskily. She turned toward Teddie. "Sweetheart . . ."

"I'm not going home with you," Teddie said miserably. "You can marry that awful man and have kids that you love."

Katy's face contorted.

"I want to stay with Parker," Teddie muttered. "He cares about me and Bart."

Parker smiled at her. "That's sweet, and I appreciate it. But it's not practical. Brave girls don't run away from trouble, you know. Your mother loves you."

"Sure she does. That's why she wants to kill my horse. Or, worse, let that horrible man take him back and beat him to death," Teddie said angrily.

Katy wrapped her arms around herself. She felt thoroughly miserable and ashamed. J.L. Denton was absolutely glaring at her.

"I won't let him take the horse," she said after a minute.

"Who'll stop him? That fancy lawyer?" Teddie asked.

"Not likely," Parker said flatly.

"Burt Dealy buys people," J.L. said icily. "He's bought off public officials for years. This isn't the first time he's been brought up on charges. He always walks. Apparently he thinks he can buy your lawyer friend off, too." He smiled coldly. "He won't buy me off. I'll have him drawn and quartered first. My attorneys are coming out here from L.A. on Monday. They'll handle the case. All you have to do, if you think you can manage it, is give me legal custody of Bart. I'll do the rest."

"She won't do it," Teddie said, glaring at her mother. "Her friend won't like it."

"Teddie, I'm sorry," Katy said miserably. "I made a mistake. I shouldn't have listened to him. It was wrong."

Teddie wasn't budging.

"Why don't you come home with us for tonight?" Cassie suggested gently to the child. "Then we'll take you back home in the morning."

Teddie looked up at Parker.

"Go," he said quietly. "J.L. has a nice big stable, much nicer than mine. You can settle Bart for the night. If your mother approves," he added. The look he gave Katy made her feel two inches tall.

"Yes, that would . . . that would be all right," Katy stammered. "If you're willing to fight for Bart, I'll thank you. I'm not really sure that Ron would fight for him, or even try to." She lowered her eyes.

"Everybody makes mistakes," Cassie said softly.

Teddie hugged Parker and walked away with Cassie. She didn't look back.

"I'll talk to you tomorrow," J.L. told Parker. "Thanks for the coffee."

"No problem. Good night, Teddie."

"Good night, Parker," she called back.

They loaded Bart into the horse trailer and within five minutes, the yard was deserted except for Parker and Katy.

She was still standing in the cold in a thin sweater, her arms wrapped around herself. She looked miserable.

"Go home," he said shortly, and turned back toward the house.

"He was kissing me," she said. "I was too shocked to

fight at first, and then you and Teddie came in and I was ashamed."

He stopped at the steps and looked back at her. "You called that yellow polecat and asked him to come out here. I figured you wanted what happened. Especially after you broke Teddie's heart with that comment about taking the easiest course and letting them put Bart down. That was cowardly."

She flushed. She drew in a breath. "Yes," she said after a minute.

"He doesn't like Teddie."

"I know."

"Maybe you'd fit in better with Washington society after all," he told her. "You'd probably be better off than living out here with barbarians. Good night, Mrs. Blake."

He went into the house and slammed the door.

Katy drove home. Her daughter hated her. Parker didn't want anything more to do with her. J.L. Denton thought she was despicable. And she'd deserved every single miserable thing that had happened to her tonight.

She could hardly believe that she'd agreed with Ron about having the horse put down, even knowing how much Teddie loved him. Teddie had loved her father, too. They'd been close in a way that Katy and Teddie had never been close. Her daughter had never warmed to her. Perhaps it was because Katy didn't know how to let people in close. She'd loved her husband in her way, but she was always alone, apart, even from her own family. Her parents had hardly ever touched. They got along, said they loved each other, but they fought a lot. They'd married to combine two huge ranch properties. They'd cared for Katy, but they didn't know how to show it. In turn, Katy had never been able to show that love she had for her daughter.

It occurred to her only then that Bartholomew had been the catalyst to bring Teddie and Katy closer together. The child had grown more optimistic, more outgoing, since she'd had responsibility for the abused horse. Parker had helped there, too. The two of them had made Katy look at the world in a different way. She and Teddie had been growing closer, more every day.

Until she called Ron to help save the horse and he'd defected to the enemy. Worse, he'd almost convinced Katy that his course of action was the right one, despite Teddie's outraged and hurt feelings. She was losing her daughter's love and trust, and for what? For a society lawyer who didn't really care about Katy as a person, only as an asset to his legal career, because she'd become a good hostess and organizer among military wives, many of whom were big in social circles. And because she had those stocks that her husband had invested in, stocks that might make her very wealthy. He'd convinced her, with logic, that terminating the troublesome horse was the quickest way out of her legal dilemma.

Quickest, yes. And an excellent venue for destroying her relationship with her only child. She saw Teddie's tearful, shocked face every time she closed her eyes. Teddie hadn't expected her mother to sell her out to a stranger who didn't even like her. Parker would never have done that. Katy was sure of it. Now the Dentons had involved themselves, and J.L. was going after the horse abuser with a firm of high-powered attorneys who made Ron look like a law student.

First, she was going to have to sign over custody of Bart in a legal manner. She thought about how that would look to her daughter and Parker and the Dentons if she got Ron to help her. No. She'd have to go into Benton Monday and find an attorney who'd be willing to do the work for her. It would be an expense, but if it would help mend the breach between her and Teddie, it was worth any amount of money.

Maybe she could win Teddie's trust again. But Parker wanted nothing more to do with her, and he'd made it very clear tonight. Until then, she hadn't realized how much a part of the family he'd become to her. It was painful to think she wouldn't see him helping around the place, teaching Teddie horse care, explaining Crow legends. Talking about the cat in the box.

She smiled sadly as she thought what a high intelligence he had, and he'd let Ron treat him like a vagrant. She couldn't imagine why. Or maybe she could. He wasn't even going to try to compete with the society attorney. He'd witnessed that impassioned kiss and he was probably convinced that Katy had chosen Ron over him. It wasn't the truth. But what did it matter? They all hated her.

Tomorrow was Sunday. She'd have to drive over to the Dentons to bring a furious Teddie home and discuss Bart's future. Ron would certainly arrive after lunch, to complicate matters. She hadn't felt such impotent sorrow since her husband's death.

She missed her late husband. She felt guilty that she'd started seeing Parker, because it was like betraying her husband's memory. But it wasn't at all. Teddie loved Parker. He was larger than life, a strong and capable man with a stunning intellect and a big heart. He never ran from a fight. Ron did. It was why he negotiated settlements out of court for most of his cases. He wasn't a stand-up fighter and he didn't like confrontation. Well, not unless he considered his adversary inferior to him. That was why he'd been so condescending with Parker. Pity, she thought, that Parker hadn't aired his views on theoretical physics. But Parker wasn't competing, because he didn't think Katy was worth the competition. That thought was like a knife in her heart. She hadn't realized how important Parker was to her until she'd alienated him. She'd alienated her daughter as well. Somehow, she was going to have to make amends, if she could.

She went back to bed and turned off the light, but she knew she wasn't going to sleep. Her life was in turmoil all over again because she'd gone nuts and invited Ron down to aid her in the struggle for possession of Bartholomew. He hadn't aided her at all. He'd helped lose part of her family.

So she closed her eyes on welling anger and considered her next course of action. Tomorrow, after she got her daughter back, she was going to have a long and very hot conversation with one eastern attorney.

The Dentons were already up when she pulled up at their front door, after calling and asking if it was all right to come fetch her daughter. She didn't want to make J.L. any madder than he already was.

Teddie was sitting at the breakfast table with Cassie and J.L. and the baby, in his high chair, when she walked in.

"Good morning," Katy said hesitantly.

"Good morning," Cassie greeted. "Won't you have something to eat? Or at least coffee?"

J.L. didn't speak. He glared.

Katy flushed. She took a deep breath and put her hands in her pockets. "I'm going into town tomorrow to see an attorney and have Bartholomew signed over to you, Mr. Denton. I'll be very grateful, and so will Teddie, for any help you can give us. I don't want him put down and I don't want his former owner to get him." She shifted her feet restlessly. "Ron is very logical. He helped me settle my husband's affairs after he was killed overseas. He seemed like a capable, trustworthy man, but he's not. He's a snake. I just didn't know it until yesterday, when he almost convinced me that I was being stupid and unrealistic."

Teddie was looking at her mother, not glaring. J.L.'s hard face softened just a little.

"Anybody can be taken in by a fast-talking lawyer," Cassie said. "My poor father was the victim of one, who helped his shady client ruin my father's reputation so they could get his position for her. The uproar caused my mother to commit suicide."

"Oh, my goodness. I'm so sorry!" Katy exclaimed.

"We were very close," Cassie confided. "It took a long time to get over it. In fact, I haven't yet."

"Teddie and I haven't really been close," Katy said, not looking at the sad little girl at the table. "My fault. My parents married to combine two ranching properties. I think they wanted me, at first, but neither knew how to show affection. I was raised with almost no touching, no sharing, no affection." She smiled. "It's hard to show love when you haven't been shown it." She glanced at her daughter. "I'm in the learning stages about that."

Teddie flushed. She squirmed in her chair.

"Coffee?" Cassie asked again.

"Thanks, anyway. But we'd better go," Katy said. Her face tautened. "I have a lawyer to parboil after lunch."

J.L. chuckled helplessly. Teddie's face lightened.

"He'll be leaving very soon, I believe," Katy added with

a glance at Teddie. "And I'm not listening to anything else he says. I'll have those papers for you tomorrow afternoon, Mr. Denton. I'll see the lawyer first thing after I dismiss my class."

"Wait and let my attorneys draw up the papers," J.L. replied. "They'll be here by noon tomorrow. I'll have Parker drop the papers off at your place when you get home."

She bit her lower lip. "Parker isn't speaking to me at the moment."

J.L. cocked his head, his eyebrows arching in a question.

"He's mad at me about the horse. He thinks I sold out my daughter. It looks that way." She searched Teddie's eyes. "When I flub up, I do a super job of it, don't I, baby?" she asked.

Teddie got up from the table. "Me, too," she confessed.

"So we'll go home and get our ducks in a row," Katy continued. She grimaced. "But it might be kinder to ask somebody besides Parker to hand over the paperwork. Kinder to him, anyway."

He shrugged.

"You'll take good care of Bart, won't you, Mr. Denton?" Teddie asked worriedly. "You won't let that awful man come and take him?"

J.L. smiled at the child. "He'd need a tank at the least to get through my security, and he's much too lazy to learn to drive one."

Teddie laughed. "Okay. Thanks. And for letting me stay."

"You're always welcome," Cassie told the little girl, and hugged her.

"Thanks, from both of us," Katy said.

Cassie hugged her, too. "Don't take life so seriously," she said gently. "Things work out, if you just give them time."

"Good advice," Katy said warmly. "We'll take it. Ready to go, Teddie?"

"I'm ready."

They said their good-byes, stopping at the stable so that Teddie could say good-bye to Bartholomew, who had a huge stall and plenty of food and fresh water.

One of the cowboys grinned at them. "That your horse?" he asked Teddie. "He's super nice."

Teddie beamed. "Thanks!"

"I'll look after him, no worries," he assured her.

"Okay."

"Thank you," Katy added. She herded Teddie out of the stable and back to the SUV, putting her in before she got behind the wheel.

"You meant it?" Teddie asked at once. "About that lawyer?"

Katy nodded. "I meant it." She drew in a breath. "I'm sorry. You were right. Daddy would have been ashamed of me."

"I'm sorry I said that," Teddie told her. "I'm sorry about it all. It's just, I love Bart and I thought you were going to let that man talk you into having him put down. I was scared."

"Nobody's putting Bart down," Katy said firmly as she started the car. "And Ron is going back home tomorrow, whether he wants to or not."

Teddie didn't say anything as she put on her seat belt. But she smiled.

Chapter Eight

It was after lunch before Ron drove up to the front porch. Katy let him in, but not with any sort of welcome. He glanced beyond her at Teddie sitting on the sofa, glaring, and he made a face.

"I thought you and I might go for a ride," he said. "To talk about the horse."

"How much did Mr. Dealy offer you, Ron?" she asked abruptly.

His lower jaw dropped. He stared at her while he searched for a reply that wouldn't get him kicked out the front door. The man was extremely wealthy and he'd offered the lawyer a whopping fee if he could convince the woman to have the horse put down. If there was no evidence, he could get out of the abuse charge, just as he'd gotten out of similar charges in the past—with money.

But it looked as if Katy was wise to the deal. He wondered who'd been talking to her. He suspected the Indian, but how would that man . . . what was his name again, Parker? How would Parker know?

"So it's true," Katy continued, nodding. "I thought so."

"It's just a horse, honey," he said softly. "An old horse. He could drop dead tomorrow."

Teddie stared at him coldly.

Odd, how guilty that stare made him feel. He didn't like kids, especially this one. He'd never wanted any, and he still didn't.

"You could get a colt and raise it," he told the child.

"That isn't your decision," Katy said quietly. "You have no place in this family except as my late husband's attorney. I was wrong to trust you. I should never have asked you for help."

"Now listen, let's not be hasty," Ron began.

"I'm signing over custody of Bartholomew to Mr. Denton tomorrow. His firm of attorneys is coming here from L.A. and they'll handle the litigation. Mr. Dealy is going to find himself in more hot water than he ever dreamed, and this time he won't walk away from the charges." She smiled coolly. "You see, we have photographic proof of Bart's injuries and at least two witnesses who can attest to them in court."

"Dealy said there were none," Ron blurted out.

"Amazing how you're willing to believe the word of a man who'll half kill a horse and lie about it. It must have been a big sum he offered you," Katy added cynically.

Ron took a long breath. He glared at Teddie. "If it wasn't for that kid, you'd have done what I asked."

"That kid is the reason I asked you to come here, to help us save her horse. And you sold us out for a promise of money," Katy added. "I'd like you to leave now, please. Don't ever come back," she added. "Don't call, don't write, don't even try to text me. If you like, I'll be happy to write you a check for all your expenses, including airfare and the rental car. Even your usual fee for representing a client," she added with icy disdain.

He shifted uncomfortably. "That won't be necessary,"

he said stiffly. "I'm not a poor man." He moved just a step closer, stopping when she moved a step away. "We could have good times together," he tried one last time, forcing a smile. "You'd shine in Washington society."

"I prefer living with the barbarians," Katy said easily. "Sorry."

He let out an angry breath. "It's the Indian, of course," he said icily. "What, you going to marry him and live on the reservation? The man is ignorant!"

"Really? What do you know about Schrodinger's cat?" Teddie asked with faint contempt.

"Schrodinger's cat?" he asked, surprised. "It's an experiment in theoretical physics."

"Parker has a degree from MIT in theoretical physics," Katy said. "His father is an astrophysicist who works for NASA."

Ron looked properly shocked. He started to speak and just gave it up. He sighed. "Okay, it's your life." He looked around the place. "It's a shack, but if you want to live here, it's your choice."

"Why, that's right," Katy said with a smile. "It is, isn't it?"

He shrugged. "If you ever change your mind, you know how to find me."

"Piece of advice," Katy said as she showed him out the door. "Don't hold your breath. Have a nice trip home."

She closed the door in his face.

Teddie let out the breath she'd been holding. She still hadn't trusted her mother not to give in to the man's persuasions.

"Thanks," she said.

Katy looked at her daughter with regret. "I've failed as a mother," she said. "I'd like to think it was someone else's fault, but it's mine. I never should have taken a stranger's part against you. You're my daughter, and you love that horse. I can't believe I agreed with Ron about putting him down. I'm so sorry, honey. So very sorry."

Teddie got up and went to her mother. "I'm sorry, too. I shouldn't have run away. But I feel sorrier for Parker. He was only trying to help, and that lawyer treated him like an idiot."

Katy sighed. "Parker won't speak to me anymore," she said. "I don't blame him. I wish I'd made better decisions."

"I thought you and Parker were getting close," Teddie said.

Katy sat down on the edge of the sofa. "We were. But I got to thinking about your dad and that it was too soon. I felt guilty."

"Daddy would want you to be happy," Teddie told her. "He wouldn't want you to be alone. He wasn't that sort of person."

Katy smiled. "You loved your dad."

"Oh, yes, I did. I miss him awfully. But I love Parker," she added. "He's very like Daddy was. He's strong and funny and gentle, and he fights for me."

Katy flushed. "Something I didn't do."

Teddie put her arms around her mother, feeling the woman stiffen. She drew back at once, but Katy caught her and pulled her close, rocking her.

"My parents never touched me," she whispered to Teddie. "It's . . . hard for me to show affection. But I'll try. Really."

Teddie hugged her back. "That's okay. I can do all the hugging. I'm good at it."

Katy laughed and fought back tears. At least one good thing had come out of the misery of the day before.

A truck pulled up in her driveway the next day when she got home from work. Her heart jumped because she thought it might be Parker. But it was the man who had the wolf. What was his name . . . ? Matthews, that was it. Butch Matthews.

"Mrs. Blake," the man said, tipping his hat. "Mr. Denton sent me over with these papers about custody of your horse."

"If you'll come in for a minute, Mr. Matthews, I'll sign them, and you can take them right back."

"That would be fine."

"Come on in," she invited.

Teddie was waiting in the living room. "You have the wolf!"

He chuckled. "Yes. I have the wolf. Sorry he scared you that time."

"I'm not scared anymore. I've been watching nature specials on wolves. Could we come over sometime and see the wolf? Maybe this weekend. If it's okay?" Teddie pleaded.

He smiled warmly at the child. "It's okay. How about Saturday just after lunch?"

Teddie looked at her mother, who'd just finished signing custody of Bart over to J.L. Denton. She looked up. "What? Saturday after lunch? That would be fine with me. But I don't know where you live," she added.

"Parker does," he said, and smiled.

Then she remembered that he'd seen her and Parker holding hands at the Halloween celebration downtown.

Obviously, he didn't know that things had cooled off between them.

"It would probably be best if you told me where to go," Katy said, and looked so miserable that Butch just smiled and gave her directions.

Katy didn't hear from Ron again. Well, except for once, when he tried to text her about rethinking her position on the horse. She blocked his number, as Parker had blocked hers. She didn't even feel guilty about it.

Things were better between her and her daughter. She opened up to Teddie in a way she hadn't been able to before. She hugged the little girl coming and going, which made Teddie happier than she'd ever been in her life. The distance that had existed between Teddie and Katy was slowly closing.

Thanksgiving Day came and was uneventful. They went to Butch Matthews's house the following Saturday to see Two Toes, the big white wolf with the dark gray ruff around his head.

"He's got dark streaks in the fur on his head," Teddie exclaimed as she stared at the enormous animal lying quietly on a rug in front of Butch's television.

"He looks like he's had a stylist color him up." Katy laughed. "He's really big, isn't he?"

"Yes, he is," Butch agreed. "Poor old thing, he's about blind and most of his teeth are gone. I take him in to see Dr. Carr from time to time. He sure does attract attention in the waiting room on a collar and leash," he added with a chuckle.

"I'll bet," Katy agreed. "Is he gentle?"

"Very," Butch said. "He can't see much, but he sits close to the television and when they run wolf stories on the nature channel, he howls," he added. "So I guess his hearing is still good. I know his sense of smell is," he murmured dryly, "because he figured out how to open my fridge and helped himself to a beef roast I was going to cook."

They both laughed.

"He likes beef. But he's a lot safer now that he's getting it fed to him," Butch told them.

"Can I pet him?" Teddie asked, fascinated with the animal.

"Sure. Just go slow. Let him smell your hand first."

Teddie got down on her knees in front of the big wolf and extended her fingers. He sniffed at them and cocked his head, sniffing again.

She ran her fingers over his thick fur, just at the side of his head, and he nuzzled against them.

"This is just awesome," Teddie exclaimed. "He's so sweet!"

"They'd have put him down if I hadn't offered to take him in," Butch told Katy while they watched her daughter pet the wolf. "Old things aren't useless, you know."

"I do know," Katy said solemnly. "My late husband's attorney came out to help us keep Teddie's rescued horse, and he sold us out to the man who beat him. I sent him packing a few days ago."

"Good for you," Butch said. "Your horse may be old, but he's got a lot of life left in him. Shame what that man did to him. Real shame. I hope he doesn't get off the hook this time."

"He won't," Katy said. "We signed over custody to Mr. Denton and his attorneys are getting ready to pin Mr. Dealy to a wall. They have eyewitnesses to the beatings, even recordings taken from cell phones. Apparently, Mr. Dealy wasn't too careful about hiding his abuse."

"If J.L.'s involved, Dealy will do time." He shook his head. "Those lawyers from L.A. are real hell-raisers. I wouldn't ever want them after me."

She bit her lower lip. "Have you seen Parker lately?" she asked quietly.

"I see him occasionally," he said. "He spends a lot of time working out with weights at the gym when he isn't working on the ranch. He's been pretty sad lately. Told J.L. he was thinking about moving back up onto the reservation in Montana."

Katy winced. She knew why he felt that way. She crossed her arms over her breasts and sighed.

"Guess you two had a dustup, huh?" he asked.

"Something like that," she replied. "I made some really stupid mistakes over the horse. Ron was so logical and he laid out the difficulties of a lawsuit in such a way that I considered taking his advice and letting them put Bartholomew down. Teddie was almost hysterical. Parker told her that nothing was going to happen to her horse. He stood up to Ron. For a few minutes," she added ruefully, "it would have looked to an outsider as if he were her concerned parent and I was an outsider trying to ruin her life. He cares a lot about her."

Butch didn't comment.

"I'm still in the learning stages about showing affection," she confessed after a minute. "My parents were ice-cold with me. I think they cared, in their way, but they never touched me. I grew up being alienated from other people. Now, I hug Teddie coming and going and I'm trying very hard to make it all up to her. Luckily for me, she has a forgiving nature."

"And Parker doesn't," he murmured dryly.

She flushed. "And Parker doesn't."

"He lived with an abusive father. His mother died young and he was left to the mercy of relatives, but they already had a son whom they loved. Parker was pretty much a beast of burden to them, from what I learned about him. He had a great brain and a teacher sent him to MIT to study theoretical physics, helped him find a scholarship that paid for everything. When he came out, he couldn't see himself teaching. And there was the war. He was patriotic to an extreme. He still is. He signed up for overseas duty and went to war with me." He sighed. "It didn't turn out the way we thought it would. War is glamorous until you see what happens to people who fight in them. After that, it's an evil you wish you could erase from the world."

"That's what my late husband said." She watched Teddie with the wolf, who was lying on his back now, letting her pet his chest. "I felt guilty, because my husband has only been dead a few months," she blurted out. "Teddie said he wouldn't want me to spend the rest of my life alone, that he was never like that. She knew him so well. They were close, in a way that she and I had never been, until just lately."

"So you backed away from Parker and now he won't talk to you," he guessed.

She nodded. "He was the best thing that ever happened to my daughter. I feel worse about separating them than I do about alienating him myself. He's a good man."

"He is. Stubborn. Bad-tempered from time to time. But he'll never desert you under fire."

They stood in a companionable silence for a few minutes. Katy looked at her watch.

"I hate to break up this lovefest," she teased Teddie, "but I have to put on stuff to cook for supper. Time to go, sweetheart."

Teddie smoothed over the wolf's head one more time and got to her feet. "So long, Two Toes," she said softly. "I'll come back to see you sometime if Mr. Matthews doesn't mind."

Butch laughed. "Mr. Matthews doesn't mind. Anytime. Just call or text me first."

"I don't have your number," Katy said.

He held out his hand. She gave him her cell phone, and he put his name in her contacts list. "Now you have it."

"Thanks very much," she said.

He walked them out onto the porch. A cold wind was blowing. "We hear that Dealy's lawyer in Denver quit and he's trying to find a local lawyer who isn't afraid of J.L.'s bunch from L.A."

She laughed. "Good luck to him. Anybody who supports that polecat is going to be in some really hot water. There are things that money can't buy. A lot of them, in fact. Beating up a poor old horse is low on my list of desirable character traits."

"Mine as well," Butch agreed. "I love horses. I'm not good with them, like Parker is. But he's got a gift. Some people have more of an affinity with animals than others do. Your daughter definitely has it," he added, watching her climb into the SUV.

"Yes," Katy said. "I was reluctant to let her adopt an abused horse. They can be problematic. But she solved that problem nicely by getting to know Parker." Her eyes grew sad. "Ever wish you had a time machine?" she wondered.

"Lots," he said.

She smiled at him. "Thanks for letting us visit Two Toes. He's a celebrity in these parts."

He grinned. "Maybe I should start hawking auto-graphed photos of him. Dip his paw in ink and put it on a picture of him."

She pursed her lips. "Lesser things have made people wealthy."

He shrugged. "I'm like you. I can take money or leave it. If I can pay the bills, that's all I want."

She chuckled. "Me, too. See you."

"See you."

She turned on the ignition and drove them home. Teddie was wired like a lamp the whole way home, enthusing about the sweet wolf.

When they got home, Katy put on her roast while Teddie looked at animal videos on her cell phone.

"I miss Parker," Teddie said sadly.

Katy drew in a long breath. "I know."

Teddie looked up. "You could call him."

Katy bit her lip as she put the cover on the Crock-Pot and set the timer. "I tried," she said huskily. "He blocked my number."

Teddie winced. "Oh."

"Sometimes, we just have to accept that things and people change, and there's not a lot we can do about it," Katy told her daughter. She sat down beside her. "We have a roof over our heads, and some cattle, and we're going to have Bartholomew back when Mr. Denton gets through having his lawyers trounce Mr. Dealy in court."

"I hope they trounce Mr. Dealy from head to toe," Teddie said angrily.

"Me, too."

"Can you take me over to Mr. Denton's place to see Bartholomew sometime?" she asked her mother. "I really miss him."

"Of course, I can. I'll text Cassie and see if it would be convenient to go tomorrow, if you like."

Teddie smiled. "That would be great! Thanks, Mom!" She hugged her mother.

Katy hugged her back, thanking God for second chances. "I don't say it much. But I do love you."

Teddie hugged her harder. "I love you, too, Mom."

"I'll bet Bartholomew doesn't miss us much, where he's living," Katy teased. "It's like a luxury hotel for horses."

Teddie laughed. "Yes, but it's the people you miss, not the place."

Katy only nodded. It was a wise comment, from a young girl. Wiser than her age denoted.

Cassie said it was all right, so Katy loaded up Teddie and they drove over to the Denton ranch, both wearing jeans and red checked shirts and down-filled jackets, because it had turned cold. In fact, snow flurries were coming down around them and heavy snow was predicted for the next two days.

"I hope it doesn't become a blizzard," Katy murmured as they got out of the SUV at the barn. "I hate driving in snow."

"They'll close the schools, won't they?" Teddie asked hopefully. "If they do, you and I could make a snowman!"

"We'll build one of Ron, with a hay mustache, and we'll pelt it with mud balls," Katy muttered.

Teddie burst out laughing.

Bartholomew was in his own spacious stall, chowing down on a mix of corn and additives to make him healthy.

Drum, J.L.'s foreman, smiled at their approach. "Missing your horse?" he teased Teddie. "He's been miserable."

"He lives in luxury," Katy pointed out.

He chuckled. "Even living in squalor where you're loved beats living in luxury where you're not," he said philosophically. "Not that you guys live in squalor. It's a good little ranch."

"Thanks," Katy said with a smile.

"Bart looks so nice!" Teddie enthused. "You guys have been brushing him!"

"Well, Parker has," Drum replied, noting Katy's sudden flush. "He comes over almost every day to check on him. He's fond of the old fellow. We all are."

"Bartholomew's special," Katy said in a subdued tone. She'd ruined everything with Parker. It was hard, remembering that.

"Have you heard about Dealy?" Drum asked, excitement in his tone.

She turned to him while Teddie petted her horse. "No. What about him?"

"He heard about J.L.'s lawyers from L.A. and ran for his life. He skipped town. Nobody knows where he went." He chuckled. "So J.L.'s attorneys got their investigator out here. Wherever Dealy ran, it won't be far enough."

"Good," Katy said shortly. "I hope they find him and

convict him and put him in chains. A man who'll beat a horse will beat a person."

"You're right about that," came a deep, quiet voice from behind her.

She knew the voice. She couldn't bear to turn and see the censure in his eyes.

But Teddie had no such reservations. "Parker!" she cried, and ran into his arms, to be picked up and hugged and swung around.

"Oh, Parker, I've missed you so much," Teddie said, her voice muffled against his broad shoulder.

"I've missed you, too, tidbit," he replied. There was a smile in his voice. "How are things going?"

"Fine." She grimaced. "Sort of fine."

He put her down. "Bart's looking good, don't you think?"

"He looks great. Doesn't he, Mom?" she added.

Katy was standing with her face down, her arms folded, feeling alone and ashamed and vulnerable. "Yes. He looks . . . very good."

"Oh, there's a calf!" Teddie enthused as she glanced over a gate farther down while Bart was eating. "Could I pet him?" she asked Drum.

He chuckled. "You bet. Come along."

They stranded Katy with Parker.

She couldn't bring herself to meet his eyes, to see the accusation she knew would be in them.

"How are you?" he asked.

She moved one shoulder. "Teddie and I are getting along better than we ever have," she said noncommittally.

"We heard that your lawyer friend left tracks heading out of town, he was in such a hurry."

"Too little, too late," she said stiffly. "I expect to spend years making it all up to Teddie."

He moved a step closer. "You won't look at me, Katy?"

She bit her lower lip. Tears stung her eyes. "I'm . . . too ashamed."

"Oh, baby." He pulled her into his arms and folded her against him, enveloped her in the scents of buckskin and smoke and fir trees. He rocked her while she cried, his lips in her hair.

"I turned against my own daughter," she choked. "Against you. I agreed to let a greedy man almost put down a horse to save myself legal problems. I hate myself!"

He drew in a deep breath. "We have disagreements. We get over them."

"Not always."

"I have a regrettable temper," he said after a minute, aware that Teddie and Drum were deliberately paying attention to the calf and not the two people down the aisle. "I'm sorry, too. I never should have blocked your number. That was low."

"I deserved it," she whispered. "I was horrible to you."

"I was horrible back."

She lifted her head. Her eyes were red and wet.

He bent and kissed the tears away. Which, of course, prompted even more tears.

"You aren't really going back to Montana, are you?" she choked out.

He laughed softly, delightedly. "Not if you don't want me to."

She looked up at him with wonder. He was saying something without saying it.

"I'd love to have a ten-year-old daughter of my own," he said solemnly. "I'd buy her pets, and drive her to parties, and take care of her horse. I'd take care of her mother, too, you understand. I mean, that would have to be part of the deal."

Her eyes widened and then she laughed as she realized what he was saying.

He understood what her eyes were saying, as well. "I'd like a son, too," he said softly, touching her hair. "Boys run in my family. Not a girl in the bunch, which is why yours would be so treasured."

"I like little boys, too," she whispered.

He bent and touched his mouth gently to hers. "We could get married. I mean, so people wouldn't gossip about us. We wouldn't want to embarrass Teddie. It's a small community, after all."

She reached up and kissed him with her whole heart. He kissed her back with all of his.

There was a loud clearing of a throat and a giggle. They hadn't heard the first cough, or the first giggle.

They drew apart, a little flushed, and stared down into a child's dancing eyes.

"Are you going to be my daddy now, Parker?" Teddie asked him.

He bent and opened his arms.

She ran into them and hugged him and kissed him and hugged him some more. "You'll be the best daddy in the whole world, next to the daddy I lost," she said against his shoulder.

"And you'll be my little girl as long as you live, even when you're married with kids of your own," he said huskily. "You won't mind, if your mom and I get married?"

"Oh, no," Teddie agreed at once. She glanced at her flushed, happy mother with teasing eyes. "It's nice to see her smile again. I thought she'd forgotten how!"

Parker only grinned.

* * *

And so, they were married. Teddie stayed with the Dentons while Parker and Mrs. Parker drove to Denver for a weekend honeymoon in a nice but not expensive hotel. Not that they saw much of it.

"Oh, my," Katy gasped as they moved together in the huge bed.

He laughed softly. "I like it very slow. Is that all right?"

She was shuddering. "I'll die."

"Not just yet," he whispered as he moved over her.

He was tender, and patient, and he knew a lot more about women than she knew about men, even after several years of marriage to her first husband. By the time she started winding up the spiral that led to an explosive, passionate culmination, she was sobbing with ecstasy she'd never experienced in her life.

He went with her the whole way, his voice deep and throbbing at her ear as his powerful body buffeted hers in the last few feverish seconds before the explosions began.

Afterward, as they lay in a sweating, exhausted tangle, she rolled over and pillowed her cheek on his broad chest. "And I thought I knew something about men."

He laughed. "You knew more than enough. We're very good together."

"Oh, yes. Very, very good." She smoothed her hand over his chest, deep in thought. "You know, we never spoke about birth control."

"We never did."

"Should we?"

"If you want to wait to start a family, we probably should."

"I'll be thirty soon."

He rolled over toward her. "Does that mean something?"

"I'd like to be young enough to enjoy our children," she whispered with a weary smile. "And Teddie will love not being an only child."

"In that case," he murmured, rolling her over again, "perhaps we should be more . . . energetic . . . about assuring that."

She laughed. "Perhaps we should!"

Predictably, a few weeks later, Katy started losing her breakfast. Parker was dancing around the room like a wild man, hugging Teddie and swinging her around.

"Parker, Mom's sick. Why are we celebrating?" she asked worriedly.

"She's not sick, honey, she's pregnant!" he burst out.

"Oh, goodness, really?!"

"Really!"

"I won't be an only child! I'll have brothers and sisters!"

"Well, maybe brothers," he said hesitantly. He put her down. "There aren't any girls in my family. Not any girl children. Except you," he teased, grinning.

"Except me," she agreed smugly.

"Could you stop celebrating and bring me a wet washcloth, please?" came a plaintive wail from the bedroom.

"Gosh, I'm sorry, sweetheart!" he said, rushing into the bathroom to wet a cloth.

Teddie sat by her mother on the bed. "I'm sorry and happy that you're sick, Mom!"

Katy managed to laugh as Parker put the wet cloth on her forehead. "Thanks, sweetheart. I'm sorry and happy myself. Goodness, how will I teach while I'm throwing up?"

"I'll get you a bucket to carry to work. Not to worry," Parker teased.

"Parker, don't you have a first name?" Teddie asked suddenly. "I mean, I call you Dad, and she calls you honey, but don't you have a real first name? Is it Crow?"

"Not really. My father didn't like my mother's family, so he insisted on naming me after a man he idolized."

"Really?" Teddie asked. "Who?"

Parker and Katy exchanged an amused look.

"Albert," Teddie guessed suddenly. "For Albert Einstein."

Parker whistled. "Sweetheart, you are a deep thinker. That's it, exactly."

Teddie grinned.

Katy laughed. "Albert." She shook her head. "It doesn't suit you. Parker does."

"It does," Teddie agreed. "But I'm still calling you Dad." She hugged him. He hugged her back.

Katy looked up at both of them and almost glowed with joy. "What a Christmas we're going to have this year," she exclaimed.

"The first of many," Parker agreed. "I can't wait to kiss you under the mistletoe!"

And it was a joyous one. The tree sat beside an open fireplace with logs blazing in it. The lights on the tree blinked in patterns and Teddie did most of the decorating, only letting Parker put the decorations and lights on the places she couldn't reach.

The result was a nine-foot-tall wonder. They took photos of it to show the coming child, when he was old enough to understand the beautiful expression of the season.

Parker put an arm around both of his girls as they stared at the end result of Teddie's and Katy's labors.

"It's the most beautiful tree we've ever had," Katy said.

"Oh, yes," Teddie agreed.

"We should bring Bartholomew in here and stand him up beside it. He could be a decoration," Parker suggested dryly.

Bart had been returned by J.L. after Dealy was pursued, caught, arrested, and charged with animal cruelty. He faced years in prison for it. J.L.'s attorneys and their investigator had managed to dig up several prior charges that had been dismissed for lack of evidence. They found evidence to convict, so he was charged in more than ten cases. No local attorney would agree to try his case, so the judge appointed a counselor for him. The consensus of opinion was that Mr. Dealy would spend a long time contemplating his brutal acts.

Meanwhile, the Parkers sat around their beautiful tree and listened to Christmas carols and drank eggnog and ate fruitcake. Parker kissed Katy under the mistletoe and she called him her mistletoe cowboy. They even took a special horse treat out to the barn for Bart.

"This was nice of you, Dad," Teddie remarked as they watched Bart nibble his treat.

Parker chuckled. "He had it coming. After all, he brought me a family of my very own," he added softly, looking from a radiant Katy to a beaming Teddie. "And it is," he added, "the nicest Christmas present I ever got!"

Blame It On the Mistletoe

MARINA ADAIR

To my dear friend,
plot partner, and sister for life, Jill Shalvis.
Whiteout conditions, roasting RVs, or
the ER . . . there's no one I'd rather
be stuck with.

Chapter One

Not much got past Noah Tucker. So he was a little embarrassed to admit that Christmas had completely snuck up on him. In fact, if a tinsel bomb hadn't erupted overhead, causing him to reach for his off-duty weapon, Christmas would have gone completely unnoticed.

Because this year, Christmas was definitely female and sporting a pair of legs that—even though they were encased in green-and-white striped tights—made him wonder if holiday miracles really did exist.

Home for the holidays was something Noah and his brothers avoided at all costs, which was why he'd waited until the cold had finally scared everyone indoors before taking a stroll through his hometown. But Santa's Helper— late twenties, five-three, whisky brown eyes, and long blond tinsel-tangled hair—didn't scare all that easily.

Nope, she was perched on a ladder, with enough twinkle lights to decorate every house from Sweet Plains to the North Pole, trying to place a snow angel atop the tree on the sheriff's station lawn. Her elf-inspired ensemble wasn't doing her any favors. Neither was the fact that she was a petite thing trying to decorate a monster of a tree all by her lonesome.

She'd donned a short, green velvet getup with a matching pointy hat and shoes, all trimmed in fur. It was like sexy collided with Christmas, making her the sexiest Elf on the Shelf he'd ever encountered.

"Son of a sleigh bell," she mumbled as another shower of tinsel drifted to the ground, causing momentary white-out conditions.

Back in Austin, Noah would have simply checked to ensure she was okay, then gone about his own business. But he wasn't in Austin. He was in Sweet Plains, Texas, and for the next three weeks his business involved returning to the family ranch, Tucker's Crossing—a place he'd spent a lifetime trying to escape—to help his brother, Cody, sort through the mess their vengeful old man had left behind.

Imagining what was to come, Noah decided to take a few additional moments of silence for himself before entering the storm.

He looked up and shielded his eyes from falling pine needles. "You need some help, Elf on the Shelf?"

"Holy Christmas!" she squeaked, nearly tumbling right off the ladder—her snow angel not faring so well in the kerfuffle.

Either, like him, she didn't take kindly to being caught off guard or she didn't like to admit when she needed help, because after she found her balance and righted her hat, she shot him a look angry enough to roast his chestnuts.

"Are you trying to kill me?" she accused in a hushed whisper.

"No, ma'am," he drawled, rocking back on his heels. "Just being neighborly is all."

"Well"—again with the hushed tone—"go be neighborly

someplace else." And, after a nervous glance around, she shooed him off with a mittened hand.

A cold chill blew off the distant rolling hills as Noah took in the twinkle-lined streets and garlanded storefronts of downtown. With not a single Who strolling through Whoville, Santa and his hooved brethren could make an emergency landing on Main Street, and no one would be the wiser. Then there was Miss Elf, the one soul brave enough to face the elements, back to stringing lights and ignoring him.

Most people would take one look at those wide doe eyes and velvet getup and assume the elf was simply spreading holiday cheer.

Noah wasn't most people.

He was a Texas Ranger, trained to be suspicious. And it didn't get more suspect than someone decorating the tree in front of the sheriff's department after sundown, when the skies were threatening to rain down some serious trouble on Sweet County.

Whistling a Christmas tune, he strolled over to pick up the tree topper and shook fallen leaves from its hair. "What about your snow angel? Seems he's lost a wing."

"Must have been the result of testosterone-induced rage. It's a growing problem in these parts."

"Is that how you lost your wings, angel?"

"You should see the other guy." That smart mouth of hers curled up into a wicked grin. "Now shoo."

"Just as soon as you tell me if Logan's aware that you're out here spreading holiday spirit all over his sheriff's station," Noah said, referring to his old friend and the recently re-elected sheriff.

"Why is that any of your business?"

Noah couldn't help but grin. It wasn't that Miss Elf didn't scare easily. She didn't scare at all.

"Santa's helper or not, you're trespassing."

"Says you."

Noah had been known to make even the most dangerous of criminals wet their pants with a single look. However, this woman was looking at him as if he were as harmless as a snowman in a Stetson. So he casually opened his jacket, sure to uncover his glimmering badge. "Says the great state of Texas."

He could tell she wanted to argue, but his badge accomplished what he hadn't been able to on his own—silence her. Only for a moment though.

With a huff, she scrambled down the ladder, her eyes two pissed-off slits as she stomped over. "You know what they say about men who go waving their pistols around?"

He hadn't intended to reveal his harnessed weapon, but now he knew why she'd suddenly gone quiet. "That you should approach with caution?"

"That their pistol is far more impressive than their"— her eyes briefly dropped below his belt buckle—"stocking stuffer."

"Well, now, angel, if you were curious about my stocking stuffer all you had to do was ask. But don't you worry, I can fire fifteen rounds before reloading."

She did her best to stare him down, a hard task since she barely reached his shoulder. Hands on hips, that red-tipped nose so high in the air he was surprised she wasn't experiencing altitude sickness, she said, "I prefer my stocking stuffers to get it right on round one. So why don't you go show your pistol to someone who cares, so I can get back to decorating my tree?"

She shimmied her cute little backside up the ladder, and

he walked over to stand behind her. "And risk getting a lump of coal for not helping an elf lady in need? Imagine what the town would say? I can see the headlines now. OFFICER OF THE LAW NEGLECTS TO REPORT SUSPICIOUS SUSPECT CAMPED OUT IN SHERIFF STATION'S TREE."

She looked down at him. "I imagine it will read more like OFFICER OF THE LAW WAVES HIS PISTOL AT UNSUSPECTING BRINGER OF CHRISTMAS CHEER—SHE WAS UNIMPRESSED."

"Either way, I need a good reason not to tell Logan that you're vandalizing his tree."

She eyed him suspiciously, as if calling his bluff. When he didn't move, she gave a sigh big enough to deflate her whole body.

"Okay, but you can't tell anyone." The words were spoken so softly, he barely heard her over the rustling tree branches.

"And why's that?"

"Because it's a surprise." Mumbling offensive things about his sex, she made her way back down. "Look, I've done this every year since the new tree went in. And every year the town erupts with excitement, trying to guess who's behind it." She looked up at him again, but this time her eyes were a warm brown. "If people know it's me, then it ruins the magic."

Noah almost told her magic didn't exist but, somehow, sensed it would be as distressing as telling his little nephew Santa was a big fat lie. Plus, starting as far back as his senior year of high school, there'd been rumors about Sweet's Secret Samaritan. An anonymous friend of the town who did little favors for people in need. Flower gardens would appear overnight, the elderly would awake to a seasonal pie on their doorstep, widows received flowers on their wedding anniversary.

He didn't think *this* Samaritan was old enough to be *Sweet's* Secret Samaritan, just as he didn't think she was telling him the entire truth about why she'd chosen that tree. But he'd done enough interrogations to know that, if he wanted the truth, he needed to soften his approach. Otherwise, she'd dig in, and they'd likely stand there all night, even though she was shivering from the dropping temperature.

He looked at his watch. "Shift change happens in about twenty minutes, so unless you want to out yourself as Sweet's Secret Samaritan to half the deputies in the county, why don't you let me help?"

"I'm not Sweet's Secret Samaritan," she said coolly. She was a pretty little liar—he'd give her that. But his BS meter was more accurate than most lie detectors. "I just like Christmas."

That was a truth. In fact, he'd go so far as to say she loved Christmas. Something about the way her eyes sparkled with childlike excitement at the admission was as adorable as it was endearing. Noah didn't normally go for adorable, but on her it worked.

"Then how about you let me help you help Santa?" he joked and, look at that, she laughed. A good sign he'd made the first crack in those glaciers she hid behind.

"Fine, but only because I have to be home in time for dinner and you're like ten feet tall. Plus, my ornaments are so big they're drooping."

As far as he was concerned, her ornaments were near perfect—in size and shape—but his mama taught him better than to argue with a lady. Plus, the sky was turning darker by the minute and their breath was starting to crystalize in the cold air.

Even though her costume was long sleeved, it wasn't nearly thick enough to stand up to the dropping temperatures. And he didn't even want to talk about her skirt and tights, which were more fashion than function.

"You're one strong breeze from turning into a Popsicle." Noah slid off his jacket and draped it over her shoulders—ignoring how good she looked in his clothes.

To his surprise, she didn't argue but immediately burrowed into it, practically disappearing beneath the shearling. She even made a sexy little sigh as she snuggled deeper.

Noah moved to zip it and she took a step back, as if startled that he'd touch her. She tried to pretend it hadn't happened by keeping her eyes on him, her shoulders ramrod straight, and that tough-girl attitude firmly in place. But it was clear that he'd startled her—and that startled him. Made him uncertain how to proceed, because there was also something similiar to fear flickering in her eyes. Something raw and habitual in her reaction that bothered him.

Deciding the best route was pretending he hadn't noticed the way she'd jumped, he casually picked up a strand of lights and went about stringing them on the higher branches that even he—at *ten feet tall*—could barely reach.

She didn't slow down long enough to defrost her fingers before hanging large plastic balls from the lower branches. But when she stepped beside him, handing over a decoration, he knew he'd made the right call.

And that's how Noah found himself during the first storm of the season, standing side by side with Sweet's

Secret Samaritan, decorating a tree in complete silence. Every so often, he'd hear her humming a Christmas tune, but then she'd remember he was there and give a dramatic huff before going silent.

The third time she did it, he laughed and she skewered him with a sidelong glance.

"If you don't answer to Secret Samaritan, then what should I call you?" he asked, and she shoved out a breath as if his presence had ruined her entire holiday season.

"Faith."

That was it. No last name. No further details. The bite in her tone suggested that one word was the beginning and end of their conversation.

Says her.

"So Faith, just Faith. I'm Noah." He stuck out his hand. "Noah Tucker."

"Well, Noah Tucker." She didn't acknowledge his extended hand. "I hope your decorating skills are better than your recall, because we've met. Many times."

His recall was near perfect. And with a woman who looked like her? She'd be imprinted on the backs of his eyelids.

So when their gazes met, he made sure his skepticism was clear as day.

"Seriously? We had an algebra class together your senior year. I sat behind you," she said. *He had nothing.* "You borrowed my notes."

Noah didn't remember a whole lot about senior year. He'd been too busy focusing on how many days were left until he could enlist and get out of this hellhole. But he hadn't been so focused as to miss a pretty girl with big brown eyes and even bigger ornaments.

Even thinking about her ornaments had him itching to

inspect them further. And no matter how many times he reminded himself they were concealed beneath the bulk of his jacket, or thought, "*Eyes up, idiot, eyes up,*" they'd eventually drift south.

Brow arched, she crossed her arms. "I was a freshman. You were a dic . . . uh, stocking stuffer. Still are."

Noah noticed her eyes were doing a little wandering of their own—from his eyes to his lips, back and forth. He winked, letting her know she'd been caught. "If I was such a . . . stocking stuffer, then why did you lend me your notes, Faith, just Faith?"

That question prompted a guilty grin. "Because you were a *senior* still taking algebra. I figured someone needed to help you pass or we'd be stuck with you another year."

"Or maybe you lent me your notes because you had a crush on me. Wait, I remember you," he said, suddenly placing her. Back then she was a quiet little thing, pretty but young as hell. She'd worked in the tutoring center after school and Noah always got the feeling that school was her way out. "You used to bring me cookies on game days."

"I brought a lot of people cookies, so don't think you were special."

"Good to know." He grinned and she rolled her eyes. "I probably didn't thank you back then. I *was* kind of a stocking stuffer."

"It's expected—all men are."

"You know, some of us learned from our mistakes and grew up."

She looked unimpressed, as if he needed to work harder. As if she didn't trust him to be anything other than a disappointment.

"You seem skeptical." He took an ornament from her

fingers and hung it on one of the higher branches. She didn't bat his hand away, but he could tell she wasn't someone who played well with others.

"So you're saying you offered to help me with zero expectations?" she asked.

"Yes, ma'am."

"And you're not going to say anything to anyone about this?"

"Trust me, your secret is safe," he said. "In fact, how about when we're done here, we grab a coffee?"

"Grab coffee? So what, we can chat about the weather? Catch up?" She looked up at him. "It's cold and late, and I don't date. All the catching up we need."

"Who said anything about a date?" he asked, finding it interesting that her cheeks turned the slightest shade of pink. "What if I was only offering you a chance to thank me for helping with the tree decorating?"

"Thank you for helping with the tree, Noah 'Let Me Show You My Pistol' Tucker." She gathered up her things, including eleven empty twinkle light boxes, a backpack, and a huge purse. "And here I thought you were still that stocking stuffer from high school." With a grin as sweet as sugar plums, she shoved a box of lights his way. "I hope these don't take too long to hang. I hear it's a crime to be merry and bright in front of the sheriff's station."

After a "good boy" pat to the arm, she turned on her elfin shoes and headed toward Main Street, still wearing his jacket, and leaving him with a ladder, six strands left to string, and a grin so wide he knew it would still be there come tomorrow.

"Hey," he called out. "How about that coffee?"

Without slowing down, she called over her shoulder, "Sorry, I'm more of a hot cocoa kind of girl."

She walked away, hips swaying like she knew he was watching. And he was. He was so focused on the way that fur trim flirted with her incredible heart-shaped backside, he didn't even notice Logan had strolled up behind him until he spoke.

Sheriff Logan Miller stood on the station's top step, looking amused as all get-out. Even though he was trained, well over six feet, and carried a badge and gun of his own, Noah could still take him. Didn't stop the sheriff from saying, "That was entertaining. Watching a Tucker go down in flames always makes for a good night."

"I was laying the foundation," Noah replied.

"Or wasting your time." Logan grinned. "In fact, you're so far in the friend zone you don't even see the zone."

"I've been getting in and out of the friend zone since middle school. I've got her right where I want her."

"Where's that? Doing her chores?" Without waiting for an answer, Logan turned and entered the station. Noah followed.

"You weren't close enough to see, but she was feeling it, too."

Logan ushered him past the front desk and into the back office, laughing the entire way. By the time the sheriff sat his annoying backside behind the desk, Noah felt like strangling him.

"Whatever you have to tell yourself to sleep at night," Logan said.

Noah blew on his hands while rubbing them together. "Are you going to ask about my feelings next or offer me a hot cup of joe?"

Logan reached behind him and in a matter of seconds a Keurig machine whirled to a start and began percolating.

Noah almost groaned when hot steam fogged the window that separated the sheriff's office from the rest of the station.

Logan handed him a mug of coffee, then released a low whistle. "Never thought I'd see the day when Noah Tucker got all out of sorts over a little chill factor. City's made you soft."

"Was going to say the same about you." Noah lifted a brow, then the coffee mug which read REAL MEN DO BALLET.

"Sidney bought me that for Father's Day," he said, grinning so big Noah couldn't help but smile in return.

Logan was dad to the sweetest five-year-old on the planet. With her blond curls and adorable tiny-girl voice there wasn't much Logan wouldn't do to make her happy. After suddenly losing his wife a few years back, Logan worked hard to fill both parental roles, trying to give his little girl as normal a life as possible. Noah guessed that meant doing daddy-daughter ballet.

"How's she doing?"

"Growing up too fast," Logan said. "She started kindergarten this year. Already negotiated extra recess time for the class with her teacher."

Noah laughed. "Sounds like you have a little lawyer on your hands."

"Bite your tongue. One lawyer in the family is enough for me," Logan said, referring to his sister-in-law, a local county prosecutor. "So what brings you home?"

"My boss had me running an Interview and Interrogation seminar up near Fort Worth yesterday, and I have another one in Texarkana a few days after Christmas. I planned on heading back to Austin in between, but Cody asked me to spend the holidays at the Crossing."

Coming home always managed to put Noah on edge. Had he been out of his mind when he agreed to spend the entire holiday at his family's ranch? He'd rather be waterboarded than spend even a night there, but when he'd heard his nephew's wish was to spend Christmas morning with his favorite uncle, Noah packed his bags for a long winter's trip.

"You been to the ranch yet?"

Noah took a sip of the hot coffee, not caring if it scorched his tongue. "Nope. Headed there now." And already he was itching to leave.

"Tell Cody I'll be there around seven."

"Is there a game on I don't know about?" Noah wasn't all that into sports anymore. He didn't have the time. But hanging out with old friends and tossing back a few sounded like a fun distraction.

"No, *Little Mermaid Live* is playing on TV tonight and Sidney asked to watch it with JT," Logan said, referring to Noah's nephew.

"How times have changed."

No game. No beer. No old times to be had, it seemed. Cody was married with a son. Logan, who Krazy Glued all the principal's furniture to the gymnasium ceiling, was now the town's sheriff. The only thing that remained the same?

Noah was still scared to go home.

Chapter Two

Growing up the daughter of a convicted felon, Faith Loren had learned that the past was bound to catch up. It was when the past beat her to the punch that really ticked her off.

"Heard you might be applying to be our evening entertainment," Faith's part-time boss bellowed from behind the pie display, then pointed a pudgy thumb over her shoulder to the silver pole that sat in the middle of the diner.

Viola McKinney was the owner of the Bluebonnet Burger, Bar & Biscuit, or the B-Cubed to the born and bred in Sweet Plains. "There's a few nights comin' up that you're not on the schedule. I can change that."

"Not even for time and a half," Faith said, balancing a tray of drinks, two orders of chicken and waffles, a pimento-cheese burger, and a B(cubed)LT with a side of onion rings. Her phone said it was Friday, but the universe was treating her as if it were a Monday. "I hardly have any days off this month, and they're already packed. I've got holiday shopping to do, Pax's holiday recital at the community center is coming up, and week after next I'm attending a wrapping party at Shelby's with the girls."

It was the final prep for the town's annual Sweet's

Holiday Shindig, an old-fashioned celebration that was over a hundred years running. The Saturday before Christmas, every one of the 9,000 residents were invited to spend a fun-filled evening with neighbors, and take part in holiday activities for the whole family.

There was a silent auction, a pie exchange, even an old-fashioned hayride around the park—best served with a steaming cup of Mrs. McKinney's hot cocoa. Folks knew to line Main Street before nine, because when the mayor lit the giant tree in front of Town Hall, Santa and his reindeer began their ride through town, waving and passing out presents.

The best part of the event was that all the proceeds went to Treats for Tots, a charity that benefitted local families in need. Last year, the silent auction alone brought in over $18,000. Sweet's Holiday Shindig had gone from a celebration to a way the town could help neighboring families experience the magic of the season, regardless of where they landed on the income scale. Because, come Christmas morning, every child in town would have a present under the tree.

Once upon a time, Faith had been one of those kids.

She was twelve when her mom moved them to Sweet Plains, and Faith could still remember the Treats for Tots present she'd found under her tree. It was a baking set for beginners, with pink bowls, measuring cups, and a coordinating apron. There was also a recipe box, pink of course, which held a family recipe from nearly every baker in town.

That one present hadn't just made Faith's holiday that year; those recipes, handwritten and shared from the heart, had made Sweet Plains feel like home. Something that didn't happen often when one's mother was a tumbleweed of the world.

Hope Loren went through husbands like most people went through calendars. Every year was a chance to throw out the old and welcome the new, and with every new man came a new city and a new house. Faith blamed her from-anywhere accent—not to mention her desperate need to belong—on a childhood spent stuck in a never-ending game of hometown roulette.

So while the wrapping party was a way for her to help other children have a magical Christmas morning, it also served as a way to connect. She was pulling so much over-time to make this holiday special for her own family, she hadn't had a day off in over a month. Faith was desperate for some down time with her friends. And in addition to wrapping, there was also going to be wine and chocolate.

Something she dared not mention to Mrs. McKinney for fear that she and her Silvered Singles posse would crash the party.

"Wrapping party?" Viola harrumphed. "Your generation is nothing but a bunch of special snowflakes, needing emotional support and twenty sets of hands to wrap a present."

"There are over five hundred donations to wrap before the auction." Including 100-plus bikes, skateboards, and other high-end gifts, many of which were donated by the Beaumont Foundation—founded by the oldest and wealth-iest families in town.

"When I was committee chair, all I got was paper bags, twine, and a bottle of bathtub gin to keep me company. And these two hands did just fine."

Faith decided not to point out that Mrs. McKinney's hands were the size of ham hocks, or that she'd wound up sleepwalking into town in nothing but her slippers and nightcap the day after the auction.

"You're an army of one, Mrs. McKinney," Faith praised. "As for the extra shifts? I'm not looking to add exotic dancer to my résumé quite yet."

"Good, because I ain't hiring anyone. Like I told that cheat Mr. McKinney, the night I strung him up on Town Hall's flagpole, the only woman who's ever going to swing on Mr. McKinney's pole again is me."

To prove how serious she was, the older woman pointed toward the cement headstone at the base of the pole, which read:

Author J. McKinney

A MAN WHOSE POLE IS PERMANENTLY CLOSED
FOR BUSINESS
Born 7.1.1941 – Died 2.17.1983

Husband, loving father
&
Devoted Fornicator

The pole was a piece of fourth-generation history left over from the previous establishment, a strip club—and a reminder to unfaithful husbands everywhere. The inscription was the result of Mrs. McKinney's discovery that her then-husband, an accountant by trade, wasn't handling people's money as much as he was exchanging it for dollar bills at his "gentleman's" club.

"Then you might want to stop prancing around town in that elf getup."

"Who told you about that?" Faith's body heated as if a spotlight was suddenly shining down on her.

What had she thought would happen? She knew better. Knew Noah wasn't to be trusted.

There were two things Faith didn't do: trust or secrets. Her childhood hadn't allowed for either. Trusting someone meant being vulnerable, and sharing secrets created an intimate bond. But she'd had no choice but to trust Noah to keep his word, because her good sense didn't allow for intimate coffee meetups with cops. Which brought her to the third thing she didn't do.

Cops.

So if he'd breathed even a single word about her being Sweet's Secret Samaritan, then he'd better watch his pistol. Because when Faith got hold of him, he wouldn't have anything left to holster.

"Mister was in here this morning flapping his lips about how you were moonlighting. He offered up a hundred dollars to anyone who'd reveal where you're dancing. He's thinking about hosting the next Moose Lodge get-together there, then announcing his candidacy for club president. He thinks your"—she waved a pie slicer at Faith's cleavage—"jingle bells will give him an edge over Mr. Woodrow Rayborn in the race."

"First, I've never danced, well, *that* way. And second—" Faith leaned in and lowered her voice. "Does Ms. Luella know about this? Because I don't want her putting a hit out on me or dumping a load of coal on my porch."

Faith shivered at the idea of letting Mister anywhere near her jingle bells. Not only was he one hair from bald, but he was also the long-standing gentleman friend of a woman who'd once tie-dyed an entire flock of sheep because their owner implied Ms. Luella's knitting was so inferior it was a waste of wool.

"Ms. Luella isn't who you need to be worried about."

This time the pie slicer was aimed at Faith's throat. "You know I don't tolerate moonlighters on my staff."

"I work fulltime at the hospital and pick up odd shifts here after work or on the weekends." Like today. Faith worked the early shift at the hospital, then raced to the diner just in time to start the swing shift, taking her work-day from ten hours to a whopping fourteen. "So techni-cally, when I'm here I'm moonlighting."

Mrs. McKinney considered that for a long, hard moment, her lips tightening even more than usual, then lowered the weapon. "Since there's no hanky-panky involved, I'll let it slide. But now you've got me thinking. After all the ruckus about you in those leggings, maybe you should wear that outfit to work. Wouldn't even have to offer Senior Sunday anymore, you'd gather a crowd. You'd have 'em wheeling their chairs right out of the nursing home."

"I have burned the costume and, not that it's any of your business, I only wore it because I was picking up some last-minute Dear Sweet letters from a few of the kids in the pediatric ward. And there was a mix-up at the costume shop, and that was the last elf costume they had."

"Bet there were a bunch of angry parents trying to dodge all kinds of elf-inspired questions today."

"It's been a week." Surprisingly, last night had been the highlight. And she meant that in the best kind of way. Seeing Noah had been exciting. Sparring with him had been as thrilling as the front seat of a roller-coaster ride.

"So that's a no on the holiday uniform?" Viola asked.

Faith dug her hands into her hips and glared down at her boss, which was impressive since, at only five-three, Faith spent most of her life looking up at people.

"Well then, shoo." Viola swatted her with the spatula.

"We've got hungry customers and the food's getting cold. Now go fetch a basket of biscuits for table five."

"Yes, Mrs. McKinney," Faith said, sweet as pie.

"Don't take that tone with me. I don't know what to do with nice."

With an even warmer smile, Faith grabbed a basket of steaming biscuits—because this was an around-the-clock biscuit establishment—and honey butter and headed toward table five, where one of her best friends was holding court.

Gina Echols was dressed in a sharp-looking blue suit, a pair of candy red heels, and enough bravado to cut steel. She was superhero worthy and ready to kick some serious bad-guy butt. Which was fitting since she worked as a lawyer for the County Prosecutor's office.

Faith set down the basket of biscuits. "On the house."

"The biscuits are always on the house. Your uniform literally says, BISCUITS ARE FREE. JUST DON'T ASK ME TO BUTTER THEM," Gina said, not bothering to look up from the brief she was reading. "Plus, no biscuits on court day. Carbs are for the weak."

"I put extra honey butter in there."

Work forgotten, Gina snatched the basket to peek in. She took a big sniff, her head sagging against her chest in defeat. "You play dirty."

"I can't help it—I'm an enabler at heart."

"Next time enable someone who didn't skip their morning run, three years in a row," Gina said around a mouthful of buttered biscuit.

"Your usual then. A coffee, eggs and bacon scramble with extra bacon on the side."

"Don't forget to hold the fruit."

"Got it." She had turned to walk away when Gina pulled

out a dollar bill and stuck it in the hem of Faith's skirt. Faith snatched the bill and glared. "What's this?"

"I was hoping you'd tell me." Her *You're busted* expression said Gina wasn't asking for a rundown on today's specials.

"I'm bringing my double-soaked bourbon balls to the wrapping party," Faith said, and Gina pulled out another bill, making a big deal about it. Faith snatched that one, too. "Who told you?"

Gina pointed to the sheriff, sitting at the counter and out of uniform, waving a few bills in the air. "According to Deputy Do Little, you were running through town dressed to impress."

Faith paused, silently repeating what Gina had said. Backtracking to be sure Gina had only accused one annoying officer of the law of being a bigmouth.

"So Noah didn't tell you anything about last night?"

She had to be sure. She also didn't know why it was so important to her that Noah had kept his word, but her heart said it was.

"Noah? As in Tucker? No, I haven't seen him since . . . God, since he blew through town last summer." Gina's grin widened and she leaned forward, resting her chin on her hands. "But clearly you've seen Noah Tucker. And from the way you're blushing, I'd say it was last night."

"I ran into him on my way home from work," she said, which wasn't a total lie. She had gone from the hospital straight to the sheriff's station. But she didn't need Gina to know she'd made a pit stop to spread some holiday cheer.

"Explain 'ran into him.'"

"Like I said, he was headed into the sheriff's station and we ran into each other. End of story."

"I see. Well, in this story, the one where you ran into Noah Tucker, what did he tell you?"

"He's not some legend who requires his surname whenever you speak of him, and I'm not on the stand. So can we call him just Noah?"

"Wow, one night and you go from mooning over him to calling him Just Noah. Impressive. That costume must have really been something."

"Can you not?" She set down the tray and shoved Gina over, scooching into the booth. "I mooned over him, past tense, like more than a whole decade in the past, past tense. So I'd appreciate it if you'd never mention it again."

"So no flutters?"

"No."

There had been no flutters. Now tingles, that was another story. So many tingles she'd almost said yes to coffee, then remembered her resolution to stop dating the wrong kind of men.

Since the right kind of men didn't exist in Sweet Plains, she'd been a little man starved of late. Which was the only logical reason she could come up with for why he'd gotten under her skin. Because Noah Tucker and his above-standard-issue pistol packed enough power to tempt her good parts to come out of hibernation midwinter.

To complicate things further, Noah had correctly guessed that she was Sweet's Secret Samaritan. Of course she'd denied it, but he hadn't believed her. When she'd left him standing there to finish her good deed, she'd felt certain he'd rat her out. Faith had successfully kept her secret identity a secret for fifteen years and seventy-two random acts of kindness, leaving but eleven transgressions to make right. But maybe Noah was the honest and decent guy

Faith had dreamed up in high school. Didn't matter. His trip home was nothing more than a drive-through howdy.

"Nope. Not a single flutter."

Gina smiled and popped half of a biscuit into her mouth. "Okay."

Faith wasn't buying it. The odds of Gina, her nosiest friend, dropping the subject so easily was about as likely as Mrs. McKinney landing on the cover of the Victoria's Secret Christmas catalog.

"Okay, what?"

"That's it. Okay." Gina's grin said it wouldn't be okay until Faith admitted that she'd felt flutters. Which she totally had—stupid hormones. "I'll take that coffee now."

Trying to figure out what just happened, Faith took two steps, then spun around to eyeball her friend, waiting for the catch. But there was no catch. Gina was back to studying her brief and Logan was elbow-deep into a bowl of Mrs. McKinney's award-winning chili.

Shaking off her rising paranoia, and residual flutters from hearing Noah's name six times in the last five minutes, Faith went back to work.

She was still thinking about those flutters long after Gina left with a suspect smile, when the early dinner crowd began—meaning every resident of retirement age arrived to cash in on the B-Cubed's BEFORE FIVE IF YOU'RE STILL ALIVE blue plate special.

Faith seated a couple in the corner booth, then saw someone at the register, waving to get her attention. Thankfully, it was Ester Rayborn, and she was waving her restaurant bill and not dollar bills. At least Faith thought it was Ester behind the dark glasses and mauve hat, which was pulled down past her eyebrows.

"How was your meal?"

"Wonderful as always, dear," Ester said, looking anything but. She was glancing this way and that, over her shoulder, around the diner, scanning the parking lot, all the while talking to Faith. "I'd like to add some *cookies* to go before you run my card, if that's all right."

"Not a problem." Faith waited but the woman didn't move. "Will that be debit or credit?"

"Oh heavens me." Ester put her credit card on the counter, then placed a hand to her chest. "I'm so nervous. I've never done anything like this before. I even sent Woodrow to the car saying I had to conduct some official bake sale business, but he doesn't ever sit still for long so we'd better hurry."

"Let me ring you up and—"

"No!" Ester was back to looking around the diner as if she were Miss Marple stuck in an Agatha Christie novel. "I'm sorry. I don't want the cookies on the bill. I'll pay cash for those. I was told that's the way these transactions go."

"Then what kind of cookies can I get you?"

"*Your* cookies."

"Oh." At the comment, a rush of pride swelled in Faith's chest. Ester wasn't merely a cookie connoisseur, she also happened to be the head of this year's bake sale committee, so she knew her baking. She also knew that Faith dabbled in cookie creations at the diner.

It was another source of desperately needed income. Especially around the holidays.

Holidays had never meant much when she'd been a kid. Her mom struggled to keep them fed, let alone buy a tree and presents. Having her mom home on Christmas morning was a luxury since Hope often volunteered to work any shift that paid time and a half. When her brother was born, Faith promised herself Pax would have a different kind of childhood—the kind Faith had always dreamed of.

She was determined to give Pax an extra special Christmas this year—only the top item on his list was way above her pay grade. Which was why she'd been working extra shifts and siphoning tip money away from her MAMA NEEDS A NEW MIXER fund into WHAT'S A NEW MIXER COMPARED TO A KID'S CHRISTMAS fund.

Six months ago, McKinney had approached Faith with an amazing opportunity. Viola would bankroll the operation, Faith would do the baking, and they'd split the profits fifty-fifty. With her own student loans to pay off and Pax only seven years away from college, accepting was a no-brainer.

Except on days like today, when Shelby was watching Pax and Faith was nearing her second shift of a fourteen-hour marathon on her feet. She had to admit she was running on fumes.

So it felt good when someone validated her hard work.

"Thank you. You kind of made my day." So much so that she felt tears prick her eyes. "If you don't have anything specific in mind, I highly recommend the peppermint bark cookies." She did a Vanna White move, displaying the tray of dog-shaped cookies with peppermint bark icing on the paws. "Or my ginger bear cookies. They come individually wrapped and make a delicious holiday gift for a neighbor or the postman. And perfect stocking stuffers."

And dang it, Gina was right. It hadn't been just tingles. The reminder of a particular stocking stuffer had parts of her, she'd thought long ago closed for the winter, whipping up a blizzard of flutters.

"No, dear, your *special* cookies." Ester lowered her sunglasses to peer over their rims, giving Faith a *You got me, right?* wink.

The only kind of *special* baked items Faith had ever heard of were still illegal in the great state of Texas. And she'd only done one illegal thing in her life—the repercussions of which were so horrifying she'd vowed to never again find herself on the wrong side of the law.

"Mrs. Rayborn, are you asking if there's marijuana in my cookies?"

Ester gasped, her hand going to her pearls. "Heavens, no. I'm looking for the cookies with the Viagra icing."

Faith choked. "You think I'm grinding up Viagra and sneaking it in my icing?"

"That's the word on the street." She wrapped her scarf higher as if the flimsy disguise would distract from her bright red canvas RAYBORN MORTUARY: TAKE THAT FINAL RIDE IN STYLE bag hanging off her shoulder. "Last night at Bea's Quilting Barn, I was getting some yarn to knit a baby blanket for Mable's granddaughter. She's expecting her first. And I overheard Luella talking to Bea about these cookies she bought for Mister. Said it was like they were teenagers again." Ester leaned all the way in and whispered, "Six hours. Feet to Jesus-style. Only taking a break to find Mister's dentures when things got a little spicy."

"Those must be some cookies."

"Cookies to get your *cookies*," Ester clarified as if Faith wasn't uncomfortable enough. "It got me thinking. What gift do you get the man who says he has everything?"

"Cookies to get your cookies?" Faith guessed.

Ester clasped her frail hands together in excitement. "So you do have some?"

"I'm sorry," Faith said. "I swapped out the traditional icing for my maple cream frosting, but these days that's as spicy as I get."

"Oh." Ester looked disappointed. "This will be my and Woodrow's fifty-fifth Christmas together and I was hoping to get the spark back. Maybe go sledding, then sit by the fire and have some hot cocoa spiked with peppermint schnapps like we did on our first date. And when the sun went down, we'd have a cookie and well . . ." Ester wiggled her brows.

Listening to Ester's plan had Faith feeling a little disappointed, too. An eighty-year-old woman was planning to seduce her husband of more than half a century with some pharmaceutical-aided romance. And the spiciest Faith had gotten lately was swapping ingredients.

She wasn't interested in Viagra-spiked cookies, but she'd welcome a little romance in her life. Someone with whom to share her day or watch the occasional movie. Someone to give her a desperately needed cookie—or two.

There wasn't space in her calendar to date. It was a stroke of luck if she had a spare five minutes to swipe on lipstick and mascara. Relationships, as far as she could tell, took a lot of time—and trust.

Two things she was short of.

Faith handed over a cookie and Ester took a big bite.

"Oh my." Ester's brows shot right over those bug-eyed sunglasses. "Viagra or not, this is the best gingerbread I've tasted in years. It's even better than my recipe." The older woman took another bite and moaned. "Have you thought about selling these?"

"I have, and I do. Here." Again with the Vanna White move.

"Have you considered selling these at the bake sale?"

Only every year when the sign-up sheet went around. But Faith was never able to scrounge up the 300 dollars to pay the booth fee. And unless she could get her hands on one of Hermione's Time Turners and be in two places at once, Faith didn't have the spare time necessary to bake fifty dozen cookies.

"Maybe next year," Faith said, more a vow to herself than to Ester.

"Why wait?" Ester clasped her hands. "I hear there's an opening for gingerbread cookies this year."

"But you've made the gingerbread cookies every year since I moved here." They were one of her favorite parts of the holiday celebration. Buying an iced gingerbread man from Ester's booth was first on her list of stops. They were as big as her hand, tasted like Christmas, and Faith loved to walk through town nibbling on her cookie while taking in all the holiday activities.

"The arthritis is getting to be too much these days. My granddaughter was supposed to fly in from Tuscola and help, but she's expecting, so her husband doesn't want her to fly."

"Congratulations, you're going to be a great-grandma."

"I'm going to be out a helper, that's what I am." Ester looked about ready to keel over from the stress. "After tasting your gingerbread and looking at your young, strong hands, I thought that maybe you'd want to take my spot."

Faith choked. "Take your spot? I thought you were going to ask me to help you."

"You would be helping me. You'd bake and ice the

cookies. We'd split running the booth. I've already done the hard part."

"What's the hard part?" Grinding the flour from wheat?

"You know, filling out the form. Paying the booth fee." Ester's forehead bunched in on itself. "I'd even cover the ingredients. You just have to do the rest."

The rest? "The event is a little more than two weeks away!" A bead of panic grew in her belly, because Faith had barely had time to brush her teeth this morning. Where was she supposed to find those kind of baking hours?

Her immediate response was to say no. But Faith couldn't turn her away. Ester had never judged Faith, even after her family's role in Hearse-pocalypse, she'd been nothing but kind and caring.

Not long after that first Christmas in Sweet, Faith's mama had met and married husband number four, Wallace Kimball, who was three years into a ten-year sentence for the third-degree felony theft of his neighbor's milking cow. He was released on a technicality—the cow was no longer lactating, dropping its value below the $20,000 necessary to make it a felony. To celebrate, Wallace partied it up with his best pals, Jack, Johnnie, and José, then led Sweet Plain's now-sheriff on a low-speed chase through town in Mr. Rayborn's hearse, before crashing it into a tree.

Wallace had gone away on DUI, evading police, and grand-theft auto charges, but the Rayborns' hearse was totaled beyond repair, leaving the couple without a way to drive their clients to the cemetery come burial day. Hope never apologized to the Rayborns for her husband's role in the damages. Heck, she didn't even acknowledge it, just walked around town as if the business of a long-standing family in the community hadn't taken a huge blow.

"Between working and caring for your brother, I know

you're busier than a one-legged cat in a litter box," Ester said. "I wouldn't even ask, but I'm afraid I'm going to let the town down."

Empathetic fear roiled in her stomach. Faith knew how paralyzing the anticipation of disappointing others could be. It was often the driving force behind many of her decisions. And kept her awake most nights, when the house was quiet, and she was alone but for her thoughts.

It was on one of those nights that the idea of becoming a Secret Samaritan had been born. That had been over a decade ago, and the more Faith learned about her parents' wrongdoings, the longer her list grew.

Mr. and Mrs. Rayborn were on that list. And while baking some cookies couldn't begin to atone for the damage her family had brought upon the Rayborns, it was a start. Faith never had a whole lot of free time over the holidays, but what better way to spend it than making Christmas cookies for a good cause?

She loved her position as a medical assistant at the hospital. Loved her patients, the staff, and the idea of caring for those who needed caring for. But she felt alive when she baked. She once read that medicine healed the body, but food from the heart could heal the soul.

"Don't say anything yet." Ester walked behind the counter and hugged her. "You have a couple of days to decide."

Which Faith would use to rearrange her schedule and hopefully convince someone to trade a few shifts with her at the hospital.

"The new schedule comes out on Tuesday. I'll let you know as soon as it's posted."

"You've always been a good girl, Faith." Ester pulled back and gave Faith's cheeks a pinch. "Now, how about you wrap me up six of your cookies? One for each grandkid and one for Woodrow." Shaking her head, Ester pulled a twenty out of her clutch. "Oh, let's make that an even dozen."

"I'll add one of my Peppermint Barks for Mr. Rayborn. Tell him it's for being patient." Faith placed the cookies in the box and was reaching for a bow to tie it closed when something caught her eye outside the diner window. Her brain couldn't exactly determine what it was that had an unsettling wave slithering down her spine, but when a black SUV drove through the parking lot, her heart jerked to a stop.

Perhaps it was the government plates or the official emblem on the door that sounded a rusty but all-too-familiar alarm. But something had gone terribly wrong.

Faith glanced around the diner, noting the people still eating their dinners and chatting with neighbors about holiday plans. The OPEN sign in the window was still flashing, Ester was still talking, and across the street Mr. Wilkins was helping a couple load a Christmas tree into a truck. Everyone was wrapped up in their daily business while Faith's world went dim.

Her heart turned to lead, the box of cookies slipping from her fingers and landing on its side. A dozen iced ginger-bread cookies tumbled onto the floor.

"Dear, are you okay?" Ester placed a hand on Faith's shoulder.

No. She was most definitely not okay. Because there, sitting in the back seat of Noah Tucker's Ranger-issued SUV, placing him on the other side of the law, was her kid brother. Her sweet and honest and oh so gentle-hearted brother, who was supposed to be safe and sound at Shelby's house riding horses and doing normal boy things, was somehow imprisoned in the back seat of a government vehicle while being escorted through town for all the world to see, as if he was like his father—

A law-breaking criminal.

Chapter Three

A painful jolt of nausea churned in Faith's gut, the same way it used to when the local police paid her family a weekly visit. Sometimes they had a warrant. Other times it was to question her mother's man-of-the-hour about some crime he'd likely committed. But Faith hadn't lived under the same roof with a convict since she was sixteen.

She worked hard to be honest and straightforward, always conscious of the decisions she made, choosing her circle of friends carefully. Her standards for men were so high that she rarely dated. When the planets actually did align, exposing a sliver of free time to go on an actual date, she never brought them around Pax.

Faith had sacrificed a lot, worked hard to be an upstanding citizen and role model in order to avoid this very situation.

"Can you watch the cash register?" she absently mumbled to Ester as she turned and hurriedly weaved through the diner and out the front door, jingle bells ringing in her wake.

Everything around her blurred together as her focus locked on the SUV, which had come to a stop right outside the diner's entrance. She reached the car as the driver came around to open the back-passenger door—that only opened from the outside.

A dull roar filled her ears as Pax hopped out, his backpack slung over his shoulder, a bright orange and black laser tag gun in his hand. A toy gun that matched the one his best friend was carrying. Faith had a strict no gun rule in place. Not in the house. Not on his person. Not ever

"Dear God," she whispered the moment his blue and white sneakers hit the asphalt. She moved quickly and, when the driver didn't restrain Pax, Faith pulled him into her arms. "Are you okay?"

"Yeah," Pax said, squirming out of her embrace.

"What is this? You know the rules." She plucked the plastic gun from Pax's hand. "Where did you get this?"

"In the Tuckers' basement," Pax said, studying the cracks in the sidewalk. "Decalin got the new Battle Rifle Pro for his Countdown to Christmas present, and he and some of the other guys were playing commando at the park."

And here Faith had been excited to find Pax a Superhero advent calendar. Behind each door was a superhero-shaped chocolate—not a 500-dollar laser gun. But Decalin was the youngest Beaumont, and that family never did anything small.

Besides donating the brand-new community center stationed in the heart of downtown, they also hosted a New Year's Eve party that was rumored to cost in the six figures. Not that Faith had ever been invited, but she'd heard all about it from her regulars at the B-Cubed. So it wasn't surprising that the budget for Decalin's advent calendar surpassed most folks' entire holiday spending.

"Decalin said it was BYOG only and" —Pax shrugged— "I don't have one."

That was the golden ticket item that sat at the top of his

Christmas list—had been for the past two years. Faith had mixed emotions about getting him a toy gun. It had never become an issue because every time she'd come close to having the money, something would come up. Last Christmas she'd needed new tires, a week before his birthday the fridge had gone out.

Pax toed the ground. "JT said we could both share his, but . . ."

But Pax would be too embarrassed.

"I remembered there were some in the basement," JT offered, being a good wingman. "They were my dad's and he never uses them anymore, so I told Pax he could have one."

Which explained why they were big, black, and incredibly realistic, instead of neon like guns the other kids had.

"Bringing them to the park was my idea," Pax admitted.

"I thought you were supposed to be helping Mr. Tucker clean out the barn and brush the horses." She cupped his face, checking him over.

"We did." Again he shrugged her off. "But we finished early and Ms. Shelby wasn't home from work yet, and JT's dad was on the other side of the ranch, so his uncle offered to drive us to the park."

Ignoring for a moment that JT's uncle, *the* one and only Noah Tucker, was standing three feet away, looking mighty fine in a pair of faded button-flies that hugged his backside to perfection, Faith pulled her brother against her.

The moment she wrapped her arms around him, and she could feel that he was safe and unharmed, Faith finally took a breath, a deep calming breath that forced her heart back into a normal rhythm.

"Why didn't you call?" she asked, not sure if she was

still scared or spittin' mad. "When plans change, you're supposed to call."

"We were only going to the park. You let me go there all the time."

She released him enough to meet his gaze. "And I probably would have. *If* you had called to check in."

"I forgot." Pax dragged out the words, his tone implying that he thought Faith was completely overreacting. The quick glances he gave the SUV said he'd rather climb back in than suffer through one more second of sisterly PDA. Even though his limbs were free of restraints and he appeared unharmed, her panic had already grown so thick she could barely breathe.

Allowing herself a final once-over, Faith forced herself to pull it together.

And she did—only to find everyone else looking back. Pax with apology for scaring her. JT with shock because the "cool" older sister was losing it. And Noah with growing concern.

Show no fear.

Those three words had gotten Faith through a lot worse than a play gun and an unofficial ride in a cop car. She took one last deep breath and buried every speck of fear, every awful memory that had been triggered, and shoved it into her TO BE DEALT WITH: NEVER file.

"I'm sorry that I didn't call to ask if you were all right with me driving him," Noah offered. Faith ignored the flutters in her stomach, too warm to blame on nerves. "It won't happen again. In fact, why don't you give me your number for next time?"

The big, imposing idiot shot Faith a smile that awoke those *Go on, I dare you* dimples of his. Faith didn't know what dare had been cast, but his gaze said it had something to do with her elf costume.

"There won't be a next time."

Ignoring Noah's grin, she plucked the laser gun from Pax's hand. "As for this. I'm okay with you playing laser tag at Ms. Shelby's house, but running around town pretending to be commandos with real-looking guns? Never going to happen." Had Shelby been home, Faith knew the guns would never have left the basement. "Why don't you give this back to JT so he can store it safely in his uncle's car? Then be sure to thank Mr. Tucker for the ride."

"I told you," Pax mumbled, handing his co-conspirator back the gun. "Thanks, Mr. Tucker, for giving me a ride."

"Anytime, kiddo. But in the future, you tell me the rules," Noah said, then reached over and ruffled Pax's hair. "Understood?"

"Yes, sir." Pax looked up at Noah, his smile so bright and eager to please, it broke Faith's heart. He was starved for a permanent male figure in his world. For a strong man to take an interest in him. Shelby and Cody were so great, always inviting Pax over to help when there was "guy stuff" to be done. But doing guy stuff with someone else's dad wasn't the same.

"Good to hear," Faith said. "Now why don't you and JT go see if Mr. Wilkins needs help loading the trees while I talk to Mr. Tucker?"

"But," Pax began, and Faith lifted a stern brow, cutting him short. His shoulders slumped with resignation. "Okay. Come on, JT. Maybe Mr. Wilkins will let us keep the tips."

When they were gone, she swallowed the big, complicated knot of heart-stomping fear and worry, then turned— to find Noah watching her.

He didn't look particularly worried. Then again, she hadn't expected him to.

Guys like Noah didn't do worry. They were too busy playing hero to be bothered with such emotions. It was evident in the way he swaggered toward her in worn cowboy boots, tossing around enough testosterone to level an all-girls' college, like he was one wink away from tipping his Stetson and saying, "Howdy, ma'am."

"I really am sorry about all this," Noah said softly. "I was about to leave for the hardware store when Shelby called saying she was going to be late, so I offered the boys a ride. They went to the store with me, seemed to have fun looking at all the tools."

Pax loved tools. Loved building things with his hands. Faith had been thinking about getting him his own little tool kit for Christmas. A hammer and wrench didn't kick her paranoia into overdrive like a gun—plastic or real.

"I'm okay with you driving him, but not in the back of your squad car," she said, ignoring how big and imposing a person he was. "Would you put your nephew in the back like a criminal?"

"I would never think that, because they're eleven." His voice was warm. "JT normally sits up front because he's been cleared in the system for ride-alongs and is a Junior Ranger. If Pax wanted to sit up front, I would have let him. But he asked, repeatedly, to sit in the back."

"Did you wonder why he wanted to sit in the back?" Faith asked quietly.

Noah stopped, his expression turning serious. "I guessed it was because we only just met and sitting next to your buddy's uncle is weird."

What he said made sense. Maybe it was her own inse-curities and experiences coming into play, but she'd worked hard so that Pax wouldn't have to overcome the same familial prejudices as she had.

"You know how small towns work," she said quietly, because she certainly did. The good, the bad, *and* the ugly. "All it takes is one person to mistake why he's in the back of your squad car and come Monday everyone will be speculating on why Pax was arrested."

"Honestly, I didn't really think of it like that," he said slowly as if he was reconsidering his decision. "And if there is any way I can make this right, let me know."

"Anything?"

She hadn't meant it as sexual, but his grin said he'd taken it that way. "You name it."

Faith rolled her eyes all the way up to the clouds before meeting his gaze. "Can I get back to you?"

"Yes, as long as you stop calling it a squad car. There's a lot of differences between my SUV and a patrol car, one of the main ones being that there's no barrier between the front and back seat."

"It still looks scary."

He lowered his voice. "He had a good time, Faith. They laughed the entire way, got a free candy cane at the store, and I may have let them flash the lights. But only when we were on my family's property, so no laws were broken."

"I know. It's just . . ." She trailed off, suddenly feeling embarrassed by the way she'd reacted to the situation. She would never admit it aloud, but maybe she had over-egged the pudding on this one.

Faith's entire childhood had been out of her control, so when she'd gained custody of Pax eight years ago, she'd promised he would have the kind of stable and happy up-bringing every child deserved. She'd dropped out of nursing school and came home to Sweet Plains to make good on her promise—even if that meant occasionally looking like a crazy woman.

He tilted his head down, meeting her gaze, his lips curved into a gentle smile. "It's just what, Faith?"

Faith stood steady, even though her instinct was to move away. "I don't like guns. Even toy ones."

"My mom didn't either."

"She sounds like a smart woman," she said, and he took off his hat. The gesture was meant to put her at ease, but Faith didn't trust well-practiced body language. Trusting meant letting down her guard and that, when standing down a giant with a weapon, was asking for trouble. So she said, "What happened to you?"

He laughed—and even that was sexy. "You know, most moms would thank me for driving their kid around town."

So he thought she was a mom. So what? It wasn't Faith's responsibility to correct his assumption. A lot of people arrived at the same conclusion. They took one look at Faith's tiny house on the outskirts of town, her late shifts at the B-Cubed, and early rounds at the hospital, and decided she must have been a teen mom.

In a way, she was. Overnight, nineteen-year-old Faith had gone from a top-of-her-class nursing student to a job-juggling single mom. Pax had barely turned three when their mom, Hope, decided she didn't have it in her to be a mother anymore.

Faith's choices? Move home and raise Pax or stay in school and watch him go into the system. It was a no-brainer. Faith chose Pax.

And she would again. Every time.

"I assure you, I'm not like any mom in town." First there were her rules, which to most seemed over the top, but to her were vital if she wanted to maintain custody.

Then there were the mandatory trips to visit Pax's father at the penitentiary three towns over, the last Saturday of the month like clockwork. And finally, there were whispers and stares that, no matter how hard Faith tried, never seemed to go away.

"I'm starting to get that." He moved so close that Faith could see little golden specks in his brown eyes. A tiny scar that started at his temple and disappeared into his thick, brown hair.

"Like I said, there won't be a next time. End of story." Exactly what she'd told Gina in the diner.

"Angel, this story's barely begun." He stepped closer. The electricity crackled between them, and she was certain he was going to kiss her—right there on Main Street. "If you want a sneak peek at chapter one, why don't we head out of here and grab that cup of cocoa so you can make good on those two thank-yous you owe me."

She arched a brow. "Two?"

"The tree." He held up a finger. Then another. "And the ride."

"Thank you and thank you. But like I said before, I don't date."

"Funny, because the way I remember it, wearing a guy's jacket was a pretty bold 'he's with me' statement. And you still have mine, angel."

"Only because I forgot to give it back." She failed to mention that she might have slept in it the night before. Perhaps pressed her nose to the fabric and breathed him in deeply. "And I didn't know you were staying. Which was why I planned on giving it to Shelby next time I saw her."

"Good news. I'm staying through the holidays," he said, and alarm bells went off. "So we can exchange clothes and anything else you had in mind. How about tomorrow?"

"I work."

"How does Sunday sound then?"

She laughed. "Like a Christmas miracle." Most Sundays started with baking before the sun rose and ended serving dinner and pie at the diner.

"Good thing miracles are my specialty," he said, and the low rumble of his voice had her good parts twinkling. "So, Sunday?"

"I'm busy."

"I didn't give a specific Sunday, angel."

He didn't need to. Noah's staying in town made her nervous. The way he called her angel had her belly fluttering as if there were six swans a-swimming in there. That he was giving her a look, the same look she'd received from men ever since the day she'd grown boobs in the sixth grade, made her downright furious.

"You're right," she said, sweet as honey. "What Sunday are you leaving?"

"Sunday after Christmas." He rested a forearm on the hood, as if he had not a single doubt that she would bat her eyes and say, *"Well then, cowboy, why don't you pick me up at five?"*

Sadly for him, Faith didn't bat—her eyelids or anything else for that matter. And she didn't date. "Sorry, cowboy, but it looks like I'm booked every Sunday from here until, well, you leave. But you enjoy that cocoa."

Chapter Four

Noah headed back toward the Crossing after the last rays of sun had disappeared behind the rolling hills, settling in for a long winter's nap. But his smile was beaming like it was high noon in July.

He rolled down the window, breathing in the crisp night air. Without the bright lights of the big city, the sky was a deep, never-ending blue, lit by millions of twinkling stars.

It reminded him of the antique glass ornaments his mama used to collect. Over her lifetime, she'd amassed dozens of them. Each a different color and size, and each with its own story of origin. One she uncovered at a yard sale, another in an antique shop in Gatlinburg, and her favorite was a gift from her granddaddy. They weren't expensive or even that pretty, but she and her granddad would drive up and down the South looking to add to their collection. She'd even bought her sons one on their first Christmas. Noah's was a twilight blue with iridescent golden specks.

Every year, they were the first thing unpacked and the last things hung on the tree, as if once in place his mama was saying that Christmas could officially call on the Tucker house.

The year she passed was the last year the ornaments had hung on the family tree. It was also the last time Christmas called on the Tucker house.

So when Noah pulled through the iron gates of his family's ranch, he let out a surprised bark of laughter. Down the rough gravel road he could make out all six horses, standing in front of the barn, wearing matching Santa hats. Big red bows topped the gas lamps that lined the drive, with garlands twirled down each of the poles.

Then there was the house—his mama's house—outlined in so many lights, it looked as if it belonged on one of those Holiday Wars shows. Strings of lights dripped down from the gutters, mimicking icicles, and soft white strands twinkled along the gabled roof down to the wraparound porch. And poking out of the chimney was a set of Santa legs, wiggling as if he'd had one too many of Ms. Luella's pies.

But what held Noah's attention was Santa's most disgruntled employee. Cody Tucker—six-one, thirties, 180 pounds, and wearing a red Santa hat—was affixing a bow to the front porch light.

Cody must have heard Noah's approach because he gave a wave from the top of the ladder. By the time Noah pulled up next to the barn, his older brother was walking down the steps, carrying a tangle of bows and lights.

Noah hopped out of his SUV and let out a laugh because he could now see that MR. DECEMBER was written across the brim of Cody's hat. "All you need is a boom box and rip-away pants and you're set. I hear the senior center's looking for some holiday entertainment."

"I'd wait until you see your hat before you start making jokes," Cody said, and Noah groaned over all the different hats Shelby could have ordered for him. "And don't think you missed all the fun. There're still seven or eight boxes of lights left on the porch. So why don't you gather them up and meet me at the barn? Shelby's holding her pumpkin pie hostage until the barn's finished."

"I could skip the lights and go enjoy your slice of pie, little brother," he said, knowing the nickname riled Cody. Although Cody was two years older than Noah, by the time Noah reached first grade, he'd gained an extra two inches on Cody—and that hadn't changed.

Cody snorted. "If you let my wife think you're some poor Tiny Tim, she'll sit you at the family table and feed you until you're nice and plump."

"That what happened to you?"

"Between Shelby's cornbread and Luella's pies"—Cody gave a low whistle —"it takes an extra two hours working in the barn just to button my pants. No more teen-hires from the neighborhood to shovel my stalls."

Cody took off a glove and when Noah went in for a shake, Cody pulled him in for a hug. Which caught him off guard. They didn't do hugs. None of the Tucker men did. But Logan had been right—things had changed around there.

A whole lot, Noah thought, taking in Cody's mud-caked work boots and jeans. It was a far cry from the uptight, loafer-wearing developer Cody had been only six months prior. Noah guessed becoming an instant father could do that to a guy.

"You hate shoveling hay."

"I also hate turning away a fine piece of pie." Cody rubbed his stomach. "One of JT's friends said I had a dad bod. I walked around like a stud at an auction until Ms. Luella explained it was one step above being called the Pillsbury Doughboy."

Noah picked up the rest of the lights and followed Cody

to the barn. "That's what happens when you become domesticated."

"Remind me, when was the last time you woke up with a beautiful woman in your arms? This morning? Oh no, wait that was me. You woke up spooning Mr. Teddy in the same bed you used to wet." Cody plugged in the strand, then started weaving it between a line of hooks, which made a grid across the barn. "In fact, the most action you've had lately would be ogling an elf up a Christmas tree."

"Did you hear that at your quilting club meeting? Or during gossip group at the Ladies of Sweet social?"

Man, he'd forgotten how fast news traveled in Sweet. His run-in with Faith had made it back to the ranch almost before he had. Wasn't that exactly what Faith had been worried about? And here he'd thought she was making a mountain out of a molehill.

"Sticks and stones." Cody handed Noah the other end and together they strung the lights around the barn doors. "So, Faith Loren, huh?"

Noah rolled his eyes. "We had a run-in."

"Town's saying two. First when you offered to show her your pistol, then today when you tried to impress her with your sirens."

"What's so wrong with a guy trying to be neighborly?" Noah argued. "I thought people in small towns got off on stuff like helping frail old ladies cross the street or rescuing kittens from trees."

"Let's be clear. There is nothing frail or old about Faith Loren. And even if you find her up a tree, don't fall for it. She's a full-grown cat with claws and isn't afraid to use them."

"I didn't even get the chance to be charming."

Cody smiled. "Don't take it personally, bro. She's had enough bad luck with men to make her wary of anyone walking around waving a pistol."

"You think you could have warned me about her issue with law enforcement before I dropped her kid off in my fancy cop car."

"Pax is her kid brother not her kid," Cody said, then took a second look at him. "Please tell me you didn't refer to her as his mom?"

"It was a logical assumption." One she hadn't bothered to correct. Probably because she'd rather have another reason to add to her TABLE FOR ONE list.

Noah had to smile because he knew, without a doubt, Faith kept a long, detailed list of all the reasons she didn't date. She probably toted it around in that enormous backpack of hers, wanting to have it on hand to add new reasons as she encountered them—like a guy letting her kid brother run around town with a toy gun that, if Noah was being honest, might cause a less experienced officer to look twice.

"For Pax to be hers, she would have had to have been, I'm guessing, like fourteen or fifteen when she had him." Cody held up a hand. "And before you remind me of how we were at that age, you knew Faith when she was in high school."

"Yeah, kind of blew that, too," Noah admitted.

"And you wonder that you're single."

Noah didn't have to wonder. He knew exactly why he was single. His last three girlfriends had made that perfectly clear. He worked long hours. Worked at home. Pretty much worked himself out of every good relationship he'd ever had. Even with his family.

But why was she single?

Faith was intelligent, down-to-earth, and didn't have a problem standing her ground. Not to mention insanely beautiful. Like a blow-your-mind, lingerie-model-meets-girl-next-door kind of beautiful—although Noah didn't remember ever having a neighbor who looked like her.

Honestly though, it was the way she presented herself, with an inner confidence that showed how comfortable she was in her own skin, that drew him in. Talk about a turn-on.

She was also the most suspicious and closed-off person he'd ever met outside of his profession. Most days were a revolving door of liars, cheaters, and the unforgivable. People stuck in a bad situation who'd made the wrong choice. And for the citizens who didn't try to evade Noah when he flashed his badge, he was usually meeting them on one of the worst days of their lives.

In his experience, there were only a handful of reasons for someone like Faith to be as wary as she was. And none of them settled well with Noah. Her fierce independence didn't seem like a statement as much as a necessity for survival. Which he respected even more.

"What's the deal with Faith and her brother?" he asked, wrapping the strand around a hook and trying hard to sound casual.

Clearly, he'd failed because Cody's expression loosely translated into *Let me guess. Asking for a friend?* Noah flipped him a finger, which needed no translation at all.

"Faith isn't really a sharer," Cody said as if Noah didn't already know. "But from bits of town gossip and talking with Shelby, I've pieced together that their mom decided she wasn't cut out for parenthood, packed up her bags, and left town. Faith moved home and adopted Pax."

"How long ago was that?"

"Eight years."

Noah let out a low whistle. "Man, she was young. That's a lot to take on."

"So she's too young to be his guardian but not too young to be his mom?" Cody asked while climbing up the ladder so he could string lights across the top of the barn door. "How does that math work?"

"What I meant is, being a teen mom's hard enough." Noah handed Cody a new strand of lights. "Being a teenager with a toddler dropped in your lap would make for one heck of a steep learning curve."

"I know how hard it was to step in as JT's dad. And he was ten," Cody said, and Noah knew his brother would give anything to get those missed years with his son back. "Plus, I had Shelby to help me through it."

Cody and his wife had had a rough start to their relationship. College sweethearts who placed their trust in the wrong friend and ended up losing a decade together. In fact, if Silas hadn't added a stipulation to his will, which required a Tucker to sleep at the ranch for a year straight, Cody still might not even know he had a son. Not that Noah was giving his dad credit for doing anything right by Noah and his brothers, but JT had been a blessing. That amazing kid had given the three brothers, whose only connection had been surviving their childhood, something new to bond over.

The love and healing that came with the next generation.

Who knew, maybe Shelby was right? Maybe Silas's intentions had been pure. Maybe he really had looked at his passing as a way to bring his sons home to heal and make new memories. Or maybe it was his final attempt to control their lives. Either way, Cody and Shelby had found their way back together and anyone looking at JT could see how much love and support the kid was surrounded with.

It made Noah wonder who Faith had in her corner. Even at the worst of times, and Lord knew there were plenty, Noah and his brothers always had each other. From the little he'd learned about Faith, she seemed to be in the thick of it all by her lonesome.

"Shelby said that Faith was off at college and decided to come home for winter break," Cody went on. "She'd barely unpacked her bags when her mom took off. One day she was a nursing student at UCLA, the next she was a single mom." Cody paused, looking down from the top of the ladder. "Wait, why are you asking me all these questions? You're the one who can pull up her entire life story with a touch of a button."

"I didn't think of it," he lied. Noah hadn't been able to think of much else since he'd caught her swinging in the sheriff's tree. "Plus background checks only give the facts. I'm looking for what wouldn't be in there."

Cody laughed. "I don't think I've seen you this into someone since Rachel Bellows showed you all her secrets behind the chem lab sophomore year."

"I'm not *into* her," he said, and Cody laughed. "Why? Because I didn't pry into her life?"

"Yes. You pry. That's what you do. You are the most suspicious person I have ever met."

"I'm a Ranger. Being suspicious keeps me alive."

"You were convinced Shelby, the sweetest, most honest person alive, had ulterior motives," Cody pointed out. "You even ran a background check on my son when I didn't ask for a paternity test."

"JT has some sketchy eyes," Noah said, climbing up the ladder at the opposite side of the door.

"Like his dad." Cody tossed Noah the lights, and he wrapped the strand around the hook and tossed it back. They made their way around the entire exterior of the barn that way, talking and laughing, and Noah had to admit, it felt pretty good.

"I didn't run a background on the lady who bought the ranch on the west side last month," Noah clarified.

"Ms. Lancaster is seventy-six and doesn't make you blush."

Looking back, Noah could admit, maybe he'd gone a little overboard when Shelby and JT showed up in Cody's life. And yes, it was true that in the past, Noah had had zero qualms about doing a thorough check on anyone who came within two feet of his family.

But he'd gotten the distinct feeling that Faith was a private person by nature, so every time he'd started to pull up her name on the national database, something stopped him.

Part of him said she'd feel disrespected if he gathered intel on her like some perp. And after today, he thanked heaven he hadn't. Another part of him, the part that couldn't stop thinking about her, knew how pissy she'd be if he somehow gained an upper hand in this little game they were playing. Plus, there was something appealing about getting to know each other at the same time, rather than Noah going in with a detailed map to all her family's hidden secrets.

But after seeing the utter terror in her eyes when she'd caught sight of Pax holding a toy gun, he knew there was a history he needed to better understand. He only hoped he could get the sexy snow angel to open up before his curious nature got him into trouble.

New rule: Check town's Facebook page before getting out of bed.

Had Faith done so, she might not have spent her Monday morning in her kitchen dressed in pajamas and yesterday's makeup, no coffee in hand, listening to Molly-Mae Beaumont, Decalin's mom and residing PTA president, blame Faith for what was now being hailed as SANTA'S BAD SECRET.

"If you had only called, I could have gotten out in front of this. But that didn't happen and now parents are concerned," Molly-Mae said, her voice sweet enough to send Faith into a diabetic coma. "A generous amount of PTA time has been dedicated to organizing the fifth grade's secret Santa exchange at the park. And while we understand some things are unavoidable, we wouldn't want some poor child missing out on account of Pax being a no-show, like he was at Decalin's laser-tag party. You understand."

The only thing Faith understood was that the slight echo happening in the background was likely a case of using speakerphone in a room full of eavesdropping PTA moms. Yay, it was a party line. As for Decalin's laser-tag party, Pax had never been invited. Knowing he was the only boy in his class who had been excluded, he'd received a call, the day of. Decalin wanted to see if Pax could "be a spare" in case anyone had to "tap out for a soda break."

Faith had said no on principle; her brother wasn't some placeholder. And she still stood behind the decision, but whenever the kids from that party got together, Pax was always the odd guy out.

"Why would you think he isn't participating?" Faith asked, looking at Pax. He was sitting at the counter in his snowflake pajamas and sleep-warmed cheeks, his precious eyes barely open as he lifted a spoonful of cereal to his mouth.

Unlike his peers, who would sleep until noon, then spend their first day of winter break at the park, Pax would be spending the morning with Viola at the diner, working off some of those community hours Faith had assigned him for his part in the toy-contraband situation. Both boys had received identical punishments, but while JT could serve his time at the ranch with one or both parents, Faith had to work.

So after a few hours clearing out the diner's storage shed, he'd head over to the community center, where he'd spend his time making reindeer heads out of pipe cleaners.

"With all the talk going around about the unfortunate situation at the diner this weekend, I assumed he wouldn't be coming," Molly-Mae said, with a genteel offensiveness that only a woman whose family owned half the town would dare use. "I mean, a patrol car and everything."

"It wasn't a patrol car. It was a work SUV."

"Is there a difference?" Before Faith could explain that, in fact, there was a difference, Molly-Mae continued. "How is Pax handling all this? He must be so embarrassed, bless his little heart. Will it go on his permanent record?"

As if he knew he was the subject of the conversation, Pax walked his barely touched breakfast over to the sink. His shoulders slumped in defeat as he disappeared into his bedroom to get dressed.

Faith wondered if Molly-Mae could feel the fury coming through the phone. This whole situation was complete madness. She wanted to ask if this was a joke, but didn't need to. The lives of everyone in her family had been out of her control the moment her daddy pulled the trigger.

But she was done taking the back seat of her own life.

She knew what Molly-Mae would say the moment she hung up, just as she knew there were a couple of different ways to handle this situation, neither of which was remotely appropriate for Pax's ears. So, tightening her robe and slipping on her house boots, Faith stepped out onto the porch, closing the door behind her.

Like Faith, the sun hadn't fully awoken, and the sky was a golden blue. A few mourning doves called to each other, and the neighbor's car was running on idle, a smokestack of steam escaping into the frigid morning air.

"You've heard the news?" Faith said, lowering her voice as if about to impart a secret of national security.

"Honey, everyone in three counties has heard by now."

"Oh boy." Her slow exhale froze on contact with the crisp air. "I know everyone saw him in the SUV, but it was part of Pax's initiation as a Junior Texas Ranger. It's a way to honor kids who display the characteristics of becoming outstanding citizens."

Faith would find a lump of coal in her stocking for that lie. But it was worth it to hear Molly-Mae choke on her jealousy. "Outstanding citizens?"

"I know. Isn't it amazing?" Faith's fingers and ears stung from the low temperature, but she didn't even consider going back inside until Molly-Mae had not one bad thing to say about her brother. "There's a lot of competition for this kind of honor, so we were over the moon when Officer

Tucker picked him up to deliver the official news. And right before Christmas, too."

"I'm president of the PTA and didn't know about this."

"No, I don't expect that you would. It's not something they advertise, as it would be a huge liability if they chose the wrong kind of kid. Part of his award was a ride-along with a real Texas Ranger. He even ran the sirens. Not in town of course."

"Oh, of course."

"The best part was that all of this came from the anti-bullying campaign Pax used when running for class president. And how important it is to win by merit and not intimidation tactics, which is why it will look so great on Pax's college application."

"But he didn't win," Molly-Mae snapped.

"He didn't need to. Being a Junior Ranger is about ethics and quality of character, not who's the most popular or who handed out personalized swag to the student body."

That candidate would have been Decalin. The swag was personalized ball caps for every fifth grader.

"They should have told the parents about this before the election."

"That's a great idea. You know who you should talk to about that? Texas Ranger Noah Tucker. I have his contact info from when he took Pax on the ride-along." She rattled off the e-mail address she'd come across on Google when stalking Noah. He didn't have much of an online presence, but his officer photo on the Texas Ranger Web site made for good dreams. "But before you reach out, I'd make sure Decalin has his essay on How to Combat Economic Prejudice in the Heartland written and edited."

Faith heard several gasps on the other end of the phone, confirming that Molly-Mae wasn't alone.

"Essay? They're eleven."

Faith grinned. "They're only looking for the best when it comes to Junior Rangers. So if I were you, I'd take the two-thousand-word minimum with a grain of salt and shoot for three or four. Anyway, thanks for calling, but Pax won't be able to make it after all. He's got another fun day of Junior Ranger stuff ahead of him. Have a good time at the park though, and Merry Christmas, Molly-Mae."

"Merry Christmas." Molly-Mae disconnected the call, but not before Faith heard someone on the other end say, "How prestigious can it be? They let a *Loren* in."

Faith's tender spots took a direct hit and that old humiliation and insecurity resurfaced from the pit of her stomach to spill over.

She'd become accustomed to the looks and whispers about her infamous family. Developed thicker skin to soften the blow. Worked tirelessly to atone for her parents' selfish decisions and insulate Pax from any of the fallout.

He was a sweet kid and at an age when other people's opinions could influence the direction of his life. And, like Faith, he hadn't had a say in who his parents were or how they behaved.

So as quickly as she disconnected, she dialed another number. She didn't think about her long hours at the hospital, her after hours waitressing and baking, or the wrapping party with chocolate and wine. She focused on what mattered—a way to change the town's opinion about what it meant to be a Loren.

Set things straight because, while Faith and Pax shared their mom's last name, that was where the similarities ended.

This new generation of Lorens didn't lie and they didn't cheat—and they sure as heck didn't run when things got tough.

So when Ester answered on the other end, Faith asked, "Do you still need help? If so, count me in."

Chapter Five

Thanks to a hailstorm and vicious winds, Faith didn't get home from her shift at the hospital until after 8:00 P.M. The house was freezing, Pax was staying at JT's, and all she wanted to do was crawl under the covers and sleep until New Year's. And it was only Monday.

But since launching Operation Cookie Monster, she'd spent every night of the past week in her kitchen, baking and freezing ginger bear cookies.

Tonight was her last night of baking, and tomorrow she'd begin the painful process of frosting fifty-dozen ginger bear cookies.

The idea of fifty-dozen cookies was far different than the reality of how much dough it took to bake fifty-dozen cookies in her stamp-sized kitchen.

After cranking the heater to Oahu-in-summer, she slipped on her apron and got to work. With the oven preheating, she pulled out the dough, which had been chilling since last night, and sprinkled flour on the cutting board. Then, one by one, she cut out each little bear face, placing it on the cookie sheet, then topped it with a dough Santa hat. The layering would give her cookies depth and make them stand out from the cookies of the past.

"You are so cute," she cooed to the first batch of the night, then slid them into the oven.

Her stomach growled, reminding her that she hadn't eaten since lunchtime. And what better late night snack than leftover apple pie? Which she popped into the microwave.

Never having much downtime, Faith didn't know what to do with leisure, so she decided to watch the plate spin around and around. Afraid she might be standing too close, she took a small step back, then watched the seconds count down.

Anticipating the *ding,* she'd just touched the handle when an ear-piercing *crack* shot through the night, filling the air with charged static. Suddenly, everything plunged into complete blackness.

Faith's stomach hollowed out as her body dropped straight to the floor, knocking over the mixing bowl, sending a cloud of flour exploding on impact. Old instincts kicked in and she covered her head with her hands, curling herself into a tight ball.

Her heart ricocheting off her ribs, her eyes tightly shut, she remained completely still, except for the involuntary chattering of her teeth. Her lungs burned to release the trapped oxygen and her pulse thundered so loudly she was certain it was audible.

And in that split second of time, Faith was a six-year-old girl again, huddled behind the couch, feeling so helpless and afraid, she was dizzy with dread.

Still unmoving, she strained to listen through the roar in her ears, waiting for glass to shatter or the sound of footsteps pounding toward her, but all she heard was a thick, suffocating silence.

Out of nowhere, a low rumble started overhead, shaking the house and rattling the windows.

Relief seeped into her tightened muscles and she opened one eye, then the other, right as another bright flash lit up her kitchen like Rockefeller Center at Christmas. It wasn't until the thunder rolled again that Faith allowed herself to breathe, to believe that it was only a storm and her life wasn't in danger.

Swallowing the wave of hysteria clogging her throat, she pushed herself up on shaky hands. Another flash of light cut through the night sky, illuminating the moist handprints she left behind on the hardwood floors, and glistening off the beads of sweat covering her arms. And only because laughing was better than crying, she allowed a small laugh to escape, which sounded a little closer to a teary croak.

"One Mississippi," she counted shakily, refocusing on the rhythm of the words and trying to slow her heart. "Two Mississip—"

Boom!

Faith let out another laugh because Mother Nature was not playing nice tonight. "Seriously, you couldn't even let me have the second Mississippi to collect my shi-gle bells?"

Boom!

Not that it would have helped. Two Mississippis didn't come close to cutting it when dealing with the haunting memories that stalked her. Which was ridiculous when she really thought about it. It had been over twenty years since that night but she could have sworn that she smelled discharged gunpowder in the air moments before everything went dark.

Then a downpour of hailstones the size of softballs bounced off the roof, confirming it was simply a winter storm; the rest of it had been in her head. That didn't mean she didn't jump when her phone vibrated in her back pocket.

"Hello?" she answered, surprised that she sounded calm and collected. Not like she was in the middle of a nervous breakdown.

"Hey, it's Shelby. Pax wanted to call and make sure you were okay."

Faith took stock of her body. She was in one piece, no one was in the room with her, and it had been nothing but a little scare.

"Tell him I'm fine," she said casually, as if she hadn't dropped to the ground like someone in the middle of a shoot-out at the O.K. Corral. "I'm fine," she repeated. It was something she'd become adept at telling people— including herself.

But instead of Shelby's answer, Faith got some rustling on the phone followed by heavy kid breathing.

"You okay?" It was Pax, and he sounded worried and small.

"You bet, buddy. I was just heating up some apple pie for dinner," she said. "How are you doing? Did you see the lightning?"

Thankfully, Pax hadn't yet been born when that awful night happened. But he'd woken Faith up from enough bad dreams to know that loud noises could sometimes freak her out. And with a heart the size of Texas, he wanted to make sure his older sister was okay after the thunderstorm.

"The lightning was pretty cool, I guess. But I told JT I might go home," he said quietly. "You know, if you don't want to eat dinner by yourself."

"And miss out on a sleepover? I don't think so."

"Ms. Luella made us clean the kitchen before we could play. And only board games. No screen time."

Exactly what she needed. A normal moment to find her

balance. "That's what happens when you break the rules. You should be happy Ms. Shelby allowed you to come over at all. You and JT are grounded, remember?"

"Yeah," he grumbled, and she could almost picture him toeing the floor, which brought a smile to her face.

"Now hand the phone back to Ms. Shelby and be sure to brush your teeth before bed." She gripped the phone to her ear. "Hey, Pax."

"Yeah?"

"I love you," she whispered.

"Love you, too."

There was more rustling and breathing—this time it was from Faith's end as she tried to keep her emotions in check—then Shelby was back. "He's a great kid, Faith. You've done an amazing job."

"Thanks." She swallowed. "And thanks for watching Pax tonight."

"Are you kidding? JT's been driving me nuts being on house arrest. I don't know who's suffered more, the kids or us," Shelby said. "Cody kept them busy, cleaning out the attic, feeding the animals. They're exhausted."

"I bet. Pax has been tired all week. Between helping Mrs. McKinney out at the diner and working off more of his hours helping Mr. Wilkins at the tree lot, he's come home tired every night. Not to mention covered in sap." Pax's community service had been meant to teach him a lesson, but it had also given Faith a place to park him while she was working extra hours.

She hated that, while his friends were home spending quality time with their family, Pax and Faith had barely had a moment together that wasn't driving to or from work. If Shelby hadn't volunteered to keep him tonight, Pax would have been sitting in the break room at the hospital until her shift had ended.

Something had to change—it wasn't fair to Pax.

"Have I mentioned what a good friend you are?" Faith said through the emotion pushing at her throat.

"Hey, it will be okay," Shelby whispered. "I remember how hard it was before Cody, juggling hours at the hospital and raising JT. You never blinked when I needed help, bailing me out more than a few times when I couldn't get home on time. Plus, you know Pax is always welcome here. So are you, Faith. Anytime you need a break, come on over."

"Thanks." Seemed like she'd been saying that a lot lately.

Faith needed to figure out a better way to juggle making a living and Pax's busy schedule. It would only get fuller the older he became. And she didn't want to miss out on the important stuff.

"But I think you're giving up more than I am," Faith said. "When I take JT, it only cuts into my *Game of Thrones* marathon, not quiet time in bed with a sexy rancher."

Shelby snorted. "Sweetie, with the house this full, we've had zero time alone. I told Cody all I want for Christmas is one uninterrupted hour of 'adult' quiet time. Although, if the house is empty, we won't have to be quiet." They both laughed.

Cody was a great guy, and he and Shelby had the kind of relationship people aspired to. Faith had never seen her friend so happy. Ever since Cody moved back to Sweet and the two reunited, it had been like watching some epic love story unfold.

And Faith had a front-row seat. Which was the only reason she believed that men like Cody actually existed, and finding a love that pure and solid was a possibility. Before meeting Shelby, Faith had never bought into the whole happily-ever-after BS. Heck, she'd never believed that love could be healthy.

Clearly, Faith had been doing it wrong. Or something was wrong with Faith. Even her relationship with her mother was complicated. Hope had done her best to raise and care for Faith, working hard to make sure Faith never went to bed cold or hungry. But when it came to making a safe home for her kids, Hope wasn't equipped with the necessary tools. Her kids came second to her need for a co-man-ionship.

Hope desperately wanted to be loved, which drove her from one man to the next. The more frogs she kissed, the more desperate she became, and the lower that bar was set. If he had a good sense of humor and good looks, Hope was game, and it didn't matter that he might also have a good reason for being incarcerated for life.

She was the type of woman who needed a man to be happy but was too afraid of men to be around them—a side effect of sustained close proximity to Faith's father. Which made Inmates.com Hope's dating site of choice, and Faith's life more and more unpredictable.

But watching Shelby and Cody, the way they put each other first, and JT's well-being above all else, was eye-opening. Looking in from the outside, Faith recognized that their relationship was helping her reconsider her self-imposed table-for-one lifestyle. She was no longer petrified at the idea of having someone to come home to, to share her day with over a home-cooked meal. What would it be like to have a person, her person, to stand next to when times were rough or, even better, when they were amazing?

Faith wasn't afraid of commitment or even love. She was gun-shy about putting herself out there, only to learn that she wasn't worthy of love, wasn't worthy of protection or care from others.

"Hey, you sure you're okay?" Shelby asked again.

"Yeah, fine. I was thinking about my fun-filled night of baking ginger bear cook . . . ies . . ." Faith froze, looked around her dark kitchen, then out the window at the other houses on her block. All dark.

She flicked the switch on the wall. A big fat nothing.

"No, no, no, no, no." She rushed to the electrical panel next to her back door and did a complete reset—three times. Still nothing.

"This can't be happening."

"What's going on?" Shelby asked, but Faith was checking on her cookies, which were no closer to frosting-ready than they had been in her refrigerator.

She put her hand in the oven, warm but not the 375 degrees her little bears needed in order to bake. She thunked her head against the stovetop. "I have no power!"

"With that wind, I doubt anyone in the county has power."

Her forehead was still pressed to the stove. "I need power to bake my ginger bear cookies. If I don't have power, they won't be ready in time for Saturday."

"Hopefully the power will come on in a few, but if not, you can skip the wrapping party to finish up."

She could, but she didn't want to. Because that meant missing girl time. And she loved girl time—almost as much as chocolate.

"Oh God." Faith's head snapped up and she looked around her mess of a kitchen, wondering what she'd gotten herself into.

The panic was back. Only this time it stemmed from disappointment. Not hers, but Ester's. The sweet great-grandma-to-be, with her apple cheeks and generous spirit, counting on her to bring the gingerbread.

A Christmas bake sale was not a Christmas bake sale without gingerbread.

"Otherwise I'll have to bake them tomorrow. And if I bake them tomorrow, then I'll have to wait until they are fully cooled before I can frost them. And then the frosting will have to harden before I can put them in their individual wrappers, which are then tied with a bow. That's six hundred cookies to frost, and harden, and tie up with a cute little bow! Six hundred—"

"Breathe," Shelby ordered. "And count to ten, or you're going to spin yourself right into a crazy lady."

She hated that her friend was right. Faith was already a little crazy by nature. If she spun herself any tighter, she'd snap. Followed by a total and complete meltdown. Two things that did not fit into her already overly crowded schedule, so she took a few deep breaths.

One.

Two.

Three. Four.

Five six nine ten! "What the holly am I going to do?"

"How about a generator?"

"Actually, I haven't gotten around to buying one. I'll add it to my shopping list. Right under NEW FERRARI and TRIP AROUND THE WORLD."

"I'll let that go since I know you're stressed," Shelby said primly. "But I was actually talking about ours. Cody keeps a spare one in the barn. It will take him twenty minutes tops to get it over there and hooked up."

"That's so sweet, but I don't know . . ." Faith wasn't used to people going out of their way to help her. She didn't like the thought of putting someone out.

"I know you hate admitting that you need help."

"I do." Even saying that made her uncomfortable.

"And *I* hate when a friend is struggling and won't let me help. So this can go down a few different ways, and you get to choose."

"Lucky me."

Shelby ignored her. "One, you don't let me send the generator over and I bring you here, to Ms. Luella's kitchen, where we finish your cookies."

"Next." Faith would rather clean Molly-Mae's toilets than cook in Ms. Luella's kitchen. The woman ran that house with an iron rolling pin.

"Two, you let Cody hook up our generator and finish your cookies there."

"Next," she said with a noticeable lack of confidence.

"Or three, you miss the party Thursday and stay up all night preparing while we laugh and eat all the chocolate."

"Now you're just being mean." Faith thought of her helpless bears in the oven and their misshaped hats and—

Why was she arguing? She needed help. Ester was counting on her and, in the end, her word was more important than her pride.

"Fine, but are you really going to make me say it?"

"Nope. That you thought it is enough," Shelby said, and Faith could all but hear her friend high-fiving herself. "One generator is headed your way."

"Fine, but you have to let me pay you back somehow." Faith didn't like owing people.

"How about after the holidays you take JT so Cody and I can catch up on some of that quiet time?"

"Deal."

Fifteen minutes, a hoodie, and a pair of pajamas she blindly pulled from the dryer later, Faith saw headlights through her front window. She secured her hair back with a hair band right as a firm knock sounded at the front door.

Not wanting Cody to stand in the rain longer than necessary, Faith padded through the front room and swung open the door. "You are my hero. Seriously, I so owe you and—"

Faith froze, because standing on her stoop, wearing a tool belt, a dark gray Henley, and looking for all the world like a sexy husband-for-hire, was Noah Tucker. And no amount of breathing was going to save her now.

His eyes ran the length of her, and he grinned. "So I'm your hero, huh?"

Faith slammed the door shut.

Chapter Six

As a Ranger, Noah had become accustomed to doors slamming in his face. It came with the territory. What he wasn't used to was this strange tightening in his chest every time he heard Faith's name or saw her around town—or thought he saw her around town.

Or saw her standing in her doorway in nothing but her bare feet and pajamas, her hair twisted into some kind of messy knot on the top of her head, and a light dusting of flour across her left cheek and forehead.

Faith Loren was the pissiest, messiest, and sexiest domestic goddess he'd ever laid eyes on. And she'd slammed the door in his face. Talk about a turn-on.

He'd been looking forward to a moment like this all week. And she didn't disappoint.

Deciding to give her a moment to figure out a strategy for how to deal with him, Noah took in the potted plants, the two bicycles leaning against the porch rail—not the smartest idea in this neighborhood—and a wreath hanging on the door. He couldn't remember the last time domesticity got him smiling. Then again, he'd never seen a wreath fashioned from those stick-on bows sold in the wrapping paper aisle, all blue, with spiky teeth in the middle and two big cartoon eyes over the top.

"Nice wreath," he called through the door.

"It's supposed to scare you away."

He could hear her pressing her face to the door, likely to look through the peephole. It made him wonder if she had to go up on her toes to reach it. And that made him smile.

"I don't scare all that easy. In fact, maybe you can teach me how to make one so I can impress JT." Silence. "No rush. Whenever you have some spare time. I can stand here all night. When I first joined the force, I pulled an eighteen-hour stakeout, didn't leave the car once. True story," he said. "I also navigated a run-in, yesterday in fact, with some locals. I went to Mable's Corner Market to pick up a few things for Shelby. It wasn't a long list, but incredibly generic, not a detail to be found. Eggs not a big deal, but apples? Do you know how many kinds of apples there are? So there I am trying to figure out what kind of toilet paper to buy, because women seem to be particular about that kind of thing."

He heard a snort.

"I wasn't about to lose to some brand with packaging that says, 'Enjoy the Go.' So I turn to the lady next to me, who had enough food to feed a family of nine. I figure, she must be a pretty good judge of TP. I didn't even get to ask my question because she says, 'Excuse me, you're a Texas Ranger, aren't you?' I figured she was a woman who appreciated a good pistol, but she wasn't interested in that in the slightest. Neither were the six of her friends she called from the store. She insisted that I wait for them to arrive before I began my detailed explanation of all the qualifications a Junior Ranger must possess."

A string of words that would have had Ms. Luella reaching for the bar of soap came from behind the door. He listened as the dead bolt was unlocked, grinned when the chain was disengaged, and was flat-out smiling when she opened the door.

"What did you say?" she asked.

Lord have mercy, those eyes could slay a man. They were bedroom eyes, he decided. Big and smoky brown and highlighted by her rich blond hair. Then there was her hoodie, which he hadn't had a chance to fully appreciate before she slammed the door. It was the softest shade of pink and clung to her breasts in a way that said she wasn't wearing a bra.

He continued his scan, lifting a brow when he got to her flannel bottoms and red tipped toes. "Pokémon?"

She looked down and cursed again. And she wasn't using the G-rated words this time either. Seemed Angel's day had been bad enough to warrant the adult kind. Which got him wondering what other kind of adult things she might be in the mood for.

"The laundry room is at the back of the house. No windows," she said, fiddling with the strings of her sweatshirt. "It was dark. I must have grabbed Pax's pajama bottoms by mistake."

Which would explain why they fit her like a second skin. Who knew Pikachu could be such a turn-on?

"What did you say?" This time when her eyes flashed to his, she looked frightened.

Faith didn't seem like the kind of woman who cared what other people thought of her. But the panic she was trying so hard to hide tore him up a little. She did, however, care what people thought of her brother. So it didn't sit well that he'd stirred up more drama in her already-complicated world.

"I mainly agreed with what the ladies were relaying," he said gently. "It was a lot of them talking and me nodding and *Uh-huh*ing and *Yes, ma'am*ing. But I did make sure to mention that the Texas Ranger organization isn't taking applications right now. It's more of a 'stand out in the crowd' kind of position and that JT and Pax were invited to participate in a small internship this summer in Austin."

"Thank you," she said right as the sky let out a supersonic boom precisely as lightning cracked overhead, turning the neighborhood to momentary morning and Faith into a vibrating ball of panic.

Noah ducked closer into the doorway and Faith nearly leapt out of her Pikachu pajamas and pink hoodie. Her face flashed to frightened, her body dialed to *run,* and her stomach bottomed out. Her reaction hadn't been solely from the storm's sudden reappearance. Nope, a good portion of that fear had been caused by Noah's rushing her. And that realization sent every one of his protective instincts into overdrive.

"Caught me off guard," he said, honestly. He was used to Faith meeting him toe to toe, not flinching away. "You okay?"

"Yeah," she said, with an embarrassed laugh, but her head was shaking hard in opposition. And that wasn't the only thing shaking. Her hands were clasped tightly together, yet trembling.

Another strike flashed and before the thunder made its presence known, Faith stepped onto the stoop and into his arms. She didn't say a word, gave no heads-up, simply released a panicked sound that broke his heart, and wrapped her arms around him.

Shocked confusion didn't accurately describe his reaction to what had transpired. One minute she was *I'm a feminist. What's your superpower?* and slamming doors in his face. The next she was burrowing into him as if he were the world's largest Snuggie and she was in need of some serious cuddle time.

Problem was, cuddling wasn't standard protocol in Interview and Interrogation, nor was it a skill the women he "dated" required. That left Noah in dangerous territory with nothing but big shoulders and sweet words at his disposal. He may have been born in Sweet, but that was the only sweet thing about him.

Now Faith was another story. Under that tough-girl shell, she was surprisingly sweet and soft. And she felt incredible in his arms, as if she was the perfect size for him, which was a little unnerving since she barely came up past his chest. Then there were her soft spots, pressing into all his hard spots in just the right way. As he ran his hands in soothing strokes down her back, he was acutely aware of how fragile she felt beneath his embrace.

After their run-ins, and the few glimpses of her around town, *fragile* was the last word he'd ever use to describe her. She was always in a rush and usually looked adorably frazzled, but never fragile.

So when Faith clung tighter, a shuddery breath or two escaping as she nestled farther into his embrace, it became clear that cuddling was not a prelude to anything. It was the actual event.

Instead of palming her delicious backside, while threading the other hand through her silky hair—a classic play from his book that, when it came to women, had a ninety-nine percent chance of ending with both sets of clothes on the floor—he decided *this* woman needed something gentler from him.

"You okay?" he asked, knowing that regardless of her answer, he wasn't the guy for the job. Then a shiver ran through her—one he was sure had zip to do with the low temperature—and he accepted that he was the only guy around, so he had to figure things out. And quick.

"Faith," he said, tipping her face up toward his and—

Pow. It was like a battering ram to the chest. Her eyes were moist, her face tense with repressed emotion, and she was working hard on what had to be the saddest smile in history.

Something bad had happened tonight. Something that left her looking like a broken angel.

Staring down into those sad brown pools did crazy things to him, like inspiring a serious internal monologue. It wasn't exactly a "What would Cody do?" conversation, but it did involve hunting down whoever had caused this heartache and ending their life. That would come later, though, after she was back to slamming doors in men's faces.

With a soft, "Whatever it is, I promise you we can fix it," his hands continued a lulling motion up and down her back. Kind of the way he hugged his sister-in-law when she was upset, using gentle, soothing passes along the friend-zone of her spine. Only, he'd never had a problem keeping himself in check hugging Shelby—or any woman for that matter.

But with Faith in his arms, he felt as if he could finally stop running.

"I'm usually not a hugger," she murmured into his

chest, her voice whisper-thin and full of a vulnerable emotion he couldn't quite pinpoint. "Or a liar." She looked up at him, her eyes brimming with apology. "But those women can be so mean. When they asked about why Pax was in your car . . . I might have gone a little overboard."

Again, she was slowly killing him. "You're not the one who made up a fake internship."

"You're not mad?" Even as she said it, her grip loosened, as if she were expecting him to back away.

He laced his fingers behind her, letting her know he wasn't going anywhere. "Why would I be mad?"

"Because I dragged you into my life drama. Not to mention, a lie that would be easy for Molly-Mae and her minions to ferret out."

"A heads-up next time would be nice but, angel, that's the sweetest lie I've ever been dragged into."

Her hands played with the zipper of his jacket, her eyes looking everywhere but at his. "Full disclosure. I gave them your e-mail address and place of work."

"So women aren't e-mailing me nonstop because they think I'm charming?" he said, and a hint of a smile teased at her lips. "It's all public record."

"It was still a pretty crappy thing of me to do, and you didn't sell me out," she said as if every man before him had done exactly that.

"What can I say? A hero's work is never done."

She laughed. And what a beautiful laugh—carefree, bold, and a whole hell of a lot better than that heartbreaking smile of a moment ago.

"If you want to talk about it, or anything."

She held up a hand and stepped back. "Nope. We're good."

He was better when she was in his arms, but he'd take

what he could get. "Then how about we take this roadshow inside and out of the rain?"

She stepped inside, then turned to block his entrance. "Depends. You got a warrant?"

"Do I need one?"

"Answering a question with a question." She rolled her eyes all the way to the peak of the house. "You're such a cop."

"Is this the part of the night where we throw out our role-play fantasies?"

She snorted. "In your dreams. And yes, you need a warrant."

"What if I don't want to search for anything? What if I come bearing presents in the form of power?"

Her fathomless eyes met his and she smiled. "You'd still need a warrant."

"You're strict, angel. Is that how you earned your wings? Following all the rules?"

"And you're a sweet talker." She opened the door and stood back. "You can come in. This once. I'm guessing you need access to my breaker box?"

"Now who's sweet-talking who?" And with a wink, Noah took off his hat and walked past her into the house, catching a hint of cinnamon and vanilla. The woman smelled like Christmas and looked like heaven, even when she was scowling at him.

With only the faint light of the moon, he could see the house was clean and well cared for, a surprise since the exterior was in some serious need of love. He kicked off his boots, chuckling over her shocked expression at his thoughtfulness, and left them and his hat by the door as he made his way farther into the room, clicking on his flashlight when she closed the door.

"Is your box in your bedroom?" he asked hopefully.

"You wish. It's in the kitchen."

He followed her lead, watching the sway of her hips. And tight didn't even begin to describe those pajama bottoms. With no visible panty lines, he had to wonder if she was wearing a thong, a G-string, or nothing at all. And while he was more of a thong than G-string kind of guy, he was rooting for commando.

"You can stop shining the light on my butt now."

"Yes, ma'am." Up the beam went, to land on—would you look at that—the breaker box.

"And it isn't that I don't know what to do in a blackout. I do. But this is our first year in this house, so I'm not familiar with how things work. And if it wasn't for the bake sale, I'd have pushed through until the lights came back on."

"Understood."

"I don't want you thinking that I'm one of those women who runs around like a chicken with her head cut off when the lights go out. I know how to flip a breaker. I have a flashlight. Normally this would be no big deal."

She talked the entire way to the kitchen, only stopping when they reached the panel in the back of the pantry, where she explained everything. She knew about her house's electrical system—which was pretty impressive.

She was still talking when he handed her the flashlight so he could familiarize himself with the setup. Faith couldn't stand not being active. Every time he'd seen her, she'd been in constant motion. So he shouldn't have been surprised when she knocked his shoulder with the flashlight because she was trying to peer around him to see what he was doing. And he didn't laugh when she placed her hands on his arm for balance as she went up on her toes, only to huff when she couldn't get a good enough view. In fact, Noah was enjoying her curiosity so much, he didn't even bother to mention that her house was already set up for a generator and there was no need for him to stand there any longer.

But her front was pressed against his back and he was in no rush to move. Then the beam of light passed over the bags of ingredients on the counter and he reluctantly stepped back.

"So?" she asked, shining the beam directly into his eyes.

"So." He placed his hand on hers and lowered the light. At the simple contact, acute sexual awareness flowed between them. "Point me in the direction of where the power comes into your house and we should be good to go."

"You didn't need to check out my box, did you?"

"I'd never pass up the opportunity to check out your box, angel." He took the flashlight before she could blind him again. "Now, what direction am I heading?"

Chapter Seven

Ten wet and blustery minutes later, Noah had the generator hooked up and running. It took nine minutes longer than usual because his beautifully independent electrician-in-training insisted on going with him. Not just going with him but taking notes on everything he was doing so she could replicate it in the event of a next time.

Noah almost told her that, night or day, he was simply a swipe on the phone away. But then he took in the crayon drawings and family calendar on the fridge, the handwritten menu on a brightly colored WHAT'S COOKIN' chalkboard, and his body started feeling twitchy.

Every detail, from the twinkling lights strung throughout the house to the holiday cards neatly lining the fridge, was a conscious choice in creating a safe and warm family environment. From the outside, the house hadn't seemed like much. But now that the lights were on, he noted how cozy she'd made her little nest. Everything was freshly painted, including the shutters and cabinets. There was a vase of garden-cut flowers on the counter, several well-kept plants on the windowsill, and every surface was covered in some phase of cookies.

The only thing out of place was Noah. Had Cody not

guilted him into coming back to Sweet, Noah wouldn't be here getting to know the most fascinating woman he'd ever encountered. He'd be back in Austin, disappearing for weeks on end into the seedy underbelly of society, tempting danger at every turn.

He'd watched as better men than he tried and failed at the family thing, leaving behind a world of hurt and disappointment. Not that he was thinking that far ahead. But if he did ever want to give the whole white-picket-fence thing a try, it would be with a woman like Faith.

Only she'd had more than her fair share of disappointment, and he didn't want to be one more guy to add to her list. So when she waltzed back into the kitchen and tossed him a dry towel, he said, "Let me grab my things and I'll leave you to your gingerbread men."

"Bears," she corrected, her face flushed from their adventure in the elements. "They're ginger bears. And you don't have to go just yet. I mean, if you don't want to. It's still coming down pretty heavy out there."

Noah wasn't interested in "out there" as much as he was in what was happening *in here*. Where Faith was not only asking him to stay but asking him while standing in those ever-so-sculpting pajama bottoms. Then there was the still rain-dampened hair and bare feet adding an adorable sweetness to that sexy coed vibe she had going on. Noah knew that staying would only lead to trouble.

But hot damn, trouble had never been so tempting.

"As long as I'm not in the way."

"Honestly, I could use the company." Her gaze fell, as if embarrassed to have asked. "Unless you have somewhere to be?"

He couldn't think of a single place he'd rather be than in this kitchen with the woman who'd consumed his every waking hour. Some of his sleeping ones too, but he didn't think she'd want to hear about that, so he said, "Why don't I make something to warm us up while you start on your cookies?"

Noticing the way her limbs sagged with exhaustion, he grabbed two mugs off the drying rack and placed the kettle on the stove. She didn't seem to mind him rummaging around her kitchen. In fact, his presence seemed to put her at ease.

Head in her cupboard, he asked, "So I assume you don't want to talk about what upset you tonight."

"Not ever."

Finding what he needed, he went to the fridge. "Okay, then, how about we start with the basics? How long have you lived here?"

"Pax and I lived in the top unit of the cute yellow Victorian across the street for about six years and loved it, but it was a one-bedroom."

Which meant, at some point Faith started sleeping on the couch so her brother could have the bed.

"Mr. Adams owned this place forever, never married, never had kids, and he loved having Pax around. Used to pay him to help with odd chores around the house. But the winters were hard on his arthritis, so last year he decided to retire to Boca Raton with his brother and sold me this house. Dated furniture included," she said. "He was a bachelor here for over fifty years, so it's definitely a fixer-upper, and there's a lot of fixing up still to be done, but we're getting there."

Faith patted the table, old and beautiful with hand-carved legs and an oval top, which he'd bet the ranch she'd refurbished herself.

"What?" she asked. "What's that look for?"

"I'm impressed is all," he said honestly. Not only had she managed to buy her own home before turning thirty, but she'd done an incredible amount of work on the place. By herself, from the sound of it, and all while raising her kid brother.

A collage of photos on the far wall caught his attention. There must have been twenty pictures of her and Pax— hiking, at the beach, in front of the Alamo. In every snapshot, the two were smiling or laughing, their love for each other contagious.

Noah enjoyed the idea of her making fun memories with her brother. Seeing her riding in some of the photos, he also liked the idea of her on his horse. He found himself smiling.

"Was this taken at the Crossing?" he asked, and when she didn't answer, he turned to face her. She was frozen in place, her eyes wide and uncertain. "Faith?"

"Where's your gun?"

"Left it in the car."

"I thought you alpha types always carry a gun with you."

He stepped around the table to stand in front of her. "Not when it makes you uncomfortable."

"You noticed that?" She rubbed the hem of her sweatshirt between her fingers, her gaze everywhere but on his.

Her unease had been hard to miss. There was a distinct difference between gun-shy and petrified, and he didn't have to look in some file to guess at the kind of history she must have survived to have that reaction to a loaded weapon.

"I seem to notice everything about you," he admitted.

The way she always put others first, the way she could

look sexy even after standing in a downpour, and the way she fidgeted when she was nervous—like now.

He placed a hand over her fingers and intertwined them with his and, *oh holy night* was right. One touch was like adding a spark to a brick of C-4. Those lush lips formed the perfect *O* of surprise, and her eyes were equally round as she looked to him for an explanation.

Yeah, angel. It really is that powerful.

And she really was that nervous. Oh, her eyes didn't stray far from his, down to his lips and back up, making the rounds every couple seconds, but he could feel the uncertainty rolling off her. She tightened her grip on his fingers and their arms swayed just enough to make him school-boy crazy.

Oh yeah, she was trouble. And he was neck-deep in it.

"What else have you observed?" she asked. "About me?"

"You look at obstacles like challenges, you like to be capable, you're actually better at electrical stuff than me. And . . ." He glanced at the scene from Santa's workshop—if Santa employed stuffed penguins—that sat on her windowsill and chuckled. "You have a bigger Christmas problem than drive-by decorating of public trees. It looks like a Christmas bomb exploded in here, but I didn't see a tree by the fireplace."

Or stockings. Or presents.

"Pax and I get up early on Christmas Eve and go get a tree, then spend the whole day decorating, wrapping presents, stringing popcorn."

"That sounds fun."

A fond smile washed over her face. "Yeah. It's kind of our tradition now. The first Christmas it was just the two of us and we were broke. I was paying tuition for a school I wasn't attending and was dealing with the cost of moving." She waved a dismissive hand as though the details of sacrificing her future for her brother were insignificant. "I'd only started waiting tables and payday was the fifteenth. I didn't want to buy a tree when I couldn't afford to put anything under it. No kid wants to stare at an empty tree. So we waited until Christmas Eve, and somehow it all ended up working out. When the next year rolled around, I asked Pax if he wanted to get a tree, and he said he wanted to wait until Christmas Eve. So now it's our thing."

She stopped talking. "What?"

"You're a pretty amazing sister," he said, loving the shy expression that stole over her face.

"You already said that once." Her voice was husky, and sexy.

"I guess I did. How about, you love baking."

"How do you know?" She feigned shock, and he laughed.

"My stellar observation skills," he joked But it was more than just the army of bears. In her kitchen she moved fluidly, calmly, as if all her worry and second-guessing and what-ifs melted away and Faith could be Faith. "They also tell me that you have a stubborn streak deeper than the Grand Canyon, especially when it comes to your independence." He looked at her over his shoulder and caught her checking out his backside. "Even more so when it comes to me."

"Because your *I'm a Big Bad Ranger* act annoys me."

"This Big Bad Ranger does something to you, angel." He flashed her a wicked grin. "But I think you're confusing your verbs."

She tossed a raw dough bear at his head and he caught

it, then popped it into his mouth. "You also have great aim. Softball?"

She floured her hands and the cookie cutter. "Skee-Ball at the arcade on Coney Island. Grand champ two summers straight."

"You lived in Coney Island?"

"I lived a bunch of places. Why?"

"Lord help me, you are more suspicious than Matlock when he's on a case," he said.

"Not suspicious, cautious," she said.

"Cautious isn't a bad thing."

She rolled her eyes, but it didn't counteract the way she'd been blushing the entire time he was talking. "How about the crazy lady part? I can't believe that you'd even want to help me tonight, especially after the way I came at you at the diner."

"Angel, you can come at me however you want, and I'd still show up on your doorstep with flowers in hand," he said as if he were the kind of guy to bring flowers. But for her, he might give it a shot. "You were protecting your brother. I can't fault you for that."

Noah peeked in the fridge, found what he was looking for. On his way back to the table, he passed by her and whispered, "Besides, you're cute as all get-out when you're crazy."

"Who told you he's my brother?" Her voice was uncertain.

Noah blinked. "What?"

She gave him a small shove back, which was cute considering he was twice her size and could bench her with one arm tied behind his back. But the hurt-filled expression gutted him.

"Uh, you said, 'You and your brother,' when talking

about getting a Christmas tree." He quickly thought back, trying to remember exactly how she'd phrased it. His recall was near-perfect, had to be in order to do his job well. But he was uncharacteristically nervous around her— lucky if he remembered his own name.

"No, I didn't." Her face drained of color. "Did you investigate me, Texas Ranger Noah Tucker? Do you have a file in your 'not-a-patrol car' listing my family's criminal history and every mistake I've ever made?"

"I did not. And I do not." And thank Christ for that. He'd been tempted, oh how he'd been tempted, but his instincts had been spot-on when it came to Faith and her privacy. And here Cody had thought himself to be the reigning expert on all things female in Sweet.

She opened her mouth and closed it, looking surprised by his answer. Her arms hugged her middle, a textbook sign of uncertainty. Silently, she studied him for a long, pressure-filled moment. Noah—to his shame—softened the muscles around his eyes and relaxed his body with his palms open by his sides. All tricks he'd learned at the academy to appear trustworthy and put the other person at ease.

But he didn't want to interrogate Faith. He just wanted her. Unfiltered and real. So it was his turn to be surprised when instead of screaming, *"Get out of my house!"* she quietly asked, "Then how did you find out?"

His opinion of her clearly mattered, which meant that his *cautious* angel was nervous about what was happening between them. And nervous meant interested—at least on some level. She wanted to trust him but didn't know how. The way she kept averting her gaze told him she was expecting him to let her down, but for now she was open to the idea that maybe he was a stand-up guy.

He had a little over a week to prove her right before he'd be heading back to Austin, so he had to tread carefully.

"Maybe I figured it out myself. Did you ever think of that?" he asked.

"Impossible. Once people create a narrative that fits their expectations, it's nearly impossible for them to reframe it."

Impressive.

It had taken him a few years on the force to learn that incredible accurate tidbit. On some level he'd known it his whole life, since he had to fight against public opinion stemming from his father's legacy.

It took active military service to rescue his reputation, then relocating to a different city when his tour was up—but it had been worth it. From what little he'd learned about Faith's past, it was a wonder she hadn't changed her name and moved to Alaska. He'd been dismayed by the fervor of the women at the market the other day.

That she'd chosen to stay in Sweet and put down roots was a testament to how committed she was when it came to her loved ones. Noah wondered how different he and his brothers' lives would have been, had Silas approached single parenthood with the same selfless devotion as Faith.

"And in this narrative you've constructed about me, I'm the kind of cop to abuse my power and spy on innocent women? Can you imagine my dates if I took that approach? The woman swipes right and walks into the bar knowing that I like cats, line dancing, and mixed martial arts. While I show up knowing her last boyfriend is in jail for a DUI, her mom is suing her dad, and she has some sordid past with a local pot dealer named Seth."

"When you say it that way . . ." She cringed. "I'm guilty of behaving exactly the way other people behave toward me. I have no good excuse. I'm not used to people being straightforward with me. People usually make their minds up before I even show up, if that makes sense. It's like living in a book about me, where everyone knows the ending *but* me."

"That would make it hard to build trust with others," he said, getting a better understanding of how she ticked, and why she ticked the way she did.

Even though he hated talking about himself, had over a decade's worth of training that went against sharing personal details, Faith was opening up—and he could tell it was a big deal for her to do so. If he wanted to keep this back-and-forth going, he needed to be forthcoming himself.

"A lot of my work is on a 'need to know' basis, where I'm the one who 'needs to know.' It can be rough to make connections when I can't talk openly about my day or what's going on at the place I devote eighty-plus hours a week to. But with everything else, you can trust that I'm a straightforward guy. What you see is what you get. And if you're not getting what you need, all you have to do is ask."

"That's refreshing."

"Better than annoying," he teased. "That's how I found out that Pax is your brother. The old-fashioned way. Asking my brother what he knows about this pretty girl in town who won't give me the time of day."

She splayed her hands out. "You're in my kitchen, aren't you?"

Huh, it appeared that his *"I don't date"* angel was flirting with him. He'd have to be annoying more often.

"See where old-fashioned courting can get you?" he said, and she laughed.

Finished with her first batch, she walked the trays over to the oven. She had three trays, which meant he got to watch while she bent over, three times, causing her sweatshirt to slide up, giving him a mighty fine view of her backside and making his Christmas wish come true.

Again, he wondered if she was commando under those pajama bottoms.

He thought on that for a moment, perhaps a moment too long, because when he lifted his gaze, she was giving him a disapproving look.

Great, he'd been caught peeking under the Christmas tree of a woman who'd been disrespected her entire life.

Wanting to clarify his intentions, Noah tipped her chin up so she could see the honesty in his eyes. "And to make it clear, angel. I am courting you. And part of courting is getting to know each other. And while I can't wait to get to *know* you, I want to make sure we get to what matters first."

She held his gaze, her lips a breath away. Then she squeezed her eyes shut and said, "How much do you already know about me?"

Chapter Eight

Faith blamed Noah for her momentary insanity.

How was a woman to think straight when surrounded by 200 pounds of muscle and alpha-man pheromones? Insanity was the only reason someone with her background would ask an officer of the law—a very hot, very male, very serious officer of the law—what he knew about her law-breaking family.

It was as if she were inviting him to look through the pile of dirty underwear in the corner of her room before leaving for their first date. No one would swipe right on that.

To be fair, he'd said he wanted to get to know her, wanted to court her—as if that wasn't the most romantic thing in the world. And to know her, he'd have to know where she came from.

Who she came from.

And wasn't that enough to make her stomach churn? But if she was really going to try this, the key word being *try*—because the last time she'd tried with a man, he'd asked her if there was another relative Pax could live with—then she wanted complete transparency. None of this bait and switch men did once they thought they had both feet in the door.

Besides, Noah wasn't like the other guys she'd dated. From what she'd read about him online, he was a rising star in the department. He couldn't have people whispering about who he was dating if he wanted to stay on the fast track.

Faith turned to face him, and since he didn't move they were pressed together with barely a breath between them.

She tilted her head up, way up so she could see his face. And what a handsome and kiss-worthy face it was. Those bright blue eyes, always calm and aware, locked on hers. Tingles sizzled all the way through her, melting away every chill left over from their time in the rain.

Stupid tingles, she thought, knowing they were the ones behind this mess. A mess she would eventually have to clean up.

"Before you say things like you want to court me—" did she just giggle? —"you might want to do that background check. Not just on me, but on my entire family."

His big hands went to her hips, his fingers splayed across her lower back, and—*hello*?—tingles turned to tension, sexual and intense. She knew the honorable Texas Ranger felt it, too, because he had to clear his throat before speaking.

Good to know she wasn't alone in this. Right?

"I don't need a file. A file isn't going to tell me that you're smart and beautiful and have such a big heart that when your mama left town, you gave up a scholarship in L.A. to move back home and raise your kid brother. Which you're doing a damn fine job of," he whispered. "A file is nothing but details of the worst moments of someone's life. And angel, you're worth a hell of a lot more than a quick glance at a screen."

"Oh," was all she said, unable to pull her focus from his lips. She couldn't help it. Noah had the most mesmerizing lips. And the words he'd spoken stole her breath.

"Now, from what I gather, you're a private person. Whether by nature or necessity, I don't know, but I'd like to find out," he said, and dread filled her chest.

Was there time to change her mind? Tell him, "Now that I've had time to think, maybe you should read my file, in the privacy of your own office, hundreds of miles away. That would be way less embarrassing than me recounting every awful, tragic, and mortifying detail while you look at me with horror."

But that was a Hope move. Draw them in, then disappear when things fell apart.

"I'm not sure where to start. All of it's pretty bad." She'd never admitted that to anyone. Most people knew bits and pieces, but no one knew the whole story. And Faith took comfort in that. "What do you want to know?" she asked, wondering why she was going down this path.

Because you can't carry it all alone anymore.

He peeked over her shoulder at the mess on her counter. "How about we start with something you enjoy? Walk me through what you're baking."

"Baking?" She blinked. "You can ask me any question and you want to know what I'm baking?"

He shrugged. "Courting usually starts with the fun stuff. The hard stuff comes later. Why shouldn't you have the same experience? Plus, I like cookies." He leaned close. "And I like seeing you smile."

With that he backed away, to stand by her side. She didn't know what to say. Or how to feel. Because for the first time since her daddy went to prison, someone who knew enough about Faith's past to get that it was scandalous, was more interested in the small things that made her . . . her.

He bumped her shoulder with his. "So bears with hats, huh?"

She couldn't hide her smile, or her gratitude. "They're my ginger bears. It's the first thing I taught myself to bake. Over the years I've made some changes, but whenever I bake them, I feel like I'm that twelve-year-old kid who still thought Christmas was magical."

"And now?"

She shrugged. "I bake them for the Treats for Tots bake sale so other kids can feel a little Christmas magic."

He stuck his finger in the bowl. "Is this something you do every year? Deliver Christmas magic?"

"Yes, on the magic, but this is my first time participating in the bake sale. They were short on bakers, so I told Ester Rayborn I'd fill in for her."

He leaned past her and went for a second dip of batter. "Ah, so a Secret Samaritan project then."

"I am not Sweet's Secret Samaritan. And stop that." She batted his hand away. "I'm already low on batter because of the blackout. Plus, eating raw dough is dangerous."

"I like a little danger."

"Danger's not my thing." She'd spent an entire lifetime trying to avoid it.

"Maybe you're trying it with the wrong people," he teased.

This time she bumped his shoulder. "Are you flirting with me, Ranger Tucker?"

"No, ma'am," he said seriously, that accent of his rolling

down her spine and making her shiver. "Not that I don't want to, but you don't seem to like it."

Her smile collapsed. Was she that out of practice? Or was he so intuitive he knew she hadn't had a whole lot of experience with men? Oh, she'd dated guys here and there, but she'd never let any of them fully into her life. That wasn't a risk she was willing to take.

But with him, it felt fun and easy. Safe even.

She looked at him with a new awareness. "Usually flirting makes me nervous, so most men think I'm cold. But with you, it's different."

"Different good or different bad?" He playfully crossed his fingers. "If you can't tell, I'm rooting for different good?"

"I'm not sure yet," she teased. "But I can tell you that I like it." She put her thumb and finger together, peeking through the tiny crack at him. "A little bit."

"Do you like me, Faith?"

She rolled her lips in. "Maybe a little?"

"I can work with that," he said softly, stepping closer, wrapping his arms around her, his embrace tender and warm. "What else do you like?"

"I like going slow."

"I can work with that, too," he said, his breath a warm caress.

Blood rushed through her heart, and anticipation of what was to come pulsed through her as he, very slowly, leaned in to her, pausing to gauge her reaction. "Slower?"

"Maybe a little too slow," she whispered against his lips.

Faith held his gaze, soaking in his touch, his strength and all that was Noah. She placed her hands on his chest, rising on her toes and, after what felt like an eternity, Noah closed the distance and their lips finally, *finally* brushed.

Once, then again, so incredibly tender and wonderful that Faith held her breath to take in every moment. It was as if she'd been starved for human contact. For someone to hold her in a way that made her feel special. Cherished.

Noah wasn't playing this hard and fast. He was making every move between them matter. His hands ran up her back and around to cup her face, sending flutters and tingles and every other kind of feeling racing through her body. She pressed closer right as he gave a final caress of her lower lip, then pulled back.

Faith didn't open her eyes quite yet, wanting to take it all in, save it for a rainy day. But when he whispered her name, she opened her eyes, surprised to find that they were still in her kitchen and she was still in her brother's pajamas. Everything looked the same, but something significant had changed.

"I meant to take it slow, but then I saw the mistletoe," he said, pointing to a strand of leaves and berries draped directly overhead.

"That's not mistletoe," she said, laughing. "That's holly. And strung together it's called a garland."

"My mistake," he said, with a boyish twinkle to his grin.

Chapter Nine

Santa's Workshop had nothing on the town of Sweet Plains when it came to present production.

Overnight, Shelby and Team Elf had transformed the Tuckers' barn into an efficient assembly line that was more suited for Ford's new manufacturing plant than a small-town wrapping party.

At one end of the barn sat a pile of toys generous enough to grace every Christmas tree from here to the county line. On the other end was an even larger stack, all beautifully wrapped and topped with shimmering, color-coded bows that made the task of pairing children with age-appropriate gifts a little easier. In the middle were several staffed stations, each with a different purpose. There was the sorting station, the boxing station, the wrapping station, the bow station, and so on. Ending with the delivery station.

And that was only the still-unclaimed gifts.

On the way in, Faith had parked next to a line of pickups being loaded with presents that were headed to the community center, where they'd be handed out. They were already wrapped and marked with personalized tags for those kids who, as Faith once had done, had sent in their Dear Sweet letters. If a child took the time to send in a letter, then the team would go to great lengths to mark off at least one item from their wish list. It wasn't always possible, and it wasn't always the top item, but Team Elf took their job seriously.

"You headed to the North Pole?" Cody joked, moseying over in a pair of cowboy boots and Santa hat with Mr. December on the brim. Unlike Faith, he was dressed in weather-appropriate jeans and a T-shirt.

"Pax already used that joke," she said. "I guess this is what I get for listening to the local weather guy." She took off her scarf to fan herself.

It was two days before Sweet's Holiday Shindig and, heeding the forecast's warning of high winds and icy roads, Faith had left the house prepared for a snowy afternoon. Her getup included a heavy sweater, a heavier coat, and enough bourbon balls for those brave enough to come to a wrapping party under the frostiest of conditions.

Only Mother Nature had decided to take a little holiday joy in keeping the townsfolk of Sweet Plains guessing, gifting them with a sunny and well-into-the-sixties afternoon.

"You know the local weatherman makes his forecast based on how his goats are acting?" Cody pulled her in for a side hug and snatched her container of bourbon balls— which she'd thankfully made the weekend before last.

"Now you tell me," she said.

"Sugar, all you had to do was hang your head out the window and you'd have thought you were back in Los Angeles."

"I haven't looked out the window for the past couple of days," she explained. She'd been up frosting cookies until 6:00 A.M. After a three-hour nap, she woke to start the painful wrapping process. She still had about twenty dozen cookies left, but she'd promised Pax he could work off some hours helping the guys around the ranch. Plus, Faith wanted to see her friends, even if it was only for an hour.

Oh, who was she kidding? It was the thought of seeing Noah that had drawn her here. She hadn't been able to stop thinking about him since their kiss, three long nights ago. When she remembered back to the way he'd held her, and the sweet words he'd whispered as he'd hugged her good night on the porch, her lips tingled.

Even the possibility of a chance encounter was enough to make her giddy. The possibility of a repeat of the other night? That had her mind working double time to process all the neurons simultaneously firing.

The Noah Tucker of her youth had been a regular in her dreams. Noah Tucker the man? He *was* the dream. The whole package. Forever material. Happily ever after in a Stetson.

He was all of those and more, wrapped into one deliciously toned package set on courting her.

She hadn't spoken to him since the kiss but when she'd awoken this morning, she'd found a single bunch of mistletoe tied with a red ribbon sitting on her porch. No note. No knock at the door. Just a sweet gift for her to claim at her own pace with no pressure to respond.

Most women might think it odd for a guy to drop off flowers without a note taking credit for the gesture. But to Faith, it was almost more romantic, because a man like Noah didn't want credit. He wanted to bring a smile to her face on a day that he knew would be taxing.

Faith looked down to find her hands in her purse, her fingers brushing back and forth over the beribboned bundle she'd placed there. A bright warmth flickered to life, lighting her up from the inside.

She was in a bad way when it came to Noah Tucker.

"Did he come with you?" Cody asked, and Faith jerked her hand from her purse.

"Ah, no. I haven't seen him since he brought over the generator."

Cody rocked back on his heels. "I was talking about Pax. JTs been asking about him all night. But if you were referring to my brother, he made a run to the store. Should be back soon."

"This is some setup," Faith said, ignoring his comment about Noah, while silently hoping he'd make it back before she had to leave.

"You know my wife." Cody popped a bourbon ball into his mouth. "She's some woman. And she's been asking for you."

Cody pointed Faith in the direction of the house before disappearing back into the barn with her container of cookies.

Faith rolled the sleeves of her sweater as she walked across the circular drive toward the yellow and white farm-house. The air was crisp and bright, and a gentle breeze danced along the tall stacks of wheat in the fields.

It appeared Faith had to exchange greetings with half the town before she even made it to the front porch. She waved back at Logan's sweet little girl, Sidney, who was practicing her princess wave from her daddy's shoulders. Mable of Mable's Corner Market, who was in charge of booth placement, gave her a stern reminder that all baked goods needed to arrive by 9 AM sharp.

"Nine sharp," Faith assured her. Even gave a salute, which Mable didn't find funny.

"There's always one every year who comes meandering

in around nine-thirty, looking like they don't have a care in the world."

"What happens if someone's late?" Faith asked, and Mable's eyes turned into two menacing slits.

"Ask Jessie McClean."

The name didn't ring a single bell, and after waiting tables for five years, Faith knew most everyone in town—at least by name. And she couldn't think of a single family in town with that surname. "Who's Jessie McClean?"

Mable leaned in, her forehead wrinkling. "Exactly."

"Good thing I'm always punctual."

"Smart girl," the older woman said. "Oh, and tell that brother of yours to stop tracking needles and sap into my store."

"Are you sure it was Pax?" He hated grocery shopping. Preferred to sit in the car if Faith had to grab something on the way home.

"As sure as the day is long." Mable nodded, and her white hair had so much spray, it moved with her. "He was in this afternoon, buying twine and a candy bar. He's a paying customer, but I ain't his mama so I shouldn't have to clear up his mess."

"No, ma'am, you shouldn't. I'll talk to him as soon as we get home tonight," Faith said. Mable's eyesight wasn't so good, and Pax had been at Community Care all afternoon, so she must have him confused with another boy. One time the older woman thought a racoon was her dog and brought him into bed with her.

After saying good-bye and exchanging another couple *howdy*s, Faith opened the bright blue front door and stepped into the house. Even though Cody said Noah wasn't home, it didn't stop her from peeking around every corner just in case. She imagined what it must have been like growing up in a house like this.

It was spacious but warm, and every nook and cranny of the historic farmhouse was tailor-made for a family. She could see a young Noah racing down the steps as he shouted to his mom that he was headed out to ride his horse. She could even see him there now as an adult lying on the floor with his nephew playing video games.

But no matter how hard she tried, Faith couldn't picture herself there. Not as anything more than a friendly guest. She wasn't sure if it was because she'd never dared to wish for a home like this growing up since it was so far out of reach, or if there was something deep down reminding her that wishes were for fools.

Faith might be a cautious romantic, but she'd never be a fool like her mom.

"Who you lookin' for?" Shelby called from the dining room, where she was wrapping a Superhero bobblehead-themed basket with clear cellophane.

Faith jumped as if she'd been caught with her hand in the Noah cookie jar. But when she saw her friend's T-shirt, Faith burst out laughing.

"ELF COMMANDER," Faith read as she set her things on one of the dining chairs.

"Wait for it." Shelby tugged on a bright red cap that had MR. DECEMBER'S embroidered across the brim. "I got one for the whole family."

"If Mr. December wasn't married to my best friend, I'd want to be his, too." She wondered if Noah had received one. And, if so, what it said. "I can't believe how much you guys have already gotten done."

"Because she's a tyrant." Their third musketeer, Gina, walked in munching on a fried chicken leg. "She came to my house at 6:00 A.M., on my day off, to bring me here and hasn't let me leave. I've wrapped more baskets for the silent auction than I've had cases this year."

"We've already taken five loads of auction items to the community center. There's a storage room off the back they're letting us use to safely store everything until Saturday night."

"See? Tyrant."

"At least you've been fed." Faith had maintained a steady diet of icing and Red Bull for the past few days. She spotted a new iPad on the table and her mouth fell open. "People are donating iPads?"

"Ten of them. Plus there's a ton of things I would bid on." Shelby picked up a beautifully embossed envelope. "A certificate for a girls' day at the spa. There's a weekend getaway for two to Padre Island. Someone even donated the new PlayStation. Can you believe it? You can't even find them in stores anymore. Everyone's sold out for Christmas, so Cody has his eye on it."

"If he wins, that's all Pax will talk about for the next six months. He'll want to move in so he can play nonstop with JT."

"Mr. *But Dad Played With Them* has his heart set on a pair of Battle Rifle Pro laser guns The Toy Box downtown donated," Shelby said. "After their little G.I. Joe stunt, I told him to dream on."

Faith's stomach flipped at the possibility of finally getting Pax his wish. She didn't want to reward bad behavior, and she sure as heck didn't want Pax comfortable holding a gun, but she also didn't want him to be excluded anymore. This might be her last chance to get him his Christmas wish.

They're toys, she reminded herself, *clearly marked as*

toys. And he had so much fun playing commando with the other kids, it would be great if he didn't have to wait for someone to "tap out" to play.

"Do all of the items go for more than they're worth?"

"Mrs. McKinney told me that it's all over the board," Shelby explained. "A twenty-dollar doll can go for a hundred. And a three-hundred-dollar bike can go for eighty bucks. The PlayStation? Cody will end up paying double for it rather than wait the two weeks for a new shipment. Plus, he hates to lose."

Faith could relate to that. She didn't care so much about winning as she did about being wrong when it mattered.

Her heart sped up on the off chance that, if she were lucky, maybe everyone would be so dazzled by the iPads, they'd overlook the laser guns. Pax would go ballistic if he found those under the tree on Christmas morning. Even if it meant cutting into her blender fund, it would be worth it to see the look on his face.

"Judge Hardy donated the iPads," Gina said. "He's a scrooge. Squeaks when he walks. He steals pens with the county logo from the courthouse to hand out on Halloween. I don't know what you did, Shelby, but I'm impressed."

Shelby had come a long way in the past few months, proving to folks around town that even though she was a big-city girl, she had a small-town heart. It wasn't until she'd single-handedly saved the Summer Spectacular bake-off that people started treating her like one of their own.

Faith hoped that being more involved in the community, in a public way, would get her a little closer to finding what Shelby had found.

"So?" Shelby wiggled her brows. "Noah got home

awfully late the other night. Said he was helping you with your cookies."

Skipping right over that, Faith said, "I only have an hour before I have to get back to baking so how can I help—"

"Uh huh. No way." Shelby stepped in front of Faith, blocking her way. "I've been dying to ask you since the storm. But I knew you were busy with the cookies, so I waited." Shelby crossed her arms. "I'm done waiting. Spill."

She turned to find Gina sitting on an ottoman, making herself at home—right in front of the doorway.

Faith sighed and plopped down on the couch. "Fine. He brought the generator over so I could—"

"Yeah, yeah, yeah." Gina twirled the chicken leg around. "Did you kiss or not?"

"Yes?" Faith said, then covered her face with her hands before ducking down.

"That was a question," Shelby pointed out.

Faith peeked through her fingers. "Yes. We did. Just a little one."

"Twenty bucks." Gina held out her hand and Shelby forked over the cash.

"You bet on my dating life?"

"So you're dating now?" Shelby turned to Gina. "One of my best friends is dating my brother-in-law and she didn't even bother to tell me."

"Stop." Faith's arms shot out, making a *T*. "We are not dating. Who said we were dating? Not me."

Shelby laughed. "Say that one more time and maybe I'll believe you."

"You also didn't deny it." Gina pointed the chicken leg at her.

Faith crossed her arms because suddenly she didn't know

what to do with them. "What, are you being Prosecutor Gina right now?"

"You bet she is. And before you try to deflect, let me remind you that she's the best prosecutor in three counties," Shelby said, and Gina grinned. "She's going to get it out of you one way or the other."

Faith took a big breath. "We aren't dating, but he said he wants to court me." God, she sounded so ridiculous saying it. Felt even more ridiculous because her lips tingled when she did.

Shelby wiggled her fingers in front of her mouth and more squealing commenced. "That is the most romantic thing I've ever heard."

"Yeah, a real Prince Charming, that one," Gina deadpanned.

"Oh stop. You're pissy because Noah took Logan's side when the Sheriff's Office blocked your attempt to redistrict some of their parking spots to the County Prosecutors' Office."

"He doesn't even live here. Why did he get involved?" Gina plopped the unfinished chicken leg on a napkin.

"Because you called and asked him to get involved," Faith reminded her.

"That's when I thought he'd see my point. The Rangers share all of their resources with their District Attorney's Office." Gina narrowed her gaze. "Now look at you, kissing the enemy."

"It was a really great kiss," Faith admitted. "And before you start squealing, let me remind everyone that he's going back to Austin in a week and I'm staying here until, well probably forever, but at least until Pax goes off to college."

"Please. A week is like a year in courting time." Shelby patted Faith's arm as if she were romantically challenged.

"Not in my world." Faith had approximately six free hours over the next seven days. "Plus, it was just a kiss. There was mistletoe, or holly, but it was raining out and he drove up in his shiny SUV like a hero coming to save the day. We got lost in the moment."

"Then you don't care that Noah is tearing down the road," Gina said, looking out the window.

All three women gathered around the window right as Noah hopped out of his not-a-patrol-car car. He walked over to one of the pickups and rested his arms—his very defined arms that had been wrapped around her—on the hood while he talked to one of the volunteers.

He wore a pair of button-fly jeans, which he filled out to perfection, and a blue and white button-down with the sleeves rolled up, giving it a casual vibe. In place of his usual Stetson was a Santa hat. Even squinting, he was too far away for her to decipher what it said, but even the sight of him had her head buzzing with anticipation.

"Just a kiss, huh?" Shelby laughed, because Faith's face was pressed so close to the window, the glass was fogging over.

Faith didn't answer. She couldn't because Noah took a case of bottled water from the back of his SUV and carried it over to the nearest tailgate. Then he hopped up into the bed of the truck and—*sweet baby Jesus*—proceeded to bend all . . . the . . . way . . . over to pick up the bottles.

His arms bulged under the weight and his shirt clung to his shoulders, exposing each and every muscle as it tightened. But what had her mouth going dry was that the best backside in the great state of Texas was on display for her viewing pleasure. Shamelessly, she watched as he repeated the process.

Three times.

"Oh my," Gina said. "I see your problem."

"Yeah." Shelby led them outside to the porch swing, getting comfortable for the show. "I wish we had some popcorn."

Cody hopped up in the truck and both brothers worked together to finish loading the bed to the brim with water for Saturday's event. A few more guys came around to help out. When finished, the group kicked back and cracked open a couple of cold drinks.

The men continued laughing and talking. About what Faith hadn't a clue, but there was something off about the way Noah held himself.

"Does Noah look all right to you?" she asked.

The two studied him for a moment and Gina snapped her fingers. "He's smiling. That's what's wrong."

Shelby laughed but Faith couldn't help but notice how he kept looking at his watch, rubbing the back of his neck. Then he looked up, spotted her, and frowned, and suddenly all the earlier flutters fizzled and soured.

"Where's the wine?" Faith asked.

"Where's your heart?" Shelby asked quietly.

Oh, it was gone. It had taken one look at Noah and rolled over in surrender. And he was checking his watch as if he'd rather be anywhere than there.

"It's so new, I don't trust it," she admitted. "I'm afraid that if I say it out loud, it won't happen. Things don't work out for people like me."

"Oh honey." Shelby put her arms around Faith. "People like you deserve the best. Plus, it's Christmas."

"I understand," Gina said, with lonely commiseration

in her eyes. She, too, had given her heart to someone who overlooked it for something flashier. Only, Gina had to interact with him every day and pretend that her heart wasn't shattered.

Faith pulled Gina into the hug and all three of them fell backward onto the swing, laughing.

"Too bad the third brother slept with my sister," Gina said. "Because I want a Tucker under my tree this year."

Faith did, too. She feared she wanted Noah Tucker for a lot longer than Christmas.

Chapter Ten

Noah was doing his best to listen to Logan, but the truth was he couldn't take his eyes off Faith. She was sitting on the front porch swing in a pretty soft blue sweater and jeans, her hair hanging long and loose around her face, laughing with her friends. And something in his brain glitched.

The last person he'd seen swinging in that seat was his mama. After she passed, none of them could handle sitting in her favorite spot without her. But Shelby looked right at home. And he couldn't help but think that Faith did, too.

Things had definitely changed at the Crossing. Cody had grabbed on to his second chance at love and run with it. Shelby had brought new life to the farmhouse. And JT . . . man, his nephew was something special. That kid could run around the ranch all day long, riding horses and playing in the hills with his buddies, doing all the things a boy should be allowed to do. And he was doing it right here, on a piece of land that hadn't seen much laughter over the years.

So why couldn't Noah stop looking over his shoulder for the Ghost of Christmas Past?

"Funny how you said it'd take you a few hours to go

pick up the bottled water, but when I texted you that Faith stopped by, you managed it in less than forty-five minutes," Cody said, reproaching his brother, his hair messed up as if he'd been smooching his wife minutes ago.

"Some good motivation there," Logan said, grabbing a beer and using the heal of his cowboy boot to pop off the top. "So Cody called it right for once, and you and Faith are a thing."

"He's courtin' her," Cody said, and Logan burst out laughing.

"Courtin'?" Logan had the stones to laugh again.

"What is this? Mayberry?" Noah asked. "You were in the house literally five minutes."

Noah had watched Cody grab his wife by the hand and drag her through the back door. He was envious at the easy familiarity Cody and his family shared. Even when his mom had been alive, Noah had never known anything like that. Never thought it was possible for a guy like him.

Being around Faith had challenged that belief.

"What do you expect? You're back in Sweet," Cody said, offering him a beer. Noah grabbed a bottle of water instead.

"You've been back in town, what? Five months?" Noah asked his brother.

"More or less."

"And you're already as bad as Ms. Luella, gossiping like a bunch of hillbilly biddies with nothing better to do than sip sweet tea and flap your lips."

"Don't let Ms. Luella hear you say that, or she'll put soap in your pie," Cody warned, a happy grin on his face.

"So I see you decided to go there." Logan leaned back in his camping chair, stretching his legs out and crossing them at the ankles, a pair of pink socks with dancing alligators peeking out from beneath his cowboy boots. "I'd say you need to get laid and blow off some steam, but as the converted father of a daughter I will teach to run from men like you until she's thirty and old enough to date, I hope that wherever you went, you didn't go there lightly."

"I don't need dating advice from a guy who dated one sister, then married the other," Noah said, and Logan's jaw clenched as his gaze landed on Gina. "But yes, I don't take dating a single mom lightly."

"So this is a thing then?" Cody asked.

How to answer that without sharing some of the private things Faith had confided in him. He grabbed the back of his neck with a hand and applied pressure to relieve the building tension—a side effect of extended time at the Crossing. "It's too early to tell."

Cody snorted. "That's about word for word what Faith said."

Noah straightened. "What else did she say?"

"Depends on whether you think I'm an old hillbilly flapping my lips," Cody said, and Noah chucked an empty water bottle at him. Cody caught it with his hand and crushed it into a ball. "According to Shelby, she said things like this don't happen to girls like her."

Cody chucked the bottle back, but Noah didn't bother to block it. He was too busy thinking about what it must have cost Faith to admit that to someone else. And what kind of disappointments she'd had to deal with to even believe that BS.

"I shouldn't have asked," he said. "She'd be so hurt if she knew people were talking about her. So this doesn't leave the circle."

"Agreed," Cody said, and Logan nodded. Thankfully,

the other guys had taken off to deliver the extra water to the event site.

"So what are you going to do?" Cody asked.

Noah looked over at Faith, still on the swing, her hair dancing lightly in the breeze, her skin glowing under the setting sun. As if sensing his interest, she met his gaze and—*merry Christmas one and all*—she was beautiful.

Even from the distance, he could feel the blast when she slid him a shy smile. He tipped his hat, acting as though his heart wasn't beating out of his chest, because in the moment he was lost—and found, all at the same time.

Suddenly, his Ghost of Christmas Past didn't matter all that much. Not when he'd been gifted with a beautiful angel sent to rescue him.

Noah stood. "I'm going to prove to her that this generation of Tuckers is trustworthy."

"He's coming," Faith whispered, unable to contain the giddiness bubbling up as he made his way across the lawn, his gaze never straying from hers.

"My word." Gina placed a hand to her chest. "That's so intense I can feel the heat."

"Are you ready?" Shelby whispered, turning to Faith and fluffing her hair.

"Do you think he knows he's doing the whole 'Heath Ledger in *Ten Things I Hate About You*' act, wearing a Santa hat that says CUFFS INCLUDED"? Gina asked.

"Doesn't matter, he's totally pulling it off," Faith breathed.

"Which"—Shelby pinched Faith's cheeks—"is why you need to be ready. Please be ready. Because I know that look. It's all Tucker and it's all aimed in your direction."

Afraid to look away, she whispered back, "What does it mean?"

"It means your world is about to change," Shelby said, then turned her attention to the new arrival. "Hey there, Noah. Can I interest you in some sweet tea?"

And there he was, standing in front of her, looking big and strong and as if there wasn't a shadow of a doubt about what he wanted. Faith swallowed, pretty sure it was her because he said, "No, ma'am," to Shelby, his voice changing a bit when he asked Faith, "Can I borrow you for as many moments as you have left tonight?"

"No sweet tea then? Great." Shelby stood, pulling Gina with her.

"Not many men could rock the hat. Kudos to you, Middle Tucker," Gina called out right before they disappeared into the house. Only to reappear in the bottom right-hand corner of the window.

"How long do you think they're going to stay there?" he asked, and Faith laughed. "Right." He ran a hand down his face, checking behind his shoulders, then said, "Stay right there. I'll be back in two seconds."

Faith looked at her pretend watch and he grinned, then took off into the house. Faith glanced at the window behind her, where Shelby was pretending to make out with her hand and Gina sang the beginning of "Can't Take My Eyes Off of You" into an invisible microphone.

"Stop," she mouthed, but they appeared nowhere near ready to stop. So she was relieved when Noah reappeared on the porch with a canvas bag in hand.

"What's that?"

"This is a surprise." He took her hand to help her up and a charged current crackled between them. "And that, angel, is chemistry."

He led her down the steps and across the lawn, their fingers completely intertwined, their steps in harmony. He didn't break contact until they reached the gate that separated the house from the grazing pastures.

Noah held it open for her to pass through, immediately taking her hand in his larger one. Heaven help her, he had great hands. Strong, firm, and work-roughened, yet absolutely tender as he ran his thumb over her skin.

"Where are we going?" she asked.

"You getting suspicious on me again?"

"Cautious," she corrected, and he brought her hand to his mouth and kissed it.

"Cautious is okay," he whispered against her fingers. "I want to show you where I used to spend a lot of time at the ranch."

"Are you taking me to the place you'd bring girls? Show them the stars, steal a kiss?" she teased.

"No, ma'am. I've never brought anyone but my brothers to this place. So, kissing was never on the agenda."

"And tonight's agenda?"

"That, darlin', is up to you."

Faith looked up to study the man who, little by little, was chiseling away the walls she'd put in place to keep her safe. He'd managed to slide right past them and into her heart. Then she thought about how he'd phrased it, "where I spent a lot of time." He hadn't said a beautiful view or his favorite spot, and his body language didn't read as if they were going to his favorite anything.

His handsome face was tense, his lips not in their usual mischievous smile. He looked determined but uncertain, and his vulnerability reached out and pulled Faith in that much deeper.

As if sensing her stare, he looked down and gave her a

busted grin, then squeezed her hands. She squeezed back, and he laughed.

"How many moments do you have left before your ginger bears call, needing you home?" he asked, stepping down onto one of the big boulders that lined the hillside next to the creek. He lifted her hand, steadying it so she could step down with him. He did it for every boulder they descended.

"If you ask Pax, he'd say all night. But I promised myself not more than two hours of fun, and then I have to get back to work."

"Not many people smile like that when they say *work*."

"Like what?"

"Like you're happy."

She touched her cheek, surprised to find it plump with joy. "I guess I am. Even though I'm exhausted and will probably never eat another gingerbread cookie as long as I live, once I put my apron on I feel, I don't know, content."

To her, contentment was almost a foreign concept. She knew discipline, resilience, and a bunch of other traits that went along with constantly being in motion. But contentment was something new.

She looked at Noah, standing on another rock with his hand outstretched, and she realized contentment was right up there with refreshing.

"It's hard not to be when surrounded by all of this," she said, taking in the rushing creek and leaves rustling in the breeze. While she'd been helping organize the silent auction, the sun had begun to set. And now that they were down in the valley, the sky had turned to a dark twilight.

"I know," he said, and Faith realized he wasn't looking at the surroundings. She was so overwhelmed by the intensity in his eyes, she found it hard to remember why this was a bad idea.

"Can you hold on?" She held up a finger and he looked thoroughly amused. "I know that was a moment and I totally blew it, but hang on." She dug through her purse and pulled out the mistletoe he'd left on her doorstep. She held it high, but he was too tall.

"I've got an idea—stay with me," she directed.

"I'm not going anywhere."

Oh boy. As if that didn't make her wish for more. Ignoring temptation for the moment, she took the bag from his hand and set it down, then led him to the last boulder of their descent. She climbed up to the top and turned to face him—

"Oh, fa-la-la." Now she was too high.

"Why don't you sit, right here?" He patted an indentation in the rock, and she shimmied down to—well, my oh my, she was at perfect lip-locking level.

She held up the mistletoe over their heads. "I think if we get the after-the-first-kiss jitters out of the way, I'll be able to breathe."

"Who am I to argue with a lady?"

Noah stepped forward, his hands sliding up her thighs, to part them as he pressed himself against her until there was no more than a whisper between them. Her hands were still holding the mistletoe, her heartbeat pounding so loudly she barely heard him when he said, "Funny, the second you took my hand was the second I started breathing."

With a small groan, he captured her mouth.

No hesitation, no gentle exploratory brushes this time. Oh no, Noah kissed her as if he had to expel everything he felt in one, single, solitary kiss.

Except his one kiss turned into two, and by the time he

went back for thirds, Faith thought she had died and gone to Tuckerland, where every kiss packed enough punch to rock her world.

And, *Lord have mercy*, he was not a man to be rushed. He teased and kissed, his hands moving from her legs to her backside, languidly taking his time to get out every . . . last . . . jitter.

And when he pulled back, they were both breathing hard, and Faith was convinced they were flying.

When she opened her eyes, she found herself wrapped around him like a pretzel while he was supporting her. Her hand was still raised in the air, clutching the mistletoe.

"That's some powerful mistletoe. I'd better confiscate it," he said, walking them over to where they'd dropped the bag, not setting her on her feet until she handed over the contraband.

With another quick smooch to her mouth, he pulled a blanket from the bag and spread it out. Faith was so in awe of his thoughtfulness she might have kissed him again.

"Why is this place special to you?"

She needed to know because her gut said this was the key to unraveling the mystery of Noah Tucker, the lethal Texas Ranger who hunted bad people by day and helped bake cookies by night. A man who loved his family but never came home. A man who looked at her as if she were a treasure to be cherished.

"This is my safe place," he said, pulling her down to lie beside him. He rolled onto his back and she nestled into the crook of his arm. "After my mom died, it was the only place I could feel like a kid. My brothers and I would fish, swim in the river, play cops and robbers, pirates. We even built a fort."

He pointed to a small opening under the old bridge that,

without being shown, she would never have spotted. She had a strong suspicion that was intentional.

She shifted to rest her cheek on his chest. "No girls allowed, I assume."

"Yeah, I was pretty dumb back then." His hand slid up her back and over the nape of her neck. He absently played with her hair while staring at the stars.

She didn't know how long they lay, with her silently watching him, but realized that she'd be content to stay right there all night long. With him holding her while the crickets chirped in the distance and the water glided over the rocks.

"I hated living here," he admitted. "I couldn't wait to get out. I had a countdown calendar with my eighteenth birthday circled and a plan of never coming back. And I didn't, for over a decade. And I don't know if it's time, or age, or you." His arm tightened around her. "But since coming back, I've realized there are a lot more good memories than bad. Turns out it wasn't this place I hated. It was my dad."

She cupped his cheek. "I'm proud of you. That's an incredibly painful realization to have. That you hate one of the people who gave you life." She leaned up and kissed his chin. "You're a good man, Noah. You've overcome so much, and you didn't let it harden you."

"I've heard the same about you," he said, and when she tensed, he gently rubbed her back. "But I'd like to hear from you instead of the people of Mayberry."

"Most of what you've heard about my family is probably true."

"I'm not asking about your family. I'm asking about you."

She looked at him through her lashes. "Let's say I've had to atone for a lot of my parents' mistakes."

"Sweet's Secret Samaritan?"

There was no point in hiding it. In fact, she didn't want to hide anything from him. "Yeah. Since the day my step-dad ran Mr. Rayborn's hearse into a tree."

"The sheriff's tree," he guessed. "So I gather you were also the mysterious person who planted the new one."

"Yup. It's finally big enough to decorate. And the cookies are my thanks to Ester for never saying a bad word about me or my family."

"That's a big list and a pretty big burden for one teen-ager to carry," he said, and she didn't comment. "That doesn't seem fair."

"Life is rarely fair. And I'm trying to balance out the bad karma from my family. I had to grow up with everyone in town hating me for my last name. I don't want the same for Pax."

He chuckled and the sound vibrated through her body. "Are you kidding? Everyone in town loves you. Do you have any idea how many people threatened me with bodily harm if I hurt even a hair on your head? Cody, Logan, Gina, even Shelby. They are more concerned about my hurting you than about my trip home."

Her head popped up and she smiled. "Really?"

"You think that's funny?" He gave her backside a teasing smack.

"Yeah." She touched his nose. "I also think it's sweet you're telling me."

"Sweet? Angel, I can feel the testosterone level drop as we lie here."

"You have plenty to spare." She sobered. "Before we go any further—"

"I'm a second-date, second-base-only kind of guy."

She smacked his chest, but inside she melted. She had something difficult to say, and he knew she was nervous, so he was doing his best to ease her anxiety. "I have to tell you something that might make you not want to see me anymore."

"You only have to tell me what you're comfortable with. For the rest, it's up to me to earn your trust, so that you want to share," he clarified, then tugged her closer while his hands slid around to lock at the small of her back. Suddenly she wasn't so afraid, because those soft blue eyes were gentle and sincere. "I'm not going to go snooping around. There's no timeline to beat."

Why did it seem like it then? Because she didn't want to get any more invested than she already was, only to find out that courting her was a conflict of interest for a Texas Ranger.

Absently, she touched a button on his shirt. "That's not how people usually go about getting to know me."

"Maybe I'm not like other people you've met," he said, and she smiled.

"I guess I'll have to find out for myself then." She pulled back. Not intentionally, but his arms tightened around her all the same.

"But?" he asked.

"I hate buts, don't you?" Realizing what she'd said, she held up a hand and he grinned. "I meant, I want to find out for myself, but I've been burned."

Too many times to count. Although her heart kept a checklist of each and every one and liked to review them whenever she watched a sappy movie.

"So have I," he said, taking her hand. "You want to know why I used to come here?"

He placed her fingers on the tiny scar at his temple that she'd noticed more than once and had chalked up to the hazards of his chosen profession. With his hand over hers, he traced the length of the wound, which started above his ear and ran deep, disappearing into his hair.

Her lips parted on a gasp as she tenderly followed the puckered skin until she was holding his head. He leaned into her palm and closed his eyes, and in that moment, she felt a connection between them that would never fade away.

"This was a Christmas gift from my old man the year after my mama passed," he began, and something inside her heart broke open. "My kid brother, Beau, was looking through my mom's stuff and came across a box of glass ornaments. He was eight, maybe nine, and had grown like five inches that summer. So he was still finding his legs—and was about as coordinated as a newborn colt."

"He broke them?" she guessed.

"No, that's what's so crazy. Beau wanted to surprise the family by stringing the ornaments under the mantel, thinking . . ." He trailed off, his accent thick with emotion. "I don't know. Maybe he thought that if he decorated the house, it would be like my mama was back, and things would return to the way they were. Heck, I don't know what he was thinking."

"We moved here a few years after your mama passed, so I never got to meet her. But Mrs. McKinney thinks the world of her." Everyone in town had loved Miz Tucker.

He smiled fondly. "She was pretty amazing. To deal with three wild, rough-and-tumble, troublemaking boys the way she did and keep my dad's beast at bay. Not many could've handled all that the way she did, and she never had to even raise her voice or a hand. Anyway, she wasn't there, and those glass balls were a reminder. When Silas came in for dinner, we could tell he'd been drinking and was already spittin' mad on account of some cattle busting through the fence. He took one look at the mantel and I knew. Ms. Luella was already gone for the night, Cody was working in the barn, so I told Beau to run and hide—"

Faith's hands flew to her mouth. "Oh, Noah, you took the blame."

"You could say that. Although it was more like the blunt end of a hoe to the head."

Faith framed his face, hating the shame hiding in his eyes. "I don't know how someone could do that to a child. To their own child. I am so sorry," she whispered, then pressed a gentle kiss to his ear. She couldn't take back what had happened, but she could hold him now. "Did you tell the police?"

Faith already knew the answer to that because, although she'd never been beaten, she'd lived through enough violent situations to know that the law doesn't protect everyone.

"Nah. Beau found me, and we hid here until Silas sobered up." He rubbed his cheek against her hand, and she held him close. They were two broken souls who'd somehow managed to find each other.

Faith closed her eyes, then took his hand, placing it under her sweater, low on her hip. She held her breath as his fingers brushed over her skin.

"My dad is Timothy Shane," she said, finding the courage to tell him the story she had never shared with another living soul. "He's serving a double life sentence in Attica for shooting an officer." Noah didn't comment, but continued tracing over the scar on her hip. "It wasn't his first offence. Hope said he liked nice things but didn't like to work. He also liked to argue. One night he got into it with a neighbor over a parking spot in front of our house. It didn't take much to rile him up. The guy refused to move his car, so my dad punctured his tires."

Faith paused for a moment, listening to the steady beat of Noah's heart. Finding strength in it. "I was six and had spent that afternoon with him at Coney Island, the two of us. I was covered in cotton candy, so Hope put me in the bath. I heard a crash downstairs and lots of shouting, so I put on my nightgown and ran to see what was happening."

It was all so strange, rattling off the facts of an event as if it hadn't happened to her.

"Later I learned the neighbor had called the cops and when they showed up, my dad refused to let them in. But since he was still on parole for a burglary charge, he wasn't allowed to deny them entry. He also wasn't allowed to have a gun."

Beneath her, Noah's body tightened, his free arm wrapping around her to hold her close.

"All I remember was thinking this man was yelling at my dad, so I ran over to help him. I didn't know I was walking into the middle of a standoff. The officer was a rookie, so when my dad moved to grab me, Officer John Harding saw he had a gun and fired, hitting me here." She placed her hand atop his again and he laced their fingers.

Even now, she remembered the searing pain in her side. Red seeping through her white nightgown and staining the carpet beneath her. She struggled to breathe, her lungs frozen from being thrust backward, and the corners of her gaze turned black. Then her daddy was there, standing over her and asking her to open her eyes. His face was contorted in anger and concern, his hands ever so gently holding her.

He whispered, "I'm so sorry," over and over.

"My dad's aim was better," she continued. "Not lethal, but accurate enough that Officer Harding retired shortly thereafter. The man who read to me every night before bedtime and braided my hair when my mom couldn't be bothered shot a policeman." Her throat closed on the last word. "And that's only husband number one. I can tell you more."

"Baby," he said, situating them so that they were both on their sides, facing each other. He wiped away her tears with the pad of his thumb. "There are so many things seriously screwed up about what you just told me, but none of that is on you."

"I know that now, but for years I played the 'what if?' game. What if I hadn't gone downstairs? What if I hadn't moved when I did? What if my dad had simply let Officer Harding in? What if he hadn't had a gun?"

"You can't go down that road—it will drive you mad. Trust me."

"The worst part is I still love him," she whispered, horrified at the admission. "He's a bad man and I still love him."

Noah rested his forehead against hers. "He's your father. Of course you still love him. People aren't all good or all bad. Some make better choices than others. But none of what you've told me changes anything about the way I feel for you."

And, right then, sitting under a blanket of stars, Faith fell headfirst into every kind of love with Noah Tucker.

Chapter Eleven

Saturday morning dawned early on the day of the Shindig, tapping a steady rhythm on Faith's eyelids for her to rise and shine.

"Five more minutes," she pleaded, pulling the covers over her head. That was her Christmas wish. Five more minutes of being horizontal and snuggled under the cozy blanket. Five more minutes to dream about Noah and his magical mouth.

That whole night had been magical. From the minute he took her hand until he helped her to her car—kissing her good-night before she drove off—the man never missed a step. Even when she'd confessed about her family. He'd been so understanding, patiently listening while she went into greater detail about her life with Hope.

She felt safe with him. No, he worked hard to make her feel safe. Every touch, look, and thoughtful word was a testament to the kind of man he was. Nothing about him was impulsive or rash, and selfishness went against his very nature. Noah was stable and honorable, and even though she had no idea how things would work between them when he went back to Austin, Faith had zero doubt there was a "them."

Faith was in a "them" with Noah. A warm burst bubbled up from her belly, leaving her dizzy with happiness. Not only were things in her love life progressing nicely, but all fifty-dozen cookies had been baked, frosted, wrapped, and were spread out on her kitchen counter, ready to go. And she'd managed to catch two whole hours of sleep.

She was tempted to add a third but wanted to check on her cookies and make sure all the frosting and piping had held under the cellophane bags.

She pulled on her housecoat, freshened up in the bathroom, and headed for the kitchen, turning up the thermostat on the way. Coffee fix satisfied, she inspected her cookies, pleased with the end result. She had frosted and painted them, adding edible sparkles in the white piping, so the trim and ball of the Santa hat caught the sunlight.

Selecting a bear whose hat was deformed from the reject pile, she took a bite, giddy at where it fell on the yummy scale. The maple frosting was a delicious contrast to the peppery hint of the ginger and rich molasses.

She took another bite as the doorbell rang. Looking at the clock, she wondered who would show up so early. Then she thought of Mable's threat and groaned.

Cinching her bathrobe belt, she peered through the peephole and her heat leapt. It was Noah.

She turned to lean against the door, a smile the size of the North Pole completely overtaking her face. She could feel the heat building in her cheeks, and her heart beat faster and faster.

Taking a deep breath, she ran her fingers through her hair, then breathed into her hand—thank God she'd brushed her teeth.

She opened the door and there he was. Looking big and beautiful—and all hers.

"Hey," she said, rolling her eyes at how lame she sounded. "This is a surprise. Not to mention, perfect timing. I have to transport six hundred cookies from my kitchen to my car and get them to the bake sale in a little over an hour."

"Hey, angel," he said, in a tone she couldn't quite place. But it wasn't good.

He ran a hand through his hair, which was going every which direction, as if he'd been tugging at it all morning. And his posture was similar to how he'd looked during the early stages of the wrapping party.

"You want to come in?" She opened the door wide and everything slowed to a stop.

Logan stood behind Noah. *Sheriff,* she corrected, taking in his uniform, grim expression, and the way his hands rested on his belt, tugging at his coat and making everything important visible.

"Is Pax home?" Logan asked.

There was no reason for the knot of terror forming between her ribs. She'd known these men for half her life. But she knew those looks as well and everything inside her screamed to lock the door and hide.

"He's asleep. Why?"

"You might want to wake him," Noah said at the same time that Logan held up a pack of papers and informed her, "We have a warrant to search the bedroom and belongings of Pax Loren on One-Eighty-Three Wildwood Lane."

Every last shred of hope dwindled in her body, like water down a drain.

"You've known my brother since he was a baby," she said to Logan. "You don't have to run through his identifiers."

"It's protocol."

Faith looked at Noah, who remained silent.

"I see." She cleared her throat. "What is the warrant for

and why do you need to search his room?" She leaned a casual shoulder against the doorjamb, slanting her body so she was blocking the entry.

"Faith." Noah reached out, and she flinched—big-time.

"Don't show up on my doorstep unannounced with a warrant and 'Faith' me. Just tell me what's going on. I will comply, but I need to know what's happening."

The men exchanged looks, a complete conversation going on between them without a word being uttered.

"Someone broke into the Treats for Tots storage room and stole property being held for tonight's event," Logan explained. "This morning, a witness came forward, claiming Pax had not only been sneaking toys into his backpack the past few days but also stole cash from the manager's office."

"There's no way. Pax would never steal anything. Plus, he's been doing the holiday camp program at the community center. I dropped him off at eight o'clock yesterday morning and he was there all day until I picked him up after my shift around six-thirty. He's been with me ever since."

"The property in question disappeared from a secure storeroom connected to the community center," Logan informed her. "One of the items missing is a laser gun set totaling three hundred dollars. There's also a PlayStation and skateboard unaccounted for. My deputies are working with Treats for Tots volunteers to search the warehouse and find out if anything else is missing."

"So you don't even know if it's missing or misplaced, but you got a warrant to search my brother's room? A warrant, Logan." Faith's body trembled all over. She held her arms tightly around herself for fear she'd shake apart.

"The boxes were found last night discarded behind a

Dumpster near the Corner Market," Logan said. "According to Pax's Dear Sweet letter, he asked for all three of those items."

"So did half the boys in town. But I guess Pax is the only one whose dad is a felon." She looked at Noah, eyes pleading. "Tell him Pax isn't like that." He remained silent. "Tell him."

But Noah didn't tell the sheriff anything. He stood stoically by, on her porch stoop where he'd left mistletoe days before, and simply said, "It's the exact laser tag set he and JT were looking at on my laptop."

"And are officers at your house, questioning JT?" she demanded.

The two men exchanged a meaningful look and Faith shook her head.

"Of course not." She laughed bitterly.

"When we rode up, we spotted a red backpack stuffed behind a planter in the side yard," Logan said, holding it up. "It wasn't hidden well and was in clear sight. Is this Pax's?"

God, no! She immediately recognized the backpack. It was her hiking backpack that she kept in the garage. Logan slid open the zipper with a pencil and Faith felt sick.

Inside were two neon blue laser guns with coordinating helmets and vests. "I don't understand. He must have borrowed them from a friend."

"I'm pretty sure we'll find they match the empty box discarded in town," Logan said, and Faith covered her mouth.

"Maybe he bought them. He's been mowing lawns all summer and fall and doing odd jobs for our neighbors." She looked at Noah. "Tell him Pax isn't like that."

Noah ran a hand over his face. "Angel, those are worth at least three hundred."

"Plus, there's another two hundred and change in the

front pocket," Logan added, and Faith sagged against the doorframe.

Where on earth would Pax get two hundred dollars?

"It all totals somewhere close to a grand," Logan finished.

"I don't know how this all got here, but there has to be a logical answer." Afraid she'd pass out, Faith placed a hand to her forehead and concentrated on slowing her breathing.

"Angel." Noah reached for her and instinctively she recoiled.

She held up a hand. "I need to know if you are here for me or to help Logan?"

Noah met her gaze, strong and steady, and a small flare of hope flickered in her chest.

"Of course I'm here for you," he said, and she nearly wept. "When Logan told me what was going on, I made him promise to call me before he issued a warrant so I could be here when he arrived."

She staggered back a step, as if her heart knew it needed space for her brain to process what he'd just said. But no matter how many different ways she came at the situation, it always ended with the same gut-wrenching conclusion. "You knew they were looking into my brother and didn't call to warn me so I could, I don't know, make sure Pax was prepared for cops to storm his house?"

"Logan called me as a courtesy," he said. "It's not my case, Faith."

Something sharp and painful tore through her chest, piercing her heart. "I'm glad someone was afforded the courtesy. And I'm glad this isn't your case, because it uncomplicates matters." She walked to the door, which was still wide open, and said, "I've been warned. You can leave now, Noah."

"Let me help." He walked over and offered her his hand. She crossed her arms so she wouldn't be tempted to take it. "I know how these things work. If Pax simply explains what happened and returns everything, I'm sure he'll get off with a warning."

Noah looked at Logan, who mumbled something about an agreement, but Faith was too busy trying to keep her heart from breaking in two to focus on the exact words. "You knew about this hours ago and decided to wait for Logan to tell me?"

"It was his call. Logan wanted—"

"Stop." She shoved at him. Logan stepped forward but Noah signaled for him to give them some space. "Oh, you don't need to step outside, Sheriff. We're done." She looked back at Noah, not bothering to hide her devastation—or anger. "I don't need to hear anymore. You answered my question." Her voice caught and she pressed a hand to her stomach. "I can't do this."

"Do what?"

"This. Us." The last word came out on a half sob. "Get out."

"Are you kidding me?" he asked, sounding as if he were the injured party. "I came here to help you."

"I don't need saving."

"Faith?" a small voice called out from behind her. "What's going on?"

Noah's breathing stopped and Logan let out a long-suffering sigh. Closing her eyes for a moment, because she would not lose it in front of Pax. He needed her strong. She cleared her throat, then turned around with a confident smile.

"Hey, buddy. Sorry we woke you." She took in his sleep-heavy eyes and the sheet print on his cheek and resolved that nothing would harm her brother. If this was going to happen, she'd make it as easy as possible. And that meant being his shield. "I have something to ask you. Sheriff Miller's here because some toys and money were taken from the community center. Do you know anything about that?"

He yawned and shook his head. "No."

Faith took the red backpack from the sheriff and Pax's gaze immediately dropped. "Did you take these from the storage room?"

"No," Pax said, the shock on his face genuine. Relief rushed through her until her legs felt as if they were about to give. She walked to the couch and sat, patting the cushion next to her. The two men followed but remained standing.

"Pax, this is serious," she began. "Our family only works on trust, you know that. So I need you to look me in the eye and tell me the truth, knowing that no matter what you say, I've got you. You understand, we're in this together."

"I didn't steal anything," he said, and she believed him.

Faith wasn't being naive. She knew that kids lied to their parents all the time, including Pax. But he'd never lie over something like this. They were more than family. They were all each other had. Pax knew how hard she'd fought to keep them together and he'd never do anything to risk their being torn apart.

"Where did you get the money?" Sheriff Logan asked.

"I earned it," Pax said, using a tone that was a little big for his britches.

"You will answer the sheriff with respect, even if he isn't affording us the same courtesy."

Pax looked the sheriff in the eye. "I can't say, sir."

Logan blinked "Can't or won't?"

Noah got down on his haunches in front of Pax. "Look, buddy, this isn't the time to hold back. If you can explain how you rightfully came by this money and the toys, now's the time to tell."

Pax's face folded with confusion. "Me telling you I didn't isn't enough?"

"I'm afraid not."

Pax looked over at Faith, worrying his lip. "So the only way you leave my house and I'm not in trouble is for me to get someone else in trouble?"

And wasn't that the worst part. That Pax was discovering precisely how backward the legal system was, and he hadn't even reached high school.

"Did this someone else steal the money and toys?" Noah asked.

Pax shook his head.

Faith watched the man who'd promised her he'd never hurt her exploit his relationship with her brother to question him.

Not going to happen.

Faith stood and put her hand on Pax's shoulder. "Why don't you take Sheriff Miller to your room and let him look around? But don't answer any questions unless I'm there."

"I know the law," Logan informed her.

"So do I, Sheriff."

She waited until they left the room, then met Noah's gaze, hers pleading for him to be the man he'd promised to be by the creek. "If he's saying he didn't do it, then can you trust me when I promise that he didn't do it?"

"I know this is hard."

"Hard? You have no idea what this is for me."

"I can imagine, and it's tearing me up inside," he said,

and there was so much compassion and concern in his tone, she prayed that what he'd said before had been a mistake. A momentary misfiring, and the Noah she'd fallen for was back. "And I know you want to believe him, believe that he'd never lie to you, but in my experience—"

"He's my family and I want him to know that his well-being is all that matters to me. I want him to know that family doesn't assume guilt and apologize later. I want him to know that when you love someone, they believe in you and let the facts reveal themselves."

"Life doesn't always work that way," he said sadly.

"Maybe not, but love does."

"I've seen people's lives ripped apart by blindly loving. In my experience anyone will lie under the right pressure."

Wow. The hits kept coming.

This hit, though, this was the one that was going to take her down—later, after Pax was okay and this mess was sorted out. The unexpected impact would shatter so many things inside her.

"That's where you're wrong, Noah. Because I would never lie to you. But clearly you lied to me, because if you cared about me the way you said the other night, you would have come straight here when you found out what was going on. You would have walked in here protecting me instead of trying to sweet-talk Pax into confessing to something he didn't do."

"What if he did?"

"Then that's for Logan to deal with. We should have been your main concern."

"Faith, we're talking about some stolen toys and a few hundred bucks. When adults ask kids hard questions, sometimes they lie. Especially to adults they don't want to disappoint. And, angel, you *are* my main concern."

Her heart gave up hoping, because his meaning came across loud and clear and was currently ricocheting around her empty chest cavity. Even if he hadn't yet realized what he'd said. She had.

And when people tell you who they are, Faith thought it smart to listen.

"I made it clear from the beginning, Pax and I are a package deal," she said, her voice shaking with heartache. "You're no different from every guy I've ever dated."

His face went completely blank, giving away nothing. "Are you seriously going to lump me in with those jerks from the past?"

"If it walks like a stocking stuffer and talks like a stocking stuffer . . ." She held open the front door. "Now get out of my house."

Chapter Twelve

There weren't many times Noah read a situation wrong. He was fluent in body language, subtext, and all things female. And when those skills failed, he always had his instincts to steer him right. But it didn't take an Ivy League education to realize he'd missed the mark. By a mile.

No matter how many times he replayed the events of that morning in his head, he came no closer to pinpointing the precise moment things had gone off the rails. He'd promised to never let her down, which was why he'd gone there in the first place—to make things easier on her. In the end, he'd only managed to break her heart.

Noah couldn't have screwed things up more if he'd set out to make Faith hate him.

Believing in people hadn't worked out so well for him in the past. But Faith wasn't people, she was his person, and he should have believed in her. He was so busy trying to remind everyone where the line of right and wrong lay, he'd overlooked the most important thing.

Love and trust were earned. Yet she'd taken a chance on him and he'd reconfirmed every fear she'd had about letting him into her world.

Noah had blown it in a way that only a Tucker could.

And that hurt worse than the unwelcome ache in his chest. He didn't stand a snowflake's chance in Austin of fixing things with her, but there was no way he was going to let her face this alone.

Hopping out of his SUV, he walked toward her front porch, regret growing with every step he took. Taking off his hat, he knocked.

"She isn't home," Pax said, and Noah turned to find him sitting on the porch rail, his eyes red-rimmed. "She's dropping her cookies off at the bake sale."

"Do you know when she'll be back?"

Pax shrugged. "Why? You here to arrest me?"

The enormity of his actions hit him like a bull busting out the gates. Noah had never felt so low. "Actually, I'm here to apologize."

"For what?"

Noah rested a hip against the railing. "Walking in here with my mind made up. That's not how friends treat each other. Friends trust one another and I blew that. So I'm hoping you'll give me another chance."

Pax studied him. "Do you think I did it?"

"Nope," he said, and meant it. "I'm giving you the benefit of the doubt, like I should have from the start. If you say you didn't steal that stuff, then I believe you."

Pax let out a breath. "Good, cuz I didn't do it."

"But you know who did?"

"You asking as a cop or my sister's boyfriend?"

Noah laughed. "I doubt your sister would take warmly to me being called her boyfriend right now. I'm asking as your friend."

Pax studied him for a long moment, most likely trying to figure out if Noah's word was any good. He couldn't fault the kid. Noah hadn't acted all that trustworthy.

"Faith's making me work off my community hours, so I started helping Mr. Wilkins move trees around his lot," Pax began. "It was supposed to be for free, you know, as part of my punishment, but Mr. Wilkins said, 'A day's work means a day's pay, and as long as it's between us men, no one will be the wiser.'"

"You weren't supposed to be getting paid and he wasn't supposed to be hiring kids too young to get a work permit?" Noah guessed because he'd once been one of those kids working for under the table pay for folks around town.

He nodded. "Faith is always going on about how we have to do things the right way on account of our dads. So I was going to tell him no, but a guy in my class offered to sell me his laser gun set for cheap. It was almost brand-new, but he said he got two sets for Christmas," he explained. "Even though I knew Faith would freak because she hates guns, I told Mr. Wilkins yes. Yesterday, I gave Decalin the money for the laser guns, but I had to swear not to tell anyone where I got them because his parents didn't know he'd sold them."

"Does this Decalin have a last name?"

"Beaumont."

Interesting. According to Logan, the witness who'd ID'd Pax was a Beaumont.

"If I promise Mr. Wilkins won't get in trouble, would you mind my going down and having a talk with him?"

"You going to tell Faith about me working for money?"

Noah ruffled the kid's hair. "No, buddy, you are."

Sweet's Holiday Shindig was in full swing and Ester had yet to show, which left Faith working the booth alone. She was dressed in a red sweater with a green snowcap, doing her best to exude holiday joy, which was difficult when inside she felt like crying.

She'd hoped today would be a game changer for her family, and it had been. Just not in the way she had envisioned. In the season of hope and joy, Faith was short on both.

Seated at the booth to her right was Gina, head of Faith's legal counsel, who worked for ginger bear cookies, lecturing her on different codes and laws. On her left was Shelby, emotional support friend and advocate for love trumps all.

"Never let a man get the best of you," Gina said. "Once they know they have you vulnerable, it's game over. Guys suck that way."

"Not all guys," Shelby argued.

"You're right," Gina said. "Just the testosterone toting, alpha-egomaniacs. You need a sweet man, who's also good in bed and isn't afraid to tap into his emotions for you."

"Noah was pretty open about his feelings," Faith said.

"Look, if you want encouraging, ask her." Gina pointed to Shelby. "I tell it to you straight."

She was right. Faith didn't need help remembering all the wonderful things about Noah. She had a mental spreadsheet already exceeding Santa's Naughty and Nice list. What she needed was someone to remind her why ending things was best for everyone.

Shelby scooched closer to Faith. "Can I ask you something?"

"If I said no, would you still ask?"

"Yes."

"Then who am I to stop you?"

"I'm not making excuses for Noah's boneheaded move because, good intentions aside, his execution had Tucker written all over it. Believe me when I say, I get it. I live with the most stubborn of the brothers." Shelby gentled her voice. "But are you really upset over him barging in like a Ranger instead of your boyfriend? Or was it that you'd started to feel something and it scared you, so you used the situation to push him away?"

"I didn't push him away." She sounded a little more defensive than intended. "I told him to go." Which he had, right out the front door and out of her life.

"Did you want him to go?"

"Yes," she said as her head shook in betrayal. "No. I don't know, maybe. He's leaving in a week anyway, so maybe it's better this way, before I become too invested."

What was she talking about? She was already so invested her heart felt as if it was pieced together by twice-used Scotch tape, ready to fall apart at the slightest breeze.

Her friends gave her identical looks of disbelief.

"You know we'll support you, no matter what," Shelby said. "But take it from someone who almost lost the best two things in her life. Relationships that really matter take work. I was so afraid of getting hurt or hurting the people I loved, I thought it would be easier to walk away. It wasn't."

"My whole life, I've been the one to put in the work," Faith said, forbidding the tears to fall. "With my dad, my mom, and even though I love him to pieces, with Pax. For once, I want to feel what it's like to have someone work for me. To know they think I'm worth the effort."

"Sweetie," Shelby said. "You are such a treasure. I don't know how I would have survived these past few years without you."

In a rare sign of emotion, Gina slipped her arm around Faith's shoulder. "You know that we love you, right?" The three of them did a group hug that had Faith sniffling. "Who needs men when you've got girlfriends like us?"

"I do," Shelby said. "But you guys are pretty great, too."

They laughed and Faith breathed in the sweet scent of gingerbread and friendship. Noah had been right about one thing. Faith wasn't alone. She'd made a family of her own. People who loved her as she was, and always had her back.

"I heard someone here hasn't had their hot cocoa yet."

Faith looked up to find Noah standing at her booth, with two steaming cups in hand and a heavy expression. Her heart pounded against her rib cage, as if it was trying to escape. Which was exactly what Faith considered doing. She started to stand, and a steady hand came down on either shoulder, holding her in place.

"You're worth it," Shelby whispered, not letting Faith get up. "But you'll never know if you run."

"I'm not above chasing," Noah said quietly.

Faith took in his long legs and knew he could easily outpace her. "It doesn't really seem like a hot cocoa–appropriate day."

"That's on me." He set the paper cups down and took off his hat. "And something I'd sure like to fix. Because if you allow me the chance, I'll make sure every day is a hot cocoa–appropriate day for you."

Faith was having a hard time seeing through the growing moisture. "You won't be here every day."

"No, probably not," he admitted. "But I'm thinking of putting in for a transfer."

"To Sweet?"

"Yeah I'm hoping to spend more time with this amazing woman I met. Actually, it was more of a reconnection and I told her I wanted to court her, then acted like a jerk.

Making her feel as if I didn't trust her. Treated her feelings like an afterthought when she's my every thought."

Gina gave him a hard look. "Big words for a man who should wear a Bah Humbug shirt to alert people that his superpower is ruining Christmas."

"Gina," Faith scolded.

"She's right," Noah said. "I should have believed you when you said Pax was innocent. Because he is."

Faith gasped. "What do you mean?"

"Turns out the eyewitness was Decalin Beaumont. He knew how the toys disappeared because he got hold of his dad's key to the storage room at the community center and took them and the money. Then sold Pax his old laser gun set."

"Why didn't Pax say that? And where did he get the money in the backpack?" When she'd left Pax at home, it was with strict instructions not to leave the house until she returned. And when she did, they were going to have a serious come-to-Jesus meeting.

"I'll let Pax tell you the rest. Just know that he wasn't lying. Another person reluctantly came forward to confirm that Pax earned every penny of the money we found."

"Reluctantly? As in you brought him to the station?"

Noah neither confirmed nor denied it, but she knew he was the reason Pax's Christmas might still be saved.

"All this because someone made a false statement, fingering my brother?" Faith wondered how one person could cause so much devastation and harm. It hadn't even been more than a few hours since she'd opened her front door, and yet it felt as if a lifetime had passed. "Does Pax know his story has been corroborated?"

"No, ma'am, I came straight here to tell you."

"Thank you." Relief shot through her, leaving her weak.

"No, angel, thank you," he said gently. "When I walked into your house, my place was by your side, not behind the badge. See, I sometimes use my badge and job to keep people from getting too close. That's why I was so set on coming to the rescue. Only, you didn't need rescuing."

"I didn't?" Faith asked on a breath, because Noah was giving that intense stare of his, the one that always made her feel as if she were the only person in the world.

He shook his head and slowly made his way around the table, taking her hands to help her stand. "I should have come directly to your house and said, 'Angel, whatever happens, I've got you. Wherever you need me, I'm there. And whenever things get rough, I will never stop loving you.'"

Flutters by the thousands took flight in her chest. "What did you say?"

"I said I love you." There was a seriousness to his tone that had that little flame of hope growing warmer. "I've never done love before, and I'm sure I'm going to make mistakes, but I'm hoping that you can be patient with me. Help me get it right."

"You seem to be doing fine on your own," she said, tugging at the zipper of his coat.

A shadow of a grin appeared. "Is that right?" He moved closer. "Because another thing I should have done this morning was this."

Noah dipped down, placing a tender kiss on her lips. His arms went around her waist and she slid her hands up his chest to his shoulders. He was holding her so gently she wanted to cry. The next moment, it shifted from a simple kiss to a silent conversation about love and belonging. Because when he held her like that, Faith felt as if she'd found home.

Eventually, he pulled back and she took the moment to look up at him. "I'm pretty sure I'm in love with you, too, Noah Tucker."

"Pretty sure?" A challenging gleam lit his eyes. "Then I'd better do that again until you're damn sure." And, man of his word, he did.

"I love you," he whispered against her lips. "I came home believing love was a weapon, but then an angel fell into my lap, showing me how wrong I was."

"I guess I was wrong about something, too," she admitted. "You're not a stocking stuffer."

With a tender smile, his thumb skated along her jawline. "I guess I'm making headway."

She wrapped her arms tightly around him. "I blame it on the mistletoe."

Mistletoe Detour

KATE PEARCE

*Thanks to Maddy Barone for pet pig help,
and Jerri Drennen for reading the novella through for
me. I hope you all enjoy this little bit of holiday magic!*

Chapter One

When his cell rang, Ted jerked upright, and almost knocked his beer over as he leaned across to find his phone. It was late, it was snowing, and he'd settled in to watch a rerun of his favorite baseball team's memorable moments from last season. From the drool on his chin he might have been napping. . . .

Even as he swiped frantically at the chips on his chest, he answered the phone in a professional manner. His father and grandfather had instilled that in him from birth.

"Baker's. How may I help you?"

"Hey, Ted, it's Nate, your friendly neighborhood sheriff. I passed a broken-down vehicle on my way out of Morgantown, and stopped to tell the driver to expect a tow truck in the next fifteen minutes. Sorry to pass the buck, but I'm on my way to a multi-vehicle pileup near Bridgeport because some idiots don't know how to drive in ice and snow."

"It's not a problem, Nate. I'll go out there right now." Ted stood and a veritable shower of orange crumbs peppered the floor. "Where's the vehicle?"

"It's a small, white rental. Hazard lights are working fine. It's pulled over just before the entrance to Morgan Ranch. Should be easy to spot unless we get more snow."

"Okay, no problem," Ted said. "I'll get out there right now."

"Thanks, Ted. I'd prefer it if the car was taken off the road so no one can drive into the back of it. Let me know if you have any problems, okay?"

"Will do. Drive safe, Nate."

Ted ended the call and glanced guiltily at the collection of empty packets on his side table. Chips, peanuts, and a protein bar counted as dinner, right? With his father being away, he hadn't bothered to cook. There didn't seem much point when he lived right opposite a pizza parlor.

He set his untouched beer back in the refrigerator and put on his heaviest jacket and boots. Whenever he was called out, he always tried to start the car and get people moving before deciding to take it into the shop. At this time of year, that usually involved standing in the snow and ice while he froze his nuts off, so he'd learned to be prepared. As the sole mechanic, with the only garage and gas station in Morgan Valley, he was called out to all kinds of situations.

He went down the stairs into the garage below his apartment, and spent a few minutes making sure he had everything he needed stashed in his tow truck before opening the doors and heading out into the inky blackness. Once he got out of the town proper, and into the sparsely populated Morgan Valley, there weren't many streetlights.

Not that it worried him. He'd lived in Morgan Valley his whole life, and knew the roads like the back of his hand. It took him less than fifteen minutes to locate the broken-down vehicle. He carefully backed up on the side of the road behind it and set his hazard lights flashing.

As he approached, the driver's door flew open, and a woman scrambled out and rushed toward him.

"Oh, thank goodness! Nate said someone would be along, but I was beginning to wonder whether he'd forgotten about me, and worrying about ax murderers, and—" She paused for breath, and a huge smile broke out on her face. "Oh, it's you! Ted Baker! How cool is that!"

She pointed at her chest. "Veronica Hernandez. We went to school together, remember?"

Still reeling from the force and brilliance of her smile, Ted nodded like a dumbass. "Yeah, I mean, hey, what's up?"

She pointed at her car. "It's embarrassing, but I ran out of gas. I thought I had enough to get me to Uncle Victor's, but I obviously miscalculated, and now I'm stuck." She gazed hopefully up at him. "Can you give me a ride into town so I can call him to come get me?"

Ted cleared his throat. "Yeah, of course, but—"

She interrupted him. "Shall I get my stuff and put it in your truck?"

"Sure, but I'll need to hitch up the car and take it with us, okay?" He surveyed the narrow, unlit road. "It's not safe to leave it out here in this weather, and on this bend. It won't take long. Do you have the keys?"

She handed them over and followed him back to the car. "Are you sure it will be quick?"

"I can't see why not." Ted opened the trunk, took out her bags, and walked them over to his tow truck. "There's no damage so it should load up easily."

Ted returned to the car and paused by the open door, peering into the murky interior, which smelled odd. A weird snuffling noise made him back up a step.

Veronica eased past him. "Oh, my little darling, are you okay? I'm coming right now."

Ted retreated farther as she emerged with a bundle of blankets and held them tenderly to her chest. It was stupid the way his heart immediately plummeted to his boots. Of course she was married and had a family. She'd always been way out of his league, and he was an idiot to think otherwise.

But if that was her kid, it had one hell of a breathing problem. . . .

She tenderly drew the blanket away and stepped close to him.

"This is Bacon, my pet pig. Isn't he the sweetest thing ever?"

Veronica waited as Ted stared down at Bacon; his mouth was working, but no sounds came out. From what she could see in the flickering lights, he hadn't changed much since school. His brown hair and eyes were as cute as ever, he definitely needed a shave, and he'd filled out his gangly frame quite nicely.

"I thought"—he paused and looked directly at her— "that was your kid."

"Gosh, no!" She gave a snort of laughter, which sounded remarkably like one of Bacon's. "He is pretty special to me, though."

"So I can see." He stepped back. "Why don't you and . . . Bacon take a seat in my truck while I get this car loaded up? There's a flask of coffee in there if you need it."

True to his word, it didn't take long for them to be heading toward Morgantown. As they drove down the deserted main street, Veronica gazed eagerly at the town she'd called home for the first eighteen years of her life.

"It looks good." She half turned to Ted who hadn't said much since they'd gotten under way. "I was worried it might have gone downhill like a lot of small towns."

"Is this the first time you've been back?" Ted asked as he drove the tow truck into a vast garage, which easily swallowed her car as well. He closed the doors, leaving them in relative silence.

Her smile dimmed. "Yeah, not that I haven't wanted to come back, but things got . . . complicated."

"I know how that goes." He grimaced. "I didn't think I'd still be here when I was pushing thirty. I thought I'd be living in a big city doing something with the motor sport industry."

Impulsively, she reached over and patted his denim-clad knee. "You could still do it. You're not that old."

"Thanks." His smile was wry as he turned off the engine and opened his door. "I feel about ninety some days."

He came around to her door and offered her his hand. "Don't want to wake the pig."

She let him help her down, her hand firmly grasping the front of his open jacket, her face momentarily buried against his chest. He smelled like motor oil, leather, and coffee, which was surprisingly comforting.

"Thanks for this." She followed him to the far corner where there was a door. "How much do I owe you?"

He unlocked the door and went up a flight of stairs into a large open-plan apartment that faced right down onto Main Street. The town was festooned with Christmas lights and looked like something out of a history book, with its raised walkways and false-fronted buildings. Ted took off his baseball cap and heavy jacket, and stepped out of his boots before turning back to her.

"No charge." His swift smile was disarmingly sweet. "Consider it a welcome-home gift."

"That's really nice of you." Veronica answered his smile with one of her own. But Ted was nice, he always had been, and it seemed nothing had changed. "Now where can I put the pig?"

He gestured at one of the doors. "How about my dad's bathroom? It's got a tiled floor."

Veronica bit her lip. "Won't he mind?"

"He's not here. He's gone on a Christmas cruise to the Hawaiian Islands." Ted went down the hallway and opened the door. "If he sends me one more picture of him drinking mai tais and basking in the sun I'll send him one of the pig."

Veronica studied the pristine tiled space. "I think this would do nicely." She gently placed Bacon on the floor still wrapped in his blankie, but he didn't stir. "I've got his food and the rest of his stuff in my luggage."

"I'll go and get that for you."

Ted was already halfway out the door before she could offer to get it herself. Considering how badly she'd disrupted his evening, he was being very kind.

After using the facilities and making sure the bathroom door was firmly closed, she wandered back down the hallway to the kitchen and family room. Although the space looked relatively new, there was very little furniture in it. If Ted and his father were the only people living there, maybe they didn't care about décor.

There was a small kitchen table with two chairs, a black leather couch, a huge TV, and an ancient recliner that desperately needed recovering. There were blinds, but no drapes, cushions, or photographs.

Ted came back with her bags and stacked them behind the couch.

"Here you go."

"Thanks." Veronica turned a slow circle. "Did you guys just move in?"

"We've been here about two years. Why?" He went into the kitchen and started making coffee.

"No reason," she said, trying not to make eye contact.

He grinned at her. "It's okay. My sister, Beth, thinks we look like squatters, too." He held up the coffeepot. "Would you like some?"

"Yes, please." She leaned against the countertop that separated the two spaces and watched him move efficiently around the kitchen. "It's been a very long day."

"Where did you drive from?" Ted asked as he scooped coffee into the filter paper.

"L.A."

"Today?"

"It's taken me a lot longer than that." She tried to relax her shoulders. "You wouldn't believe how many hotels wouldn't let me bring Bacon in with me."

"I think I would."

"And I was trying to avoid the freeways because who knew that pigs get carsick?"

"Not me." Ted opened the fridge. "Do you take cream in your coffee?"

"Yes, please." She turned back to her bags. "I'll just get Bacon settled in, and I'll be right back."

* * *

Ted fussed around with the coffee and wondered whether he should offer Veronica something to eat. Not that he had much to tempt her with, but Beth had left some meals in the freezer, and he was perfectly capable of reading a set of cooking instructions. Luckily, Beth was an excellent cook and even her frozen food turned out great.

Having Veronica in his apartment made Ted painfully aware of how he and his dad were still living out of boxes like two people who weren't sure they were really home. When he'd rebuilt the mechanics shop and gas station, he hadn't intended to live in one of the apartments. One was for renting out, and the other was for his dad. But after everything that had happened with his father's health, he couldn't leave the old guy to fend for himself, so he'd moved in with him—just for a while.

Two years later, he was still here, and his dad had gone off on a cruise to Hawaii. . . .

"He's still sleeping." Veronica came back into the kitchen. "I left out some food and water just in case he wakes up."

She wore a thick, knitted blue sweater over jeans and her long, dark hair was pulled back into a ponytail. Her earrings were large gold hoops that swung as she talked and her lipstick was bright red. There was more color in her than in his entire apartment or life—and far more warmth.

She glanced over at the phone on the kitchen wall. "Is it okay if I call Victor? My cell phone battery died somewhere around Bridgeport."

Ted paused as he set out two mugs. "Is he expecting you?"

"No, but I don't think he'll mind. Do you?"

He caught the hint of uncertainty in her voice and

looked up. "Seeing as he's always talking about you, I doubt it, but . . . he's not there right now."

"He's out for the whole day?"

"Nope, he's gone for the next two weeks."

She went still. "But he's *always* there."

"Not this Christmas. He's gone on a cruise to the Hawaiian Islands with my dad."

She gulped. "*What*?"

"That's exactly what I said." Ted poured out the coffee and slid a mug across to her. "Apparently, they both had the same crazy idea and decided to go for it together."

He'd tried to be pleased that his dad felt well enough to travel, but he was worried about him. Victor had reassured him that he'd keep an eye on his old friend, and yet it still hadn't felt right.

"Is there anyone out there at the ranch?" Veronica asked, breaking into his thoughts.

"No one's living there while Vic's away, if that's what you mean." Ted hesitated. "If you're contemplating heading out that way, I don't think your rental would make it through the snowdrifts. I wouldn't recommend you trying to go out there without four-wheel drive." Ted took a sip of his coffee. "I know your uncle asked the Garcia family to deal with any produce or stock issues. It's the end of his growing season, so he doesn't have a lot left in the ground."

Vic ran a small organic farm that provided produce and free-range eggs to many of the local towns, businesses, and farmers' markets. He also kept a few horses, which meant that Ted and his father got to keep up their riding skills so they could cowboy up and help out on the ranches during branding and herding operations.

Veronica stared down at her coffee as if it held the key to the universe.

"Is the Hayes Hotel still open?"

"Yeah, but it's full to bursting right now seeing as Ry Morgan is getting married to Avery Hayes this weekend, and the wedding is being held there."

"Oh." She frowned. "Is there another hotel nearby?"

"You'd have to go back to Bridgeport, and I'm not sure they'd take a pig," Ted said tactfully.

She swallowed hard and worried at her lip.

"You okay?" Ted asked. He sure was out of practice dealing with other people's feelings.

"Not really." Veronica slowly raised her head, and to his horror there were tears in her eyes. "I was kind of hoping . . . I mean I was *depending* on Victor being there so I could stay with him." A tear rolled down her cheek. "I don't know what to do."

Ted stared at her in fascination as another perfect tear followed the first, and then another.

"You could stay here with me," he blurted out.

She gazed at him for a long moment. "What?"

"Until Victor gets back," Ted hastened to explain. "It will only be a couple of weeks, and then you can talk to him and sort things out."

"But I'd be taking advantage of you."

"How?" Ted shrugged. "I'm here all by myself. We could keep each other company over the holidays while our relatives float around the Pacific without a care in the world."

"What about Bacon?"

"What about him?" Ted raised an eyebrow. "As long as he doesn't get out and crap all over my apartment I'm good with him being here, too."

Veronica grabbed his hand and held it fast. "You are so *kind*, I can't—"

He returned the pressure of her grip. "Yeah, you can. In fact, you'd be doing me a favor."

"Won't your girlfriend mind me being here with you?"

"I don't have a girlfriend." Ted held her gaze. "And even if I did, how could she object to me helping out an old friend? You can sleep in Dad's room and use his bathroom so you won't even have to see much of me if you don't want to."

"Thank you." She brought his hand to her lips and kissed his knuckles. "Are you sure?"

"Absolutely. Stay here, and let's make this a Christmas to remember."

Chapter Two

After she'd unpacked, checked on Bacon, and taken a quick shower, Veronica went back into the family room and found Ted with his head in the refrigerator. He was muttering something, so she waited politely until he straightened up and slammed the door.

Even though she felt a little guilty, it was no hardship looking at his rather fine Wrangler-covered ass as he bent forward, or the dip of his spine where his T-shirt had ridden up. He was a big, strong, solid guy, and she was so grateful she'd found him again. His offer to give her a roof over her head until her uncle returned was a lifesaver. No one would think to look for her here, or ever make a connection between her and Ted.

After her panicked exit from L.A., she needed time to think, and make a new plan. What better place to do that than here in her sleepy hometown, which would soon be cut off from civilization by snowstorms, mile-high drifts, and closed mountain passes? As a kid, she'd hated that isolation, but now it might be crucial to her and Bacon's survival.

"I don't have a lot of food in." Ted grimaced. "I wasn't expecting company." He rubbed at an orange spot on his

T-shirt that looked suspiciously like powdered cheese. "We could order pizza in, or I can check out the meals Beth left in the freezer?"

"There's pizza in Morgantown?" Veronica advanced toward him. "Since when?"

"About a year ago." He touched her shoulder, pivoting her toward the windows where she could just see a neon sign opposite. "It's real close."

"Perfect." She checked her pocket for her credit card. "And it's on me, okay?"

"Sure. Do you want to order off the menu? I'll call it in, and then I can walk over and pick it up." He handed her a well-folded piece of paper splattered with tomato. "I usually get the deep crust, the works one, but I have a feeling you might not eat pork."

Veronica shuddered. "I just can't do it anymore," she confessed. "When I look at his sweet little face . . ." She perused the menu and handed it back to Ted. "I'd like a small pineapple and cheese thin-crust pizza and a side salad."

"Pineapple on pizza?" His revolted expression made her want to smile. "Gross."

"All the more for me, then."

He phoned in the order and looked over at her. "Fifteen minutes."

"Great. Plenty of time to set the table."

Even as she spoke, he was dumping paper plates and napkins onto the countertop. He obviously wasn't a great one for formal dining.

"Beer?" he asked.

She finished her coffee, considered how her day had gone, and nodded. "Thanks."

He clinked his bottle against hers and took a long swallow. "Can I ask you something?"

Veronica immediately tensed. "Sure."

"Why did you name your pig Bacon?"

"I didn't."

He studied her carefully. "Okay."

"My ex called him Bacon, as a joke, and it kind of stuck." Her mouth twisted.

"You don't look like you found that joke particularly funny." Ted was watching her face.

"I didn't, but that's one of the many reasons why that man is now my ex-husband."

"You're divorced?"

"Two years ago." She managed a smile. "Best two years of my life since I left home at eighteen—hardest two years of my life, as well, but I don't regret anything."

"My sister, Beth, says the same thing. She came home a few years ago. I don't think she regrets it." He fiddled around with the napkins.

"Beth and I were always the smart ones." Veronica said.

His slow smile made everything inside her go still for a moment before she continued talking.

"I got married too young, and left college to be with Jason. Within a couple of years, I knew I'd made a mistake, but I was too proud to admit it, and too stubborn to come home and ask for help from my family."

"That's why you didn't come back?" Ted asked.

"Yes, because if I had, they would've known something was wrong, and tried to help me. At the time, I didn't think I had any choice but to hang in there, put my head down, and make things work."

"You really should talk to Beth," Ted said as he went to wash his hands. "Her ex beat the shit out of her. She didn't tell us because she was afraid one of us would go after the bastard, kill him, and end up in jail."

Veronica's hand flew to her mouth. "Poor Beth."

"She left when he started in on their son."

Ted's normally good-humored expression had disappeared, revealing the strength of the man beneath—a man who valued his family, and wouldn't put up with anyone hurting someone he loved. He'd been like that in school, defending his sister and her friends from any guy who tried something. He'd even defended Veronica, and she'd never forgotten it.

His cell buzzed, and he took it out of his pocket to check the message.

"Pizza's ready."

She went toward the hall door. "Then let's go and get it."

Despite the fact that they hadn't seen each other for ten years, walking across the street beside Veronica felt like the most natural thing in the world. Her being in his apartment also felt right—as if she'd brought something with her that lit up his life. She'd always been the most positive person he'd known, and, despite her jerk of an ex, she'd obviously retained that quality.

He held the door of the pizza place open and followed her inside. The rich smell of bubbling cheese, garlic, and roasted tomatoes hit him square in the face and he breathed it in like oxygen. In his opinion, pizza made everything better.

"Hey!" His nephew grinned at him. "Back again? You should take shares in this place."

Ted pretended to frown at his favorite relative. "Don't tell your mother, okay?"

"I'll think about it if you give me a decent tip," Mikey replied, his amused gaze falling on Veronica who was openly laughing up at Ted.

"This is Veronica. She's staying with me over the holidays." Ted pointed at his nephew. "This is Beth's son, Mikey. He's a pain in the ass, but I still love him."

"I can tell." Veronica smiled at Mikey. "It's good to meet you."

Mikey nodded, his eyes wide as saucers. Any second now Ted figured he'd be getting a call from his sister about the strange woman in his life and why hadn't he told her?

"Did you guys meet online?" Mikey asked totally innocently as Veronica handed him her credit card.

"Nope, we went to kindergarten together. I grew up on the Hernandez farm."

"Victor's place? We get a lot of our pizza ingredients from him. Gina says his tomatoes are the best." Mikey eyed Ted speculatively. "Well, I can tell you that my uncle's a good guy, and that my mom says he needs to stop being so boring, get out there, and live a little."

"Thanks for the rec, Mikey." Ted raised his eyebrows. "Maybe you could check on that pizza?"

He braced himself as Mikey went to the back of the store, and Veronica looked up at him, a smile dancing on her lips.

"You need to get out more?"

"Apparently." Ted tried to keep his cool. "But please don't listen to my nephew. He's hardly an unbiased source."

"He's charming," Veronica added as she signed the receipt and placed it back on the counter. "Must run in the family."

Luckily for Ted, who was definitely starting to blush,

the door behind him opened and he turned in relief to greet whoever was coming in.

"Hey." Tucker Hayes, who was the general manager of his family's historic hotel and Ted's best friend, nodded at him. "You ready for the big day? I was just going to knock on your door so you saved me a trip. Avery said to come by and pick up your shirt tomorrow."

His interested gaze went past Ted and focused on his companion.

"Veronica, right? Vic's niece."

"Wow, you have a good memory." Veronica stepped forward and shook Tucker's proffered hand.

"It helps in my business." Tucker shrugged modestly. "Are you here for the holidays?"

"Yes, I was supposed to be staying with my uncle, but he's gone off on a cruise, so I'm staying with Ted." She smiled at him. "I hear Avery's getting married?"

"Yeah, to Ry Morgan. They've been engaged for ages. Avery wanted to get through her last set of surgeries, and make sure she felt one hundred percent before she walked down the aisle."

"I remember her barrel-racing accident," Veronica said softly. "I also remember how sweet Ry Morgan was on her at school. I'm not surprised they've fallen in love."

"You should pop by with Ted tomorrow and say hi. She'd love to see you," Tucker said.

She looked hopefully at Ted and he nodded. "We'll walk over after breakfast."

As they left with the pizza, Ted realized how nice it was not having to explain everything and everyone in Morgan Valley to his companion. She knew all his friends and most of his family. And they all had a sense of her because she was already part of their community.

"Everyone's being so nice," Veronica said as if aware of the direction of his thoughts. "I feel like I've never been away." She sighed, her breath frosting in the frigid air. "I wish I'd come back sooner. Jason, my ex, wouldn't let me go anywhere without him. If I'd brought him here, my family would've seen what a miserable excuse for a human being he was, and defended me."

Ted tucked her hand in the crook of his elbow as they crossed the street, the snow crunching beneath their booted feet.

"Was he afraid you wouldn't come back if you went alone?" Ted reached the side door and took off his glove to find the key in his pocket.

"I'm not sure I would've gone back." Veronica followed him inside, wiped her feet on the mat, and took off her knitted hat. "But he didn't let me have any money or access to the bank account so I couldn't go far without him."

"That's . . ." Ted tried to think of something that wouldn't come out as a curse and failed miserably. "Awful."

"Yes, it was." She unbuttoned her coat and followed him up the stairs, her cheeks red with cold. "He told me his first wife left him for another man, and that he was just being extra careful with me. It didn't matter how many times I told him I'd never do that, he'd made up his mind." A wry smile tugged at her lips. "The funny thing is, that in the end, it turned out he was the one who was having an affair, not me."

"Wow, what a piece of shit." Ted was done trying to be polite.

"She turned up at our house one day, and told me to set him free so that she could love him properly." Veronica hung her coat on the hook. "She was so young, and so deadly earnest that it was really hard not to laugh in her face."

"What did you do?" Ted asked.

"I started making the plans I should've made years before. I set up my own bank account, made sure my employer started sending my checks to it, and went out to find an apartment of my own." She grimaced. "It was hard because I didn't have much of a credit history, but my employer stood by me, and I lucked out with a rent-controlled apartment in a decent neighborhood close to work."

She walked into the kitchen, her head held high. "I retained a divorce lawyer, moved out, and served Jason the papers before he even knew what hit him."

"Good for you," Ted said, his admiration increasing with every second. He got two more beers out of the refrigerator. "It sounds like you made the right decision."

Jeez, Ted knew it wasn't his fight, and that Veronica didn't need his help, but he wished he could meet her ex in a dark alley and explain a few things to him. . . .

"His new girlfriend, Marissa, moved in with him two days after I left." Veronica searched the drawers for the pizza cutter and brought it over to the counter where Ted had placed the boxes. "She kind of reminded me of myself when I first met him and was so dazzled by his charm that I wouldn't have believed anything bad about him."

"She'll probably work it out eventually." Ted passed Veronica a paper plate. "Or, when he meets wife number four."

"Who will be even younger than Marissa if he stays true to form." Her smile was sad. "I wasted ten years of my life on that jerk, so in a weird way she did me a favor by turning up on my doorstep."

"Well, I'm glad you're rid of him." Ted held her gaze. "He didn't deserve you."

"Totally agree." She picked up her beer and clinked it

against his. "Now, what about you? Why aren't you married and settled down?"

Fifteen minutes later, after Ted had done everything possible to avoid answering her original question, Veronica finally had him cornered and sitting opposite her at the table.

"So why aren't you in a relationship?"

He blew out a breath and slowly shook his head. "You don't give up, do you?"

"Nope. You're a good-looking guy, you run a successful family business, and from what I can tell, you're not afraid of talking to women. So what is it?"

"I live in an apartment with my dad."

"So you can't bring anyone back here?" Veronica frowned. "Don't the women in Morgan Valley have their own homes?"

"Of course they do." He looked down at his pizza and started on another slice. "I just haven't met anyone who's made me want to get serious with them, and in a small town, if I mess up, I still get to see them every day and that could get awkward."

"You have dated though, right?"

His head came up. "I'm not a complete loser."

"I didn't think you were—in fact I'm surprised you haven't been inundated." She chewed thoughtfully for a moment. "I seem to remember you were like that at school, totally oblivious to any hints us girls put out to you."

"Oh, I noticed." He took a swig of beer. "Hard not to when you come back to your truck after a football game and there are two half-naked cheerleaders in your back seat."

Veronica's mouth fell open. "Who was it?"

"The Hardcastle twins. They always did everything together."

She leaned forward. "Did you—"

"Dude, no!" He looked revolted. "I wasn't into that. I sent them HW Morgan's way." He set his pizza down. "Maybe I wasn't the only one who didn't get the hints."

Veronica wrinkled her nose. "How so?"

"Maybe the girl I wanted to look back at me only saw me as a friend."

"Who did you like?" Veronica asked. "Because if she's still in town, and I know her, maybe—"

He suddenly stood up, picked up his plate, and headed for the kitchen. "Do you want any more pizza? Or shall I put on some more coffee?"

She stared at the back of his head as her brain finally caught up with her mouth.

"Ted?"

"What?" He didn't turn around.

"Were you talking about me?"

"Might have been." He shrugged, still keeping his back to her. "But it was a long time ago."

Veronica picked up her plate and joined him in the kitchen. "It never occurred to me that—"

"Of course it didn't. You were one of the popular kids, and I was just one of the crowd. That's why I didn't say anything. You probably would've laughed at me."

Instinctively, she reached out and touched his back. "I wouldn't have laughed. You were always so kind to me."

"Kind, yeah, but not boyfriend material." He finally turned to look at her, and slowly grinned. "I bet you wish you hadn't started this conversation now. And for the record, I haven't spent the last ten years pining over you."

"I would hope not," Veronica rallied. "Because that would've been stupid, and you're not that kind of guy. And, considering the choices I *did* make when I was a teenager, you should probably be relieved you weren't my type."

He got down two mugs and leaned back against the countertop, his arms crossed, and a thoughtful look on his face.

"What?" Veronica asked.

"I didn't think I was going to stay in Morgantown. I never looked for a permanent relationship because I guess I didn't want anyone to tie me down here." He grimaced. "That's probably the closest to the truth I've ever come to admitting to anyone including myself."

"Then why did you stay?" Veronica held his gaze.

"All kinds of reasons." He smiled and turned back to the coffee. "Too many to bore you with right now. Do you want to get some cream out of the refrigerator for your coffee?"

Chapter Three

After taking Bacon out for a short morning stroll on his leash around the rear of the gas station, Veronica went back up to the apartment. She couldn't stop thinking about her conversation with Ted the night before. Why hadn't he left town, and why did she care that he seemed to have somehow given up? She hadn't seen him for ten years; she had no right to pry into his life. But, as her uncle Vic had always told her, sometimes a person appeared in your life for a reason, and maybe her purpose was to get Ted out of his rut.

She walked into a cloud of steam and the sound of whistling and almost dropped Bacon as Ted came out of his bathroom with just a towel around his hips and nothing else.

"Sorry." He took such a hasty step backward that he collided with the bathroom doorframe. "I forgot you were here."

"It's okay." Veronica waved away the steam, feeling as if she was in one of those dream sequences from a movie when a handsome hunk stepped out of the shower. "It's not like I've never seen a man's body before."

Feigning nonchalance, she walked past him and into

the second bathroom where she put Bacon on the floor and checked the mirror to make sure her tongue wasn't actually hanging out.

Jason was short and lean, and Ted . . . was definitely neither of those things. He had actual abs, and those line thingies that she could never remember the name of that angled diagonally down from his hip to his . . . groin.

Veronica fed her pig and then splashed water on her flushed face. The only reason she was reacting so *positively* to Ted's body was because she hadn't had sex with an actual person for three years. It was perfectly understandable and natural and nothing to worry about.

She went back into the kitchen and opened the refrigerator door, appreciating the wave of cold air.

"I thought we could get breakfast at Yvonne's, and then walk over to see Avery at the hotel. I'm one of Ry's groomsmen so I've got to look the part."

She turned as Ted came up behind her. He was now completely dressed in jeans, a T-shirt, and a thick flannel shirt. He'd also shaved, which was a pity in her opinion.

"Is that a new café?" She took her time closing the refrigerator door.

"It's been here a while. Yvonne did her culinary training in France so she's an amazing pastry and bread maker."

"Sounds awesome." She smiled brightly at him, mentally picturing those fine abs hidden by his shirt. "I'll just get my coat."

Ted glanced down at his companion as they walked along the street toward Yvonne's. He could already smell the coffee, but that wasn't the only reason he was feeling so upbeat and optimistic. There was something about Veronica that just made him wake up and appreciate life more. Sure, she asked him awkward questions, but she also didn't judge his answers, or make him feel guilty. He liked that, and she was definitely making him think.

The trouble was, the more he thought, the more ashamed he became of how he'd sat back and let life pass him by.

"Hey!" Yvonne approached the table as he and Veronica sat down. "I heard you had someone staying with you. I'm glad you brought her in."

Veronica held out her hand. "I'm Veronica Hernandez. I'm waiting for my uncle Victor to come home from his cruise because we got our dates mixed up. Ted very kindly let me stay with him."

"You're Victor's niece? He has the best local produce." Yvonne winked at Ted. "I do hope you're going to persuade Veronica to stick around and continue the family business."

Ted held up his hands. "Nothing to do with me."

Yvonne gave them both menus. "What can I get you to drink?"

By the time they'd refilled their coffee twice and eaten their food, Ted reckoned that half the town had come by their table to say hi or just ogle his guest. Who would've thought him bringing a woman into the café would've caused such a stir? Was he really such a loner?

And Veronica had been great with everyone; her interest in their lives was not feigned, but completely genuine, and it showed. A number of people had given him a thumbs-up behind her back or an encouraging wink, which was totally embarrassing. They were all going to be disappointed when they realized he and Veronica were just friends. He stared at her as she finished her coffee.

Dammit, he was going to be disappointed if that's all they ever were.

"What's wrong?"

Ted started, as she looked him right in the eye.

"Nothing, I was just . . ." He wasn't stupid enough to share his revolutionary thought. She'd probably go running out the door and back to L.A. before he finished the sentence. "Thinking we should get a move on. I've got to take a shift at the gas pumps at lunchtime, so I'll need to get back."

"Sure!" She immediately pocketed her phone, and stood up to put on her jacket. "I can't wait to see Avery."

He helped her with her coat, and then put on his own before waving good-bye to Yvonne and heading back out onto Main Street. The snow had hardened into a firm crispness that made walking on it far easier than the night before. Veronica looped her arm through his and he slowed his pace to accommodate her shorter strides.

"It's so beautiful here." Veronica sighed as she looked around and then out at the towering black peaks of the Sierra Nevada. "It makes you forget that you're soon going to be cut off from civilization, and praying every night that the power stays on."

"I hear you." Ted chuckled. "I've got my own generator, if that makes you feel any better. And I kind of like it— the isolation and the quietness that descends when the gold country tourists can't get to us. It's like we've stepped back in time."

"And the hotel is a saloon and the sheriff is gathering a posse to go after some bandits?" Veronica grinned at him. "Who would've thought you could be so romantic?"

They reached the hotel, which was four stories high,

and much bigger than it looked behind its old, faux western façade. Ted had spent his childhood running in and out of the place so he had no hesitation in taking Veronica through the kitchens.

Keeping hold of Veronica's hand, he went up the steep backstairs and emerged two stories higher, slightly winded. The sound of laughter reached him from along the narrow corridor and he headed for the open door.

Avery Hayes stood in the middle of the room with a clipboard in one hand and a pen in the other. She was talking to January Morgan who had her small son, Chase William, with her.

"I don't want to throw flowers." The little boy stuck out his lip. "I want to ride my pony."

Ted paused in the doorway and kept quiet as he waited to see how the bride-to-be and her new sister-in-law handled the stubborn three-year-old.

"You know, I'd love it if you could do that." Avery sat down beside him and sighed like she really meant it. "But as it's winter, we're holding the wedding inside, and not out at the ranch. I don't think it would be fair on Muggs. He might get scared with all the noise and the people."

"I wouldn't let him be scared," Chase William insisted.

"I'm sorry, honey, but horses aren't allowed inside hotels," January added firmly. "Mr. Hayes said so. Wouldn't you just like to throw the flowers? I know you'd be really good at it." She paused. "Unless you'd prefer baby Elizabeth to do it?"

"She's too small!" Chase William protested.

"But she could do it if Daddy or I carried her, and then you could just sit in the row with Grandpa, and not have to do anything, or have anyone look at you, and think what a big, grown-up boy you are."

"Masterful," Veronica whispered in Ted's ear as a hundred different expressions crossed the little boy's face. "That's TC Morgan's wife?"

"Yup, January. She's awesome."

Chase William turned back to Avery who had been waiting patiently despite the fact that she must have a million things to organize.

"I'll do the flowers."

"That's so good of you," Avery said admiringly. "I can't think of anyone who could do a better job." She looked up at January who winked. "Then, that's settled. We'll see you here on Saturday at two."

As she stood, she glanced back at the door and spotted Ted.

"Hey! What's up? Tucker said you had a surprise for me." Her gaze slid past him to Veronica.

"Ronnie?"

"I guess I'm the surprise!" Veronica rushed forward to envelop Avery in a giant hug. "It is so good to see you again."

"Likewise." Avery turned to Ted. "I didn't realize you two were long-distance dating." She grabbed Veronica's hand. "You did come for the wedding, right? I guess that's why Ted didn't reply about his plus one because he wanted it to be a surprise."

"I—" Veronica looked uncertainly up at him, and he shrugged.

"If you have room for Veronica, I'd love to bring her," Ted said.

"Of course I do." Avery grinned at them both. "It will

make my wedding even better—if that's possible." She glanced back at January who was helping her son into his coat. "Is it okay if I bring Veronica out to the ranch this evening for my party?"

"Sure!" January straightened up, keeping a firm hand on the back of Chase William's collar. "The more the merrier. Now, I have to get back to feed Elizabeth, but is there anything you need me to take with me, or any messages I can relay?"

"I think I'm good."

"Then we'll see you tonight." January smiled at Ted and Veronica. "Have a great day."

Half an hour later, they were walking back to Ted's apartment, his new blue shirt and cowboy hat tucked securely under his arm. Veronica squeezed his sleeve.

"Are you really okay about me coming to the wedding with you?"

"I can't think of anything I'd like better." He unlocked the door and walked ahead of her up into the apartment.

"Because I feel a bit like you were put in an impossible position, and—oomph."

Veronica, who'd been looking down, concentrating on the steps, walked straight into Ted's chest as he turned around to talk to her. His arms closed around her, stopping her from falling backward, and she just stayed where she was, enjoying the heat of him and feeling far safer than she had in a long while. She knew somewhere deep in her soul that if Ted Baker gave you his trust and support, you were set for life.

But she'd have to tell him what she'd done, and the

thought of him recoiling from her made her attempt to gently push him away.

"Veronica?"

He took a step back, but still reached out a hand to cup her chin so that she had to look up at him.

"What?"

"I—" His smile was crooked. "I just have this crazy idea that I want to kiss you."

"Definitely crazy." She tried to smile.

"You wouldn't want that from me?"

She considered him carefully, the strong line of his jaw, his warm brown eyes and the mixture of confusion and desire behind his stare.

"What are we talking about here exactly?"

"I don't know. I haven't thought that far ahead." He sighed. "That's me all over, right? That's exactly why I'm stuck here pleading with the most beautiful woman I've ever met to feel sorry enough for me to kiss me."

"I don't feel sorry for you." Veronica moved past him into the apartment and took off her hat and coat. *He thought she was beautiful?* "I'm just trying to get my head around this whole thing." She slowly unwrapped her scarf, took a deep breath, and turned to face him. He surprised her by speaking first.

"I was thinking, that seeing as everyone wants us to be a couple, we could oblige them during the wedding."

He fixed his gaze on her and he looked so hopeful that she didn't know whether to laugh or cry.

"Or not, if you think that's a stupid idea," he added hastily. "I know you've only just got here. It's just that I'm having such a great time hanging out with you, that—"

Veronica held up one finger. She might sound confident, but after a year of crappy dates she wasn't sure of the right approach to take anymore. And as this might be her last Christmas of freedom, maybe she'd better go all out and enjoy it.

"I don't have any major objections to that idea."

"You don't?" Ted let out his breath. "That's . . . *awesome*."

"But I do have a few questions." Veronica went into the kitchen and started making coffee purely to have something to do with her hands as her thoughts skidded around like a car on ice.

"Sure." Ted followed her and leaned up against the countertop, arms folded over his chest. "You get to set the rules."

"I do?" After having a man running her life for ten years, Veronica couldn't even tell Ted how much that idea appealed to her.

"Yeah, like what's okay, and what's not okay for us to do together."

A few ideas sprang to life in her head involving him maybe being naked, and Veronica's cheeks heated. She hurried to get out two mugs and the creamer.

"Maybe we should play that bit by ear?"

"Fine by me." He nodded. "We could go with the idea that we've been dating online for a while, and that one of the reasons you came back for Christmas was to size me up in person."

"Sounds reasonable."

Ted's phone buzzed and he took it out of his pocket and made a face. "I've got to relieve Mano at the gas pumps for a couple of hours. Can I take my coffee to go?" He opened one of the cupboards and produced a metal flask. "You can stick mine in there."

"Don't you need some lunch?" Veronica called after

him as he went down the hallway to his bedroom to change into his work clothes.

"Still full from breakfast!" he shouted back at her. "I'll need to go grocery shopping at some point if we're not going to eat pizza every day."

As Veronica had been in the refrigerator, she knew he had a point. She poured the coffee, added sugar to hers, and waited for him to return to the kitchen, which he did in very short time.

He was wearing a dark blue coverall with the word *Baker's* embroidered on the pocket and thick work boots. She instinctively went over, stood on tiptoe, and flattened down his mussed-up hair. He caught her around the waist and held her still until she looked shyly up at him.

"May I kiss you?"

"Yes, please."

He slowly lowered his head, giving her all the time in the world to say no, and set his mouth over hers. As he angled his head, the subtle scrape of his stubble against her skin made her knees go weak and the polite kiss turned wild. Within seconds, she had her hands in his hair and was demanding more.

He only stepped back when his cell phone buzzed again, his lips slightly parted, which made her want to drag him right back and keep him there until they were naked and horizontal. Who'd have guessed that Ted Baker would be a phenomenal kisser?

"Gotta go." He cleared his throat and swallowed hard. "Spare key's by the door if you want to go out and explore."

"Okay." She turned to hand him his coffee. "See you in a couple of hours."

After he'd left, she remained in the kitchen, her gaze fixed on the door, her senses still reeling from the kiss they'd shared—a kiss that had felt both natural and incredibly hot. He tasted right, and his body fitted against hers in all the correct places.

She smiled. Maybe she had been a fool not to notice he was attracted to her in school. She could've stayed in Morgantown, built a happy life with him, and never had to deal with the awfulness of Jason. But maybe the experience of a Jason made a woman appreciate the finer things in life such as coming back to her hometown and finding Ted Baker all grown up.

A loud piglet snort from the bathroom reminded her not to get carried away until she'd sorted out the current mess her life was in. She set down her coffee and went to find Bacon, who was extremely pleased to see her. She sat on the floor and let him climb into her lap. His happy little pig snuffles and wet nose made her want to hug him tight and never let go.

At least she hadn't crossed any state lines and was still in California. Was it actually illegal to transport a single, lovable pet pig into another state? Did Bacon need papers? Did she need a lawyer?

Veronica patted Bacon, set him back on the floor, and got up. There was no point staying inside worrying about everything. She'd wait until Uncle Victor returned, and share all her troubles with the man who'd brought her up after her parents had died in a car accident. If he couldn't help her, no one could. Until then, she'd keep an eye on the news, enjoy her time with Ted, and make sure he at least had something to eat for dinner before she went out with Avery.

* * *

Ted returned the credit card receipt to his customer and waited until he signed it.

"Thanks. Drive safely now."

He discreetly made sure the guy hadn't taken his pen, and checked that the credit card machine was set back in place. He couldn't wait for the day when everything became paperless. There were still several people in Morgan Valley who insisted on writing him a check, but he never rushed them. They'd known his beloved grandpa and his father and were as much a part of the valley as he was. One day, when he could afford it, he'd upgrade the remaining pumps to take credit card payments right there on the forecourt.

"Hey."

He looked up to find Tucker grinning at him.

"Hey, yourself. What's up?" As customers were scarce because of the weather it was nice to see a friendly face. "Aren't you supposed to be running a hotel or something?"

"It's a madhouse right now what with Marley telling everyone what to do and Dad countermanding her orders while Mom and I rush around frantically getting in each other's way." Tucker let out an aggrieved breath. "If they'd all sit down and stop arguing, we'd be in much better shape."

"You guys could organize a wedding in your sleep," Ted reminded him. "You've done hundreds of them."

"But not like this one. Marley's taken it as a personal challenge to show that the Hayes family can outdo Morgan Ranch, which is stupid when there is plenty of room for both venues. Avery made the right choice to organize the Morgan Ranch end of things and keep out of the way." Tucker checked his phone and groaned. "And they keep texting me like I have all the answers."

Ted chuckled. "You usually do. What time do you want us there on Saturday?"

"Two? There's a big crowd coming and we'll need to manage them."

"I've herded a few cattle in my time." Ted shrugged. "I can wrangle a few rowdy cowboys."

"Once the wedding is over and we've had the champagne toast, everything's moving up to Morgan Ranch for the main reception and dance. We just don't have the capacity, and seeing as Avery and Ry know every damn family in the valley, and most of the professional rodeo community between them, it's going to be wild."

"I'm looking forward to it," Ted confessed. "I can't think of any couple I'd rather see make it than those two."

"I wonder why?" Tucker winked at him. "You suddenly hoping these old schoolyard romances always work out well?"

Ted gave him a withering look. "If you're talking about me and Veronica, we never went out in school."

"But you always had a thing for her."

"Yeah, but she always saw me as a friend." Ted rearranged some of the gum at the front of the counter to avoid looking at Tucker. "And that's primarily what we still are—friends."

"Yeah, right." Tucker wasn't having any of it. "You've been happier than I've seen you in years since she arrived."

"She's only been here a day, and she's a very positive person to be with," Ted said.

"She sure is." Tucker hesitated. "Is she coming back to live here?"

Knowing he was the worst liar in town, and was currently facing the man who knew him best in the world, Ted desperately tried to think of a reply.

"I'm not sure. I think it depends on a lot of different factors."

"Like you?"

"No, way more important things than that," Ted said hastily. "I think Victor would be thrilled if she decided to stay. He definitely could do with some help with the business, and some company."

"That's true." Tucker looked over his shoulder as another customer came into the store and sighed. "I'd better get back before Marley and Dad come to blows. Avery will pick Veronica up around six, okay?"

"I'll let her know." Ted smiled at the woman approaching the counter. "Afternoon, ma'am, how can I help you?"

Even as he attended to business, his thoughts were racing. Veronica did make him feel more optimistic about everything, but he still knew very little about her. The fact that she'd turned up in Morgantown without alerting her beloved uncle was definitely suspect, and why had she brought a pig with her? His smile died as the woman left the shop. He wanted Veronica to tell him the truth. He wanted her to trust him, and that meant he was already in way over his head.

Chapter Four

"Did you have a good night?" Ted came into the kitchen to find Veronica sitting at the table eating a bowl of cereal. She looked far too awake and chirpy for him.

"It was awesome. Avery hasn't changed a bit, and everyone was so kind and welcoming. They're all really pleased you've found yourself a girlfriend, by the way."

"Funny, I never realized how interested the whole town was in my love life until you turned up."

He helped himself to coffee and opened the refrigerator to view the now-filled shelves. "Thanks again for getting all this stuff. I really appreciate it. Let me know how much I owe you."

"It's on me." She waved her spoon in his general direction. "You're saving me a packet on hotel costs, so it's the least I could do."

Ted grabbed a bowl, filled it with the granola stuff, which looked way too healthy, added milk, and took the seat opposite his guest. Her hair was coiled in two braids on either side of her head and her sweater was red and fluffy.

He pointed at her head. "Princess Leia, right?"

"Kind of." She gave him an approving smile. "With a touch of manga realness."

Ted nodded like he knew what that was, and dove into his cereal.

"Can I ask you something, Ted?"

"Sure." He wiped milk from his chin and gave her his attention.

"Is there a reason why you haven't put up any holiday decorations or got a tree?"

He looked blankly around the bare apartment and then back at her. "I guess I just haven't gotten around to it. Dad usually does that kind of stuff."

"Would you mind if I did it?" She must have seen something on his face that made her rush onward. "I've always loved the holidays, and this one feels kind of special to me. But I can totally understand if you don't want to do anything. It's your place."

Ted set his spoon down. "The thing is—it doesn't *feel* like my place. I built it for Dad, and I still feel like I'm a guest here. I bought land to build my own house just behind the shop and I've done nothing with it." He tried to smile. "I bet you think that's lame."

"Not at all." She shook her head. "Because that's exactly how I felt living with Jason. He wouldn't let me make any decisions about the furnishings, or décor, or anything. I always felt like he didn't trust me, you know?" She looked away. "When I got my own place, I spent a year staring at the bare walls, too terrified to change anything in case I did it wrong. Then I realized that even if I got it wrong, it didn't matter because there was no one to see it but me. I went out and bought all my holiday decorations, and finally made it feel like home—*my* home."

Ted reached over and took her hand. "Maybe we both should decorate this place?"

Her face lit up. "I was thinking I'd ask to borrow your truck, but if you can come with me, that will make it even more special."

"It's my day off." He grinned back at her. "We can go whenever you want."

Ted helped himself to more coffee and sat back down again. "The tree is the easy part. We just head up to Morgan Ranch, check in with the family, and go and help ourselves."

"They still do that?"

"Yeah, Billy and Chase have continued the tradition the first William Morgan started back in the eighteen hundreds. The Christmas decorations might take a bit more planning because we'll need to go to a bigger town."

"Don't you have any in storage?" Veronica asked.

"I guess so," Ted considered. "Dad definitely got some out last Christmas. I'll check around the apartment."

"Maybe we should do that before we go shopping so we'll know what we're missing."

"Sure." Ted resigned himself to a morning investigating the closets and finished his cereal, which hadn't been too bad after all. "I'll get on that right now before I have my shower."

Veronica fed Bacon and took him out for his morning walk. There had been more snow the previous night, but someone had already been out and cleared a path from the body shop to the gas station. Having grown up with the snow and ice, Veronica wasn't too worried, but she did put little pig boots on her pet to make sure he didn't damage his hooves.

She hadn't lied when she'd said how much she'd enjoyed her evening with Avery. Jason hadn't encouraged her to have friends and had gradually cut her off from her family and hometown. She'd tried to apologize to Avery for her long silence, but her friend had brushed aside her admission of guilt with a gentle understanding that had almost made Veronica want to weep.

Having friends again—having the support of a local community who watched out for each other—was something she desperately wanted. But would Victor let her stay when he learned what she'd done? He was a man with great respect for the law, and he'd firmly insist that Veronica should tell the truth and accept the consequences for her actions.

She got out her cell and anxiously checked her old local channel, but there was no news. Should she call her boss and just casually inquire if anyone had been asking after her? Like the police? But Leon wasn't stupid, and he'd definitely want to know what she'd done. And, as she still wasn't sure exactly what she'd done, she wasn't going to confess and incriminate herself.

She returned to the apartment, and found Ted standing on one of the chairs in the hallway in front of a closet packed with boxes. He glanced down at her after she'd put Bacon away.

"Can you take these from me? They aren't heavy at all."

"Sure."

Veronica reached up to take the box, which was helpfully marked "Christmas Decorations," and took it through to the family room. She came back to receive the second box, sneezing as the dust rose to tickle her nose.

She washed her hands and brought a damp cloth to wipe down the two boxes while Ted put away the chair and came to join her on the rug. He carefully opened the first box and peered inside.

"This is definitely the Christmas stuff."

"Is it okay to just take it out and put it on the floor?" Veronica asked as she cut the tape on the other box.

"Sure. It's not as if this is a new rug. I think my dad brought it with him from our old place." Ted started unwrapping newspaper parcels and Veronica took the other box and did the same.

After a while, she glanced over to see Ted staring down at a star-shaped ornament. His smile had disappeared as he gently ran his finger over the metal. He must have sensed her interest because he looked up.

"I'd forgotten about this one. My mom got it for me." He held it up so Veronica could see it better. "She had it engraved with my name, hers, and the date." He grimaced. "Shame she didn't stick around to see me actually open my present that year."

"She left at Christmas?"

"Two days before." Ted shrugged. "I don't think Dad ever got over it. She resurfaced in Fresno a few months later, and asked Dad for a divorce."

"I remember you getting really quiet at school and Beth crying a lot," Veronica said carefully. "You know what small towns are like—we all knew your mom had left Morgantown."

"Yeah, well." He turned the star over in his capable hands, his head bent low. "I did get to see her again occasionally after things settled down, but it was never the same."

"Did she remarry?"

"No, which, to be honest, kind of surprised me because I was pretty sure she'd left Dad for another guy, but there never was anyone. I guess she just couldn't stand living with us anymore."

Wincing at the echo of pain in his voice, Veronica took the ornament from Ted to read the inscription.

"'I'll always love you, Teddy Bear.'" She met his gaze. "Maybe she was trying to leave you with something to remember her by?"

A muscle twitched in his cheek. "I'd rather she'd stuck around to be honest. If she'd loved me, she wouldn't have left, would she?"

Veronica considered the ornament, the metal warm from Ted's fingers. "Have you ever asked her about that?"

"Why would I?" He raised an eyebrow. "She went and she didn't come back. What else is there to say?"

Veronica wanted to tell him that there obviously was a lot that needed to be said, but knew it wasn't her place.

"She picked out most of these ornaments." Ted gestured at the box. "I think Dad must've only used the ones he'd bought after she left because I haven't seen these since then. She loved to buy a new one for each of us every Christmas—something special, or a private joke, or nickname."

"Like Teddy Bear," Veronica said softly.

"Yeah." He reached over and took the star from her, wrapped it back up, and started on the rest of the pile he'd already accumulated.

"What are you doing?" Veronica asked.

"Putting them back where they belong—in the closet gathering dust." He abruptly stood up and went into the kitchen. "I need some tape."

Veronica waited for him to return, her hands palm down

on her crossed knees. How could she have been stupid enough to forget that Ted's mother walking out on him when he was twelve would have affected him so deeply? She'd been so eager to accept him at face value that she'd forgotten that everyone had hidden scars, and this one was a doozy.

Eventually, after Ted resealed the box and put it away again, he returned to sit opposite Veronica on the rug.

"I suppose I should apologize." He made himself meet her gaze. "I didn't think something as stupid as a tree ornament would bring back so many memories."

"We're good." Veronica reached out to pat his knee. "I'm the one who should be sorry, badgering you to decorate your apartment."

"It's fine." He hastened to continue. "I'm totally over what happened with my mom, so I don't know why I got so bent out of shape about it."

"Because feelings aren't always logical," Veronica said softly. "Because adults sometimes do shitty, selfish things without thinking about their kids? I lost both my parents when I was four, Ted. I know how it feels to be abandoned."

"Your parents died in a car crash. That was hardly their fault," Ted reminded her.

"Why do you think they were driving so fast?" Veronica let out her breath. "They'd decided they didn't want to stay with Victor because the work was too hard, and they wanted to be free."

Ted frowned. "But what about you?"

"They just left me there. Two days after they were confirmed dead, Victor got a letter in the mail they must have posted the day they left, explaining it all to him," Veronica said flatly. "I didn't know any of this until I was eighteen and Victor told me the truth. I thought it was all a tragic accident."

Ted reached over, picked her up, and deposited her on his knee. She pressed her face against his chest and he wrapped his arms around her.

"I'm so sorry," Ted murmured into her hair. "At least I got to see my mom again."

She placed her palm over his heart. "We both lost something, Ted. We can both grieve that loss."

Had he ever grieved for his mother? He couldn't consciously remember doing so. He'd had his dad, his school stuff, and his part-time job at the gas pumps to keep him busy. And he hadn't wanted to upset his father who was barely hanging on as he struggled to understand why his wife had left him.

Veronica raised her head to look up at him. "I was lucky to have Victor and the rest of the family. I was so young when my parents ran off that I never really felt the lack of them. You were twelve when your mom left. That must've been hard."

"It was." Ted couldn't believe he'd actually said the words out loud. "And I still don't know why."

"You should ask her." Veronica looked him right in the eye.

"I'll think about it."

Ted kissed her nose and then when he had her attention, her mouth, until she kissed him back. It was way better to show how he felt rather than talk about his feelings, and way more enjoyable.

When she eventually eased away, they were both breathing hard, and she somehow had her hand up the back of his T-shirt while he was cupping her breast.

"You sure you want to stop right now?" he asked softly. "Because I have a real nice comfortable bed where we could get naked."

She bit her lip and brought her hand up to his jaw. "I think I need to tell you something first."

"Okay." He took his hands off her and resisted the impulse to readjust his jeans. "Shoot."

"I stole Bacon," she said in a rush.

Ted blinked at her. "As in your pet pig, and not the stuff from the supermarket?"

"Yes." She nodded. "When I lived with Jason, he had a pig called Perry. Jason didn't like her when she got big, so I ended up looking after her."

"How big does a pet pig get?" Ted asked suspiciously.

"About two hundred pounds. And they can be really badly behaved if they aren't cared for properly." Veronica shrugged. "Jason lost interest in Perry when she stopped looking cute, but he was too scared to do anything to upset her, and he liked breeding her and selling off her piglets."

"Okay," Ted said cautiously. "So where does the pig stealing part come in?"

Veronica looked down at her clasped hands. "I . . . kept an eye on Perry after I left because I was worried Jason wouldn't treat her right."

"How exactly did you do that?"

"My old next-door neighbors hated Jason and were quite happy to send me regular updates on Perry whenever they saw her in the backyard. I couldn't take her with me because my apartment didn't allow pets."

"Hard to hide a two-hundred-pound pig." Ted nodded. "So what happened?"

"Jason kept breeding her and eventually, Perry became ill." Veronica swallowed hard. "I ended up texting him because I was so worried, which was a terrible mistake because he's never forgiven me for divorcing him. He said Perry wasn't worth keeping anymore because only one of her piglets had survived." Ted winced. "I offered to come over and take Perry to the vet to see if there was anything that could be done for her. I even offered to pay the bill, but Jason wouldn't let me."

"So what did you do?" Ted prompted her gently.

She raised her chin. "I went around to the house. There was no sign of Perry, which was bad enough, so I took Bacon."

Ted considered what to say next. "So basically you stole his pig."

"That's what I told you in the beginning!" Veronica held his gaze. "He's going to be furious! What if he comes after me?"

"I suppose he could do that," Ted acknowledged. "But do you really think he's going to come all the way out here just to get his pig back?"

"I don't know!" Veronica said. "That's why I came here. I thought Uncle Victor would be able to help me."

"But Vic's away."

"Yes." Veronica didn't look very impressed with his impeccable logic or speed of thought. "I know that *now*. I didn't at the time."

"Okay, so what does this have to do with whether or not we go to bed together?"

Veronica scrambled off his lap and paced the worn rug, her arms wrapped around herself before turning back to Ted.

"Are you being deliberately annoying?"

Ted shrugged. "Nope, I guess it just comes naturally to me."

"I'm trying to be honest with you."

"I get that."

"Do you not care that you might be having sex with someone who stole a *pig*?"

Ted looked from her flushed face down to her pink kitten socks and slowly shook his head. "I can't say that it bothers me."

"Uncle Victor will be so disappointed," Veronica whispered.

Ted held up one hand. "Just clarifying that I'm not related to you, and I didn't bring you up, so I'm not conflicted about this at all."

She spun away from him and looked out of the window, her shoulders hunched almost up to her ears.

"Should I tell Nate?"

Ted got up from the floor. "Do you want to?"

"Of course I don't. I wish I could go back in time and change everything that happened, and—" She sighed. "Well, maybe not all of it because I do have Bacon."

"What else happened?" Ted asked slowly. "You stole the pig, and you don't regret that. What do you regret?"

She drew herself up. "The *stealing* part, Ted? That I should have taken the time to negotiate some deal with Jason and not just . . . taken him. I panicked."

From the way she was avoiding his gaze, Ted had a strong suspicion that she might have done something else, but seeing as his opinion of Jason couldn't get any lower, he didn't have a problem if Veronica had trashed the house a little on her way out.

"Do you want me to talk to Nate for you?"

"No, I'm a big girl. If it comes to that, I'll talk to him

myself." She blew out a breath. "Thanks for offering, though."

"You're welcome." Ted paused. "Anything else you want to tell me?"

She looked so guilty that he almost wanted to laugh.

"I . . . don't know yet."

"Well, at least that's honest." He waited again. "Are you sure you don't want to spill the beans? Because you'll probably feel much better if you let it all out."

She reached for his hand. "I just *can't*."

"That bad, eh?"

She squeezed his fingers hard. "Maybe." She met his gaze. "Would you prefer it if I moved out?"

"Dammit, no!" Ted frowned at her. "Why would you even think that?"

"Because I don't want to get you into trouble."

"For harboring a *pig* stealer?"

Her eyes filled with tears. "I've ruined everything because I didn't think things through properly. I should have kept this to myself. I wanted this Christmas with you to be special, and now I've made you mad."

"I'm mad because you're trying to leave, not because of the stupid pig," Ted said patiently. "Hell, you could have brought ten pigs with you and I wouldn't have noticed. I just want to spend Christmas with you, too."

She bit her lip and eyed him hopefully. "If I promise to tell you the rest of it the moment I can, will that do?"

"I'm not the one putting up barriers here, Veronica," Ted reminded her. "That's all you."

She studied him for a long moment and then slowly nodded. "Okay, then."

"Okay, what?" Ted wanted to make sure they were on the same page.

"I'll stay."

"And consider my offer of my nice big bed? I changed the sheets this morning."

Her smile made something inside him relax. "How about we start with the Christmas shopping and see how that goes?"

Ted kissed her cheek. "Okay, you win. Let's get going."

She should have told him everything. Veronica couldn't get that thought out of her mind as they headed to the nearest town with a decent mall. Why had she stopped? He'd been surprisingly calm about the pig stealing and she had an instinctive sense that he'd be okay about the rest of it. But he also reminded her very much of her uncle Victor who, while being totally on her side, would expect her to do the right thing, step up, and accept the consequences of her actions.

She glanced down at her cell phone. Should she text her old neighbor Sharon who'd always kept an eye out for Perry? Or would it be better to talk to Leon who was a little more removed from the neighborhood, but disliked Jason enough to help her out? She'd been gone for over a week now and no one had contacted her about anything—which could be a good or a bad thing. . . .

Ted made the turn into the parking lot and looked over at her.

"You okay?"

She found a smile somewhere. "Yes, sorry, I was just thinking about what we need for the apartment, and I also have to get something to wear for the wedding. It's not going to be super dressy, is it?"

Ted chuckled. "You know Avery. She doesn't like a fuss

and neither does Ry." He slotted the truck into a corner parking spot and turned off the engine. "The groomsmen are wearing the same Western shirts, and the bridesmaids are wearing whatever they like as long as it's green, because that's Avery's favorite color."

"I'll definitely need something. I haven't been to a wedding for years." Veronica glanced down at her jeans and sweater. "I didn't bring anything formal with me because I knew Victor would have me out there working the moment I arrived."

"Yeah, he probably would have. I've pulled a few carrots out of the ground for him once or twice when I just went up there to deliver his mail." Ted grabbed his jacket from the back seat and checked if he had his phone and wallet. "You ready to go?"

Veronica got out of the truck and headed toward the mall entrance, Ted by her side. The interior was decked out in red, gold, and green. Christmas music was playing, and judging from the line of excited little kids curving around the corner, Santa was already in residence hopefully handing out presents. Veronica paused to check out the illuminated mall map while Ted swiped a paper copy of the same thing.

"Let's do the dress shopping before we end up with too many bags," Ted suggested. "According to Beth, there are a couple of decent places here."

"So I see." Veronica braced herself. "You don't have to come if you don't want to. You could start on the decoration side of things."

He looked down at her from his considerable height, his brow creased. "I'm happy to tag along—unless you'd rather be alone?"

"I . . ." Veronica grimaced. "Jason always came shopping with me and basically bought and chose all my clothes, so I guess I'm a bit skittish about it."

"Understandable." He nodded. "How about I do the same thing I do when I shop with Beth?"

"What's that?"

"Keep my mouth shut unless she asks for an opinion."

Veronica blinked at him. "You'd do that?"

He shrugged. "It's your body."

She went up on tiptoe and planted a kiss on his mouth.

"What was that for?"

"For being so *nice*." Veronica kissed him again.

"Don't they say that nice guys finish last?" Ted asked.

"*They* are completely wrong." She mock frowned at him. "Trust me on this."

She took his hand as they went up the escalator to the second floor and held on to it as they went into the big department store that anchored one end of the mall. She still didn't enjoy shopping for clothes. Years of Jason criticizing her taste and judgment were hard to shake off.

True to his promise, Ted didn't say a word as he followed her through the racks. He did volunteer to carry the ever-increasing pile of garments she gathered as she went and she was very grateful for that. A salesperson glided up and offered to set her up in a dressing room, which Veronica accepted.

Eventually, she found herself in her own space and quickly set about trying on all the things. Most of them she discarded immediately, but there were three she liked. She glanced doubtfully at the door. Should she go out there and show Ted? Would he really be able to keep his mouth shut?

She reminded herself she'd been a free woman for two years now, and that what she wore was totally up to her.

She unlocked the door and went out to where Ted and a couple of other guys were all sitting staring glumly at their phones. He looked up as she approached and smiled.

She did a little twirl. "What do you think?"

"It's great," Ted said. "I like the color."

He continued to smile approvingly while she waited for the *but*, which never came. Eventually, she went back to try on dress number two. It was a soft pink color with an embroidered skirt and a red sash that complemented her coloring nicely.

This time, he stood up and his smile was definitely hotter. He didn't need to say anything because she already knew he liked it, but she still asked.

"It looks good on you," he finally said, his gaze firmly on her face. "How do you like it?"

"I think it's my favorite," Veronica confessed and lowered her voice. "You don't think it's too revealing, or too juvenile for me, or anything?"

"Nope."

"That's it?" She looked up at him.

"Yup. Did you say there was one more contender?" He gently turned her around and pointed her back at the dressing room. "Let's see it, then."

Chapter Five

"Hey, Dad." Ted waved at his phone as his father, Kevin, who had finally conquered FaceTime, appeared on the screen. He looked tanned, relaxed, and way healthier than he had in years. Despite his initial concerns about the trip, Ted was beginning to believe that it had been a good thing for both of them.

"Hi, son! How's snowy Morgantown?"

"Snowy." Ted grinned back at him. "How's Hawaii?"

"We've just left Maui and we're heading to the Big Island overnight. It's all been great. The food is good, the weather, the company . . ."

"Awesome. Is Victor there?"

His dad looked around. "I can find him if you want me to. What's up?"

"Maybe you could just give him a message? His niece Veronica turned up, thinking he'd be there."

"Vic wouldn't have come if he'd known Veronica was visiting." Kevin frowned. "He loves that girl."

"I think it was a sudden decision," Ted said tactfully. "Anyway, just tell him that she's staying with me over the holidays, and that he can see her when he gets back, okay?"

"With you?"

Ted shrugged even though his father couldn't see all of him. "Yeah, everywhere else is all booked up for the Hayes wedding of the year."

Kevin's grin widened. "Nice going, son. You always liked her, didn't you?"

"We were always good friends. What's your point?"

"No, you *really* liked her. I remember Vic and I joking that we were going to be in-laws one day."

"Dad . . ." Ted blushed like a teenager. "Stop. She's just staying here until Victor gets back."

"You're a fool if you don't take advantage of that, aren't you? She's a nice girl and that ex-husband of hers was a dirtbag."

"So I hear."

"Then reach out to her! Get off the couch and live a little, okay?"

"That's hardly fair," Ted pointed out. "I stayed here for a reason. I'm not the kind of guy who walks away when his family needs him."

"Beth is doing great now, and so am I. It's time for you to reach out for what *you* want."

"Fine! Great! I'll do that, okay?" Ted scowled at his father. "Pass my message on to Victor, will you? If he wants to talk to her, he can call my cell or try hers."

He abruptly ended the call, feeling more unsettled than he should have been. He walked out into the family room where Veronica had set up the ironing board and was carefully pressing the skirt of her dress she'd bought at the mall.

She looked up as he came in and set the iron down. "Everything all right?"

"Dad said he'd tell Victor you were here." He wandered

into the kitchen, looked aimlessly into the refrigerator, and then poured himself some coffee.

"I hope he's okay with me turning up like this."

"Why wouldn't he be?" Ted stirred his coffee so forcefully, half of it swirled right out of the mug. "I bet he'd leave the cruise right now to get back to you if he had the choice."

He added more coffee to his mug and mopped up the pool on the countertop.

"Did you and your dad have a disagreement or something?" Veronica had returned to pressing her skirt and had her back to him. "You seem a bit tense."

"He just . . ." Ted let out an aggrieved breath. "I stuck around because he needed me, and now somehow *I'm* the one who is at fault for not getting out and doing more with my life."

"Are you talking about what happened with your mom?"

"Not just that. Three years ago Dad had prostate cancer. It's gone now, but it took him a couple of years to really get back to his old self, you know?"

He set his mug down and went over to her, taking the iron out of her hand. "You've missed a bit." He angled the skirt and eased the tip of the iron toward the gathered waistband. "Can you fetch my wedding shirt? I left it on my chest of drawers."

"Sure!" Veronica was looking at him like he was crazy; he wasn't quite sure why as he turned the fabric and repeated his action.

By the time she returned, he'd finished her dress and put it back on the hanger. He unwrapped his new shirt, placed it on the ironing board, and sprayed it with water.

"Beth was busy looking after Mikey, so I was the one

who took Dad to all his appointments—not that I minded doing it—but with that, and running the gas station, and the shop, I didn't have a lot of free time."

"I bet you didn't." Veronica perched on the arm of the couch and watched him work. "You don't have to explain yourself to me."

Ted smoothed a hand over the creases in the arm of his shirt and straightened it out. "I know. I just hate it when I'm suddenly the one at fault for supposedly sitting around when all I've tried to do is take care of everyone else." He tried to smile. "I guess I owe you an apology, for losing my temper over something that isn't your fault."

"That's you losing your temper?" She raised an eyebrow and clutched at her chest. "Ooh, I'm terrified."

He picked up the bottle and sent a mist of spray right at her head, which made her duck and squeak. His smile turned into a genuine grin as she came off the couch and squared up to him.

"Hey!" He held up his hands. "Let me finish ironing my shirt, and then you can fight me all you like."

She retreated to the couch. "Seeing as watching you iron is a huge turn-on, I'm happy to wait."

"Someone had to do it when Mom left." Ted turned the shirt over and applied steam and firm pressure. "I find it really soothing."

"I bet you fold your laundry the moment it comes out of the dryer as well," Veronica commented.

"Doesn't everyone?" He looked up to find her gazing at him like he was some kind of rock star. "It's not exactly hard."

He checked the shirt, decided it looked okay, and threw it over his shoulder before unplugging the iron. "I'm going to wash it and iron it again when it's dry. Do you have anything to put in the washing machine?"

"You're going to do it all again?" She followed him out into the hallway.

"Yeah, I find the creases go away more quickly." He added detergent to the machine as she came back with an armful of her clothes. "As long as they're not white, stick them in. I don't think the shirt is going to bleed any color out, but you never know."

"I don't have any whites." She placed everything in the machine and stood back to let him push the right buttons. "Thanks."

He turned around and bumped right into her, his hands coming automatically to her elbows to hold her steady. She looked up at him, wrapped her hand around the back of his neck, and brought his head down for a kiss.

After letting his dad rile him up, Ted certainly wasn't in the mood to stop her. He kissed her until he was pressed against her from knee to forehead and she was practically glued to the washing machine. With a groan, he set her on top of the dryer, and she parted her knees to let him even closer. Within seconds, he was hard and undulating his hips in the same rhythm as his kisses.

Her fingers curled around the bottom of his T-shirt and tugged. He shucked off his plaid shirt and bent his head to allow her to pull the cotton undershirt off him. She scraped her nails over his back and he shuddered, wanting more.

"May I?" he breathed against her shoulder, and bit her neck as she sighed his name.

"Do what?"

"Take some of your many layers of clothing off?"

She enthusiastically helped him remove her big sweater

and T-shirt, and undid her jeans. He slid his hand past her open zipper and cupped her mound.

"Here?"

"God, yes." She arched her hips, letting him pull the denim down her legs to expose her plain, cotton panties.

Ted had never seen anything more alluring in his life. He leaned in, breathing the scent of her arousal, and set a wet kiss over her already-damp panties. His fingers followed his questing mouth and soon he was in heaven, his tongue tasting her, his thumb planted firmly on her bud until she was writhing against him. He pushed deeper, and was rewarded with her cry of release and a hand in his hair that demanded everything.

He eased her down, kissing his way along her now-lax thighs until he was able to look up at her. She'd planted one hand behind her and was leaning back like an arched bow, her mouth soft and her eyes still glazed with pleasure. Ted felt a flicker of pride that he'd helped put that particular expression on her face.

She caught his eye. "You iron, do laundry, *and* put a woman's needs first? Why hasn't any sane woman snapped you up?"

He shrugged and kissed his way up over her stomach. "I have no idea."

She stroked the back of his neck as he gave one hundred percent of his attention to her lush breasts.

"Any chance we can make use of those nice clean sheets on your bed right now?" Veronica breathed.

He picked her up, making her gasp, and planted a smacking kiss on her cheek. "I thought you'd never ask."

She bit her lip, that sense of uncertainty still there. "That is, if you don't think we're moving too fast, or—"

"I don't." He laid her in the middle of his big bed and

went to shut the door. "I'm totally okay with this as long as you are."

He climbed onto the bed and settled himself over her, his elbows locked, his hand flat on the mattress. She reached out and ran her fingernail along the waist of his jeans, making him suck in a breath.

"You look kind of uncomfortable. Can I help with that?"

He nodded wordlessly as she dealt with his belt, button, and zipper, and released the aching pressure on his cock. He helped by pushing his jeans down and somehow getting them off, leaving him in just his black boxers.

"Nice." She breathed against his most precious possession and stroked her finger up the hard thrust of his covered shaft. He gently took her hand in his.

"If you touch me right now, I'll come, so can we get back to this bit?"

She grinned at him. "If you're sure."

"Oh, I am." He nodded fervently and reached out to the drawer on his nightstand to find protection. "Just give me a minute and I'll prove it to you."

Veronica lay back on the crisp sheets and watched the flex of Ted's muscles as he loomed over her. She reached behind her to undo the clasp of her bra and freed her breasts. His breath stuttered as he stared down at her. There was no mistaking the absolute adoration and heat in his gaze. For the first time in forever, she felt completely at ease with her body in front of a man.

She hooked a finger in the waistband of her panties and gave him an inquiring glance. He nodded silently, one hand cupping his erection, the other reaching to caress her breast. And then he was all over her, kissing, fondling, and learning every inch of her skin until she was rubbing up against him in unspoken invitation.

"You good?" he managed to ask between kisses. "You want me?"

"Oh, yes," she breathed back at him. "Please."

He slowly eased inside her, his gaze intent as he noted every nuance of her expression. She walked her feet up his thighs sending him even deeper, and with a soft growl he moved faster. She closed her eyes and clung to his shoulders as his powerful body took her higher and higher until she climaxed and gasped his name.

He didn't stop, but drove her on to another high and they came together, which was something Veronica had read about, but never really believed could happen in real life. Ted slumped over her like a plank hit him. She had to give him a polite nudge to make him roll off her.

"Sorry," he muttered.

"It's all good."

Without the heat of his body covering her, Veronica suddenly felt cold, but the feeling didn't last for long as he gathered her into his arms and pulled the covers over them. She settled against him, her cheek against his chest and her palm over his still-racing heart. She waited for the guilt, or recriminations, or self-doubt to wash over her and felt nothing but a sense of righteousness.

Ted wasn't Jason. Whatever happened between them next, he would never react like her ex.

He stroked her hair away from her face and tucked it behind her ear.

"You okay?"

"I'm good." She kissed his chest. "You?"

"Also good." He went quiet for a minute before asking, "You want to stay here tonight?"

"In your bed?"

"Yeah, I wasn't planning on kicking you out of the apartment."

She nipped his nipple and he fake-growled.

"I need to go and check in on Bacon, and brush my teeth, but I'll definitely come back if you'd like me to."

"I would."

Neither of them made any effort to move and Veronica's eyes closed as she drifted toward sleep. The sound of her phone buzzing made her abruptly sit up.

"Where did I leave my cell?"

Ted looked around the clothes-strewn floor. "I have no idea." He obligingly got out of bed and searched through her clothing. "It's not here. Your jeans are still in the laundry room, I think."

She grabbed a T-shirt from his chair and rushed into the hallway, but her phone had already stopped ringing. She paused to investigate her jeans, which didn't reveal her cell, and then went into the kitchen where her phone sat on the countertop. The unknown number had an L.A. code. She checked for a message, but whoever it was hadn't left one, which left her imagination running riot. She didn't recognize the number. Had it been the cops, or one of Jason's friends?

"Everything okay?"

She jumped when Ted came up behind her, and immediately shut down her phone and clutched it to her chest.

"Great!" she said brightly. "I'll go and check on Bacon now that I'm up."

* * *

Ted watched Veronica rush down the hallway, his brow creased. He didn't want to be that guy, but she'd looked guilty as hell when he'd come up behind her. Who was calling her, and why was she so keen to talk to them that she'd leapt out of bed like a rocket? Was it possible that she still had some other guy in L.A.? He'd told her he didn't have a girlfriend, but he hadn't inquired about her relationships. . . .

Ted rubbed a hand over his unshaven jaw and stared unseeingly down the hallway toward his dad's bathroom. For the first time in his life, he'd jumped in with both feet. Up until about five minutes ago, he'd loved every second of his free fall, but now he was back wishing he'd stayed put. Maybe this was why he was the slow and cautious type— keeping up with Veronica was already giving him heartburn.

He strolled casually toward his own bedroom door, which was past his dad's. He could hear Veronica talking to the pig, so she wasn't back on the phone. He paused at his open door and surveyed the rumpled sheets. Should he ask her what was going on, or should he leave things be, and just enjoy being with her? He didn't want to mess things up, but he also didn't want to be a complete fool.

The bathroom door opened and he pretended to be busy sorting out the clothes on the floor. He looked up as she came toward him, her cheeks flushed, and her hair falling down around her shoulders. She was wearing his T-shirt, which was too big for her and almost came down to her knees.

Just the glorious sight of her made any questions impossible. He wanted her back in his arms, and if there was trouble coming, maybe he'd just have to deal with it when it exploded in his face, or pray she'd tell him what was going on.

She paused at the side of the bed and looked over at him. "I'm sorry about that."

He shrugged. "No worries."

"I've been hoping that Sharon, my neighbor, would let me know if she'd spotted Perry again."

"Oh, right." Ted concentrated on sounding neutral. "Did she leave you a message?"

"Unfortunately not." She sighed and set her phone on the bedside table. "I should just call her, but I'm scared about what she's going to say."

Ted felt some of the tension in his shoulders disappear. Whatever was going on, her concern for the momma pig was very like her. Maybe he was overthinking things after all. He set his clothes on the chair and turned to face her, offering her another chance to tell him the rest of it.

"Sometimes it's better to deal with things head-on than worry yourself to death over them."

"I know." She managed a smile. "As I said, it's complicated. Maybe I'll call her tomorrow." She hesitated, her hand hovering over her phone. "Are you still okay with me sleeping here?"

Ted smiled and patted the mattress. "I wasn't thinking we'd be doing much sleeping, but you're more than welcome to try."

Chapter Six

The wedding day started with clear skies and weak sunshine, which settled in, wrapping the small town in a cocoon of white snow and soft light that made it feel almost magical. Veronica leaned against the frosted window, her breath condensing on the glass and allowed herself to imagine living in Morgantown again. Leon wouldn't be happy, but he'd understand, and what else was there to keep her in L.A.? She didn't want to be bumping into Jason and his new girlfriend every five minutes. He'd keep on rubbing it in her face if she stayed; he was just that kind of guy.

She could live at her uncle's place, help him out, and maybe find a job locally. She glanced back at the bed where Ted softly snored, one arm flung out over the pillows as if looking for her. They'd spent the last three days together, and she'd never been happier. She could see Ted every day. . . .

The thought of all that—of having a family again, or being with a man who respected her—was so tempting. But she had to be brave and deal with the mess she'd left behind. At some point today, she was going to call Sharon and find out exactly what was going on.

She grabbed Ted's soft-lined plaid shirt from the chair and put it on, enjoying the scent of him surrounding her, and went out into the kitchen. It was still early, but she knew Ted had to put in a stint at the gas station before the wedding kicked off at the hotel around two. She'd wait until the wedding was over, when they were curled up together in his big warm bed, and tell him everything. It didn't feel right him not knowing any more because she wanted them to have a future together.

Veronica let out a long breath. There—yes, she'd said it. She wanted more. And if he found what she'd done unacceptable, then that was okay, too. Except it would break her heart. . . .

"Hey."

Ted's sleep-roughened voice came from behind her, and she turned to smile at him. He wore nothing but his boxers slung low on his hips and looked so hot she wanted to jump his bones.

"What?" He cocked an eyebrow at her as she advanced toward him.

"When do you have to be at work?"

He glanced over at the kitchen clock. "In about an hour. Why?"

She hooked her finger in the front of his boxers. "Plenty of time then."

"For what?"

"This." She eased down onto her knees, bringing his boxers with her.

He made a strangled sound as she cupped his balls and then went gratifyingly quiet.

* * *

Ted checked his reflection in the mirror and fiddled with the top button of his blue shirt. His new, brown cowboy hat sat on the bed along with his thick winter coat. As transport was being provided up to the ranch after the ceremony, he and Veronica had decided to walk over to the hotel. Ted paused to say a quick prayer that no one would need his services today. Mano was standing by, but Ted was the only one around with the expertise to fix anything complicated. He reminded himself that the whole valley would be at the wedding so they were unlikely to be getting up to any other kind of mischief.

His bedroom door opened, and Veronica came in wearing the pink dress she'd bought at the mall. She'd put her hair up on top of her head, allowing soft curls to tumble down and brush her shoulders.

"I think I'll bring my shoes in my bag and—" She stopped talking and smiled at him so openheartedly that he couldn't look away. "Wow, you look so good in that color. It really brings out the hazel in your eyes."

Ted instinctively stood up straighter and sucked in his gut. "Why, thank you, ma'am. You look pretty awesome yourself."

She smoothed the velvet of her long sleeve with her fingertips. "For once, I'm not going to argue with you about that. I *feel* beautiful."

He gently cupped her chin and brought his mouth down to hers. "You are beautiful, inside and out, and I—" He kissed her before he blurted out the *L* word. Even he knew it was way too early to go down that path, though he was certain to his soul. "And we need to get going. You know I've got to do the groomsman thing so I won't be with you all the time?"

"That's okay." She patted his shoulder. "I'm a big girl. I can take care of myself."

"I'm sure you'll be too busy talking to everyone you haven't seen in Morgan Valley yet to miss me much." Ted made a sad face as he picked up his hat and coat.

"Oh, I'll miss you." Veronica swatted his butt as he went past her. "You can count on that."

They put on their boots, scarves, and gloves before opening the door and going down to the garage where Ted checked in with Mano who had his cell number for emergencies. The town was quiet, and the snow lay relatively undisturbed, giving the place an old-time vibe. A lot of the shop owners, including Yvonne at the café, Daisy at the florist's, and Gina at the pizzeria, had closed up for the afternoon to attend the wedding.

Veronica slid her arm into the crook of Ted's elbow as they crunched through the foot-high ridges of snow, her breath condensing in the freezing air in puffy white clouds.

"It's beautiful here." She sighed. "I'd forgotten how much I love this time of year. You don't get much of a snow season in L.A."

"Sunshine and heat will sound really good after a couple of months of this," Ted reminded her. "But by then it's too late to get out."

He guided her up onto the planked walkway, which someone had cleared of snow and salted.

"So practical." She grinned up at him. "Just let me enjoy my little fantasy, okay?"

Ted grimaced. "Sorry, I'm a real Debbie Downer, aren't I? My dad is always getting at me for it."

She stopped, turned to face him, and placed her palm on his chest. "It's okay. There's nothing wrong with being a realist. I haven't lived here for years so I have forgotten the bad things. I don't mind you pointing them out to me."

"But I don't want to *be* that person," Ted exhaled. "I don't want to be the grumpy old guy in the corner."

She met his gaze head-on and raised her eyebrows. "Then stop. That's on you, okay?"

He nodded and she turned around again, took his hand, and walked forward. He followed as meekly as a besotted calf. Was it really that simple? Was it time he stopped weighing up every issue and exploring every possible outcome before he dared take a step?

"I had to be cautious when I took out the loans for the rebuild." Ted couldn't quite believe he was still yapping, but there it was.

"I totally get that." She nodded, but didn't slow down. "Financial decisions that affect your whole family and your business deserve a lot of thought."

"But that's why I didn't borrow enough money to build my own house and ended up living with my dad." Even as he said the words, Ted realized how he'd held himself back. "I didn't want to take that risk, and I could've afforded it."

"You can always refinance," she said gently.

"Don't be nice to me," he grumbled. "I'm trying to be honest here."

That earned him a laugh and a squeeze of his hand. "They say confession is good for the soul."

"I'm so not feeling it." He paused at the end of the walkway to study the bright lights of the Hayes Hotel. "Here's where all the action definitely is. The place is lit up like a Christmas tree!"

"Marley's really going for it," Veronica said in awed tones. "The whole front is a mass of lights, and there's literally a red carpet running from the street into the hotel."

A battered truck pulled up, and a bearded cowboy got out and came around to open the passenger door. He handed his keys off to the valet and paused to chat as he helped his female companion step down.

Beside Ted, Veronica went still. "That's—"

"Ben Miller's girlfriend." Ted gave the couple a casual wave. "They've built a new house out on the Gomez Ranch, which Ben is managing."

Veronica poked him in the side. "That's Silver Meadows!"

"Yeah, I know." He frowned down at her. "They probably got here early to avoid any gawkers."

"She's one of the biggest film stars in the world!" Veronica squeaked, almost jumping up and down with excitement.

"So what?"

Veronica shook her head and started down the steps, her mouth still open. "This place is nuts. Tech millionaires, rodeo stars, Navy SEALs. . . ."

"Always has been, always will be." Ted followed her onto the red carpet where they paused to allow a photographer to take their picture. "Now, *I* feel like a movie star."

The inside of the hotel was still relatively quiet because the ceremony wasn't due to start for almost an hour. A sign directed them to a large room where they could shed their outerwear and change their shoes. Settling his hat under his arm, Ted turned to Veronica. "I've got to go upstairs and find Ry. Will you be okay?"

"I'm pretty sure I will," Veronica kissed his mouth, which was much easier in high heels. "I'll save you a seat?"

"That would be awesome."

She watched him leave, aware that in his wedding garb

he looked more like a cowboy than a mechanic. She wondered if she'd spot him again in the crowd of ranchers. She had a feeling that she'd be able to find him anywhere now, and that he'd make sure he was there to be found. How could she have come to care for him so deeply in such a short space of time? Was she just not used to a man being a decent human being anymore? She reminded herself that she had dated a few guys since her divorce, and that none of them had made her feel like Ted had.

"Hey, you."

She was jerked from her thoughts by the appearance of Tucker Hayes looking very smart in a three-piece suit. He bowed and offered her his arm.

"May I escort you through to the wedding venue?"

She found a smile. "That would be lovely, thank you."

"Ted's really sweet on you," Tucker said conversationally as they went back through the lobby and toward the connected rooms that ran the length of the hotel. "I hope you're going to stick around."

"I'm definitely thinking about it," Veronica confessed, and was rewarded by a delighted grin. "And I promise I won't mess him around."

"Good to know." Tucker paused near the row of seats. "He's a great guy who sometimes needs a kick in the pants to get going. I think you're just what he needs."

Veronica sat down and allowed herself to take in the amazing floral arrangements and classic Christmas decorations themed in silver and red that covered the dining room and adjacent drawing room. Even the chairs had garlands of scarlet ribbon with silver bells entwined across their backs. There was a table set at the front of the room next to a large fireplace where Veronica assumed the pastor would stand. Marley really had done the Hayes family proud.

As Veronica sat, taking everything in and just enjoying being back in her hometown, the rows started to fill up with the residents of Morgan Valley in their best formal Western wear. She recognized some of the women she'd met at Avery's party, and was touched when several came over to speak to her, and make her feel welcome.

As the murmur of conversation grew to a muted roar, a trio of musicians started playing quietly in the corner, and the front seats containing the Morgans and Hayes family were gradually occupied. Veronica received a wave from Ruth Morgan, and a wink from Roy, the ancient ranch manager who accompanied her to her seat.

Eventually, there was a stir at the back, and everyone craned their necks to watch Ry Morgan, the groom, accompanied by his identical twin brother, HW, walk down the aisle. Ry looked his usual, calm self, but HW was grinning and yakking away like he was still trying to wind his brother up. It occurred to Veronica that people didn't really change that much after all.

Ted was the same kid who'd looked out for his sister and her friends, and worked hard to support his family business, but was Veronica the same girl? Despite everything that had happened in her life so far, she liked herself better now. She was a resilient woman who had been tested and emerged stronger than ever.

The music paused, and then started again, this time with a country tune from a star Veronica knew Avery loved. Everyone stood, and HW Morgan took the opportunity to elbow his twin in the side. There was a very long pause, and then Chase William appeared, a furrow on his brow as he delved into his basket, crouched down, and carefully placed one rose petal on the center of the carpet before moving another six inches forward and doing it again.

January, who was Avery's matron of honor, bent to whisper in his ear, and made a hurry-up kind of motion, which didn't go down well with her son. After another consultation, he scowled, shoved his hand in the basket, threw out a whole load of petals, and stomped up the aisle scattering them everywhere. Behind him, January laughed, hoisted her daughter, Elizabeth, higher on her hip, and followed him up to the front where she handed the baby over to her husband, and grabbed hold of the collar of Chase William's blue-checked Western shirt.

The maids of honor, accompanied by the groomsmen, progressed at a more regular pace. Veronica spotted Ted accompanying Marley Hayes at the back. The blues and greens of the bridal party offered a soothing contrast to the silver and red of the décor, like a promise of spring after a hard winter.

There was another pause, as Ry Morgan stared straight ahead, and then a gentle sigh of appreciation as Avery Hayes and her father came down the aisle. Avery wore a simple, white, high-necked dress that finished just below the tops of her white and red cowboy boots. She also wore a white hat with a vivid silver and red sash that trailed down the back.

Veronica gave a shaky sigh as Ry Morgan spotted his bride. His whole face lit up with such adoration that Veronica knew her friend would never have a moment's regret in her choice of husband. He worshipped her, and had waited patiently for her to decide when she was ready to marry him without a word of complaint, or expectation of anything. Veronica was truly happy for her friend.

She sniffed and a tissue appeared under her nose. She

looked up to discover Ted had slipped into the seat next to hers.

"Here you go," he whispered. "I knew you'd cry."

"So did I," she whispered back, and pointed at her purse. "I have a whole packet of tissues in there."

"We'll probably need them before the end of the ceremony," Ted murmured. "I'm getting a little misty-eyed myself."

She wiped her eyes and reached for his hand when the pastor asked them all to sit. Whatever happened between her and Ted, she knew that true love did exist; she was watching it happen in real time.

As the wedding progressed, Ted couldn't help wondering how it would feel if it was him up there saying vows to Veronica. He'd never imagined finding someone he could stick with for the rest of his life. What was funny was that the idea of it didn't even scare him. He knew he was getting dangerously ahead of himself, but for once he wasn't prepared to put the brakes on.

Veronica just fitted right: with the town, with his family and friends, and, most importantly, with him. She was everything he wasn't, and somehow that worked. And she was beautiful with her dark hair, her olive skin, and that breathtaking smile.

After the ceremony, there was champagne and tiny little sandwiches and cakes that just made Ted hungrier. He stopped himself from downing too many, and focused on re-introducing Veronica to everyone she hadn't yet met who was attending the wedding. They all knew who she was, so it was mainly a remember-fest, and a hope that she would stick around that Ted could only silently echo.

Eventually, Ry and Avery reappeared looking radiant. Tucker stood at the bottom of the main staircase and cupped his hands.

"Transport up to Morgan Ranch will be arriving shortly out front! I suggest you all wrap up warm if you want to use it!"

Ted glanced out of the window as he heard the faint chiming of bells. He grabbed Veronica's hand.

"Let's go see what Tucker's talking about."

They hurried through the groups of guests to the front door. It had snowed again, and the sun had come out, bathing the whole town in a bright, white glow. Around the corner came a sleigh drawn by two horses in full Christmas regalia. Three more sleighs arrived, stretching the length of Main Street. Just to complete the picture, all the drivers were dressed as Santa Claus.

"I can see why we need to wrap up warm." Ted chuckled. "You want to ride in a sleigh with me?"

"Oh, yes," Veronica said fervently. "I can't think of anything I'd like more."

He guided her back inside where Tucker was directing guests who preferred the speed and convenience of four-wheel drive to the delights of an open sleigh around to the parking lot where they could either pick up their own vehicle or take the Morgan Ranch shuttle.

Ted joined the line for the sleigh ride while Veronica finished getting ready, enduring the good-natured teasing from the locals about his wonderful girlfriend. He wasn't going to argue about that. He and Veronica might have started their relationship in an unconventional way, but he sure as hell intended to make it a long-term commitment.

If she stayed—and if she finally told him everything that was going on in her life . . . He pushed those thoughts to the back of his mind. Just for once, he was going to allow himself to appreciate the day without self-sabotaging. Veronica was here, she was happy to be with him, and he was darn well going to enjoy it.

Avery and Ry were escorted into the first sleigh, along with their best man, maid of honor, and Chase William who obviously wasn't prepared to wait any longer to get home. There was just enough room for Ted and Veronica in the fourth sleigh. Tucker promised the rest of the line that if they didn't mind a wait, the sleighs would be re-turning.

Ted lifted Veronica onto the seat and squeezed in next to her, wrapping one arm around her shoulder to keep her steady as the sleigh jolted to a start. He couldn't remember the last time he'd been out on the snow like this. These days he preferred the safety and convenience of his big tow truck.

Beside him, Veronica shivered, and Ted drew her closer against his side before wrapping her scarf securely around her neck. She wore her knitted hat with the big pompom and he squished it down hard until it reached her nose.

"Better?"

"Yes, apart from the fact that I can't see or speak any-more." Veronica's reply was muffled until she pulled the scarf away from her chin. "I've forgotten how cold it gets here."

"You'll get used to it," Ted reminded her, bracing his arm against the side of the sled as it turned out of Main, and onto the county road. The sound of the chiming bells and the feathers nodding in the horse's brow pieces made him feel like he was in some kind of movie.

"Or I'll buy a thicker coat."

He smiled down at her. "You thinking about staying then?"

"I'd have to talk to my uncle first."

"You do that," he said softly, his gaze lingering on her face. "I'm sure he'd welcome you home with open arms."

Chapter Seven

Veronica allowed Ted to lift her out of the sled onto the well-packed snow, and took in the amazing scene around her. The circular drive between the ranch house, the old barn, and the new guest center had been transformed into a winter wonderland of decorated pine trees, multicolored fairy lights, and enough tinsel to fill a gift shop.

The sleigh behind her moved off, following the others back to town. Veronica took Ted's proffered hand and walked over to the all-weather red carpet leading to the reception area and bar. Arches of lit branches entwined over their heads and soft bells chimed in the breeze perfumed by pine, Christmas spices, and apple cider.

"Hey, look up!" Ted stopped at the entrance.

"Why?"

Veronica's next words were lost in the wonder of Ted's kiss. When he finally released her, he pointed over her head. "Mistletoe."

"Oh, now I get it." Veronica grinned at him and he winked.

"Couldn't pass that opportunity up."

In the main lobby they were directed toward a cloakroom

to drop off their outer garments and change their shoes. Ted waited for her to join him back in the hall.

"I've got to help out in the receiving line. Will you be okay?"

She gave him a mock frown. "As I said already, I'm a big girl. Go off and do what you need to do."

In fact, she was quite happy to see him occupied with his wedding duties so that she could finally fulfill her promise to call Leon and Sharon. One of them must know *something*, and she really wanted to set her mind at rest. She had a sense Ted wanted to talk to her about staying permanently in Morgan Valley. She wanted to stay, but she couldn't make the commitment until she knew everything was all right in L.A.

Ignoring the reception in the big room off the lobby, she turned instead toward a long hallway of what looked like offices, and wandered down there, her phone in her hand as she typed her messages. There was no immediate response from either of her friends, so she pocketed her cell, and walked back toward the receiving line.

She was welcomed by a grinning Ted, hugged, squealed over, and passed along the line like a Christmas parcel until she ended up in Avery's arms. Her friend wore a red velvet cloak with a hood over her wedding dress and looked like a fairy-tale princess.

"I'm so glad you could come," Avery whispered. "And I really hope you marry Ted and stick around."

"You're getting a bit ahead of yourself, now." Veronica laughed and hugged her back. "You just want everyone to be as happy as you are."

"Of *course* I do!" Avery winked at her. "Now, go and get something to drink, and we'll send Ted to find you before you know it."

Veronica went over to the bar and was offered a champagne cocktail, which she happily accepted. She wandered across the crowded room to the large picture window that looked over the snow-covered pastures and toward the towering black heights of the Sierra Nevadas. Even as she sipped her cocktail, she considered what it might be like waking up to such a familiar view every morning—maybe with Ted sleeping by her side.

Her cell buzzed, and she took it out of her pocket to see a message from Leon.

No scandal mentioning your deadbeat ex's name around to my knowledge. What did you do to him? LOL.

Veronica winced as she typed a reply.

I just wondered if he'd come by the practice, or was looking for me? If he comes near me again, he knows he'd get an earful and a restraining order slapped on his ass.

Do you want me to find out anything I can?

That would be really good of you.

Veronica took a hasty sip of her cocktail.

I'll be super discreet. X.

Veronica knew that was almost impossible for her boss. He was a talker, and he loved nothing more than a good bit of gossip. Would he march right up to Jason's front door and demand to know what was going on? He'd probably consider that discreet as opposed to hopping over the back fence and spying through the windows.

Veronica groaned and downed the rest of her drink. She wished she hadn't sent the text now.

"Everything okay?"

She spluttered as Ted spoke over her shoulder and hastily ditched her glass before she dropped it.

"Yes! I'm great! You?"

He eyed her like a man attempting to defuse a bomb.

"You sure about that?"

She summoned her best smile. "I'm just . . . working on that problem I told you about back in L.A. There's nothing to worry about."

For some reason, the concern in his eyes only deepened. "I wish you'd just tell me what's going on."

She reached for his hand. "I will! I mean, I will as soon as I've sorted it out, which will be very soon, because I've got people on it."

"People?"

She nodded as she squeezed his fingers. "People. I just need a couple of answers to the . . . problem, and then I'll be fine. I promise."

His brow creased. "Look, if all this is moving too fast for you—I mean the stuff between us—and you want to step back, it's okay. I won't be offended. Maybe I've been pushing you too hard, and—"

"Ted, please listen to me." She met his gaze. "The reason I'm being so careful is that I don't want to mess this up, and by this, I mean you, and us, and staying here, and all that stuff that I can't talk about until I've tied up some loose ends."

"So you keep saying." He gently released his hand from hers. "The thing is, Veronica, I can't help feeling that if you really trusted me you'd tell me everything anyway."

She bit her lip at the hurt in his voice. Before she could reply, someone called his name. He looked back over his shoulder and grimaced.

"Sorry, I've got to be in some pictures. We can talk about this later, okay?"

There was nothing she could do but nod and let him go. She turned back to the view and struggled to compose herself. Was she being stupid not telling him? But what could she say when she wasn't even sure what had happened since she'd left? She already knew Ted was wary about relationships; would her refusal to give him a direct answer make him back off completely? It sure was looking that way, and she couldn't quite blame him.

Her cell buzzed, and she took it out of her pocket to see a message from Sharon.

Hey, neighbor! What's up?

Veronica sank down onto one of the cushioned benches that framed the window and replied to the message.

Any news from next door? Is Perry still around?

She waited impatiently for the small bubbles in the corner of the text to appear, indicating that Sharon was responding to her.

I haven't seen her or her piglet since you left. I did wonder if you'd taken them both with you ☺ but couldn't figure out how you'd get them in your car. LOL

Is Jason still there?

Yeah, and whatshername, Marissa, who is kind of sweet tbh, and always says hi, and asks after the kids.

Veronica gripped the phone tighter as she typed.

But Jason's okay?

Yeah, why wouldn't he be? Did you hire an assassin or something?

Ha ha. Is there any way you could ask Marissa what happened to Perry, like asap?

There was a longer pause before Sharon replied.

Sure, her car's on the drive, so I'm fairly sure she's home and the dickhead is out. I'll get back to you when I can, okay?

Thanks so much. I owe you one! Veronica typed even faster. Feel free to give her my cell number if she wants to talk to me directly. She did say she wanted us all to get along.

Like Veronica had believed that for a second, but maybe she had misjudged her ex-husband's new girlfriend. . . .

Even though his mind was not on the wedding, Ted smiled like a champ in all the pictures. He sighed in relief when they were finally released back into the dining room for the beginning of the reception, only to find that he was at the top table, and Veronica was way over in the opposite corner.

He tried to get her attention as he sat down beside Marley, but Veronica was looking down at her phone as if it held the secrets of the universe, which he supposed it did. But who was she waiting to hear from, and why did she look so worried? Had he spoken out too strongly? But what else was he supposed to do when his tentative dreams of future happiness might blow up in his face?

Marley elbowed him in the side.

"I know you've got a girlfriend and that you're besotted,

Ted, but do you think you could give me your attention for two minutes, and tell me whether the Hayes Hotel decorations were better than these?"

Ted turned to face her. "I'm sorry, Marley. From now on, I promise I'll be the most attentive wedding partner you've ever had. Now, what were you asking me?"

It wasn't hard to lose himself in two of his oldest friends' happiness. One look at Ry's face was enough to remind him that love did exist, and that some people, unlike his mom, were capable of staying together through the storms of life. But even as he contemplated their happiness, it only hardened his resolve to have it out with Veronica. If she wasn't one hundred percent all in, then he wasn't going to pretend that was okay with him.

The food was amazing, the company perfect, and the speeches almost made him choke up. By the time he was free to circulate, he was optimistic about his chances to clear the air with Veronica and make things right. He was in love with her—there was no point in pretending otherwise—and he needed her to know that.

He approached her table. She looked up and smiled, and he knew in his heart that everything was going to be all right.

"Hey," she said softly, and patted the seat next to her. "Want to share some of this amazing dessert?"

He took the vacant chair. "It's not like you to share the sweet things."

"I've had six different kinds. Even I'm getting full." She handed over her fork. "Be my guest."

He ate the creamy cheesecake in three bites while Veronica looked on.

"It's good. I didn't get to try everything because I was too busy trying to find tactful ways of assuring Marley that her decorations were just as good as the Morgans'." Ted wiped his mouth with her napkin.

"Then let me get you some more." Veronica stood up. "Would you like coffee? I'm going to get myself a cup."

He touched her arm. "You don't need to get me food."

"Since I'm already getting the coffee, it's hardly a problem, is it?"

He let her go, and she made her way through the tables, stopping to speak to various people, her smile lighting her way.

Something buzzed, and Ted looked down at the table to see Veronica's cell phone lit up with a text. He wasn't even aware that he had starting reading it until it was too late.

Hey, babe, drove by but nothing to report, except when are you coming back? The kids and I are missing you!! Xxx

"Here you go." Veronica set the two coffees on the table along with the plate of desserts. "I hope they've got more in the kitchen because with all these hardworking, outdoor-living cowboys, the food's going down fast." She glanced over at Ted who was staring at her, his expression unreadable. "What?"

He pointed at her phone. "You got a text."

She leaned in to read it and turned back to Ted with a grin. "Leon is such an idiot."

"Is he?"

He definitely wasn't laughing.

"Did you read it?" Veronica asked. "Because—"

"I didn't mean to. It just caught my eye." He sat back

in his chair and crossed his arms over his chest. "Anything you need to say to me right now?"

Veronica bristled at his tone.

"I would've thought you'd be the one apologizing for reading my private messages."

"As I said, it was an accident, and I can't say I'm sorry I read it, because who the hell is texting you, and what's that about you having kids? Is this the 'little problem' you have to deal with back in L.A.?"

Veronica reached over, picked up her phone, and slid it into her pocket, her whole body trembling. "Excuse me."

She rose to her feet and he stood too, towering over her, one hand reaching for her elbow.

"Veronica . . ."

She flinched away. "Don't touch me, okay?"

She slammed her chair in, stepped away from him, and headed for the exit. It took her only a minute to reach the cloakroom and start searching for her belongings. She only looked up when the door clicked shut, and she found Ted leaning up against the inside of it. He held up one hand.

"Look, I know what I did was wrong."

She didn't reply as she finally found her boots and outerwear.

"I shouldn't have read your text."

"No, you shouldn't have." She clutched her coat to her chest and glared at him. "I spent ten years with a man who monitored all my calls, texts, and e-mails and I *hated* it!"

"*Shit.*" He grimaced. "I'm sorry, I didn't think about it that way."

"I don't want to be with a man who constantly doubts me, okay? It would destroy me."

"I get that." He nodded slowly, his whole attention

fixed on her face. "But are you really going to lay all of this on me?"

"Maybe." Veronica stared right back at him.

"Rather than have an honest conversation?" He shrugged. "I'm usually the one running away from those hard truths, but I'm trying here."

"Trying to accuse me of something I haven't done, from one text?" Veronica wasn't quite ready to be reasonable yet.

"You said you'd explain things when you could." He paused. "Wouldn't you say this was maybe a good time to do that?"

Veronica slowly released her death grip on her coat. Okay, maybe he had a point. He wasn't Jason, and she couldn't blame him for everything that had happened in her previous life.

"Leon's text doesn't have anything to do with the other matter I'm concerned about."

"Okay." He didn't look any more relaxed. "Are you saying you're still not ready to talk to me about what's going on?"

"I will be by the end of the day," Veronica offered.

"Got it." He nodded and opened the door. "If you want someone to take you back to Morgantown early, speak to Tucker. He'll get you down there."

"Do you want me to leave?" Veronica asked.

He paused to look back at her. "Honestly? Right now, I don't know what the heck I want. I get that I invaded your privacy, and I'm sorry as hell about it, but I still hate you for not being honest with me." He sighed. "It feels like you're using this as an excuse not to be straight, and that doesn't make me feel good about anything."

"That's not fair," Veronica whispered.

"Maybe it isn't, but it's how I feel, and I can't help that any more than you can help getting mad at me for reading your texts."

He abruptly stopped speaking, stepped back, and threw the door open to let some guests come in. After exchanging pleasantries, he looked over at Veronica.

"I'll check in on you later, okay? I've got to help get the groom ready to leave before HW gets up to his tricks." He hesitated, his voice rough. "The apartment keys are in my pocket if you want them, or just ask Mano for the spare set in the gas station safe."

Still clutching her coat, she watched him leave, her heart thumping hard as she tried to work out what to do next. He'd read the text and drawn all the wrong conclusions from it—which, considering what Leon had said, wasn't exactly hard.

Should she leave? Was there any point in staying when she'd already made him doubt they had a future together? He might not believe her even if she did try to explain. Jason never had. Maybe she'd been stupid to think that any man would ever trust her.

"You okay, Veronica?"

She looked over to the door to find Tucker observing her.

"Ted said you might need to leave early because you weren't feeling too good." He paused. "I've got a fleet of vehicles going back and forth between here and the hotel so if you want to go, it won't be a problem."

"Thanks." Veronica let out a shaky breath. "I think maybe I *should* go. Ted's not very . . . happy with me right now."

"I kind of got that," Tucker said tactfully. "If I can just

say something in his defense, he's a good guy, and he doesn't get mad easily. If you can bear to stay and talk this out, he'll definitely listen to you."

"I know." She offered him a smile. "He's not the problem, it's me. And I can't give him the answers he needs right now."

Chapter Eight

"She said to tell you that she was sorry, and that it was all on her, and that you weren't to worry about anything," Tucker said and then hesitated. "But she looked like she was about to burst into tears, and I don't think she really wanted to leave."

Ted nodded slowly as he tried to deal with the fact that Veronica had left the wedding. The reception had finished and the evening party with a band and a free bar had commenced, leaving everyone, except him, full of food and happy to dance the night away.

"It wasn't all on her."

Tucker grimaced. "It rarely is."

"I read a text on her phone and got mad about it, forgetting that she'd dealt with an abusive ex who controlled her life, and that she might not take what I did too well."

"Unfortunate."

"Yeah, that's one way of putting it. She asked me to be patient and wait until she could explain everything to me, and I wanted more." Ted shook his head. "So damn stupid!"

"You're in love with her—you get to be stupid." Tucker

gently punched his arm. "Now, all you have to do is think of a way to fix this."

Ted looked over at the dance floor where the happy couple was swaying gently to some romantic song. "I can't go after her right now. I have duties."

"Like those two would even notice you'd gone," Tucker scoffed. "If they ask where you are, and they won't, I'll tell them you had to pull someone's truck out of a snow-bank, and you'll be back when you can."

"But—"

Tucker punched him again, this time harder, and shoved him toward the door. "Don't even go there. Veronica needs you, and that's more important than anything."

Veronica let herself into the apartment and gently closed the door behind her. She hadn't taken Ted's keys and had borrowed the spare set from Mano, who had told her he'd been up to check on Bacon, whom he'd taken quite a shine to. She went straight to see the piglet, who immediately climbed into her lap. She held him close, burying her face into his neck, and just breathed him in.

She should have stayed and had things out with Ted, but she hadn't wanted to disrupt the wedding even more than she already had. Ted deserved to enjoy the day with people he loved and trusted, and she wasn't sure she was one of those people anymore. She took down Bacon's leash. She wished she could say she'd overreacted to Ted reading her text, but that wasn't something she could control because it was so tied up with the person she'd been, and had tried to get past.

When he returned, she'd tell him everything, even though Sharon hadn't yet gotten back to her. And then they could be friends again, wish each other well, and move on. She swallowed hard. He'd only asked her to be his girl-friend for the wedding after all. . . .

Making sure she had her keys, she took Bacon out for his walk. The town was quieter than usual as almost every-one was still at Morgan Ranch enjoying the wedding. She didn't see a single soul, which, in her present mood, suited her just fine.

By the time she got back, her face was chilled from the wind and the thought of crawling into bed with a mug of hot chocolate was incredibly appealing. She stomped up the stairs, her boots leaving wet patches of snow on the steps, and unlocked the door to the apartment.

There was a light on in the kitchen she was certain she'd turned off before she'd left. Hugging Bacon to her chest, she eased off her boots and walked through to find Ted sitting at the counter staring right back at her.

"Hey." He still wasn't smiling.

"Why aren't you at the wedding?" Veronica asked.

He shrugged. "This seemed way more important."

She held Bacon up like an offering. "I'll just put him into the bathroom and then I'll be back, okay?"

"I'll make some coffee."

She contemplated making a mad dash for the stairs but only for a second. This was Ted, her *friend,* and whatever else happened between them, Tucker was right. She could rely on him to at least hear her out.

When she got back, he was sitting in one of the chairs and had placed two mugs on the kitchen table in front of him. He gestured at her cup.

"I made you hot chocolate. You always like it when you're cold."

"Thank you." She cradled the cup in her hands as she

settled into the chair opposite him, and tried to decide where to begin. "About Leon . . ."

He held up his hand. "You said that didn't have anything to do with what happened, so why don't you move on?"

"But—" She took a good look at his face and sighed. "Okay, then I'll start with Jason. I thought he was dead."

"What?" He blinked at her.

"As in no longer living, but from what I've found out today, that doesn't appear to be the case."

"Did you . . . *try* to kill him?" Ted asked.

Despite the seriousness of the moment, it was such a Ted question that Veronica's sense of humor surfaced, and she fought a smile.

"What if I did?"

He sat back. "Then you didn't succeed, and you're in the clear, right?"

"Doesn't that worry you at all?"

"Look, I've already accepted that you stole his pig, so adding a probably justifiable homicide isn't that big of a stretch."

She stared hard at him as his lips twitched.

"You think if I had killed him, he would probably have deserved it?"

He nodded. "I'd still make you turn yourself in, but I suspect you'd get a minimum sentence."

"You sound like my uncle Victor."

"I'll take that as a compliment." Ted sipped his coffee and then set the mug back down. "What exactly happened to make you think Jason might be dead?"

Veronica let out a relieved breath. Here came the hard part. "As I already told you, I went around to see how Perry and her piglet were doing. I still had my keys so I kind of ended up inside the house."

"Ended up." Ted raised a skeptical eyebrow.

"I looked through the back windows. Perry was lying on the floor with the piglet next to her. I thought Perry was dead. I rushed in without thinking or realizing that Jason had taken the day off and was still at home."

"That explains how Jason comes into the story. Go on." Ted nodded.

"He grabbed hold of Bacon, and held him up in the air with one of the kitchen knives at his throat." Veronica shuddered as she recalled the scene. "He said he was going to send both pigs to the slaughterhouse, and that he'd only stayed home to wait for the truck to arrive.

"I . . . lost my temper, lowered my head, and tried to tackle him to the floor. I made a grab for Bacon, who was squealing his head off, but Jason shoved me backward so hard that I fell on my ass next to Perry, who definitely wasn't dead. She didn't like Jason much by this point, and seeing him hurting her baby made her mad. She charged him and he went down like a stone."

Veronica gulped for air. "Luckily, Bacon fell on top of Jason when he hit the ground and Perry was more interested in saving her piglet than finishing Jason off."

She glanced over at Ted to find his shoulders were shaking, and that he had one hand covering his mouth.

"It *wasn't* funny!" She glared at him.

"Sure sounds like it from this side of the room."

She shot to her feet and marched over to him, hands on her hips. "I was afraid!"

He slid an arm around her waist and pulled her onto his

knee, which, she realized, was exactly where she wanted to be.

"I guess you had to be there," he said.

She punched him hard in the chest and he obligingly grunted.

"I'll shut up now. You didn't know whether Jason was okay at that point, so I get that it was stressful." He smoothed his hand over her back. "I guess this was when you stole Bacon and made a run for it?"

"Yes." She tangled her fingers in the buttons of his shirt and wouldn't look up at him. "I did call nine-one-one and left the back door open for the paramedics."

"Of course you did." Another tremor rumbled through his frame but this time he kept his voice even. "I suppose, after you left like that, you couldn't just call his cell and ask him if he was okay?"

"No, which is why I couldn't tell you everything. Today I asked Sharon to find out what happened to Perry. She's supposed to be getting back to me anytime now." Veronica finally looked up at him. "Do you think Jason went through with it, and sent her to be killed?"

"I don't know, love." Ted held her gaze. "Do you want to call him and ask?"

"*Call* him? Ted, I've spent the last two years avoiding him like the plague!"

Even as he opened his mouth to reply, her cell rang. She jumped like she'd been shot and yanked it out of her pocket.

"Oh my God, it's Jason."

"Well, pick up," Ted said. "Put him on speakerphone." She glared at him, but did as he suggested.

"Hello?"

"You've got my pigs, haven't you?"

"Hi, Jason, how are you? Long time no speak," Veronica said airily, hoping her ex wouldn't notice the tremor in her voice.

"I hear you've been looking for me. If you don't return my property, I'm going to the cops. I'm going to tell them how you broke into my house and attacked me. I had a concussion!"

Veronica offered Ted a stricken glance and he wrapped his hand around the one of hers holding the phone, which steadied her.

"I thought you were sending the pigs to be slaughtered."

"And I *will* be doing that after you return them," Jason countered. "Perry's too dangerous to keep."

"You'd better keep your stories straight for the cops, Jason. Which is it? Did Perry attack you, or was it me?" Veronica asked. "Maybe that bump on your head really did confuse you."

"I'm not confused, sweetheart, you just—oh, hi, Marissa, how was your day?"

Veronica glanced over at Ted and raised her eyebrows as Marissa started talking.

"I've just been speaking to Sharon, and now I hear you threatening your ex-wife on the phone over a *pig?* You told me she'd ambushed you and stolen them, and that you wanted them back because you *loved* them—not that you intended to send them off to be slaughtered! You *know* how I feel about animal cruelty. How could you do such a thing?"

"Marissa, sweetheart, darling—"

"Don't you Marissa me. If Veronica did take those pigs, she's welcome to them!"

"But—I didn't . . ." Veronica tried to interrupt, but the couple at the other end of the conversation was too busy shouting at each other to hear her. She looked over at Ted and shrugged. "She's got more guts than I ever had, I'll give her that."

"Hello?"

Veronica jumped as Marissa came on the line.

"Er, hey. What's up?"

"Jason's stormed out in a huff."

"Okay . . ." Veronica said cautiously.

"Don't worry about Perry," Marissa continued. "She's safe on my parents' farm."

"I beg your pardon?"

"You've got the piglet, right? You're welcome to keep him—although you do know he'll get big like his mother?"

Veronica took a firmer grip on her phone. "Can we back up a bit here? Did you just lie to Jason?"

Marissa chuckled. "Who do you think came home and found Jason being attended to by the EMTs while he rambled on about Perry trying to kill him? While we were at the ER I called my folks and asked them to come get Perry and keep her safe. Jason doesn't remember any of it."

"How did you know I had Bacon?" Veronica asked.

"I didn't until I talked to Sharon today and realized you'd been in the house on that fateful day and that you'd probably taken him to safety. I was just glad to hear he was okay. I was worried he'd run away." Marissa paused. "Thanks for doing that. If he does get too big for you, let me know, and he can come live on my parents' farm. They kind of collect rescue animals and they already love Perry."

"Marissa, Jason said he was going to call the cops and say I attacked him if I didn't bring Bacon back," Veronica said.

"He won't be doing that," Marissa said.

"You sound very confident," Veronica commented.

"He'd never live it down if I went to the cops with him, and insisted that he'd been brought down by a pig. And I would do that for Perry who doesn't deserve to suffer because of Jason's actions."

Even though Marissa couldn't see her, Veronica nodded. "Jason sure hates looking stupid."

"Yeah . . ." Marissa sighed. "Although I think the stupid one is me. I really messed up believing all those lies he told me, and thinking I was the one who'd finally be the woman he needed."

"Trust me on this." Veronica snorted. "The women aren't the problem, Marissa. The common theme is Jason."

"I realize that now, and I'm truly sorry for all the harm I caused you."

"You didn't cause me harm. I was already looking for a way out of the door before you came along. In fact, you helped me realize how relieved I would be to go." It was the first time Veronica had voiced her feelings on the matter, and they rang true. "I'm sorry you had to find out he's a rat-tailed ass."

It was Marissa's turn to snort. "Look, I'd better go. I have some packing to do before Jason gets back. I'll get your number from Sharon, and maybe we can keep in touch?"

"I'd like that," Veronica said sincerely. "And maybe, one day I can come and see Perry in her new home."

"Awesome. Happy holidays."

Veronica ended the call and got up to set her phone on the countertop before facing Ted.

"Well, that didn't go *quite* how I was expecting it to, but I think everything's okay now."

"You do?" Ted asked, his slow smile warming her heart. "Like, *everything*?"

"Everything that was stopping me from telling you that I want to stay in Morgan Valley—if Uncle Victor will have me." She met his gaze head-on. "I'm sorry. I should have told you everything up front instead of making you doubt me. But I didn't want you ending up with a criminal being tried for murder."

He winced. "A lot of that's on me, okay? I'm . . . not great at trusting people, and I always look for the worst possible outcome."

"You do?" She fluttered her eyelashes at him. "*Really?*"

He rose to his feet in one strong motion and hoisted her over his shoulder.

"That's it."

"What? Put me down!"

He carried her through to his bedroom and gently dropped her on his bed before straddling her hips and looming over her.

"One question."

"What is it?" Veronica asked.

"Leon."

"I thought you didn't care about that because it didn't have anything to do with the pig situation."

"I care now, so give it up."

"He's my boss," Veronica said.

"Go on."

"We work together."

Ted flicked her nose with his finger, which made her grin.

"I'm a specialist pediatric nurse. Leon's a doctor."

Ted considered her for a very long minute. "So, the 'kids' are your patients?"

"Yes." She nodded. "Go to the top of the class."

"Dr. Tio is desperate to get a pediatric nurse here at the new health center," Ted mused. "You should go and talk to him after you've settled things with Victor."

"Sounds like a plan." Veronica pretended to try and sit up. "Now, shouldn't we be getting back to that wedding?"

Ted shook his head. "Not quite yet." He leaned in and kissed her. "I need to sort a few things out here, first— with you."

"I thought we just did that?" Veronica breathed against his lips.

"Other things." He kissed her again. "More important things, like 'I think I might be falling in love with you' kind of things."

She opened her eyes wide. "Well, that's good to know because, despite everything, I've been kind of feeling that way myself."

"Yeah?" He ran a finger down her throat to the bodice of her dress. "Like sticking around, and making things work between us?"

"Definitely." She bit her lip. "If you think you can trust me after all this mess I've involved you in."

"I think I can. Even when I knew you weren't quite being straight, I never gave up hope that you would change your mind and trust me." He hesitated. "And I promise I'll never treat you like Jason did."

"I know that." It was her turn to pause. "We've both had our reasons not to trust the people who were supposed to love us the most, but I want to move past that—to believe in someone. To believe in *you*."

He took her hand and placed it over his heart, his voice hoarse. "I swear I'll do everything in my power to make you the happiest woman in Morgantown."

"And I'll make you the happiest man," Veronica promised in return. "I've learned a lot about myself since I left Jason. I know I can stand alone, but I'm not stupid enough to ignore an upstanding, honest, honorable man like you."

He swallowed hard. "I need you to keep pushing me, yeah? To share your strength and remind me how lucky I am."

"You already know all that in your heart," Veronica said softly. "I'm just here to help you remember it."

With a groan, he lowered his head, and Veronica stopped thinking about anything other than the delights of their lovemaking for a very long time.

"Hey, you."

Ted opened the bathroom door a crack and went in, sitting on the pillow Veronica had left near Bacon's bed. The little piglet came over and immediately jumped into his lap, making Ted wince as he only had his robe on, and who knew little pig hooves were hard?

He stroked Bacon's head until he settled down and Ted got used to the unique odor of pig again.

"It's all going to be okay, little buddy," Ted murmured to the pig. "We're going to take you out to your great-uncle Victor's place. You'll love it there. I guarantee it."

Bacon snuffled happily and Ted relaxed against the wall. He'd sent a text to Tucker telling him that everything was okay, but that he and Veronica weren't going to make it back to the wedding, and to make their excuses to everyone.

Tucker's reply was short, to the point, and too rude to share with Veronica, who was currently fast asleep in his bed. He owed his friend one, that was for sure. The night had passed without any callouts for his tow truck services, mainly because everyone in the valley, including the deputy sheriff, was up at Morgan Ranch enjoying the wedding.

Glancing out of the small window, Ted noticed snow was falling, meaning they'd be getting their usual white Christmas—the best one he could remember since his mother had left the family. Careful not to disturb Bacon, he slid his phone out of his pocket and sent his dad a text wishing him a Merry Christmas, with a selfie he'd taken with Veronica earlier, which he knew his father would love.

He paused, his smile lingering before scrolling through his contacts with his thumb, and eventually stopping, and typing.

Happy Holidays, Mom. x

To his surprise, she replied immediately.

Same to you, son. Thank you for thinking of me. x

Ted hesitated and then channeled Veronica telling him to be brave.

Am thinking of popping up to see you before Dad gets back from his cruise. Would that be okay?

That would be wonderful. I always miss you most at Christmas.

Ted wondered whether she regretted what she'd done, but knew it wasn't the right time to bring the subject up. That conversation would have to take place in person.

I might bring Veronica Hernandez with me.

You're dating?

Yeah. Ted couldn't help smiling even though he was alone.

That's wonderful to hear, Ted. I can't wait to meet her again. I have to go walk my dogs now. Let me know exactly when you think you might be coming, and I'll clear my calendar. Love you, Mom. x.

Love you, too.

Ted stared down at the exchange, trying to read nuance into his mother's words and failing. Maybe they'd finally get around to having that all-important conversation when he visited, or maybe he'd just let it go and forgive her. He was older and wiser now, and, he hoped, more willing to listen, understand, and accept her view of what had happened, even though it might still hurt him.

Bacon let out a snore, and Ted laid him gently back in his bed, checked that he had water and food, and let himself out into the hallway. He paused in his doorway to appreciate the sight of Veronica sleeping soundly in his bed. He wasn't falling in love with her—he was one hundred percent fallen, and he didn't regret that.

If things stayed like this, he'd no longer be the one dreading Christmas—he'd be celebrating it as the time when all his dreams came true. . . .

Christmas Peanut Clusters for Ted
(You'll need a 4-quart slow cooker for this recipe.)

Ingredients:
- 2 lbs white almond bark, broken or chopped up
- 12 oz bag semi-sweet chocolate chips
- 4 oz bar German chocolate, chopped
- 32 oz dry roasted or cocktail peanuts
- Christmas sprinkles

Method:
1. Spray slow cooker lightly with oil; add almond bark and both kinds of chocolate. Place a clean, dry kitchen towel over the top of the cooker, place lid on top.
2. Cook on high for one hour, reduce heat to low, and cook for one more hour, stirring every 15 minutes until everything is melted.
3. Carefully remove lid and towel and add peanuts. Stir well.
4. Line baking sheets with waxed/parchment paper. Drop candy mix by spoonful onto sheets and add Christmas sprinkles before it sets.
5. Refrigerate for an hour, then store in an airtight container for a week, or freeze.

Makes 20+ servings.

Please turn the page for an exciting peek at:

THE SNOW MAN

by
Diana Palmer

Available at bookstores and e-retailers

Meadow Dawson just stared at the slim, older cowboy who was standing on her front porch with his hat held against his chest. His name was Ted. He was her father's ranch foreman. And he was speaking Greek, she decided, or perhaps some form of archaic language that she couldn't understand.

"The culls," he persisted. "Mr. Jake wanted us to go ahead and ship them out to that rancher we bought the replacement heifers from."

She blinked. She knew three stances that she could use to shoot a .40 caliber Glock from. She was experienced in interrogation techniques. She'd once participated in a drug raid with other agents from the St. Louis, Missouri, office where she'd been stationed during her brief tenure with the FBI as a special agent.

Sadly, none of those experiences had taught her what a cull was, or what to do with it. She pushed back her long, golden blond hair, and her pale green eyes narrowed on his elderly face.

She blinked. "Are culls some form of wildlife?" she asked blankly.

The cowboy doubled up laughing.

She grimaced. Her father and mother had divorced when she was six. She'd gone to live with her mother in Greenwood, Mississippi, while her father stayed here on this enormous Colorado ranch, just outside Raven Springs. Later, she'd spent some holidays with her dad, but only after she was in her senior year of high school and she could out-argue her bitter mother, who hated her ex-husband. What she remembered about cattle was that they were loud and dusty. She really hadn't paid much attention to the cattle on the ranch or her father's infrequent references to ranching problems. She hadn't been there often enough to learn the ropes.

"I worked for the FBI," she said with faint belligerence. "I don't know anything about cattle."

He straightened up. "Sorry, ma'am," he said, still fighting laughter. "Culls are cows that didn't drop calves this spring. Nonproductive cattle are removed from the herd, or culled. We sell them either as beef or surrogate mothers for purebred cattle."

She nodded and tried to look intelligent. "I see." She hesitated. "So we're punishing poor female cattle for not being able to have calves repeatedly over a period of years."

The cowboy's face hardened. "Ma'am, can I give you some friendly advice about ranch management?"

She shrugged. "Okay."

"I think you'd be doing yourself a favor if you sold this ranch," he said bluntly. "It's hard to make a living at ranching, even if you've done it for years. It would be a sin and a shame to let all your father's hard work go to pot. Begging your pardon, ma'am," he added respectfully. "Dal Blake was friends with your father, and he owns the biggest

ranch around Raven Springs. Might be worthwhile to talk
to him."

Meadow managed a smile through homicidal rage.
"Dariell Blake and I don't speak," she informed him.

"Ma'am?" The cowboy sounded surprised.

"He told my father that I'd turned into a manly woman
who probably didn't even have . . ." She bit down hard on
the word she couldn't bring herself to voice. "Anyway,"
she added tersely, "he can keep his outdated opinions to
himself."

The cowboy grimaced. "Sorry."

"Not your fault," she said, and managed a smile. "Thanks
for the advice, though. I think I'll go online and watch a
few YouTube videos on cattle management. I might call
one of those men, or women, for advice."

The cowboy opened his mouth to speak, thought about
how scarce jobs were, and closed it again. "Whatever you
say, ma'am." He put his hat back on. "I'll just get back to
work. It's, uh, okay to ship out the culls?"

"Of course it's all right," she said, frowning. "Why
wouldn't it be?"

"You said it oppressed the cows . . ."

She rolled her eyes. "I was kidding!"

"Oh." Ted brightened a little. He tilted his hat respectfully and went away.

Meadow went back into the house and felt empty. She
and her father had been close. He loved his ranch and his
daughter. Getting to know her as an adult had been great
fun for both of them. Her mother had kept the tension
going as long as she lived. She never would believe that
Meadow could love her and her ex-husband equally. But
Meadow did. They were both wonderful people. They just
couldn't live together without arguing.

She ran her fingers over the back of the cane-bottomed rocking chair where her father always sat, near the big stone fireplace. It was November, and Colorado was cold. Heavy snow was already falling. Meadow remembered Colorado winters from her childhood, before her parents divorced. It was going to be difficult to manage payroll, much less all the little added extras she'd need, like food and electricity . . .

She shook herself mentally. She'd manage, somehow. And she'd do it without Dariell Blake's help. She could only imagine the smug, self-righteous expression that would come into those chiseled features if she asked him to teach her cattle ranching. She'd rather starve. Well, not really.

She considered her options, and there weren't many. Her father owned this ranch outright. He owed for farm equipment, like combines to harvest grain crops and tractors to help with planting. He owed for feed and branding supplies and things like that. But the land was hers now, free and clear. There was a lot of land. It was worth millions.

She could have sold it and started over. But he'd made her promise not to. He'd known her very well by then. She never made a promise she didn't keep. Her own sense of ethics locked her into a position she hated. She didn't know anything about ranching!

Her father mentioned Dariell, whom everyone locally called Dal, all the time. Fine young man, he commented. Full of pepper, good disposition, loves animals.

The loving animals part was becoming a problem. She had a beautiful white Siberian husky, a rescue, with just a hint of red-tipped fur in her ears and tail. She was named Snow, and Meadow had fought the authorities to keep her in her small apartment. She was immaculate, and Meadow brushed her and bathed her faithfully. Finally the apartment manager had given in, reluctantly, after Meadow offered a sizable deposit for the apartment, which was close to her work. She made friends with a lab tech in the next-door apartment, who kept Snow when Meadow had to travel for work. It was a nice arrangement, except that the lab tech really liked Meadow, who didn't return the admiration. While kind and sweet, the tech did absolutely nothing for Meadow physically or emotionally.

She wondered sometimes if she was really cold. Men were nice. She dated. She'd even indulged in light petting with one of them. But she didn't feel the sense of need that made women marry and settle and have kids with a man. Most of the ones she'd dated were career oriented and didn't want marriage in the first place. Meadow's mother had been devout. Meadow grew up with deep religious beliefs that were in constant conflict with society's norms.

She kept to herself mostly. She'd loved her job when she started as an investigator for the Bureau. But there had been a minor slipup.

Meadow was clumsy. There was no other way to put it. She had two left feet, and she was always falling down or doing things the wrong way. It was a curse. Her mother had named her Meadow because she was reading a novel at the time and the heroine had that name. The heroine had been gentle and sweet and a credit to the community where she lived, in 1900s Fort Worth, Texas. Meadow, sadly, was nothing like her namesake.

There had been a stakeout. Meadow had been assigned, with another special agent, to keep tabs on a criminal who'd shot a police officer. The officer lived, but the man responsible was facing felony charges, and he ran.

A CI, or Confidential Informant, had told them where the man was likely to be on a Friday night. It was a local club, frequented by people who were out of the mainstream of society.

Meadow had been assigned to watch the back door while the other special agent went through the front of the club and tried to spot him.

Sure enough, the man was there. The other agent was recognized by a patron, who warned the perpetrator. The criminal took off out the back door.

While Meadow was trying to get her gun out of the holster, the fugitive ran into her and they both tumbled onto the ground.

"Clumsy cow!" he exclaimed. He turned her over and pushed her face hard into the asphalt of the parking lot, and then jumped up and ran.

Bruised and bleeding, Meadow managed to get to her feet and pull her service revolver. "FBI! Stop or I'll shoot!"

"You couldn't hit a barn from the inside!" came the sarcastic reply from the running man.

"I'll show . . . you!" As she spoke, she stepped back onto a big rock, her feet went out from under her, and the gun discharged right into the windshield of the SUV she and the special agent arrived in.

The criminal was long gone by the time Meadow was recovering from the fall.

"Did you get him?" the other agent panted as he joined her. He frowned. "What the hell happened to you?"

"He fell over me and pushed my face into the asphalt," she muttered, feeling the blood on her nose. "I ordered him to halt and tried to fire when I tripped over a rock . . ."

The other agent's face told a story that he was too kind to voice.

She swallowed, hard. "Sorry about the windshield," she added.

He glanced at the Bureau SUV and shook his head. "Maybe we could tell them it was a vulture. You know, they sometimes fly into car windshields."

"No," she replied grimly. "It's always better to tell them the truth. Even when it's painful."

"Guess you're right." He grimaced. "Sorry."

"Hey. We all have talents. I think mine is to trip over my own feet at any given dangerous moment."

"The SAC is going to be upset," he remarked.

"I don't doubt it," she replied.

In fact, the Special Agent in Charge was eloquent about her failure to secure the fugitive. He also wondered aloud, rhetorically, how any firearms instructor ever got drunk enough to pass her in the academy. She kept quiet, figuring that anything she said would only make matters worse.

He didn't take her badge. He did, however, assign her as an aide to another agent who was redoing files in the basement of the building. It was clerical work, for which she wasn't even trained. And from that point, her career as an FBI agent started going drastically downhill.

She'd always had problems with balance. She thought that her training would help her compensate for it, but she'd been wrong. She seemed to be a complete failure as an FBI agent. Her superior obviously thought so.

He did give her a second chance, months later. He sent her to interrogate a man who'd confessed to kidnapping an underage girl for immoral purposes. Meadow's questions, which she'd formulated beforehand, irritated him to the point of physical violence. He'd attacked Meadow, who was totally unprepared for what amounted to a beating. She'd fought, and screamed, to no avail. It had taken a jailer to extricate the man's hands from her throat. Of course, that added another charge to the bevy he was already facing: assault on a federal officer.

But Meadow reacted very badly to the incident. It had never occurred to her that a perpetrator might attack her physically. She'd learned to shoot a gun, she'd learned self-defense, hand-to-hand, all the ways in the world to protect herself. But when she'd come up against an unarmed but violent criminal, she'd almost been killed. Her training wasn't enough. She'd felt such fear that she couldn't function. That had been the beginning of the end. Both she and the Bureau had decided that she was in the wrong profession. They'd been very nice about it, but she'd lost her job.

And Dal Blake thought she was a manly woman, a real hell-raiser. It was funny. She was the exact opposite. Half the time she couldn't even remember to do up the buttons on her coat right.

She sighed as she thought about Dal. She'd had a crush on him in high school. He was almost ten years older than she was and considered her a child. Her one attempt to catch his eye had ended in disaster . . .

She'd come to visit her father during Christmas holidays—much against her mother's wishes. It was her senior year of high school. She'd graduate in the spring. She knew that she was too young to appeal to a man Dal's age, but she was infatuated with him, fascinated by him.

He came by to see her father often because they were both active members in the local cattlemen's association. So one night when she knew he was coming over, Meadow dressed to the hilt in her Sunday best. It was a low-cut red sheath dress, very Christmassy and festive. It had long sleeves and side slits. It was much too old for Meadow, but her father loved her, so he let her pick it out and he paid for it.

Meadow walked into the room while Dal and her father were talking and sat down in a chair nearby, with a book in her hands. She tried to look sexy and appealing. She had on too much makeup, but she hadn't noticed that. The magazines all said that makeup emphasized your best features. Meadow didn't have many best features. Her straight nose and bow mouth were sort of appealing, and she had pretty light green eyes. She used masses of eyeliner and mascara and way too much rouge. Her best feature was her long, thick, beautiful blond hair. She wore it down that night.

Her father gave her a pleading look, which she ignored. She smiled at Dal with what she hoped was sophistication.

He gave her a dark-eyed glare.

The expression on his face washed away all her self-confidence. She flushed and pretended to read her book, but she was shaky inside. He didn't look interested. In fact, he looked very repulsed.

When her father went out of the room to get some paperwork he wanted to show to Dal, Meadow forced herself to look at him and smile.

"It's almost Christmas," she began, trying to find a subject for conversation.

He didn't reply. He did get to his feet and come toward her. That flustered her even more. She fumbled with the book and dropped it on the floor.

Dal pulled her up out of the chair and took her by the shoulders firmly. "I'm ten years older than you," he said bluntly. "You're a high school kid. I don't rob cradles and I don't appreciate attempts to seduce me in your father's living room. Got that?"

Her breath caught. "I never . . . !" she stammered.

His chiseled mouth curled expressively as he looked down into her shocked face. "You're painted up like a carnival fortune-teller. Too much makeup entirely. Does your mother know you wear clothes like that and come on to men?" he added icily. "I thought she was religious."

"She . . . is," Meadow stammered, and felt her age. Too young. She was too young. Her eyes fell away from his. "So am I. I'm sorry."

"You should be," he returned. His strong fingers contracted on her shoulders. "When do you leave for home?"

"Next Friday," she managed to say. She was dying inside. She'd never been so embarrassed in her life.

"Good. You get on the plane and don't come back. Your father has enough problems without trying to keep you out of trouble. And next time I come over here, I don't want to find you setting up shop in the living room, like a spider hunting flies."

"You're a very big fly," she blurted out, and flushed some more.

His lip curled. "You're out of your league, kid." He let go of her shoulders and moved her away from him, as if she had something contagious. His eyes went to the low-cut neckline. "If you went out on the street like that, in Raven Springs, you'd get offers."

She frowned. "Offers?"

"Prostitutes mostly do get offers," he said with distaste.

Tears threatened, but she pulled herself up to her maximum height, far short of his, and glared up at him. "I am not a prostitute!"

"Sorry. Prostitute in training?" he added thoughtfully.

She wanted to hit him. She'd never wanted anything so much. In fact, she raised her hand to slap that arrogant look off his face.

He caught her arm and pushed her hand away.

Even then, at that young age, her balance hadn't been what it should be. Her father had a big, elegant stove in the living room to heat the house. It used coal instead of wood, and it was very efficient behind its tight glass casing. There was a coal bin right next to it.

Meadow lost her balance and went down right into the coal bin. Coal spilled out onto the wood floor and all over her. Now there were black splotches all over her pretty red dress, not to mention her face and hair and hands.

She sat up in the middle of the mess, and angry tears ran down her soot-covered cheeks as she glared at Dal.

He was laughing so hard that he was almost doubled over.

"That's right, laugh," she muttered. "Santa's going to stop by here on his way to your house to get enough coal to fill up your stocking, Dariell Blake!"

He laughed even harder.

Her father came back into the room with a file folder in one hand, stopped, did a double take, and stared at his daughter, sitting on the floor in a pile of coal.

"What the hell happened to you?" he burst out.

"He happened to me!" she cried, pointing at Dal Blake. "He said I looked like a streetwalker!"

"You're the one in the tight red dress, honey." Dal chuckled. "I just made an observation."

"Your mother would have a fit if she saw you in that dress," her father said heavily. "I should never have let you talk me into buying it."

"Well, it doesn't matter anymore, it's ruined!" She got to her feet, swiping at tears in her eyes. "I'm going to bed!"

"Might as well," Dal remarked, shoving his hands into his jeans pockets and looking at her with an arrogant smile. "Go flirt with men your own age, kid."

She looked to her father for aid, but he just stared at her and sighed.

She scrambled to her feet, displacing more coal. "I'll get this swept up before I go to bed," she said.

"I'll do that. Get yourself cleaned up, Meda," her father said gently, using his pet name for her. "Go on."

She left the room muttering. She didn't even look at Dal Blake.

That had been several years ago, before she worked in law enforcement in Missouri and finally hooked up with the FBI. Now she was without a job, running a ranch about which she knew absolutely nothing, and whole families who depended on the ranch for a living were depending on her. The responsibility was tremendous.

She honestly didn't know what she was going to do. She did watch a couple of YouTube videos, but they were less than helpful. Most of them were self-portraits of small ranchers and their methods of dealing with livestock. It was interesting, but they assumed that their audience knew something about ranching. Meadow didn't.

She started to call the local cattlemen's association for help, until someone told her who the president of the chapter was. Dal Blake. Why hadn't she guessed?

While she was drowning in self-doubt, there was a knock on the front door. She opened it to find a handsome man, dark-eyed, with thick blond hair, standing on her porch. He was wearing a sheriff's uniform, complete with badge.

"Miss Dawson?" he said politely.

She smiled. "Yes?"

"I'm Sheriff Jeff Ralston."

"Nice to meet you," she said. She shook hands with him. She liked his handshake. It was firm without being aggressive.

"Nice to meet you, too," he replied. He shifted his weight.

She realized that it was snowing again and he must be freezing. "Won't you come in?" she said as an afterthought, moving back.

"Thanks," he replied. He smiled. "Getting colder out here."

She laughed. "I don't mind snow."

"You will when you're losing cattle to it," he said with a sigh as he followed her into the small kitchen, where she motioned him into a chair.

"I don't know much about cattle," she confessed. "Coffee?"

"I'd love a cup," he said heavily. "I had to get out of bed before daylight and check out a robbery at a local home. Someone came in through the window and took off with a valuable antique lamp."

She frowned. "Just the lamp?"

He nodded. "Odd robbery, that. Usually the perps carry off anything they can get their hands on."

"I know." She smiled sheepishly. "I was with the FBI for two years."

"I heard about that. In fact," he added while she started coffee brewing, "that's why I'm here."

"You need help with the robbery investigation?" she asked, pulling two mugs out of the cabinet.

"I need help, period," he replied. "My investigator just quit to go live in California with his new wife. She's from there. Left me shorthanded. We're on a tight budget, like most small law enforcement agencies. I only have the one investigator. Had, that is." He eyed her. "I thought you might be interested in the job," he added with a warm smile.

She almost dropped the mugs. "Me?"

"Yes. Your father said you had experience in law enforcement before you went with the Bureau and that you were noted for your investigative abilities."

"Noted wasn't quite the word they used," she said, remembering the rage her boss had unleashed when she blew the interrogation of a witness. That also brought back memories of the brutality the man had used against her in the physical attack. To be fair to her boss, he didn't know the prisoner had attacked her until after he'd read her the riot act. He'd apologized handsomely, but the damage was already done.

"Well, the FBI has its own way of doing things. So do I." He accepted the hot mug of coffee with a smile. "Thanks. I live on black coffee."

She laughed, sitting down at the table with him to put cream and sugar in her own. She noticed that he took his straight up. He had nice hands. Very masculine and strong-looking. No wedding band. No telltale tan line where one had been, either. She guessed that he'd never been married, but it was too personal a question to ask a relative stranger.

"I need an investigator and you're out of work. What do you say?"

She thought about the possibilities. She smiled. Here it was, like fate, a chance to prove to the world that she could be a good investigator. It was like the answer to a prayer.

She grinned. "I'll take it, and thank you."

He let out the breath he'd been holding. "No. Thank you. I can't handle the load alone. When can you start?"

"It's Friday. How about first thing Monday morning?" she asked.

"That would be fine. I'll put you on the day shift to begin. You'll need to report to my office by seven a.m. Too early?"

"Oh, no. I'm usually in bed by eight and up by five in the morning."

His eyebrows raised.

"It's my dog," she sighed. "She sleeps on the bed with me, and she wakes up at five. She wants to eat and play. So I can't go back to sleep or she'll eat the carpet."

He laughed. "What breed is she?"

"She's a white Siberian husky with red highlights. Beautiful."

"Where is she?"

She caught her breath as she realized that she'd let Snow out to go to the bathroom an hour earlier, and she hadn't scratched at the door. "Oh, dear," she muttered as she realized where the dog was likely to be.

Along with that thought came a very angry knock at the back door, near where she was sitting with the sheriff.

Apprehensively, she got up and opened the door. And there he was. Dal Blake, with Snow on a makeshift lead. He wasn't smiling.

"Your dog invited herself to breakfast. Again. She came right into my damned house through the dog door!"

She knew that Dal didn't have a dog anymore. His old Labrador had died a few weeks ago, her foreman had told her, and the man had mourned the old dog. He'd had it for almost fourteen years, he'd added.

"I'm sorry," Meadow said with a grimace. "Snow. Bad girl!" she muttered.

The husky with her laughing blue eyes came bounding over to her mistress and started licking her.

"Stop that." Meadow laughed, fending her off. "How about a treat, Snow?"

She went to get one from the cupboard.

"Hey, Jeff," Dal greeted the other man, shaking hands as Jeff got to his feet.

"How's it going?" Jeff asked Dal.

"Slow," came the reply. "We're renovating the calving sheds. It's slow work in this weather."

"Tell me about it," Jeff said. "We had two fences go down. Cows broke through and started down the highway."

"Maybe there was a dress sale," Dal said, tongue-in-cheek as he watched a flustered Meadow give a chewy treat to her dog.

"I'd love to see a cow wearing a dress," she muttered.

"Would you?" Dal replied. "One of your men thinks that's your ultimate aim, to put cows in school and teach them to read."

"Which man?" she asked, her eyes flashing fire at him.

"Oh, no, I'm not telling," Dal returned. "You get on some boots and jeans and go find out for yourself. If you can ride a horse, that is."

That brought back another sad memory. She'd gone riding on one of her father's feistier horses, confident that she could control it. She was in her second year of college, bristling with confidence as she breezed through her core curriculum.

She thought she could handle the horse. But it sensed her fear of heights and speed and took her on a racing tour up the side of a small mountain and down again so quickly that Meadow lost her balance and ended up face-first in a snowbank.

To add to her humiliation—because the stupid horse went running back to the barn, probably laughing all the way—Dal Blake was helping move cattle on his own ranch, and he saw the whole thing.

He came trotting up just as she was wiping the last of the snow from her face and parka. "You know, Spirit isn't a great choice of horses for an inexperienced rider."

"My father told me that," she muttered.

"Pity you didn't listen. And lucky that you ended up in a snowbank instead of down a ravine," he said solemnly. "If you can't control a horse, don't ride him."

"Thanks for the helpful advice," she returned icily.

"City tenderfoot," he mused. "I'm amazed that you haven't killed yourself already. I hear your father had to put a rail on the back steps after you fell down them."

She flushed. "I tripped over his cat."

"You could benefit from some martial arts training."

"I've already had that," she said. "I work for my local police department."

"As what?" he asked politely.

"As a patrol officer!" she shot back.

"Well," he remarked, turning his horse, "if you drive a car like you ride a horse, you're going to end badly one day."

"I can drive!" she shot after him. "I drive all the time!"

"God help other motorists."

"You . . . you . . . you . . . !" She gathered steam with each repetition of the word until she was almost screaming, and still she couldn't think of an insult bad enough to throw at him. It wouldn't have done any good. He kept riding. He didn't even look back.

* * *

She snapped back to the present. "Yes, I can ride a horse!" she shot at Dal Blake. "Just because I fell off once . . ."

"You fell off several times. This is mountainous country. If you go riding, carry a cell phone and make sure it's charged," he said seriously.

"I'd salaam, but I haven't had my second cup of coffee yet," she drawled, alluding to an old custom of subjects salaaming royalty.

"You heard me."

"You don't give orders to me in my own house," she returned hotly.

Jeff cleared his throat.

They both looked at him.

"I have to get back to work," he said as he pushed his chair back in. "Thanks for the coffee, Meadow. I'll expect you early Monday morning."

"Expect her?" Dal asked.

"She's coming to work for me as my new investigator," Jeff said with a bland smile.

Dal's dark eyes narrowed. He saw through the man, whom he'd known since grammar school. Jeff was a good sheriff, but he wanted to add to his ranch. He owned property that adjoined Meadow's. So did Dal. That acreage had abundant water, and right now water was the most important asset any rancher had. Meadow was obviously out of her depth trying to run a ranch. Her best bet was to sell it, so Jeff was getting in on the ground floor by offering her a job that would keep her close to him.

He saw all that, but he just smiled. "Good luck," he told Jeff, with a dry glance at a fuming Meadow. "You'll need it."

"She'll do fine," Jeff said confidently.

Dal just smiled.

Meadow remembered that smile from years past. She'd had so many accidents when she was visiting her father. Dal was always somewhere nearby when they happened.

He didn't like Meadow. He'd made his distaste for her apparent on every possible occasion. There had been a Christmas party thrown by the local cattlemen's association when Meadow first started college. She'd come to spend Christmas with her father, and when he asked her to go to the party with him, she agreed.

She knew Dal would be there. So she wore an outrageous dress, even more revealing than the one he'd been so disparaging about when she was a senior in high school.

Sadly, the dress caught the wrong pair of eyes. A local cattleman who'd had five drinks too many had propositioned Meadow by the punch bowl. His reaction to her dress had flustered her and she tripped over her high-heeled shoes and knocked the punch bowl over.

The linen tablecloth was soaked. So was poor Meadow, in her outrageous dress. Dal Blake had laughed until his face turned red. So had most other people. Meadow had asked her father to drive her home. It was the last Christmas party she ever attended in Raven Springs.

But just before the punch incident, there had been another. Dal had been caught with her under the mistletoe . . .

She shook herself mentally and glared at Dal.

Connect with Us

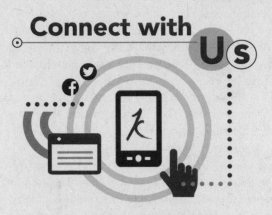

Visit us online at
KensingtonBooks.com
to read more from your favorite authors, see books
by series, view reading group guides, and more.

Join us on social media

for sneak peeks, chances to win books and prize packs,
and to share your thoughts with other readers.

facebook.com/kensingtonpublishing
twitter.com/kensingtonbooks

Tell us what you think!

To share your thoughts, submit a review,
or sign up for our eNewsletters, please visit:
KensingtonBooks.com/TellUs.